Praise for *The Rice Mother*

'A first novel of Eastern exoticism and unforgettable characters
. . . You'll struggle to find a more powerful, moving read this
year.' *Glamour*

'*The Rice Mother* deserves the hype. The novel moves through
generations in its vivid, imaginative description of the frailties of
human nature and the consequences of war . . . The book looks
certain to become a massive success.' *Sunday Business Post*,
Dublin

'It would be difficult not to be seduced by the evocation of setting,
family life, clothes, food and the intriguing mixture of myth,
religion and superstition . . . there is a freedom and freshness in
the manner in which the author explores the interior life of her
characters whose idiosyncrasies and many failings are sympathetically and sometimes humorously observed . . . It possesses
a genuine intimacy and passionate involvement.' Elizabeth
Buchan, *Times Play*

'*The Rice Mother* is exactly the kind of absorbing, cross-
generational read that will pass away a few more train journeys
than the average popular paperback . . . brimming over with
colourful imagery, mythology, unfeeling men and vivid descrip-
tions of cooking . . . Emotionally satisfying, complex books like
this are harder to find.' *Heat*

'A vivid storyteller . . . Unfolding over four generations like a
Greek tragedy, it's a compulsive and often harrowing tale.' *In
Style*

'Echoes of *Memoirs of a Geisha* in this exotic family saga.' *Mirror*

'Powerful.' *Sunday Mirror*

Rani Manicka

The Rice Mother

SCEPTRE

Copyright © 2002 by Rani Manicka

First published in Great Britain in 2002 by Hodder & Stoughton
A division of Hodder Headline
First published in paperback in 2003 by Hodder and Stoughton

A Sceptre paperback

A CIP catalogue record for this title is available from the British Library

ISBN 0 340 82383 6

Typeset in Sabon by
Phoenix Typesetting, Ilkley, West Yorkshire

Printed and bound in Great Britain by
Mackays of Chatham plc, Chatham, Kent

Hodder & Stoughton
A division of Hodder Headline
338 Euston Road
London NW1 3BH

For my parents, watching gods at the
beginning of all my journeys

Acknowledgements

Thank you, to my mother for each and every one of the precious scars she shared with me; Girolamo Avarello for believing before anyone else; the team at Darley Anderson Literary Agency for being simply the best; William Colgrave for his support and encouragement; Joan Deitch for adding that special something; and the inimitable Sue Fletcher at Hodder & Stoughton for actually buying my manuscript.

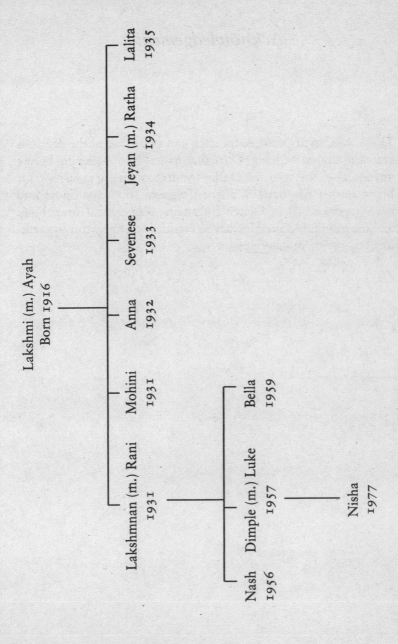

Lakshmi (m.) Ayah
Born 1916

Lakshmnan (m.) Rani   Mohini   Anna   Sevenese   Jeyan (m.) Ratha   Lalita
1931   1931   1932   1933   1934   1935

Nash   Dimple (m.) Luke   Bella
1956   1957   1959

Nisha
1977

It was on my uncle the mango trader's knees that I first heard of the amazing birds' nest collectors, living in a faraway land called Malaya. Without torches they bravely climb up swaying bamboo poles hundreds of feet high to get to the roofs of mountain caves. Watched by the ghosts of men who had plunged to their deaths, they reach out from their precarious perches to steal a rich man's delicacy – a nest made of a bird's saliva. In the terrible blackness even words like fear, fall or blood must never be uttered for they echo and tempt demon spirits. The nest collectors' only friends are the bamboo poles that support their weight. Before the men take their first step, they tap the bamboo gently, and if it sighs sadly the men abandon it immediately. Only when the bamboo sings will the nest collectors dare their quest.

My uncle said, my heart is my bamboo, and if I treated it kindly and listened for its song the highest, biggest nest would surely be mine.

Lakshmi

Contents

Part 1

Little Children Stumbling in the Dark

Lakshmi

I was born in Ceylon in 1916, at a time when spirits walked the earth just like people. Before the glare of electricity and roar of civilisation had frightened them away into the concealed hearts of forests. They dwelled inside enormous trees full of cool, blue-green shade. In the dappled stillness you could reach out and almost feel their silent, glaring presence, as they yearned for physical form. If the urge to relieve ourselves beset us while passing through the jungle, we had to say a prayer and ask their permission before our waste could touch the ground, for they were easily offended. Their solitude broken was the excuse they used to enter an intruder. And walk in his legs.

Mother said her sister was once lured off and possessed by just such a spirit. A holy man from two villages away was sent for, to exorcise the spirit. He wore many chains of strangely twisted beads and dried roots around his neck, testaments to his fearsome powers. The simple villagers gathered like a human ring of curiosity around the man. To drive the spirit away he began to beat my aunt with a long, thin cane, all the time demanding, 'What do you want?' He filled the peaceful village with her terrified screams but, unmoved, he carried on beating her poor body until it bled streams of red.

'You are killing her,' my grandmother howled, held back by three appalled yet horribly fascinated women.

Ignoring her the holy man fingered a livid pink scar that ran all the way down his face and walked his determined, tight circles around the cowering girl, always with the darkly whispered query, 'What do you want?' Until eventually she screamed shrilly that it was a fruit she wanted.

'Fruit? What sort of fruit?' he asked sternly, halting before the sobbing girl.

A shocking transformation occurred suddenly. The little face looked up at him slyly and perhaps there was even a bubble of madness in the grin that slowly and with unspeakable obscenity spread its legs on her lips. Coyly she pointed to her younger sister, my mother. 'That is the fruit I want,' she said, her voice unmistakably male.

The simple villagers united in their gasp of stunned shock. Needless to say the tall man did not give my mother to the spirit for she was surely her father's favourite. The spirit had to make do with five lemons, cut and flung into its face, a searing sprinkling of sacred water and a suffocating amount of myrrh.

When I was very young I used to rest quietly on my mother's lap listening to her voice remember happier times. You see, my mother was descended from a family of such wealth and influence that in their heyday her English grandmother, Mrs Armstrong, had been called upon to give a posy of flowers and shake the gloved hand of Queen Victoria herself. My mother was born partially deaf but her father put his lips against her forehead and spoke to her tirelessly until she learned to speak. By the time she was sixteen she was as beautiful as a cloud maiden. Proposals of marriage came from far and wide to the lovely house in Colombo but she fell in love with the scent of danger. Her elongated eyes lowered on a charming rogue.

One night she climbed out of her window and down the very neem tree upon which her father had trained a thorny bougainvillaea bush when she was only a year old in an effort to deter any man from ever scaling the tree and reaching his daughter's window. As if his pure thoughts had fed the bush it had grown and grown until the entire tree, ablaze with flowers, became a landmark that could be seen for miles around. But grandfather had not reckoned on his own child's determination.

That moonlit night thorns like bared fangs shredded her thick clothes, ripped her hair and plunged deep into her flesh but she couldn't stop. Beneath was the man she loved. When at last she stood before him there was not an inch of her skin that didn't burn as if aflame. Silently the shadow led her away but every step was like knives in her feet so she begged in terrible pain to rest. The wordless silhouette swung her up and carried her away. Safe inside the warm circle of his arms she looked back at her home, grand against the vivid night sky, and saw her own bloody footprints leading away from the tree. Stains of her betrayal. She cried, knowing that they would hurt her poor father's heart the most.

The lovers married at daybreak in a small temple in another village. In the ensuing bitter quarrel, the groom, my father, who was in fact the resentful son of a servant in my grandfather's employ, forbade my mother even the mere sight of any member of her family. Only after my father was grey ash in the wind did she return to her family home, but by then her mother was a widow grey with loss.

After issuing his heartless sentence my father brought

my mother to our backward little village far away from Colombo. He sold some of her jewellery, bought some land, built a house and installed her in it. But clean air and wedded bliss didn't suit the new bridegroom and soon he was off. Lured away by the bright lights in the cities. Summoned by the delights of cheap alcohol served by garishly painted prostitutes and intoxicated by the smell fanned out of a pack of cards. After each absence he returned and presented his young wife with jar upon jar of all manner of white lies pickled in various brands of alcohol. For some obscure reason he thought she had a taste for them. Poor Mother, all she had left were her memories and me. Precious things that she used to take out every evening. First she washed off the grime of the years with her own tears then she polished them with the cloth of regret. And finally, when their wonderful sparkle had been returned to them, she laid them out one by one for me to admire before carefully placing them back in their golden box inside her head.

From her mouth issued visions of a glorious past full of armies of devoted servants, fine carriages drawn by white horses and iron chests filled with gold and rich jewellery. How could I, sitting on the cement floor of our tiny hut, even begin to imagine a house so high on a hill that all of Colombo was visible from its front balcony, or a kitchen so huge that our entire house could fit into it.

My mother once said that when she was first placed into her father's arms, tears of joy streamed down his face at the sight of her unusually fair skin and her full head of thick, black hair. He held the small bundle close to his face and for a while all he could do was breathe in that strange, sweetish odour that is a newborn baby. Then he strode into the stables, his white *veshti* flapping against his strong, brown legs, jumped onto his favourite stallion and galloped off in a cloud of dust. When he returned it was with the two largest emerald pieces that the entire village had ever seen. He presented them to his wife, little baubles in return for a marvellous miracle. She had them fashioned into diamond-encrusted earrings that she was never seen without.

I have never seen the famous emeralds but I still have the black and white studio photograph of a sad-eyed woman standing stiffly in front of a badly painted background, a coconut tree growing on the edge of a beach. I look at her often, frozen on a piece of paper long after she is no more.

My mother said that when I was born she cried to see that I was only a girl, and my disgusted father disappeared to make more pickled lies, returning two years later still roaring drunk. Despite this I still retain crystal-clear memories of a village life so happy and so carefree that not a day goes by in adulthood when I don't think about it with a bitter-sweet ache. How can I even begin to tell you how much I miss those carefree days when I was Mother's only child, her sun, her moon, her stars, her heart? When I was so loved and so precious that I had to be coaxed into eating. When Mother could come out of the house with a plate of food in her hand and search the village for me so she could feed me with her own hand. All so that the tedious business of food would not interrupt my play.

How not to miss those days when the sun was a happy companion that stayed to play all year round and kissed me a careless nut brown. When Mother caught the sweet rain in her well behind the house and the air was so clear that the grass smelt green.

An innocent time when the dusty dirt roads were surrounded by slanting coconut trees and dotted with simple village folk on rickety bicycles, their reddened teeth and gums stretched inside untroubled laughter. When the plot behind each house was a supermarket and one slaughtered goat was adequate for eight households blissfully unaware of an invention called the refrigerator. When mothers needed only the gods who gathered in the white clouds above as babysitters to watch over their children playing in the waterfall.

Yes, I remember Ceylon when it was the most magical, most beautiful place in the world.

I suckled at Mother's breasts until the age of almost seven, running wild with my friends until hunger or thirst nudged me and then I dashed back into the coolness of the house impatiently crying out for my mother. And regardless of what she was doing I pushed aside her sari and let my mouth curl around the unbound mounds of soft, toffee brown. My head and shoulders burrowed inside the safety of her rough cotton sari, the clear scent of her, the innocent love in the milk that flowed into my mouth and the warm comfort of those quiet sucking sounds that I used to make inside the envelope of her flesh. Try as they might, the cruel years have not managed to rob my memory of either taste or sound.

For many years I hated the taste of rice or any kind of vegetables, content to live on sweet milk and yellow mangoes. My uncle was a mango dealer of sorts and crates of them used to sit in the storeroom at the back of our house. A skinny mahout on an elephant would deposit them and there they waited until another arrived to pick them up. But while they waited . . . I sprinted to the very top of those wooden crates and sat there cross-legged without the slightest fear of the spiders and scorpions that inevitably lurked within. Even being bitten by a centipede and turning blue for four whole days didn't deter me. All my life I have been driven by the blind compulsion to walk barefoot down the difficult path. 'Come back,' people would scream desperately at me. My feet bleeding and torn, I would grit my teeth and press on in the opposite direction.

Dissolute and untamed I tore the skins off the succulent orange flesh with my teeth. It is one of the most powerful images I still carry with me. Me all alone in the cool darkness of our storeroom, high atop those wooden crates, with sticky, sweet-warm juices running down my arms and legs, gorging my way through a heap of my uncle's wares.

Unlike boys, girls didn't have to go to school in our day and except for the two hours of every evening when mother taught reading, writing and arithmetic, I was mostly left to run wild. Until, that is, at the age of fourteen when the first drop of menstrual blood proclaimed me suddenly and distressingly a grown woman. For the first week I was shut up in a small room with the windows nailed shut. It was the custom, for no self-respecting family was prepared to risk the possibility of adventurous boys climbing up coconut trees to peek at the newly found, secret charms of their daughters.

During my confinement period I was forced to swallow raw eggs, washed down with sesame seed oil and a whole host of bitter herb potions. Tears were to no avail. When Mother came in with her offerings from hell she came equipped with a cane that I quickly found to my utter amazement she was prepared to use. At teatime, instead of her delicious sweet cakes I was handed half a coconut shell filled to the brim with hot, soft aubergines cooked in a surfeit of the dreaded sesame oil. 'Eat it hot,' Mother advised as she closed and locked the door. In a fit of defiance and frustration I purposely let it get cold. Between my fingers the cold, slimy flesh of the aubergines squashed satisfyingly but in my mouth they were utterly disgusting. It was like swallowing dead caterpillars. Thirty-six raw eggs, a good few bottles of sesame seed oil and a whole basketful of aubergines must have slid down my throat before the small-room confinement was over. I was then simply confined indoors and made to learn to do women's things. It was a sad transition for me. The deep loss of sun-baked earth under my running feet is impossible to explain. Like a prisoner I sat and stared longingly out of small windows. Almost immediately my long, matted hair was combed and plaited and transformed into a sleek snake down my back and my skin suddenly pronounced too sun-darkened. My real potential, my mother decided, lay in my skin. Unlike her I was no Indian beauty but in a land of coffee-coloured people I was a cup of very milky tea.

A prized, precious colour.

A colour surely to be actively sought after in a wife, subtly encouraged in a daughter-in-law and lovingly cherished in one's grandchildren. Suddenly strange middle-aged ladies began to appear in our home. I was dressed to the nines and paraded in front of them. They all had the shrewd look of buyers in a diamond store. Their sharp, beady eyes looked me over carefully for flaws, without the slightest trace of embarrassment.

One hot afternoon, after Mother had tugged, pulled and expertly rolled my stiff, awkward body into a great deal of pink material, decorated my hair with bruised, pink roses from the garden and dribbled me in precious stones set in dull-yellow gold I stood scowling by the window, marvelling at how quickly and completely my life had changed. In a day. No, less. And without warning.

Outside, the wind rustled in the lime tree and a playful breeze flew into my room, teased the curls on my temples and blew softly into my ear. I knew him well, that breeze. He was as blue as the baby god Krishna and as cheeky. Whenever we dived from the highest rock into the waterfalls in the woods behind Ramesh's house he always managed to reach the icy cold water first. That's because he cheats. His feet never touch the dark-green velvet moss on the rocks.

He laughed in my ear. 'Come,' his voice tinkled merrily. He tickled my nose and flew out.

I leaned out of the window, craning my thin neck as far as I could, but to me the shining water and the blue breeze were lost for ever. They belonged to a barefoot child laughing in a dirty dress.

Standing there nursing my frustration I saw a carriage stop outside our house. Wheels creaked in the dry dust. A heavy woman in a dark-blue silk sari and slippers too dainty for her frame heaved out. Stepping back into the gloom of my room, I watched her curiously. Her dark eyes roved around our small house and meagre compound, with some secret satisfaction. Surprised by her strange expression I stared at her until I lost sight of her cunning face. She disappeared behind the bougain-villaea trees fringing the path that led to our front door. Mother's voice inviting her in wafted into my room. I stood pressed to my bedroom door and listened to the stranger's unexpectedly musical voice. She had a lovely voice, one that belied the sly, small eyes and the thin compressed lips. Presently my mother called out to me to bring in the tea that she had prepared for our visitor. As soon as I reached the threshold of the front room where Mother received visitors I felt the stranger's quick, appraising glance. Once more it seemed to me that she was satisfied by what met her searching eyes. Her lips opened into a warm smile. Truly if I hadn't seen the smug, almost victorious look she had thrown at our poor dwelling earlier I might have mistaken her for the adoring aunt that Mother smilingly introduced her as. I dropped my glance demurely as I had been instructed to do in the presence of benevolent adults and sharp-eyed diamond buyers.

'Come and sit by me,' Aunty Pani called softly, patting the bench beside her. I noticed that on her forehead was not the red kum kum dot customary for married women but the black dot signifying her unmarried status. I walked carefully lest I should trip in the six yards of heavy cloth that swirled dangerously around me, humiliate my mother and amuse the sophisticated stranger.

'What a pretty girl you are!' she exclaimed in her musical voice.

Mutely I looked at her from the corner of my eye and felt a strange inexplicable revulsion. Her skin was unwrinkled, smooth and carefully powdered, her hair scented with sweet jasmine and yet in my enchanted kingdom I imagined her a rat-eating snake woman. Oozing like thick tar out of trees and gliding into bedrooms like a silent ribbon. All the while, black and hunting. She flicks out a tongue long, pink and cold-blooded. What does she know, the snake woman?

A plump, be-ringed hand delved into a small beaded

handbag and snaked out with a wrapped sweet. Such treats were rare in the village. Not all snake women were poisonous, I decided. She held the morsel out to me. It was a test. I didn't fail my watching mother. I didn't snatch. Only when Mother smiled and nodded did I reach out for the precious offering. Our hands touched briefly. Hers were cold and wet. Our glances met and held. She hastily looked away. I had outstared the snake. I was sent back to my room. Once the door had closed behind me I unwrapped the sweet and ate the snake woman's bribe. It was delicious.

The stranger didn't stay long and soon Mother came into my room. She helped me with the complicated task of getting out of the long swathes of beautiful material, folding them and putting them away carefully.

'Lakshmi, I have accepted a marriage proposal for you,' she said to the folded sari. 'A very good proposal. He is of a better caste than we are. Also he lives in that rich land called Malaya.'

I was stunned. I stared at her in disbelief. A marriage proposal that would take me away from my mother? I had heard of Malaya. That land of birds' nest thieves many thousands of miles away. Tears welled up in my eyes. I had never been parted from my mother.

Never.

Never. Never.

I ran to her and pulled her face down to mine. I put my lips on her forehead.

'Why can't I marry someone who lives in Sangra?' I asked.

Her beautiful eyes were wet. Like a pelican that claws at its own breast to feed its young.

'You are a very lucky girl. You will travel with your

husband to a land where there is money to be found in the streets. Aunty Pani says that your husband-to-be is very wealthy and you will live like a queen, just like your grandma did. You won't have to live like me. He is neither a drunkard nor a gambler like your father.'

'How could you bear to send me away?' I breathed, betrayed.

There was aching love and pain behind her eyes. Life had yet to teach me that a child's love could never equal a mother's pain. It is deep and raw but without it a mother is incomplete.

'I will be so alone without you,' I wailed.

'No, you won't because your new husband is a widower and he has two children aged nine and ten. So you will have much to keep you busy and plenty of companionship.'

I frowned uncertainly. His children were almost my age. 'How old is he?'

'Well, he's thirty-seven years old,' Mother said briskly, turning me around to release the last hook on my blouse.

I wriggled around to face her. 'But Ama, that's even older than you!'

'That may be, but he will be a good husband for you. Aunty Pani says he owns not one but a few gold watches. He has had plenty of time to amass a huge fortune and is so rich he does not even require a dowry. He is her cousin, so she should know. I made a terrible mistake and I have ensured that you will not. You shall be more. More than me. I will begin preparing your jewellery box immediately.'

I stared mutely at Mother. Her mind was made up.

I was doomed.

The five hundred burning oil lamps at my grandmother's wedding nearly fifty years ago had surprised the awakening sun for five lavish days of merrymaking, but mine was to be a one-day affair. For a whole month wedding preparations kept everybody busy and despite my earlier misgivings I came around to the idea of a mysterious husband who would treat me like a queen. I was also rather pleased with the idea of lording it over my two new stepchildren. Yes, perhaps it would all be a wonderful adventure. In the gorgeous fantasy I created, Mother came to visit once a month and I took the boat back perhaps twice a year. A handsome stranger smiled tenderly and showered me with gifts. I bent my head shyly as a thousand romantic notions partly clothed and blushing ran through my silly, teenage head. Of course none of them involved actual sex. No one I knew talked or even knew of such things. The secret process of making babies did not concern me. Curly headed they would turn up when the time was ripe.

The big day arrived. Our little house seemed to sigh and groan with the weight of fat middle-aged ladies whirling about. The aroma of Mother's famous black curry filled the air. I sat in my little room quite caught up in the hustle and bustle. A little ball of excitement was growing in my stomach and when I laid my palms on my cheeks they were hot, very hot.

'Let's have a look at you then,' my mother said after Poonama our next-door neighbour's clever hands had pleated and neatly pinned down the six yards of my beautiful red and gold sari. For a long while Mother simply looked at me with the oddest mixture of sadness and joy, then she dabbed the corners of her swimming eyes and, unable to speak, simply nodded her approval. Efficiently, the lady she had engaged from a different village to do my hair moved forward. I sat on a stool as her quick hands threaded strings of pearls through my hair and added a wad of coarse, false hair, twisting the whole thing into a large round bun low on the thin nape of my neck. It looked like a second head had popped out of the back of my neck but I could see that mother seemed pleased with the idea of a two-headed daughter so I said nothing. The lady then produced a little tub that she unscrewed to reveal a dense, red paste. She dipped her fat forefinger into the vile-smelling product and applied the sticky grease carefully on my lips. I looked as if I had kissed somebody's bleeding knee. I stared fascinated.

'Don't lick your lips,' she instructed bossily.

I agreed solemnly but the temptation to wipe off the layer of thick smelly paint persisted until the moment I saw my bridegroom. That was when I forgot not just the annoyance of the blubber on my lips but everything else as well. When time stood still and my childhood fled for ever, screaming with horror.

Decked in jewellery I was escorted into the main hall where my bridegroom waited on a dais, but as we reached the second row of seated guests I could hold back my curiosity no more. Brazenly, I lifted my head and looked up at him. That ball of excitement that had bubbled and bounced so playfully in my stomach shattered. My knees went weak and my step faltered. Both my smiling escorts simultaneously tightened their grip on my arms. I could hear their disapproving thoughts in my spinning head: *What on earth is the matter with the tea-coloured girl now?*

The matter with the tea-coloured girl was that she had seen the bridegroom.

Sitting on the dais awaiting me was the biggest giant of a man I had ever seen. So dark his skin shone like black oil in the night. On his temples, like a bird of prey, rode large wings of grey. Beneath his broad nose, long yellow teeth jutted forward, making it impossible for him to completely close his mouth.

Fear coursed through my child's body at the thought of that man as my husband. My silly, romantic dreams desperately gasped their last breaths and I was suddenly very small, alone and tearful. From that moment on, love for me became the worm in the apple. Whenever my seeking mouth meets its soft body I destroy it and it in turn disgusts me. Panic-stricken, I searched through the blur of watching faces for the one person who could make it better again.

Our eyes met. My mother smiled at me happily, her eyes shining proudly in her poor face. I could never disappoint her. She had wanted this for me. In the face of our abject poverty his wealth had blinded her to everything else. My feet took me ever closer. I refused to hang my head like other shy brides. I stared hard at my new husband-to-be with a mixture of fear and boldness.

I must have been but one third his size.

He looked up. He had small black eyes. I caught the small black beads in my bold gaze. In them I found an irritating expression of proud possession. I stared unblinking at him. Show no fear, I thought, my stomach in angry knots. I locked him into a childish game of who could outstare whom. The beating of drums and the sound of trumpets faded away and the watching people became so much background grey as my eyes blazed ceaselessly into his. Strangely I felt a shift in my new husband's eyes. Surprise swallowed proud possession. He dropped his eyes. I had defeated the ugly beast. He was the prey, and I the hunter, after all. I had tamed the wild beast with a look. I felt fire rush through my body like a fever.

I looked around at my mother. She was still smiling that same proud, encouraging smile that she had been smiling before. Before my momentous victory. For her the moment had never been. Only my new husband and I had sensed it. I smiled back at her and, raising my hand slightly, let my middle finger tap my thumb three times, our secret signal, 'everything is grand'. Reaching the decorated dais I let my knees give way on the bed of petals beneath me. I could feel the waves of heat that emanated from the body of the tamed beast but there was nothing to fear.

He didn't turn his head to look at me. The rest of the ceremony passed in a blur. He never sought the fierce blaze in my eyes again. And I, I spent the entire ceremony diving tirelessly again and again from the highest rock into the cool waterfall behind Ramesh's house.

That night I lay very quietly in the dark as he pushed aside my clothes clumsily and mounted me. He muffled my cry of pain with his large hand. I remember his hand smelt of cow's milk.

'Shhh . . . it only hurts the first time,' he consoled.

He was gentle but my child's mind reeled in shock. He did to me what the dogs in the streets did . . . until we threw water on them and they parted grudgingly, disgruntled pink bits still distended. I concentrated my thoughts on the clever way he could completely dissolve into the darkness. His long teeth hung in the night without support and his watching eyes glistened wetly without expression like a rat in the dark. Sometimes the gold watch that had impressed Mother so much flashed. I stared into his open, watching eyes until he blinked and then I stared at his teeth instead. And in this way it was over very quickly.

He lay back and cuddled me like a bruised child. I lay as rigid as firewood in his arms. I had only known my mother's soft embrace and his hardness was unfamiliar. When his breathing turned even and his limbs heavy I carefully inched out from under his sleeping body and tiptoed to the mirror. I stared at my own tear-streaked, shocked face in confusion. What was it he had just done to me? Had Mother known that he would do *that* to me? Had Father also done that disgusting thing to Mother? I felt dirty. There was still sticky liquid and blood soiling my thighs, and soreness between my legs.

Outside, in the light of oil lamps, the most dedicated merrymakers still laughed and drank. I found an old sari in the cupboard. My face hooded, I cautiously opened the door and slipped outside. My feet were noiseless on the cold cement floor and nobody took notice of my slight figure moving close to the wall, hugging the silent shadows. Very quietly I ran out through the back door and was soon standing beside Poonama's well. I stripped in a mad frenzy and drew a bucketful of glinting black water from the deep hole in the earth. As the icy cold water cascaded down my body I began to sob, great racking sobs that made my body heave uncontrollably. I poured black water over my shivering body until it turned numb. And when the sobs were all washed into the hungry earth I dressed my wretched body and made my way back to my husband's bed.

He lay peacefully asleep. My eyes slid to his gold watch. At least I would live like a queen in Malaya.

Perhaps he had a house on the hill so big that our entire house could fit into his kitchen. I was now no longer a child but a woman and he, my husband. Tentatively I reached out a hand and stroked the broad forehead. Under my fingers his skin was smooth. He didn't stir. Comforted by my thoughts of a kitchen bigger than our entire house I curled up into a ball as far away from his large body as I could and fell into a deep sleep.

We were to set sail in two days and there was much to do. I hardly saw my husband. He was the dark shadow that spread its great wings over me at the end of every day shutting out even that curious, thin ray of light that usually stayed at the bottom of my door to watch me fall asleep.

On the morning of our departure I sat by the back doorstep and watched Mother in her silent world. She was cleaning the stove as she had done every morning for as long as I could remember. But that morning tears dripped off her chin and made round dark patches on her sari blouse. I had always known that I did not love my father, but I did not know that I loved my mother so deeply it could hurt. I saw her all alone in our small house, cooking, sewing, cleaning and sweeping but there was nothing I could do. I turned away from her and watched the last of the thunderstorm retreat. In the woods, hundreds of frogs joined in song, begging the skies to open once more so the puddles on the earth could become frog-sized swimming pools. I looked around at all that was familiar; the smooth cement floor of our home, the badly built wooden walls, and the old wooden stool where Mother sat and oiled my hair. I felt bereft suddenly. Who would comb my hair? It was almost a ritual. Dashing back tears I promised myself that I would

not forget a single thing about my mother. The smell of
her, the taste of the food that came off her work-worn
fingers straight into my mouth, her beautiful, sad eyes
and all the precious stories that she stored inside the
golden box inside her head. I sat for a while imagining
my grandfather on his white horse, tall and proud, and
imagined what he would have made of me. Puny me.

In the yard Nandi, our cow, oblivious and unconcerned with the details of my departure, rolled her eyes
mournfully at nothing and the newly hatched baby
chicks were already at ease in the role life required of
them. Part of me couldn't believe it. Couldn't believe that
I was leaving that day, leaving everything I had ever
known to sail away with a man who said, 'Call me Ayah.'

We arrived at the agreed meeting point in the harbour.
I stared mesmerised at the massive liner rising out of the
water, gleaming importantly in the sunshine. Ready to
cross the ocean. Aunty Pani, entrusted with the task of
bringing my stepchildren, was late. Creased with worry,
Ayah glanced once more at his resplendent watch. Just
as the great horns were about to blow she arrived in her
carriage but minus the children. 'They are quite ill and
not fit to make the journey. They shall stay with me for
a few more months,' she announced cheerfully to my
stunned husband. 'When they are better I will bring them
to Malaya myself,' her musical voice added.

Ayah looked around helplessly like a lost baby elephant.
'I can't leave without them,' he cried desperately.

'You must,' she insisted. 'They are not seriously ill. No
harm will become them, to stay for a few more weeks
with me. You know how fond I am of them. No one
could possibly take better care of them.'

For a painful moment my husband stood hesitant,

undecided. All around him were watching faces. Aunty Pani's unrepentant face suffused with victory when he finally picked up a small case by my feet and prepared to board. Incredible as it seemed, he was going to leave them. It was obvious to me, as it was to everyone else watching, that the mysterious illness was no more than a ploy of some kind. Why didn't he insist that someone hurry to her home and get the children? I followed him slowly, not understanding but silent. She was not a good person. I felt it clearly, yet deep inside me flowered a black thought that perhaps it was all for the best. I had seen my stepchildren at the wedding and they were small copies of their father. They wore sluggish expressions on their poor faces and moved with irritating slowness. I didn't like conceding victory to the Pani woman but my dread of my simple-minded stepchildren was greater.

I turned around and kissed my mother on her fore-head. 'I love you with all my heart,' I said to the smooth surface. She grasped my face in both her hands and looked at me long and hard as if memorising the lines of my face because she already knew that it was the last time she would ever see me or touch me again. That we would never again meet for the rest of our lives.

From the ship I watched my mother till she was a small speck of sobbing green among a crowd of waving, wailing relatives.

Oh, the journey.

The journey was horrible beyond description. I was delirious with fever for almost the entire voyage. My head swam and my dizzy stomach rolled and heaved. Sometimes I felt so bad that I wished I was dead. My husband was a helpless rock by my side as I twisted like a snake in the small bunk bed with the endless need to retch. A sickening, sour smell permeated everything. My hair, my clothes, the bedclothes, my breath, my skin . . . everything felt grimy with the sticky sea air.

I awoke in the lurching darkness with a raging thirst. A gentle hand rested on my forehead.

'Ama,' I called out weakly. Disorientated, I imagined my mother had come to nurse me. I turned to smile at her. My husband stared into my eyes with the strangest expression. Taken aback by the intensity of his regard I blinked and stared back, unable to look away. My mouth dried.

'How do you feel?' he asked softly.

The spell broke.

'Thirsty,' I said hoarsely. He turned away and I watched him, loose-limbed and large, pour me some water. I studied his expression as I drank but his ebony face was filled with nothing more than kindness. I remember that incident because for the rest of our life together I was never ever to see that naked wanting in his eyes again.

The sky was clear cerulean and the surface of the sea a thick piece of sparkling glass in the bright sunlight. Concealed at the bottom of its green depths were, I knew, mysterious, wondrous cities studded with fine palaces, dazzling minarets and exquisite sea flowers, home to the powerful demigods of Mother's stories. Up on the ship, hundreds of people strained against the rails and stared fiercely at the approaching land. The air vibrated like the beating of a thousand wings. The wings of hope.

To my incredulous eyes Penang Harbour looked like the most exciting place on earth. More people than I had ever seen in my life swarmed and scurried about like a colony of ants on a sand dune. And what strange sorts of people they were too. I gawked, delighted.

Here were olive-skinned Arab merchants in long flowing robes and headdresses of white and black. Even from afar their prosperous mien stood out like a red kite in a blue sky. Their dressed heads they held at an arrogant tilt and their fat fingers, crammed with huge rings, glittered red, green and blue fire under the blazing sun. They had come to trade in spices, ivory and gold. The wind cupped their strange, guttural language and flew it up to my ears.

Then there were the Chinesemen. Slit-eyed, flat-nosed and determined. Not a moment to spare in idleness. Shirtless and sunburned to a deep bronze, they hunched low and staggered under heavy gunnysacks that they unloaded from barges and trawlers. They were tireless in their task. To my young eyes that had learned only to appreciate the sharply accentuated features and the large soulful eyes of my native land, their moon-faced flatness appeared the epitome of deformity.

Locals the colour of ripening coconuts hung about with a mildly subservient demeanour. There was something instinctively noble in their faces and yet they were not masters of their own land. I didn't know then that their war against the white man had been lost quickly, subtly, on covert violence alone.

First to disembark were the Europeans. While segregated in first class they had apparently dined so well that they had swelled into larger-than-life proportions. Tall, haughty and elaborate of dress they strode forward with sunlight in their hair like gods. As if the world owed them an oyster. Their beige and inaccessible lips I found oddly absorbing. The men were unusually solicitous towards the women who, high-nosed, tightly corseted and carrying tiny frilled parasols pathetically incapable of the job at hand stepped, straight-backed, into fine cars and fancy carriages. My last glimpses of them were fascinatingly white wrists and fluttering lace handkerchiefs.

Strong men in white loincloths and brown swarthy faces came forward to help the passengers. Big iron boxes were loaded into covered rickshaws and sinewy, barefoot men with triangular hats and screaming muscles pedalled people and their belongings into the town.

I felt a tap on my shoulder and looked up into my husband's broad, dark face. I must have shone with youth and eagerness for his small eyes looked at me with almost fatherly tolerance.

'Come, Bilal will be waiting,' he shouted into the din. I followed his huge figure as he easily carried along all that belonged to me in his hands. He stepped in front of a large black car parked under the shade of a tree. Bilal, the driver, was Malay. He spoke no Tamil and as he could pluck no Malay from my tongue he studied me curiously, nodded and summoned a yellow grin for the master's child bride. I climbed into the motor car with its pale leather seats. I had never been in a motor car before. And this is the beginning of my rich new life, I thought with an indescribable sense of adventure.

The streets weren't paved with gold but thick with dust and dirt. Warehouses with curved Oriental roofs and bold Chinese letters at the entrances dozed in the burning sun. Rows of narrow shop-houses stood on either side of the street, congested with a marvellous array of wares. Fresh produce in baskets spilled out onto the pavement and on specially built wooden steps sat large bottles of dried goods. Tailors, shoemakers, bakers, goldsmiths and the grocery store were all in one long row of colour, noise and smell. Inside coffee shops stringy old men with leather faces and baggy shorts lounged, cigarettes dangling from their stained fingers. Disappearing around corners were tattered dogs with moist noses and scavenger eyes. In a makeshift stall by the roadside a row of ducks hung by their broken necks and in a wooden cage on the ground a flock of live ones squawked and quarrelled noisily. A huge butcher's knife buried in a chopping block glinted crazily. Men, coloured midnight blue by the sun, swept the drains by the road with long brooms.

At a set of traffic lights in the middle of town, two old women squatted in the shade of a tree and gossiped, the loose skin on their faces wobbling. On the other side of the road a creature more glorious than I could have imagined alighted from a car. She was delicate of bone and fair, so fair, she was almost white. Dressed in a bright red Chinese costume she had pinned in her midnight hair jewelled combs and trailing beads. Her eyes were almond-shaped and large but slanting and coy and her small mouth was shaped like a tiny rosebud. She had painted it very red and it glistened in the sun. Everything about her was perfect and doll-like until she took a small tottering step forward. One of her minders shot out a steadying hand. Ungratefully she cracked her fan on the helping hand, pulling away haughtily. It was then I realised her feet were no bigger than my balled fist. And I have small hands. I blinked and stared incredulously at her misshapen feet clad in black silk shoes meant for a very small child.

'Her feet were bound when she was a little girl,' my husband said into the terrible heat inside the car.

I whirled around in shock. 'Why?'

'So they wouldn't grow big and clumsy like yours,' he teased lightly.

'What?' I cried in disbelief.

'It is the custom in China to bind a girl's feet. The Chinese consider bound feet beautiful and desirable. Only the poor peasants who have a need for an extra pair of hands in the rice fields have daughters with unbound feet. As early as the age of two or three the best families bind the feet of their young girls so tightly that the growing bones mangle into a painful arch. And throughout the rest of their lives they pay the price of indescribable pain for this hint of femininity. Once bound their feet can never be unbound again or they grow into deformed shapes that would make even their strange rocking steps impossible.'

I had left my innocent village behind for ever.

Instantly I decided that the Chinese race was barbarous. To bind one's own daughter's feet as she howled in agony, to watch her through the years hobbling along painfully must take a particularly cruel heart. What depraved taste had first hankered for a deformed foot? I looked down at my sturdy feet in their brown slippers and was glad for them. These feet had run free through forests and swum in cool water and had never even considered the possibility that somewhere in the world little girls sat helplessly in pain all day and wept softly all night.

Soon our car was making its way out of the bustling town. A man in muddy clothes led a water buffalo by the nose along the side of the road. Small huts dotted the flat landscape. My husband relaxed back into the hard seat and his small eyes closed into sleep. In the blazing midday sun the road stretched out like a silvery grey snake, twisting through rice paddy fields, spice plantations and eventually through the bright orange soil of virgin forests. On either side rose walls of tangled dark-green vegetation. Giant ferns threw their fronds out into the yellow light and fat creepers swung untidily from tree branches in an effort to snatch at pieces of dappled sunlight like children reaching for birthday cake. And here and there rough bark peered out like old faces frowning with worry. Between the flat leaves all was still and quiet. Mile after mile. Water mirages appeared and disappeared on the road. The forest wisely slept but I couldn't even blink for fear of missing something momentous.

The two hours of constant vigilance paid off.

On the horizon I saw first one then two and then a whole line of people on bicycles. They were all dressed from head to toe in black. And every single one of them was frighteningly faceless, lurking inside the shadows their black headdresses threw over their faces. The headdresses were kept in place with red handkerchiefs tied under their chins. On top of the black headdress and red handkerchiefs they wore enormous straw hats. Their black sleeves they wore longer than their hands. Not a tiny strip of flesh was exposed. Unhurriedly they approached.

I shook Ayah urgently awake.

'What? What is it?' he muddled, bewildered into sudden wakefulness.

'Look!' I cried fearfully, pointing at the obvious menace in the black procession ahead.

His eyes followed my finger. 'Oh them,' he sighed, relieved, and settled back sleepily. 'They are dulang-washers. They work in the tin mines and sieve tin ore in large trays from the mining sites. Underneath all that black material are some of the fairest Chinese girls you will ever meet. You should see them at night, when they squeeze into their tight cheongsams.'

The slender trail wheeled past. Silent. Harmless.

I was intrigued. They wrapped themselves like the mummies in an Egyptian pyramid so they could remain rice-powder white. We rattled along on roads meant for carts, passed small towns and lazy villages. Once Bilal slowed down for two small, wild pigs that snorted and scurried across the road in a moment of curiosity. Brown children, naked, ran to the side of the road to watch us and wave enthusiastically. Sweating freely inside six yards of material anchored on a firmly tied white petticoat I loved them instantly. Inside me a barefoot girl longed to get out. Even now I think I remember those velvet-eyed children best. Mid-afternoon we passed a Chinese temple with granite pillars, a deep-red interior and intricately carved stone dragons resting on its ceramic roof.

At length we reached Kuantan, our final destination. Bilal drove into a potholed road strewn with sharp white stones. A cul-de-sac of sorts. The road encircled an untidy clump of wild bushes, a bamboo grove, a rather splendid rambutan tree, and served the five dwellings built around it. The house closest to the main road was the grandest, obviously mine. Under a shady angsana tree nestled a table and chairs made of stone. It was beautiful and I loved it. Inside the coolness of its thick walls I imagined soft-footed servants. I noticed red Chinese lanterns hanging by the door and pondered the reason for them.

Bilal slowed the car down next to the big, black gates but as I prepared to get out, two savage Alsatian dogs ran out to bark threateningly at us. Then, having negotiated a large pothole, Bilal drove on, right past the beautiful house. A small brown face at one of the windows watched us pass with avid curiosity. I turned towards my husband but he deliberately avoided my searching gaze and stared ahead. Confused, I turned away. We bumped along the terrible road. The other four houses were poor and wooden. Bilal stopped outside a small house on low stilts.

My husband got out and I clambered out in my brown slippers, a crumpled, dazed little person. The bags came out of the trunk of the car and Bilal, who was not my husband's trusted driver at all, bade us goodbye and drove off. Ayah fished around in his baggy trousers and produced a set of keys. He smiled into my reduced face. 'Welcome home, my dear, dear wife,' he said softly.

'But . . . but . . .'

But he was gone, striding ahead on those ridiculously long legs of his. The wooden door of the wooden house opened and swallowed him whole. For a moment I could only stare at the dusky interior of the house then I followed slowly. At the first step I stopped. Mother had been tricked. The thought was heavy: *My husband was not rich, he was poor*. Pani had duped us. I was all alone in a strange country with a man who was not what he was supposed to be. I had no money of my own, didn't speak a word of English or the local language and hadn't the least idea of how to return home. The blood ran very fast in my veins.

Inside it was cool and dark. The house was sleeping. Quietly and softly. Not for long, I thought. I opened all the windows in the small living room. Fresh air and weak, slanting evening sunlight streamed into the little house. Suddenly it didn't matter at all that it wasn't a grand house or that I wouldn't have servants to command. In fact, the challenge of making something out of nothing beckoned, far more exciting. I could still be the lady of the wooden house.

Ayah had disappeared somewhere at the back of the house. Curiously I began to explore. I walked on a concrete floor and looked at wooden walls. The small living room held two rickety armchairs cradling tired old cushions, a small ugly side table, a dilapidated old dining table and four poor chairs slumped around it. I went into the bedroom and was amazed to find a huge, iron four-poster bed painted silver. I had never seen such a big bed in all my life. Surely it was a bed fit for a king. The curtains were faded to an ailing green. The cotton-filled mattress was lumpy but to me it was heavenly. I had never slept on anything but a woven mat. An old intricately carved cupboard made of very dark wood with a mirror on its left door creaked when I opened it. Silver cobwebs hung inside. I found some of my husband's clothes and four saris belonging to the first wife. I took them out. They were plain and dull, the discreet colours of a dead woman. Standing in front of the mirror I loosely draped a grey one around my body and I thought of her for the first time. Once she had lived in this house and worn these clothes. I touched the cool material and sniffed it. It smelt of the earth during the dry season. The hot smell made me shiver. The saris reminded me of her and her children whom I had so easily left behind. I put the sari back inside the cupboard and closed it quickly.

In the second bedroom two old beds crouched by the

window. A shelf had been turned into a prayer altar with framed pictures of Hindu deities. Bunches of dead flowers crowned the pictures. There had not been a woman in the house for a long time. Automatically I pressed my palms together in a gesture of respect and prayer. Two pairs of children's slippers lay by the door. Two small faces looked up to me. 'We have no shoes,' they murmured sadly, their eyes desolate. Quickly I backed out, closing the door behind me.

The bathroom, I was surprised to note, was connected to the house. Back home I had to walk to an outhouse. I heard my husband moving onto the veranda. I inspected the smooth grey walls, turned on a small bronze tap and beautiful, clear water rushed out into the built-in, cement water container in the corner. It looked like a waist-high well and I was pleased with it. I flicked the old-fashioned, round black light switch and yellow light filled the tiny, windowless space. Truly I was delighted with my new bathroom. I left the bathroom and walked into the kitchen where I gave my first cry of joy. For in the far corner was the most beautiful bench I had ever seen. Made of hard wood with beautifully carved legs, it was as big as a single bed. I examined it minutely with real pleasure, running my fingers over the aged, smooth surface, not realising that that piece of furniture would survive me and one day hold on its dark surface my dead husband's body.

From the kitchen window I could see a cemented area for washing and outdoor tasks like grinding and milling, and a vast, neglected backyard with mature coconut trees. A large monsoon drain divided our property from the fields covered in spear grass beyond. A small path could be seen leading away into woodlands.

With the energy of a fourteen-year-old I began to clean, clear, wash and wipe. My house became my new toy. My husband sat on an easy chair on the veranda outside, lit himself a long cheroot and proceeded to enjoy it. The aromatic smell wafted into the house as I bustled about importantly. Soon the small house looked neat and tidy, and finding some ingredients in the kitchen I made a simple curry of lentils and cooked some rice.

While the food bubbled gently I closed myself in my new bathroom, turned on the tap and luxuriated in my indoor well. Clean and fresh I removed all the dead flowers from the prayer altar. From the jasmine shrub at the end of our terribly overgrown backyard I plucked a plateful of flowers and decorated the altar with them. I prayed for blessings. Ayah came in and I served him the simple meal. He ate heartily but slowly, as was his way in all things.

'What work do you do?' I asked.

'I'm a clerk.'

I nodded but it didn't mean anything to me. Only later would I learn the level of meniality the word represented.

'Where did the bed and bench come from?'

'I used to work for an Englishman and when he was returning home for good he gave them to me.'

I nodded slowly. Yes, it was a superior bed and a superior bench meant for people who caught sunlight in their hair.

That night, as I lay in the unfamiliar bed, I closed my eyes and listened to the night sounds. The wind rustling in the bamboo reeds, the crickets gossiping in the dark, a lemur scratching in the rambutan tree and the snake-charmer's flute. The lonely melody reminded me of Mother. It made me think of her all alone in her small hut. Tomorrow I would write to her. I would tell her everything from the lady with the crushed feet to the black-clad mine workers. And I wouldn't forget the barefoot children or the row of ducks, their necks broken. I would tell her everything, except perhaps that her daughter had married a poor man. And I would never tell her about the soft clink that the shining gold watch, which had so impressed her, made when it fell into Bilal's upturned palm, just before he nodded and returned to his real master. I heard the stiffly starched sheets rustle in the dark and felt his heavy hand rest on my stomach and sighed softly.

My neighbourhood was a circle of five homes. The splendid house that I had coveted on my arrival in fact belonged to the third wife of a very rich Chineseman called Old Soong. Next to her, in a house similar to mine lived a Malay lorry driver and his family. He was away a lot but his wife, Minah, was a good-hearted and neighbourly woman who welcomed me with a plate of coconut jelly on the second day of my arrival. She had the open, smiling face one comes across in every Malay kampong, a truly astounding hourglass figure and a genteel manner neatly folded inside her person. She wore soft grace like a long, beautifully cut costume. There were no hard edges about her. Everything was refined, her voice, her manners, her movements, her walk, her language, and her skin. When she left I stood behind my faded curtains and watched the slow sway of her hips until her figure disappeared behind the bead curtain hanging over her doorway. Inconceivable but she was the mother of four children. It was only much later, after the end of her fifth pregnancy, that I learned about the nightmare of a traditional Malay confinement. Forty-two days of bitter herbs, a smoking, hot stove under the bed to dry out excess fluid and tighten vaginal muscles, a tenaciously bound stomach and merciless, daily massages from freakishly strong, wrinkled old women. But hardship has its rewards. Minah was living testament.

Next to her house was a confusingly plentiful Chinese household. All manner of people seemed to appear and leave from that small house, making me wonder where they all slept. Sometimes one of the women from the household would run out into the pathway after a screaming child and, catching it, pull down his or her pants and slap its white flesh till it turned bright red. Then, still cursing and swearing, she would leave the child sobbing pitifully on the roadway. Sometimes they punished one of the older girls by making her run around their house naked. She might have been nine or ten and I felt very sorry for the poor mite as she streaked by my window, scrawny, red-eyed and sniffing. They were uncouth and brazen but the reason I hated them with foul vengeance was because every day in the half-light of dusk the man's two wives took turns to fertilise their vegetable plot with human waste. And every time the wind blew in our direction the horrible stench disgusted me, put me off my food and made me want to retch.

To the right of us lived an old hermit. Sometimes I glimpsed his face, long and sad at the window. Next to him lived the snake-charmer, a small, wiry man with blue-black straight hair and a hawk-like nose in a stern, wild face. At the beginning I was fearful of this man with his dancing cobras and poisonous snakes from which he made snake medicine for sale, worrying that his escaped snakes were lurking in my bed. His wife was a small, thin woman and they had seven children in total. One day while I was at the market I found myself at the fringe of a big circle of curious onlookers. Manoeuvring my purchases I pressed my way forward. In the middle sat the snake-charmer closing the lids of his baskets, his act apparently finished. He signalled to one of his sons. A boy, no more than seven or eight years old, came forward. Curly locks hung low obscuring bright, laughing eyes. Dressed in a grubby white shirt and a pair of khaki shorts he looked like a street urchin. In his hand he held a beer bottle. Suddenly, without warning, he smashed the bottle on the ground, picked up a piece of glass, put it in his mouth and began to chew. The crowd gasped and went silent.

Blood began to pour from the boy's mouth. It poured down his chin and seeped into his grubby white collar. Red trickled down his shirtfront. He picked up another broken piece from the dirty ground and stuffed it into his mouth. As I stood horrified and transfixed, he opened his mouth wide to show the blood-filled cavity then pulled out a little red cloth bag from his pocket and, still crunching, began to collect coins from the crowd. I pushed my way out frantically. The feat, the trick was beyond me. I felt disturbed and upset and physically ill. Ever since that incident I avoided contact with the snake-charmer family. I was convinced there was skullduggery and black magic being practised in that strange household. That in their half-darkened house lay a presence that could not be described but made my flesh crawl and creep.

I sat on the veranda and watched the snake-charmer's son run barefoot to the lorry driver's house, his curls flying in the wind. I could still see him standing in the middle of a group of gaping spectators, a mess of crushed glass and blood in his poor mouth, his eyes not laughing but grave. He saw me watching him and waved. I waved back. The smell of my neighbours' cooking blossomed in the air. The sweet fragrance of pork sizzling in hot lard made me yearn for something other than vegetables and rice. The cupboards were all bare but fortunately Mother had written down in meticulous detail her best recipes and we had been living on my ability to turn an onion into a tasty dish for the last two weeks. But that day I was expectant with waiting. It was pay day. I sat on the veranda waiting for Ayah to come home, impatient to feel housekeeping money in my hand for the first time. Just like my mother I too would plan and spread the money wisely, but first I wanted to treat us to some good food for a change. I saw Ayah turn into our road, his big body clumsy on the rickety bicycle as he manoeuvred it on the loose stones. I stood up quickly.

He parked his bicycle unhurriedly, smiling at me. I smiled back restlessly. In my hand I had a letter from Ceylon for him, and as I held out the light blue envelope to him, he delved into his pocket and brought out a thin brown envelope. We exchanged envelopes and he passed me by and went into the house. I stared at the brown envelope in my young hands in complete surprise. All of it. He had given me his entire salary. I tore open the envelope and counted the money. Two hundred and twenty ringgit in all. A lot of money. Immediately I began to make plans in my head. I would send my mother some money and a nice chunk I would hide together with my jewels in my square tin that once held imported chocolates. I would save and save and soon we would be as rich as Old Soong. I would make a rosy future for us. I stood there grasping the money and my fabulous dreams in both hands, when a man in a Nehru-cut jacket, a white *veshti*, leather slippers and holding a huge black umbrella turned into our dirt road. In his other hand he carried a leather briefcase. He was walking towards me with a big smile. Soon the squat man with the bulging pot-belly stood before me. His eyes drifted to the money clutched in my hands. I lowered my hands slowly and his greedy eyes followed the money. I waited until his gaze managed the journey up to meet my eyes. The round face filled with false cheer. I disliked him on sight.

'Greetings to the new lady of the house,' he said cheerfully.

'Who are you?' I asked sullenly, unforgivably rude.

He didn't take offence. 'I'm your moneylender,' he explained with a large smile that showed reddish brown teeth. From a pocket he produced a small notebook, licked a fat finger and thumbed through the soiled pages. 'If you will just give me twenty ringgit and sign against today's date I shall not bother you any longer and be on my merry way.'

I practically snatched the notebook from his pudgy hands. Bemused, I saw my husband's name at the top left-hand corner and a row of his signatures against different amounts. For the last month he had paid nothing while he was in Ceylon looking for a new wife. The man's eyes gleamed as he reminded me about the arrears and interest. In a daze I handed over the twenty ringgit for that month, the arrears and the interest he demanded.

'Good day to you, madam, and see you next month,' he chirped as he turned away to leave.

'Wait,' I cried. 'How much debt is left?'

'Oh just another hundred ringgit,' he sang merrily.

'A hundred ringgit,' I mouthed silently and looking up saw another two men coming towards our house. As they passed the moneylender they nodded.

'Greetings to the new lady of the house,' they chorused.

I shuddered. That day the 'visitors' didn't cease until well after dark. At one point there was even a queue outside the door until eventually I was left clutching fifty ringgit. Fifty ringgit to last me an entire month. I stood silently in the middle of our shabby living room, embarrassed and fuming.

'I have only fifty ringgit to last me the whole month,' I announced as calmly as I could to my husband as he ate his last mouthful of rice and potatoes.

Dull eyes regarded me, for a minute. I thought of a heavy animal, its lumbering slowness, its stoic endurance in the face of persistent flies and its filthy, swishing tail as it just stood there. Stupidly.

'Don't worry,' he soothed finally. 'Whenever you need money just ask me and I can borrow some more. I have good credit.'

I could only stare incredulously at him. A sudden gust of wind blew into our kitchen the smell of human waste. The food inside my stomach did a small back-flip, and somewhere inside my head a hammering began. A loud insistent hammering that would last me for the rest of my life with only short breaks in between. I gazed away from the dull black eyes of the lumbering beast and said nothing.

That night, in the light of a kerosene lamp, I sat cross-legged on my beautiful bench and made a list of debtors. I couldn't sleep for the plans I was making. Finally, when all the night demons had flown over to the other side of the world I lay on my stomach and watched through the open window a red dawn break over the eastern sky. The hammering in my head had relented a little. The plan was clear in my head. I made a strong brew of black tea and sitting at my good table I slowly sipped it like my mother and her mother before her had done at the end of a long day. Before the birds began their day I bathed in icy cold water, washed my hair in coconut milk and, dressed in a clean cotton sari, walked the one mile to the Ganesha temple just behind Apu's provision shop. In the small temple by the dirt road I prayed with all my heart. So sincerely that tears escaped from my closed eyelids. I begged Lord Ganesha to make my plan work and my new life a happy one. I then put ten cents into the donation box by the Elephant God who was ever merciful and tender-hearted, and rubbing holy ash on my forehead walked back.

When I arrived home my husband had just awakened. The crackle of the radio filled the small house. I made gruel and coffee for him and sat to watch him eat. I felt strong and protective towards him, our house and our new life together. After my husband had left I sat down and composed a letter, a very important letter. Then I walked into town. At the post office I posted the letter to my uncle, the mango dealer. He lived with his wife in Seremban, another state in Malaya. I had a proposition for him. I wanted to borrow the total amount of debt that was owed by my husband plus a little more to tide me over until the next pay packet arrived. In exchange I would pay him some interest and he could keep my box of jewels as collateral. My jewels I knew were worth far more than the amount I was asking. My mother had given me a ruby pendant nearly as large as my smallest toe and that alone I knew was worth a great deal of money. It was a beautiful stone with a strange hot light inside that, in the sunlight, breathed red fire like a live thing. After I had posted the letter I went to the market, a fascinating place full of splendid things I had never seen before.

I stood before piles of black salted eggs, one or two on top of the pile left open to expose yolks the colour of blood. Chinesemen in wooden clogs squatted on the ground selling little clouds of birds' nests. Inside wire cages large lizards scurried about with nervous, jerky movements at the sight of slithering snakes in other cages. There was fresh everything in woven baskets and Malay women traders with gold teeth sold soft turtle eggs in wire baskets.

In one corner an ancient Chinesewoman, barely able to walk, hobbled about her strangely twisted mud-coloured sea cucumbers, hardened black seaweed, and a whole cornucopia of unidentifiable creatures swimming in water-filled wooden buckets. Trappers chewing betel nut waited patiently behind stacks of all sorts of wild roots, wild creatures still struggling and bunches of medicinal leaves. Sometimes in their hands they held the tails of four or five live snakes that writhed and stretched themselves out on the pavement in front of them. People bought those multicoloured, slim snakes for medicinal purposes. There were vats full of yellow noodles and rows of roasted ducks hanging by their greasy necks still dripping fat. Of course the frogs were the real surprise, white and disembodied they lay spread-eagled on slabs of wood. But on that day I didn't linger. I was on a mission.

I quickly purchased a very small piece of meat, some

vegetables, a bag of tamarind and a dulang-washer's large, broad-brimmed hat for five cents and made for the jetty where I bought a handful of prawns. Mother had a very special recipe for prawns and I was certain I knew how to make it. Head bent and totally lost in my own thoughts of a rosy future I retraced my steps home. In front of me my shadow was very long and eager. I was so intent upon the execution of all my carefully hatched plans that I jumped when another shadow joined mine. I looked around and found the face that had stared so curiously from the open window of Old Soong's house, smiling a shy, uncertain smile. Two long black plaits ending in childish pink bows hung on either side of her face. Why, she was only as old as I was. A pair of jet black eyes sparkled in her round face.

Mui Tsai (little sister) in reality, I later found out, was a pitiful domestic slave. I smiled back tentatively. I had found a friend but it was to be the beginning of a lost friendship. If I had known then what I know now, I would have treasured her more. She was the only true friend I ever made. She tried to communicate with me in Malay but the language was still an unfamiliar mixture of sounds to me and we only managed a series of complicated hand gestures. I decided to ask Ayah to teach me to speak proper Malay. We parted company at the gates of her house. I saw her hurry indoors with her basket full of market produce.

As soon as I got home I hunted around in the kitchen and found a very long, rusty old knife that in its heyday had probably been used to crack coconuts. Then I donned the petticoat that one wears inside the sari. On top of that I wore an old frayed shirt that belonged to my husband. The shirtsleeves came over my hands and I looked at the overlap with satisfaction. Then I placed a huge man's handkerchief over my head and tied it under my chin. I popped my new dulang-washer hat on top of my head and, satisfied that I was completely protected from the cruel sun, I opened the green back door and began to clear away the weeds, long grasses and nasty brambles that cut my hands and made them bleed. Stinging plants grew abundantly in every square yard but I was absolutely determined. I didn't stop until the entire place was clear and the hard earth tilled and softened by my curving knife. My back ached horribly and muscles in innocent places screamed with pain but I felt pleasure, real pleasure at a job well done.

When I finally came in, sweat dripped off me and ran down my body in rivulets. After a cold shower I soothed my swollen hands with sesame seed oil before I began to cook. I marinated the meat in spices and left the potent mixture to gently simmer in a heavy closed pot for the next few hours. While it simmered I cleaned and pounded the prawns. Then I grated fresh coconut and made Mother's special sambal with chillies and onions. Afterwards I cooked aubergines in a little water that had turmeric and salt in it and when it became soft I crushed it into a chunky paste, added coconut milk, and let it come up to the boil. I sliced potatoes and fried them with a little curry powder. The onions and tomatoes I chopped and mixed with fresh yoghurt. A meal fit for a king nearly ready, I set about cleaning the house. I was feeling quite pleased with all the lovely aromas coming from the cooking meat when I found a letter ripped to pieces inside Ayah's tobacco tin. I know I shouldn't have but I couldn't help myself. I scooped up the pieces and, laying the fragments of curly blue handwriting flat on the bed, I read the letter that had arrived for my husband yesterday.

Dear Ayah,

The village is poorer than ever but I can never hope to leave and prosper as you have done. This impoverished land is where the funeral pyre for my old bones shall light the skies for a short while. But the past few weeks have been a joyful godsend for me for I have learned to love your two children like my very own flesh and blood. At least now I will not die alone.

I hope that in the youthful arms of your new happiness you have not forgotten your responsibilities. The children are growing fast and need new clothes, new shoes and good food. As you know I am alone with no husband to lean on and now I have two new hungry mouths to feed. I hope you will send some money urgently as the situation is getting quite dire for me.

I stopped reading. The rest of the letter from Aunty Pani was a blur. My legs felt suddenly weak and I sat down heavily on the bed. Then I understood why she had come for me that day, the speculative look in her sly eyes and the instinctive revulsion I had experienced at the sight of her. She had wanted to keep the children as her means of income for many years to come. She had come to a poor woman's house looking for a malleable young bride. One she could manipulate. At that moment I felt as if I hated her. How hateful her demanding tone. Did she fancy my husband's head a footstool? It made my blood boil with anger. I had barely had a good meal since the day I got married, and for the next eight months, if my plan was to work, I would have to save and scrape to get by, let alone send more money. Wouldn't it be a good lesson for her if we simply didn't send the money? But then in my mind rose the picture of two small children, their eyes barren and hopeless, their dark skin stretched tight over wide cheekbones. The innocence and stupidity indisputable for all to see. Even their teeth were so bored with sitting inside such empty heads, they jutted out in two uneven yellow rows to stare at the world outside. Doubtless the children were nothing more than slaves to the crafty woman, but the truth, no matter how horrible it makes me look, was that I didn't want them to live with me.

I closed my eyes and experienced profound defeat. I had been spectacularly used by the woman. Had it not been for her pretty lies, I could still have been at home with my beloved mother.

We would have to send the money. We had no choice.

Then the beauty of youth stepped in. As spring touches new leaves onto withered branches, youth decided that my plan could stretch to an allowance for my step-children. My mother and I suffered because my father did not bother to send us money. I would do better than my father. We simply wouldn't have meat until all our bills were settled. We would live on our vegetable patch outside and from the eggs our hens laid when we had our chicken coop installed. By the time I went into the kitchen to stir the meat, the bounce was back in my step.

That evening my husband returned with cash that he had borrowed from the moneylender to send to his children, a newspaper-wrapped present for me and a piece of wood that he said he was going to carve. He put the present beside me on my bench and waited. I looked at his expectant face and then at the unwanted newspaper-wrapped present and I wanted to scream in pure frustration. At this rate we would never climb out of our snake-pit of debts. How to explain that I'd rather starve for a month than endure a queue of moneylenders outside the house every pay day? I took a deep breath, bit my tongue and untied the string. The newspaper tore open and my animosity died in my throat. Inside was the most adorable pair of high-heeled gold slippers adorned with coloured beads I had ever seen in my life. With something akin to reverence I placed them on the grey concrete floor. Enchanted, I slipped my feet between the dainty gold ropes. They fitted perfectly. The heels would take a bit of getting used to but I already loved my unnecessary acquisition.

'Thank you,' I whispered, my head bowed with humble gratitude.

He was a good man, my husband, but we were still doing it my way. First he had his sumptuous meal and then I told him of my plan. He listened in silence. Finally, taking a deep breath and looking him directly in the eye, I told him that from now on I would be the only one paying the bills. He would receive a small allowance to buy a newspaper or a cup of coffee from the canteen at work, but he could borrow no more money and was to refer to me on anything pertaining to our financial health. He nodded and gently stroked my hair with his big hand but his dull eyes were ravaged. 'As you wish, my darling wife,' he agreed.

'And one more thing. Will you teach me to speak Malay?'

'*Boleh*.' He smiled at me.

I knew that word. It meant 'can do'. I smiled back.

'*Terima Kasih*.' Thank you, in Malay.

By the end of that week, my vegetable garden was

planted. A man from across the main road had built me a chicken coop and I housed it with soft, yellow chicks. As I stood under my dulang-washer's hat proudly surveying my new plot of cultivated land, my uncle, the mango merchant, arrived groaning under the weight of a huge sack of mangoes. At the sight of his familiar brown face I dashed away tears of joy and ran to hug his round figure. I didn't know how lonely I was until I saw him. He had brought the money I had requested, heartily laughing away as ridiculous my idea of collateral. After he left I ate six mangoes in quick succession and then, inexplicably, walked to the stove, picked up some charcoal pieces and began to nibble at them.

That was when I knew I was pregnant.

The weeks were swallowed by the hungry months that lay waiting in my garden. My little plot prospered. I ran my fingers down the velvety skin of a new crop of lady fingers, was surprised by the redness of my bird's-eye chillies and grew especially proud of my shiny purple aubergines. And my chicken coop was a success even before my belly filled out the space in front of me. I was happy and satisfied. The debts were taken care of and I had even begun to save a modest amount inside a small tin that I hid in the rice sack.

At night, after all the human voices died down, the plates washed, light switches turned off and the neighbourhood put away to sleep, I lay awake. Sleep refused to rest awhile upon my eyelids. He crossed his arms and looked at me wickedly from afar. So I spent many hours laying flat on my back staring out of the window at the star-filled night sky, learning Malay and filling my head with impatient dreams of my unborn baby. I imagined a cherubic baby boy with gorgeous ringlets and sparkling eyes. Always in my daydreams he would have clever, large eyes that darted about in alert intelligence, but always in my nightmares a thin, emaciated infant with small, dull eyes and stretched shiny skin would stare beseechingly at me. Begging for a little love. I would jerk awake suddenly, guilt for my abandoned stepchildren like a small furry bee inside my heart. Trapped, lonely, it lifted its furry front legs and knocked softly on the door of my heart. And my young heart would miss a beat in pure shame. Before dawn I would bathe and make my way to the temple. There I would make offerings and earnestly pray that my child would look nothing like the waif of my nightmares.

My husband was solicitous to a degree that made me want to scream. He would worriedly enquire after me every morning and every night, and wait for my answer expectantly as if I might say something other than, 'I'm just fine.' For nine months it never crossed his mind not to ask worriedly and wait expectantly for my reply. He refused to let me walk to the market and would insist on going himself. At first he came home with old fish, grey meat and rotting vegetables, but after a few false starts and cold sulking silences from me he made friends with a kind stallkeeper who felt sorry for his predicament. After that he returned with fish whose silver-bright eyes were still bloody with freshness, fruit ripe with colour and choice pieces of meat that I myself would have been pleased to have chosen.

One day he brought home some strange fruit called durian. I had never before seen a fruit covered in such menacing-looking long thorns. A durian falling off a tree onto a man's head can kill him, he told me. I had no trouble believing him. He carefully prised open the prickly skin and inside lay rows of flesh-covered seeds. I fell in love with the creamy taste of the golden flesh instantly. I even loved its astonishingly unique smell that I am told prompted an English novelist to describe it as eating a sweet raspberry blancmange in a lavatory. I am perfectly capable of finishing five or six fruit in a single sitting.

By the time I was eight months pregnant I was so uncomfortable that I would lumber out of bed as quietly as possible and lie on the hard coolness of the bench in the kitchen. Through the window the inky blackness of the Malayan night would reach in and caress me, its touch heavy and moist. Sometimes my husband would come in to peer worriedly in the gloom and to enquire after me. And on those wretched nights I would swallow my nasty spurt of irritation and remind myself that he was a good man.

At least I did not have little Mui Tsai's terrible sorrows. She was also pregnant. Her stomach bulged through the thin high-necked blouses she always wore to denote her status as a 'little sister'. She tied her loose black trousers underneath the smooth white bulge. In the shadows cast by the oil lamp her story was enough to make Despair itself despair. It all started in a little village in China when her mother died suddenly from a strange fever. Mui Tsai was eight years old. In less than a month, a new silk-clad mother came to live with them. In the tradition of good Chinese omens, a small red mouth flowered in her pale round face. The Chinese favoured brides with small mouths, believing that women with big mouths were harbingers of ill fortune. A woman with a large mouth spiritually swallowed her husband and caused his early death.

The new bride's mouth was reassuring but the thing that made Mui Tsai's father melt like a dollop of yellow ghee in his new wife's presence was her bound feet. The bride's feet were smaller than her eight-year-old step-daughter's feet, for Mui Tsai's mother had been too soft-hearted to bind her daughter's feet. The new bride sat in a scented room quite helpless to the calls of ordinary housework. Mui Tsai ended every long, arduous day with the task of taking off her stepmother's restraining bandages and bathing her feet in warm fragrant water. So many years later, Mui Tsai's elongated shadow shuddered on my kitchen wall with the memory of her stepmother's bare feet. A sight wisely denied to all men and especially one's husband, for the stark deformity without the dainty little shoes was unbearable. Twisted, bruised and reeking of decaying flesh, they had the power to repel the most ardent suitor. Every day some dead skin and in-grown nail had to be clipped away before the ugly things were re-bandaged with rose petals.

For three years Mui Tsai fetched, cleaned and cooked for her new mother. After her thirteenth birthday her stepmother's gaze turned from ill-concealed dislike to one of calculation. Mui Tsai's sister had just turned eight and could now take over her duties. If the elder girl remained in the household there would be the worry of a marriage. Marriages meant dowries. One morning while Mui Tsai's father was at work her stepmother made the young girl dress in her best and sit in the front room. She sent word to the market and a passing merchant came to the house. Mui Tsai was sold to him. A legal and binding document was drawn up on thin red paper. From the moment her stepmother's soft white hands signed the paper Mui Tsai became the exclusive property of the merchant. For the rest of her life she would have no will of her own.

The merchant with the hard eyes and long yellow fingernails paid for her and she was taken away with nothing but the clothes on her back. He caged her. In the same room there were other cages with other crouched, frightened children. For weeks she lived like that, a sullen maid passing bowls of food and receiving containers of waste through the same hole in the cage. In that dark room, together with girls from other villages, she cried and moaned with fear and sickness. Yet none of them could understand each other's dialect. Then they were all thrown on a junk boat set for South East Asia. The old boat tossed wildly on the South China Seas made turbulent by strong monsoon winds. For many days the wretched children screamed in terror. The sour smell of ocean sickness plunged them into the sure belief that they would all perish at sea to become food for the sons and daughters of all the white-fleshed fish that they had unthinkingly consumed during their lifetimes. Miraculously they survived. Still wobbly from the miserable voyage, they were efficiently disposed of in Singapore and Malaya, sold as whores and domestic slaves at a handsome profit.

Old Soong, Mui Tsai's new master, paid the princely sum of two hundred and fifty ringgit for her. She was to be a gift for his new, third, wife. Thus little Mui Tsai came to live in the grand house at the top of our cul-de-sac. For the first two years she did the housework and lived in a tiny room at the back of the house. But, one day the master, who had until then concentrated on running his chubby hand up his wife's ivory thighs and teasing morsels of food from the ends of his chopsticks into her sulky mouth, suddenly began to smile at Mui Tsai in a manner not quite wholesome. Then, about the time I moved into the neighbourhood, his greedy eyes began to follow her at mealtimes with an intensity that was frightening to the young girl, for he was a repulsive creature.

On my way to the market I had sometimes seen him sitting in the cool of his living room under the whirling fan, sweating profusely while reading the Chinese newspaper, his extra-large singlet stretched across his bulging belly. The tightly packed fat reminded me of his insatiable penchant for dog meat. He often brought home the flesh of puppies wrapped in waxed brown paper. The cook made it into a stew laced with expensive ginseng imported specially from mainland China.

Every evening the master played the same game. With both his pudgy hands covering his mouth he picked his teeth while his hot eyes like fleshy hands roved over his servant's youthful body. Her eyes carefully averted, Mui Tsai pretended not to notice. She did not realise that that was her role in the game. Reluctance. The wife, her eyes downcast, saw nothing. She sat in her fine garments, and like an eagle she poised with elbows on the table waiting patiently for the arrival of each new dish, whereupon her waiting chopsticks moved with quicksilver speed, spearing the choicest morsels with unerring accuracy. Once the best pieces were in her bowl she proceeded to eat with alluring daintiness.

Soon Old Soong was finding occasions to let his fingers accidentally brush his wife's 'little sister' and, once, his fat hand slid up her thigh while she was serving the soup. The soup spilled on the table. Still the wife saw nothing. 'Stupid wasteful girl,' she muttered angrily into her full bowl of tender suckling pig.

'Tell her,' I urged, horrified.

'How can I?' Mui Tsai whispered back aghast, her almost eyes shocked. 'He is the master of the house.'

As his attentions grew bolder Mui Tsai began to leave her room at night. She only slept in there when her master was at one of his other wives' homes. When he came to visit her mistress, Mui Tsai curled up under one of the beds in one of the rooms in the large sprawling house, and in this way for many months she managed to evade her master's sweaty grasp. Often she climbed through my kitchen window and we sat on my bench talking about our homeland into the wee hours of the morning.

I couldn't believe that what was happening to Mui Tsai was legal and I was determined to report the matter. Someone had to do something to end her suffering. I told Ayah about it. He worked in an office. Surely he knew someone who could help, but he shook his head. The law could do nothing as long as the domestic slave was not abused.

'But her mistress slaps her and pinches her. That's abuse, isn't it?' I demanded hotly.

He shook his head and the words that walked onto his thick tongue appeared like uncouth foreigners who came into a temple with their shoes on. 'Firstly that is not considered abuse and secondly, although Mr Soong himself does not come to collect the rent, he is our landlord. He owns every house along this curving road.'

'Oh,' I said giving up all my revolutionary ideas of marching into strange offices to denounce Old Soong. The problem really was much bigger than me.

One night when the trees were silvery with ghostly moonlight Mui Tsai's mistress called her into her bedroom. She wanted a massage. Her back, she said, ached from eating too many cooling foods. She took off her satin garments and lay face down on the bed. Mui Tsai began to massage her. She ran her firm brown hands down the soft white skin of her mistress's back. Without her clothes, the mistress was inexorably running to fat.

'I shall let you massage the master tonight. He is very tired and you have such an excellent way with your hands,' she said, gathering up her satin robe. As if choreographed beforehand the master walked into the bedroom in his silken yellow robes that had the black embroidered dragons on them. His robe whispered against his flabby white legs. Mui Tsai froze with shock. Her mistress did not meet the master's eyes; instead she fixed Mui Tsai with a warning stare and admonished in an irritated voice, '*Ai Yah*, don't make such a fuss.' At the sound of her soft slippers dying on the terrazzo tiles the master sat on the slightly ruffled bedspread. Mui Tsai kneeling on the floor by the bedside looked up at him in disbelief. After months of hot looks the game was about to be won. The winner sat in a yellow robe. The robe parted further and his belly, large and hard in front of him, he reached over and switched off the little bedside lamp. In the moonlight his face with its sheen of moisture was suddenly mask-like. Mui Tsai was filled with terror. Intoxicated by the forbidden excitement implicit in the situation the eyes deeply buried in pale folds of flesh glittered hot. He stank of liquor. She felt the first small prick of loathing.

'Come, come, my dear,' the master invited gently, patting the bed beside him, his voice quickening. She knew his thoughts as if he had spoken them: *The girl was not destined to be a great beauty but in the first charming flush of youth undoubtedly pretty, and being a virgin would give him much-needed vitality. Always good for a man of his age to take the first drink of a girl's essence.* Her purity and innocence was like a flower waiting to be picked. And in that garden he was master.

He smiled an encouraging smile and disrobed his rotund body.

Poor girl, she was still staring at the small worm nestled between his legs in frozen disbelief when he lowered his white flesh over her tiny figure. Something small and hard entered her painfully and to her surprise loose wet flesh jiggled all around her. He grunted like a wild pig and groaned very close to her ear until without any warning his whole weight suddenly collapsed on top of her. Crushed, she gasped for breath. He rolled over and panted for a glass of water.

It was over. In a daze she pulled her trousers back on and went to get water for the master. Tears stung the back of her eyes and her chin wobbled with the effort not to cry. When she returned with the water he made her disrobe completely. While he drank his water the hot dark slits in his face studied her with unsmiling intensity. She felt his sticky passion running out of her and down her bloodied inside thighs. She stood naked and vacant in the pale moonlight until he reached out a fat hand and pulled her down once more. When he fell asleep, snoring heavily, Mui Tsai stared up unseeingly into the silver shadows on the ceiling until quite suddenly and with a start she found herself staring into the disgusted face of her mistress. Barefoot the woman had come into the room so stealthily that Mui Tsai had not heard her footsteps.

'Get up, you shameless hussy,' she hissed angrily. Her envious eyes roved the youthful body on her bed. Humiliated, Mui Tsai tried to cover her breasts.

'Get up and cover your itchy body and don't ever dare fall asleep in my bed again,' she spat. Mui Tsai stumbled to the back of the house to wash. She lay awake and ashamed in her small back room until the morning came. After that it was often that the master required a massage. Sometimes the master had a need for a massage twice in the same night. On those dreadful days she would hear his footsteps outside her door and the creak of it as it opened in the dark. For a second in the secret light of the moon and stars she would glimpse the richness of his yellow robe. Then the door would close and in the darkness of her windowless room she would hear only the soft slapping sound of his silk slippers on the concrete floor and his laboured breathing. Then a hand chilled with cold sweat would fall upon her small breasts. In no time she would be enveloped in cold wet flesh and her nostrils filled with his hot stale breath. The odd jiggling movement would begin all over again.

Very soon Mui Tsai was with child.

The master was extremely happy, for his three wives were barren. For a long time now it had been whispered that he was to blame but now it was obvious that the old hags were responsible. Ecstatically he ordered that Mui Tsai be fed with the best so his seed would grow strong and healthy. The mistress was forced to be kind to Mui Tsai though deep within those slanting eyes lay grievous envy. Often Mui Tsai hid some of her very expensive but horribly bitter special herbs for me.

'To make the baby strong,' she said in her happy, lilting voice.

One morning the master came with the news that First Wife wanted to meet the fertile tree that had given life to her husband's seed. She was a large woman with loose folds of flesh around her jowls, an arrogant tilt to her flat nose and small, shrewd eyes. Old Soong's home was filled with furious activity. Choice dishes were cooked, the floors washed and polished and the best china cleaned and laid out for the scrutiny of sharp eyes.

'Have you eaten?' she asked in the customary, polite Chinese greeting. Her voice was gruff and her face though proud had known sorrow. The sorrow of being replaced in her husband's affections, the sorrow of being unable to bear children.

'Yes, she has a very good appetite, elder sister,' Mui Tsai's mistress replied quickly.

'How many months more till the baby comes?' First Wife asked regally.

'Three months more. Have some more tea, elder sister,' Third Wife replied with humble politeness borrowed for the occasion. She rose gracefully to pour the tea.

First Wife nodded her approval and thereafter she made a few more visits, always sitting under the Assam tree with Mui Tsai. She was kind, seemed genuinely concerned and showed more and more interest in the unborn baby. She even brought it presents, expensive imported baby clothes in blue and a small quacking duck. Mui Tsai was pleased to have the grand old lady visit. It was an honour to be accepted by First Wife. Perhaps her luck had changed after all. Things would be different after the baby was born. She would be the mother of the heir to the vast fortune of the master.

A fair came into town and settled in the football field by the market. Mui Tsai and I slipped away when the heat was at its worst while her mistress, sluggish after a heavy lunch, dozed under the whirling fan.

Twenty cents to get in.

The sweet smell of egg and nut cakes mingled with the greasy smell of fish cakes frying in large vats of oil. The makeshift stage where, nightly, comely girls sat in a smiling row waiting for bashful young men to pay fifty cents for the pleasure of an energetic dance with his chosen girl, was deserted that hot afternoon.

'*See the amazing python lady!*' screamed a big poster of a giant snake wrapped around a beautiful girl with fiercely pencilled eyes. We paid ten cents and entered the covered tent. Inside it was stifling. A naked bulb burned in the stuffy air. In an iron cage, a middle-aged, lacklustre Malay woman sat cross-legged on a bed of straw. She held a disappointingly small snake in her hands and tried to drape it around her but the bone idle thing only flicked its tongue and slithered lazily back into the straw. Bored and hot we left quickly.

The drinks vendor filled the enamel containers we handed over with chilled coconut water and Mui Tsai persuaded me to join a queue to enter a Chinese fortune-teller's tent. Outside his tent were drawings of different types of palms sectioned off into various categories, their relevance to one's fortunes explained in green Chinese writing. We were handed red tickets with numbers on them. Mui Tsai and I shared a ticket, as we wanted to be seen together. Mui Tsai's head brushed the wind chimes at the tent flap and we were still giggling when we entered the brown tent.

An old Chineseman with a sparse goatee beard smiled

enigmatically from across a folding table. His skin was very yellow and his eyes flat. He indicated towards some chairs in front of the table. We sat awkwardly, sliding our containers of coconut water to the grass, our silly giggles swallowed by his staring eyes. On his desk was a small red altar with burning joss sticks and a small bronze figurine.

He raised his right hand and said, 'Let the ancestors speak.'

The wind chimes trilled softly.

Expressionlessly he reached for Mui Tsai's hands first, clasping them between his own wrinkled hands and drawing deep breaths. Mui Tsai and I shrugged and made faces at each other to relieve the sudden tension in that oppressively hot tent. I rolled my eyes comically and she pouted back.

'Sorrow, much sorrow, much, much sorrow,' he cried hoarsely.

We were startled by the sudden cry in the still tent.

'You will have no children to call your own,' he added in a strange, hollow voice.

The air in the room died. I felt Mui Tsai go rigid with fear. As if her small hands had burned him, the old man released them suddenly. Then he turned his vengeful eyes on me. Caught off guard and unnerved, I automatically slipped my hands into his outstretched, waiting ones. I felt dry leathery skin close over my damp hands. His eyes closed. In the stifling heat he was as still as a statue.

'Strength, too much strength. You should have been born a man.' He stopped to frown. Behind his closed lids his eyeballs moved wildly. 'You will have many children but never happiness. Beware your eldest son. He is your enemy from another life returned to punish you. You will know the pain of burying a child. You will attract an ancestral object of great value into your hands. Do not keep it and do not try to gain from it. It belongs in a temple.' He dropped my hands and opened those expressionless two-dimensional eyes. They looked at us blankly. Both Mui Tsai and I stood up shocked and frightened. Goose pimples spotted my arms. The heat was unbearable.

We stumbled outside, our limp plastic bags of drinks forgotten in the grass. I looked at Mui Tsai and her eyes were round with fear, her hands cupping her abdomen. Though seven months pregnant her bump was not obvious like mine. In her loose samfu, she could fool anyone.

'Look,' I stated bravely, 'it's obvious that he's a fake. Why, he said you would never have children when you are already pregnant. We've just thrown good money away. Everything he said was rubbish.'

'Yes, you are right. He must be a fake. A horrible fake who likes scaring young girls.

We were silent on the walk home. I tried to forget about the old man with the lips that hardly moved, but his eerie words were branded into my memory like a curse from a stranger. I held the bulge in front of me protectively. It was ridiculous to think that my unborn eldest son, already so beloved by me, could possibly be my enemy.

Pure nonsense if ever I heard any.

And life went on. My husband's wood-carving very slowly became an oval face. At first I looked at it every day and then because progress was so slow my impatient nature took over and I lost all interest.

Oh wait, I must tell you about my encounter with a proper python. It happened one muggy afternoon while I was sitting on the cold kitchen floor separating and cleaning the insides of dried anchovies. Anchovies were cheap and plentiful and I used them a lot in my cooking. Curried anchovies, aubergines with anchovies, and anchovies in coconut milk. Almost without thinking I added the nutritious things into everything. Anyway, that afternoon, Mui Tsai's face appeared at my kitchen window. Her eyes were big in her face and her hands waved excitedly about. 'Quick, come and look at the python.'

'Where is it?'

'Behind Minah's house.'

We rushed out to the back of Minah's house and in the bushes quite far away from the house three small boys were huddled together, pointing at something on the dry ground, their eyes shining with a mixture of fear and excitement. Although aware of our presence a thick, curled python appeared unable to move. The sun and a very big meal had made the beast sluggish and heavy. Unblinking, burnt-orange eyes in a diamond-shaped head observed us malevolently.

It was huge and beautiful.

So beautiful I wanted to keep it. Inside me was no fear of snakes.

In a flurry of urgent shouts some men arrived and beat its head to a pulp. Its thick, shiny body writhed and twisted in pain before it died a bloody death. They uncurled the dead animal and measured it by using the length from the tip of their fingers to their elbows as a ruler. They declared it more than twelve feet long. Then they ripped open its belly and found a half-digested goat bloodied and crushed almost beyond recognition. I stared in pure fascination at the absurd lump of mangled mauve flesh covered in slimy stomach juices with the odd hoof and horn sticking out of it. A strange thought occurred to me. Soon my belly would be bigger than that, I thought. And sure enough my belly grew at a rate that alarmed me. By the ninth month I was so big and uncomfortable I felt sure that I would burst like a smashed melon any time.

Finally the real pains began. Water gushed out of me like cheap rice brandy in a busy brothel. The back of my neck tingled. It was time.

Oh, but I was brave. I called out to my husband to summon the midwife. For a few seconds he stared at me with a blank expression then he turned suddenly and dashed out of the house. I stood at the window and watched his speeding bicycle wobble dangerously on the stone-filled path.

In the kitchen I put two fresh towels out and some old but clean sarongs. In a large pot I boiled water. Clean water to wash my son. I bent my head and prayed once more for a son. While waiting for my baby's arrival I sat on my bench and unfolded an old letter from Mother.

My hands were trembling. I stared at them, surprised. I thought I was being adult and calm. Seven thin pages rustled in my hands like a secret. A gorgeous sprite walking over dry leaves. Mother's small neat handwriting shook and blurred in my hands.

A sharp pain tore through me. My hand jerked. Seven tissue-thin pages filled with Mother's longings, hopes, prayers, love and wishes whispered softly and scattered onto the kitchen floor.

Very quickly the pains turned vicious. And still I was calm. Even Mother would have been proud for I bit hard on a piece of wood and stifled all my screams so that the neighbours would neither see nor hear anything. Suddenly I would be standing on the veranda with a flat stomach and a baby in my arms. How they would marvel. But another lightning cramp inside my body made me clutch my stomach in helpless pain. Beads of sweat grew on my forehead and upper lip. Then another one. So quickly.

'Ganesha, help me, please,' I prayed through clenched teeth.

Worse than the pain was the fear. Fear for the baby. Fear that everything was going wrong. Another ferocious spasm and I began to panic. I was standing inside a small Ganesha temple with not a soul in sight and ringing the bell for a god's pleasure. I rang it until my hands were bloody. 'Oh Lord Ganesha, remover of all obstacles, let my baby be safe,' I begged over and over again.

I felt the baby kick inside and hot tears squeezed past my tightly closed eyelids.

I cursed my slow, stupid husband. Where was he? I imagined him sitting in a ditch somewhere. The baby began moving inside me, urgent, impatient and dangerously vulnerable. A painful pressure was building up between my hips and freshly brewed, all-consuming terror bubbled in my brain.

The baby was coming. There was no midwife and the baby was coming.

Without any real warning I was standing in the eye of the whirling storm. The stick fell out of my mouth. The edges of the room were going black.

God had forsaken me.

I became certain I was dying. Abruptly I forgot the neighbours and the seductive idea of suddenly appearing on the veranda with a flat belly and a baby in my arms. I forgot to be brave or proud. The hard coconut shell of pride is so easily smashed and into so many pieces when it is hurled on the hard cement of pain.

A shivering mass of sweat and terror knows no pride. Squatting like a frightened animal I opened my mouth to howl long and hard but a sudden tearing pain knocked the breath out of me. I could feel the crown of the baby's head.

'Push. Just push,' the midwife's grey voice said inside my head. Her voice made it all sound so simple. Easy. The storm in my brain ceased unexpectedly. It was magic. 'Push. Just push.' I gripped the edges of the bench on either side, took a deep breath and pushed. I pushed and I pushed. The head was in my hand. The frightening lonely struggle I have now forgotten but I remember the magic of quite suddenly holding a whole, purple baby in my bloody hands. I held the slime-covered thing up over my stomach and looked in dazed wonder at it. 'Oh Lord Ganesha, you've given me a boy,' I gasped happily. My hands as if they had done it a thousand times before reached for the knife lying by the chopping board. That morning I had sliced an onion with it and it was stained with onion juices. I grasped it firmly in my hand and severed the umbilical cord. The cord dangled from the baby. The baby was free from me.

His eyes still tightly shut he opened his tiny mouth and began to howl, the thin sound going right through me. I laughed with joy.

'You simply couldn't wait, could you?' I asked with pure wonder. I looked at that toothless, ridiculously angry little creature and thought him the most beautiful thing I had ever seen. Motherhood ripped open her body and showed me her furiously beating heart. And I knew from that moment on that for this wrinkled stranger I could tear the heads off male lions, stop trains with my bare hands and scale snow-peaked mountains. Like a surreal comedy, Ayah and the midwife appeared in the doorway, breathless. I smiled broadly at their gaping faces.

'Go home,' I told the midwife proudly, thinking of the fifteen ringgit I had saved by forgoing her services. I turned my beaming face impatiently away from their plain faces so I could drink in the beauty of my new, wonderful creation. In fact I wished they would go away for a little while longer but just then a hard, bunched-up fist smashed into my lower belly making me double up in agony. The midwife ran forward. She grasped my baby expertly and laid him on the pile of clean towels. Then she bent over me. Her hands on my body were quick and precise.

'Allah, be merciful,' she prayed under her breath before turning to my husband and muttering, 'There is another baby in her belly.'

And that was how simply my son's twin was born. She slipped easily out of me into the midwife's waiting arms. The midwife was an old Malay woman Minah had recommended called Badom. 'Her hands are her gift,' Minah had said and nothing could be truer. I shall never forget the strength that flowed like a charging river inside her sinewy hands or the confident knowledge that shone from the depths of her rheumy eyes. She knew everything there was to know about mothers and babies. In her withered skull lay intimate and vast knowledge of all that counted. From forbidden cucumbers and powdered flowers to shrink the womb to magical potions of boiled nettles and herbs to return a stretched body to its former bloom.

She put into my arms two gorgeous babies.

My son was everything I could have hoped for. A gift from the gods. All my prayers answered in fine black ringlets of hair and a perfectly formed hearty yell to proclaim his health – but it was really my daughter that I stared at in something amounting to disbelief. I should tell you straightaway how incredibly special she was. For she was fair beyond anything I could have imagined. Badom, when she put the tiny bundle into my arms, raised her sparse eyebrows and said in an astonished voice, 'But her eyes are *green*.' In all her years of delivering babies she had never seen a baby with green eyes.

I stared in amazement at her pink skin and the beginnings of a curtain of shiny, straight hair. It could only be Mrs Armstrong's blood that ran through her veins – Mother's famous grandmother who had been called upon to give a posy of flowers and shake the gloved hand of Queen Victoria all those years ago. I looked at the small, fair creature in my arms and decided that all the names my husband and I had spent hours discussing were useless. I would call her Mohini.

Mohini was the celestial temptress of ancient legends, so incredibly beautiful that one accidental sip from the liquid depths of her eyes was all it took to cast even a god forgetful. In Mother's stories they drowned one by one in their urgent desire to possess her. I was too young then to know that excessive beauty is a curse. Happiness refuses to share the same bed as beauty. Mother wrote back to warn me that it was not a good name for a girl. It was bad luck. Now I know that I should have listened to her.

I can't even describe those first few months. It was like walking into a secret garden and discovering hundreds and hundreds of beautiful new flowers, the colours, the incredible new scents, and the wonderful shapes. They filled my day. From morning to night I was happy. I went to bed with a smile on my lips, stunned by the beauty of my children, and dreamed of running my awed fingers down their silky skin.

Perfect from the top of her soft little head to her tiny toes my Mohini was without flaw. People stared at her with unconcealed curiosity when I took her out. They looked at plain old me, then at her ugly father, and then I watched envy drop sharp roots into their small, petty hearts. I took the responsibility of my daughter's beauty very seriously. I bathed her in coconut milk and scrubbed her skin with lime quarters. Once a week I crushed hibiscus flowers in warm water until the water turned the right shade of rust and then I lowered her wriggling little body into it. She splashed and laughed and threw hand-fuls of reddened water into my face. I won't bother to tell you what great lengths I went to, to protect her milky-white skin.

No little girl could have been loved more. Her brother simply adored her. While lacking in any kind of physical similarity, there was a special, invisible bond between them. Eyes that spoke. Faces that understood. An in-describable something. They didn't finish each other's sentences, rather it was the pauses they shared. As if in those stolen moments of pure silence they communicated with each other on a different, deeper level. If I close my eyes now I can still see them sitting opposite each other grinding rice in the stone mortar. Not speaking. Not needing small talk. He turned the heavy stone and she pushed the rice into the hole in the stone with her bare hand. Silent and perfectly in tune as if they were one person. I could have watched them for hours. Every other day, late evening. Dangerous work. A crushed hand was always a possibility.

When they were alone with just each other for company, that stillness settled around them, a magic circle called 'us' that excluded everyone else. I remember that there were even times when it wasn't comfortable to watch.

If I was inordinately proud of my daughter her father worshipped the very ground she walked on. She made his soul tremble and reached so deep into his delighted being that it confused and surprised him. When she was first born she was small enough to completely fit into his large, cupped hands and it was a sensation he never forgot. Scarely able to believe such a marvel had sprung from his loins he stood and stared for hours as she slept. He woke up two, sometimes three times in the middle of the night to gently change her clothes if they were damp with perspiration. Often in the morning I found a pile of her clothes at the foot of her suspended cloth hammock.

If she fell or hurt herself in the smallest way he picked her up with large gentle hands and rocked her slowly in his arms, her tears mirrored in his own eyes. How much that man suffered when she was ill! He loved her so much that even a moment of pain endured by her was like a terrible thorn embedded deep into his simple heart.

When she was very young she spent many of her waking hours in his lap as they listened to the static-filled voices on the radio. She sat for hours twirling a lock of his thick hair in her fair fingers, never suspecting that it was a magic trick that had the power to turn gentle giants into babbling fools.

My little boy I named Lakshmnan. First-born, gorgeous, clever, precious and indisputably my favourite. You see, even though Mohini was beyond anything I could have hoped for, she was undeserved. The feeling never left me that I had somehow stolen into someone else's garden and plucked without permission their biggest and best bloom. There was nothing of her father or me in her. Even when I cuddled her in my arms I felt as if she was borrowed and that at some date someone would knock on my door to reclaim her. Hence I held back a little. I was awed by her perfect beauty but I didn't, couldn't, love her the way I loved Lakshmnan.

Ah, but the way I loved him. How I loved him! I built an altar in my heart just for his laugh. I recognised myself in his bright eyes and when I held his kicking, sturdy body against mine you could not tell where he began and I ended for he was exactly the same shade as me. Very milky tea.

Mui Tsai gave birth to her baby. She smuggled him into my house late one night while the neighbourhood slept so I would be able to see how bonny he was. The male child she had prayed for at the red temple by the market. He was very fat and very white with a shock of black hair. Exactly what she had prayed for.

'You see, the fortune-teller *was* wrong,' I crowed joyfully, hiding the pure relief I experienced when I heard her son was born, healthy and alive. If the fortune-teller was wrong about Mui Tsai then he could be written off as a charlatan, his predictions reduced to cruel lies. I put my finger into the child's tiny palm and he kicked energetically, gripped my finger in his little hand and refused to let go.

'Look how strong he is,' I complimented.

She nodded slowly as if not daring to provoke the gods with excessive pride even though I saw her bliss. In the light of the oil lamp her skin appeared luminous as if someone had switched on a bulb inside her skull; but one must never boast about one's good fortune. That was the belief. It was bad luck, she had once said. So that happy night she kissed her baby and complained half-heartedly about the picture of health in her arms being too scrawny. When she left tightly clutching her precious bundle, I was happy for her. Finally she had something to call her own.

Exactly one month later, to correspond with the end of her confinement period, her master gave her baby to his first wife. Mui Tsai was too shocked by the betrayal to protest. Completely devastated and unable to refuse, all that was left for her to do was accept the customary red *ang pow* packet with the crisp, folded, fifty ringgit note inside in exchange.

'How dare he? Has a mother no rights?' I demanded, appalled.

She informed me dully that it was simply another long-established custom in China that the first wife was entitled to claim the first-born of any secondary wife or concubine.

'It is a great honour when the eldest wife asks for the son of a Mui Tsai. I think it is best for the boy. Now he will have a proper place in the family without any questions,' Mui Tsai added sadly. Her poor heart was broken and the bright light inside her skull had blown a fuse.

Aghast, I stared at her. It was simply monstrous.

She still came to sit with me some nights when she couldn't bear the lonely calls of the lemur in the rambutan tree any more, and she still climbed into my window with the old agility that I remembered, but everything was different now. The giggling girl packed to bursting with mischievous intentions was gone and in her place was a lost round face. Like a dejected puppy she sat in my kitchen with her chin buried in her palms. Sometimes she replayed the entire scene when the baby was taken away from her.

'What do you expect? To be higher than First Wife?' her loathsome mistress had scolded scornfully. She would look at me bravely and assure me that she did not expect to be higher than First Wife. Of course, she knew her place. She was a Mui Tsai. Poor Mui Tsai. I had my two beautiful babies and she, the knowledge that some other woman cradled her child. Sometimes when she looked at the twins asleep and breathing softly inside their cotton blankets, bitter tears poured unchecked down her face. She would sniff audibly, wipe her face with the ends of her sleeves and in a small, meek voice declare, 'It is the will of the gods.'

Then one day she was pregnant again. Gloating with the second sign of his manly fertility, the master readily promised that this time she could keep the baby. First Wife never came to visit which Mui Tsai took as a good sign. She had learned her lesson well. No news from the old matriarch was good news.

I stopped breastfeeding and became pregnant too. Mui Tsai and I were once again united playing Chinese chequers and giggling quietly in the dim light of my kerosene lamp. In the afternoons, while her mistress slept, she sat on my windowsill and we dreamed together. Impossible dreams of our children in high places. Other afternoons she helped me dig up the groundnut beds. We washed the mud off the nuts, boiled them and ate them piping hot in my kitchen. It was then that she used to sigh and dramatically declare that all her happiest times were in my kitchen, but as her delivery date loomed closer she became increasingly agitated. Deep inside her heart the bones of her ancestors rattled and reminded her of the prediction that had been spoken inside a stuffy tent more than two years before. A whole lot of dead relatives stood, arms outstretched, and wished her childless. Had the master made an empty promise?

Often she woke up during the night, her heart pounding hard. Leaving her bed, she walked along the outside of her room looking into the inky night for the light of my kerosene lamp. And if she saw its glimmer she sighed with relief, closed her door quietly and walked towards it. Very heavily pregnant she climbed through the low window of my kitchen. Like a sweet, dim voice from the past I can still hear her saying, 'Lakshmi, you are my lamp in the night.'

I was always glad to see her round face. Sometimes we whispered and sometimes we simply shared the silence. When I think of that time now I realise how precious it was. If only I knew then what I know now . . . I would have whispered in her ear that I loved her. I would have told her she was my best friend. I wish I had said, 'You are my sister and this is your home.' Maybe I was too young, too absorbed in the selfish business of mothering my own. I took our closeness for granted and never gave it a second thought. Sometimes for no reason at all she would burst into tears and say in the most pitiful voice, 'I was born under a very bad star.'

Mui Tsai gave birth to another boy. She said he had a full head of black hair. And that he smiled at her. She held him very close to her breast for the first day. On the second day her mistress came into her room. There was a spiteful gleam in her eyes when she told Mui Tsai that Elder Sister's baby died a month ago and it was their duty to sacrifice and help Elder Sister. Mui Tsai must give her baby to the grieving woman. The shock of hearing that her first son had died was even harder to accept than the idea of giving up her second child. She shook her head in confusion and gave her sweet-smelling bundle away. In her heart Mui Tsai knew her first son had died of a broken heart.

She was grey-faced but dry-eyed even when the malicious woman had the gall to say, 'You are young and very fertile. There are many more sons in your belly.'

'Would you have them all?' Mui Tsai asked so softly that it was certain that Third Wife did not hear it.

Two months later, Anna came into my hot and freezing malaria-struck world, caramel-coloured and saucer-eyed. The nights were the worst. First delirious with slow-burning fever, then shivering uncontrollably in my own sweat. During the day, weak behind the haze of quinine, I felt the children in Mui Tsai's arms. For seventeen days Ayah was a moving shadow and the children bright specks of whispering anxiety by the bedside. Sometimes I felt my husband's cool, hard lips on my clammy skin and sometimes curious little fingers prodded my face, but it always seemed easier to turn away and dive into the forgiving blackness. When it was all over I had lost my milk, my breasts were small rocks under my skin. My exploring fingers found them hard and painful. I felt tearful and weak. The only person who could tweak a smile out of my face was my darling Lakshmnan.

I looked at little Anna and felt pity. Poor thing. Not even mother's milk was to be her right but she was a good, good baby with enormous, shining eyes and I was once again grateful that another child had escaped the simple genes of my hulking husband. I lay in bed and watched Ayah pick her up gingerly as if he was afraid of dropping or hurting her even though he had picked up and held Mohini like an experienced midwife from the very first time.

Mui Tsai was totally enamoured by the new baby. She responded to Anna in a way that she had never done with Lakshmnan or Mohini. She found charm and joy in the littlest things. 'Look at her tiny tongue. It's so pretty,' she would exclaim, her round face lighting up with simple delight. One day I came back from the market and found her breastfeeding Anna. She looked up guiltily. 'I'm sorry but she was crying with hunger.'

In a flash I knew why Anna hated tinned milk. I listened with burning ears to Mui Tsai's explanation. How her milk had dried when her baby was taken away and how the first primal cry Anna emitted suddenly filled her breasts. Right then and there in front of my awkward husband her blouse had been embarrassingly wet.

Of course. It had never occurred to me before but it was she who fed Anna during the seventeen days when I lay delirious with fever. Only with the greatest difficulty did I manage to quell my instinctive revulsion that someone other than me had breastfed my child. I told myself that it was her terrible loss that made her assume such a liberty. I understood. I told myself I did, anyway. I wanted to be magnanimous. She had lost so much. Where was the harm if she fed my baby? My breasts remained parched and hers rich and plentiful for many weeks to come. So it was Mui Tsai's small, undeveloped breasts that Anna's little pink mouth suckled. It is a strange thing, motherhood. It gives and takes away so much. I should have been grateful but I wasn't. Even though I did not say anything I wasn't big enough to let the matter pass.

I built a low wall between us.

It wasn't a high wall, but every time the poor girl wanted to get to me she had to climb it. I regret building the wall now. I was the only friend she had and I turned my back on her. Of course it is all too late now. I tell all my grandchildren never to build walls, because once you start, the wall takes over. It is the nature of the wall to build itself until it is so high that it cannot be scaled.

When Mohini was three years old she caught a cold. In less than a week the cold had turned into a frightening asthmatic rasp. She sat small and utterly defenceless, propped up by three pillows in my large, silver bed and laboured through the task of breathing, her beautiful eyes full of fear and her mouth a ghastly blue line. In her tiny chest I heard the rattle of a dangerous snake pretending to be a child's toy. The snake's rattle made her father cry.

I tried all the traditional remedies I could think of and everything else the ladies at the temple advised. I rubbed tiger balm on her wheezing chest, held her screaming body over the fumes of pungent herbs and forced little black ayurvedic pills down her throat. Then her father travelled all the way to Pekan on a bus to buy green pigeons. They looked so adorable in the cage cooing and nodding their pretty heads but I trapped their struggling bodies full of tiny bones under the palm of my hand and chopped their heads off. Baby Mohini had the purplish flesh diced and roasted with cloves, black root and saffron. Then First Wife from the confusing household next door brought a flat newspaper packet of specially dried insects. Closer inspection revealed dead bugs, ants, bees, cockroaches and grasshoppers tangled together in a surfeit of legs, so bone dry they clicked against each other and rasped hoarsely against the paper they arrived in. I cooked them in water until the brown mixture boiled down to a third of its original amount and that I poured into the child's mouth. All to no avail.

There were certain frightening hours in the dead of night when she turned a nasty blue for lack of oxygen. In our backward hospital a doctor gave her small pink pills that made her body tremble and shake uncontrollably. The shakes frightened me more than the rattlesnake inside her chest. Two hellish days passed. Ayah buried his head in his hands like an old man, destitute and helpless. The radio stayed silent. He blamed himself. It was he who had taken her out for a walk and let her get wet when the sudden rain came.

I wanted to blame him but there was no one to blame. It was me who had asked him to take the children out. I prayed. How I prayed! I spent hours kneeling on the cold temple floor and, prostrating myself on the floor, rolled across the temple to show my utter devotion. I am nothing but a bug. Help me please, dear God. Surely the good lord would not abandon me now.

On the third afternoon Mui Tsai burst into my kitchen with the most preposterous idea. I stopped stirring the lentils cooking in yoghurt, clutching my growing stomach, for I was pregnant again, and listened half in shock and half in disbelief to the quick, excited words shooting from her small mouth. Even before she had finished I was already shaking my head. 'No,' I said, but my voice lacked conviction. The truth was I was ready to try anything. I wanted to be persuaded.

She wasted no time. 'It will work,' she insisted fiercely.

'It's a disgusting idea. Ugh. Whoever came up with such a sick idea?' Yet . . .

'It will work. Please try it. My master's *sinseh* is very, very good. He has come directly from Shanghai.'

'It is an impossible idea. How can I make the poor little thing do that? She can hardly breathe as it is. She might choke to death.'

'You have to. Do you want her to be cured from this terrible disease?'

'Of course, but . . . '

'Well then. Try it.'

'Is it just an ordinary rat?'

'No, of course not. It is a specially bred, red-eyed rat. And when it is newly born it has no fur. It is pink and only as big as my finger.'

'But she has to swallow it live?'

'In the first few minutes of it being born it does not move. Mohini can swallow it with some honey. Don't tell her what it is.'

'Are you sure that it will really work?'

'Yes many people in China have done it. The *sinseh* is very clever. Don't worry, Lakshmi. I shall ask Mistress Soong for help.'

'How many rats will she have to swallow?'

'Just the one, OK?' she said very quickly.

But little Mohini never had to swallow Mui Tsai's live rat after all. Her father refused. For the first time since I had known him, his small black eyes flashed angrily. 'Nobody is feeding my daughter with a live rat. Bloody barbarians,' he thundered angrily before going in to see Mohini where he reverted back to his crooning, babbling self.

Ayah hated rats. The mere sight of them from afar revolted him terribly. For no real reason that I can think of, Mohini began to recover and in a few days she was better and I did not require the children of the specially bred, red-eyed rat until many years later.

Sevenese came into the world at the stroke of midnight. When he was born the snake-charmer was playing his flute and the sweet, lonely notes that accompanied his birth were almost like an omen for the strange person that he swelled into. The midwife packed him, dark red in a clean towel, and presented him to me. Under his transparent skin his blood pounded through a web of minute green veins. When he opened his eyes they were dark and strangely alert. I breathed another sigh of relief. He did not look like my stepchildren.

When he was a child Sevenese had a winning smile and a cheeky answer ready on his tongue at all times. With his head of curly hair and mischievous grin he was irresistible. I was proud of his quick mind in those early days. Even very young he was already attracted to all things unusual. The snake-charmer's house stood on the curve of the road and pulled him like a magnet. Even after I forbade him that house he slipped away on the sly and spent hours there, tempted and tantalised by their strange charms and potions. One moment he would be in the backyard and the next he would have disappeared to that horrible house. There was something missing or unfinished or different inside him that propelled him on, searching, searching and never finding. Many nights he came running into the kitchen awakened by morbid dreams that made the hairs on my forearms stand on end. Huge snarling panthers with glowing orange eyes that sprang out of his chest and then turned around and feasted on his face. Once he saw my death. He saw me lying inside a box. On the lids of my closed eyes were coins, and people he didn't recognise were walking around the coins with burning sticks in their hands. Old ladies were singing devotional songs in hoarse voices. Mohini, grown up and with a child on her lap, was crying in a corner. When he dreamed my death he had never seen a Hindu funeral yet he described it in such amazing detail that my back chilled. He lay beyond my understanding.

When Anna was two and a half I walked in from the garden unexpectedly one day and stopped dead in my tracks. Anna was burrowed deep inside Mui Tsai's blue and white patterned samfu. I stood astonished, for I had imagined that Mui Tsai had stopped breastfeeding her a long, long time ago. This secret was like a betrayal. I didn't think it normal for my two-year-old to be still breastfeeding. Anger rose up from the black mud in my stomach. The red-hot resentment made me forget that I had suckled at my mother's breast till the age of almost eight. Ugly, cruel words gathered in my throat. They were bitter in my mouth. I opened my lips but suddenly realised that Mui Tsai, unaware of my searing eyes, was staring far into the horizon, silent tears rolling down her grieving cheeks, her anguish such that I had to turn away and bite my tongue. The blood was racing in my veins. She was still my friend. My best friend. I swallowed the poison in my mouth.

Standing behind the kitchen door I breathed deeply and in the most normal voice I could manage, called to Anna. She came running with nothing but innocence in her face. There was no betrayal on her part. In my breast I still felt that strangely ugly beast of jealousy stirring. He is a pitiless thing. Why we hold him so close to our hearts, I will never know. He pretends to forgive but he never does. Unmoved by the wolves he had seen crouched and waiting in her destroyed future, or the black crows of despair circling overhead, he whispered in my ear that she longed to steal my child for her own. I held little Anna close to me. She smacked a wet kiss on my cheek. 'Aunty Mui Tsai is here,' she said.

'Oh good,' I said cheerfully, but from then on I was loath to leave Anna alone with Mui Tsai.

Time burned into the months like lighted joss sticks and left fine white ashes on my body, changing it. I was nearly nineteen. A woman. My hips had broadened with creation and my breasts were full and tender with milk. My face too was changing. Cheekbones appeared. A new sense of confidence had entered and settled inside my eyes. The children grew quickly, filling the house with laughter and childish shrieks. I was happy. It was a good feeling to sit outside in the evening watching them play, the square white cloths that I used as nappies, Lakshmnan's small shirts and Mohini's tiny dresses billowing in the wind. I hugged very close to me the knowledge that I had made a silk purse out of a sow's ear. My children were all beautiful, none of them afflicted with that which my stepchildren bore uncomplainingly.

Mui Tsai cut her long hair to a shoulder-length bob. We were both pregnant again. In those days every unguarded moment in the dark had, in its sticky ending, years of responsibility and pain. Baby Sevenese's big round eyes watched as Mui Tsai walked with the heavy walk of the condemned.

This time definitely, the master had promised. 'He looks sincere this time,' Mui Tsai said. There was nothing I could do or say. Her dull eyes looked at me with a blankness that I had never seen before. She was a small animal, her foot trapped in a mangle. Even in the shadows cast by my oil lamp I saw her silent, pitiful cries glittering in her eyes. Before, we had discussed everything. Even bedroom secrets; nothing was large enough to be a secret between us. Now there was my silent, petty wall, and on the other side she stood woeful, alone and watching. I had my brood of children and she had her master's visits and her empty pregnancies.

But we are still friends, I told myself, stubbornly refusing to tear the wall down. When you are young it is difficult to destroy a wall you have built with the red bricks of selfishness and cemented with grey pride.

After she gave birth I kept the kerosene lamp burning late into the night and sat by the window listening for her footsteps, for her sing-song voice to whisper, 'Are you still awake?' Weeks went by, but her round face never appeared at my window. Of course in my heart I knew what had happened. Quite by chance I saw her.

I was very pregnant then but from my veranda I saw her sitting on one of the green stone chairs, her elbows resting on the heavy stone table. Head bent, she was staring at the ground. Her straight hair had fallen forward, hiding her face. Slipping my feet into my slippers I hurried clumsily to the wall that circled Old Soong's property. I called out to her and she turned her head dully. For a moment she simply stared at me. At that moment I felt as if I didn't know, had never known her. She was a different person. Then she stood up reluctantly and walked over to me.

'What happened?' I asked although I knew.

'Second Wife has the baby,' she said expressionlessly. 'But the master says I can keep the next one. Where is Anna?' she asked and a trace of emotion came into her face.

'Come and see her. She's getting very big very quickly.'

'I shall come to visit soon,' she said softly with a small smile. 'You had better go before the mistress sees you. Goodbye.'

The curtains at one of the windows twitched and fell back into place. And before I could say goodbye Mui Tsai had already turned away and was walking back towards the house. I didn't worry about Mui Tsai for long because that afternoon word came that my husband had met with an accident. While cycling to the bank a motorbike had crashed into him. I swallowed the news that he had been taken unconscious to hospital as if it were a solid object. It had the feel of a weathered brown stone in a shrinking riverbed. Tasteless and hard but smooth.

The stone was very heavy in my stomach when the children and I took a taxi to the hospital. I was sick with fear. The thought of bringing them up on my own without a breadwinner stretched like an enormous black hole in front of me. I herded the children into the Emergency Ward and arranged them on one of the long benches in the waiting room. They squeezed their small bodies between a groaning woman and a man with a terrible case of elephantiasis. I left them staring at the poor man's hugely bloated leg and walked along a corridor. There I saw Ayah's still body lying on a narrow trolley pushed up against the corridor wall. I ran towards him but the closer I got the more frightened I became. A gash had opened his head like a coconut and red blood had gurgled out, matting his hair, spilling on his shirt and pooled under his head. I had never seen so much blood in all my life. In his bloodied face, four of his front teeth, the very ones that I had taken such exception to at our wedding, were gone. A hole blacker than his face gaped at me but the real shock was his leg. The bone had broken clean off and was pushing through his pink flesh. The sight of it made me feel faint and peculiar. I had to grab something to stay upright. The nearest thing was the corridor wall and I fell back against it heavily. With the wall solid against my back I called his name, but he was unconscious.

Some male orderlies came rushing along the corridor and they wheeled him through the swinging double doors of the Emergency Ward. I stood leaning against the wall in a daze. My knees felt weak. The baby inside me kicked and I felt tears start at the back of my eyes. I looked at the bench and the children were sitting quietly in a row staring at me with large, fearful eyes. I smiled at them and walked back to the bench. My knees felt like jelly. They huddled around me.

Lakshmnan put his thin arms around my neck. 'Ama, can we go home now?' he whispered in an odd little voice.

'Soon,' I said in a choked voice, hugging his small body so tightly that a whimper slipped past his lips. The children and I waited for hours.

It was night before we left with no news. He was still unconscious. In the rickshaw the twins looked at me solemnly. Anna fell asleep sucking her thumb and baby Sevenese blew bubbles. I watched them and felt as if I knew how the widow who threw her sixteen children and then herself into a well had felt. The thought of bringing my children up on my own was terrifying. I stumbled alone in a pitch-black tunnel, the voices of my children echoing around me.

Listlessly I fed them and put them to bed. I was too shocked to eat so I sat on my bench staring out at the stars. 'Why me?' I asked again and again. 'Why, dear God, do you throw so much hardship my way?' That night I waited for Mui Tsai and missed her desperately when she did not come.

When the children awoke the next morning I fed them and we went back to the hospital. A grey, unconscious figure with a very white bandage lay on a bed. I brought the children home for lunch and, unable to face the trip back to hospital, sat down and cried. That evening I took the children to the temple. I laid baby Sevenese on the cold floor and stood my children in a row in front of me and together we prayed. 'Please, Ganesha, do not forsake us now. Look at them,' I begged. 'They are so innocent and so young. Please give them back their father.'

There was no news the next day. He was still unconscious.

When I looked down I saw that someone had lined the glass bangles of worry and fear on my hands. They caught the light and sparkled from afar. Distracted by their soundless jangle I did the unthinkable. I stopped eating. I had forgotten about the little person inside me. For four days I starved my blameless baby. On the fifth day I woke up disorientated on my bench, my body aching all over.

I watched my children eat their favourite breakfast of sweet purple root broth. The sight of children eating is heartbreaking when you are frightened and alone. They chewed with their mouths open, purple goo swirling around small pink tongues. More purple dribbled on to Sevenese's white shirt. I looked at them, so young and so unprotected, and felt sick with fear. Tomorrow I would be nineteen. Tears prickled the back of my eyes and blurred the wounded picture of my children, their virtuous mess and their tiny teeth. Sometimes a face cried while its owner stood apart and made terrible plans, saw terrible things. That was what happened to me. I saw in the distance all the dreams and hopes that I had nurtured so carefully, dying. I watched the flesh come off my dreams. It was a frightening sight. And when I turned my eyes away from the horrible sight, I saw my fate sniggering in a corner, my fleshless dreams imprisoned inside his iron box.

Fear exploded into violence.

I rushed into the prayer room. At the altar I dipped a shaking finger in the silver bowl of red kum kum and drew such a large, uneven red dot that it nearly covered my entire forehead. 'Look, look,' I cried to the picture of Ganesha. 'I still have a husband.' He stared back at me calmly. All the gods I had prayed to for as long as I can remember, stared back at me with exactly the same inwardly gratified expression they had worn all these years. And all these years I had mistaken that half-smile for gentle munificence. Inside my skull, the violent emotions bubbled into angry words on my tongue. 'Take him if you must. Make me a widow as a birthday present,' I challenged, my voice incoherent with rage, my hand rubbing away at the red dot on my forehead. 'Go on,' I screeched fiercely, 'but don't ever think I will drown my children in a well or lie down and die. I will go on. I will feed them and make something of them. So go on. Take the useless man. Have him if you must.'

The instant my mouth closed on those harsh, ugly words, and I swear this is the truth, someone called my name from outside the house. At the door was a lady that I knew from the temple who worked as a cleaner in the hospital. She had come to tell me that my husband was awake. Muddled but asking about the children and me.

I gazed at her, mystified. God's messenger? Then I saw her eyes flick to the red mess on my forehead and remembered that I had not bathed for three days. 'Let me have a quick shower,' I said to her, my heart beating very fast. Hyenas padded over to me bearing celestial flowers in their vicious jaws. God had answered my prayers. He had heard me. I was light-headed with joy. God was only testing, playing with me as I did with my children.

I poured a bucket of cold water over my head and, suddenly, I couldn't breathe. Perhaps it was the shock of the cold water on my weakened body or the fact that I had hardly eaten for five days, but my lungs froze. Refused to take in air. My knees gave way beneath me and I fell to the wet floor, my hands urgently banging on the door. God's messenger came running to help me. Mirrored in her eyes was horror, and no wonder. A horrendously pregnant naked woman with blue lips and a twisted expression was writhing on a bathroom floor. Oddly there is no clarity any more but I can remember very clearly seeing the edges of the messenger's lime-green sari turning bottle green as it came into contact with water. She pulled me up with some difficulty, panting with the effort. My wet limbs kept sliding out of her small hands. Terrified I was dying, I leaned against the grey walls gasping like a fish until inexplicably the muscles in my chest loosened and the tight bands of constricting steel relaxed. Small breaths became possible. The messenger covered my body with a towel and slowly I learned to breathe normally like all God's children. Suddenly my children, dumbstruck and traumatised, lunged at me sobbing and screaming.

A few days later we brought him home. And a few weeks later he took a rickshaw to work. Things slowly got back to normal except for a slight wheezing in my chest on very cold nights.

Jeyan when he was born was a great shock. He had small dull eyes in a large square face and painfully thin limbs. I kissed him gently on the dewy eyelids of his tiny half-closed eyes and hoped for the best but I knew even then that he would never amount to much. Life would treat him with the same contempt it had reserved for his poor father. I didn't know then that I would be the instrument that life would use to torment my own son. In Jeyan's head God had seen fit to release only a few words and a whole lot of spaces in between them. He didn't speak until he was almost three years old. He moved as he thought. Slowly. He reminded me of my stepchildren whom I had so successfully pushed into the back of my mind. Sometimes it came to me to wonder guiltily if the terrible shock that I experienced in the bathroom when I poured that bucket of cold water on my head or the glass bangles that made me neglect food was responsible for his condition.

Mohini thought him enchanting. She cradled his dark, still body in her fair arms and told him his skin was as beautiful as the blue skin of baby Krishna. He stared at her curiously. He was a watcher. Like a cat he followed you around the room with his eyes. I wondered what went through his head. Unlike my other children he refused to smile. Tickling him brought forth only short barks of involuntary laughter but smiling as an art eluded him.

Eight months after Jeyan was born Mui Tsai had another baby. The tiny infant screamed until he was red in the face when First Wife came to claim him. He was needed as a companion for 'her' first child who, in the absence of brothers and sisters, was becoming too spoilt and unruly for her to control.

December came rolling in bringing not just its usual monsoon rains but also a new baby. Mrs Gopal, who was present at the delivery, was very brisk and practical. 'Better eat less of expensive prawns and start saving now for the child's dowry instead,' she advised, jangling the keys hanging from her petticoat. My poor daughter was the colour and texture of bitter chocolate. Even as a baby Lalita was extraordinarily ugly. The gods were getting careless with their gifts. First with Jeyan and now with this tiny mite who looked at me through sorrow-filled eyes. Like the fading eyes of a very sad old woman they looked at me as if saying, 'Ah, you poor fool. If only you knew what I know.' It was as if my Lalita already knew then that unhappiness awaited her flat face.

My brood, I decided, was complete. The pot was full. No more unguarded moments in the dark. The months put little flesh on Lalita. Limbs thin to the point of emaciation waved peacefully about her body. She was as quiet as her father. She was never exuberant with her affection but I think she loved Ayah dearly. In his eyes she saw all that was wrong in her forgiven unconditionally. Notoriously shy and impossible to provoke she lived in her own fantasy world. She spent hours in the vegetable patch turning over leaves and stones, peering underneath them and whispering secrets to the invisible things she found there. When she grew up and her invisible friends deserted her, life was very unkind to her but she withstood all that it threw at her without a fight. Nay, without a murmur.

When Jeyan was one and a half he tired of crawling and wanted to stand but his legs were too weak to support his own weight. Mother advised me to dig a hole in the sand and stand him in it. Buried thus, his limbs would slowly grow strong and sturdy. I dug a hole a foot and a half deep just outside the kitchen window where I could keep an eye on him while I cooked, and lowered him into the hole in the mornings, leaving him there for hours at a time. Often Mohini sat beside him to keep him company. Slowly his limbs improved until one day he could stand on his own two feet.

When Lakshmnan and Mohini were six years old they started school. In the morning they went to mainstream school where they learned English, and in the afternoon to vernacular school where they were taught to read and write Tamil. Lakshmnan had to wear navy-blue shorts and a white short-sleeved shirt and Mohini a dark-blue pinafore with a white shirt beneath. White socks and white canvas shoes completed the outfits. Hand in hand they walked beside me. My heart swelled with pride to see them full of nervous excitement. First day at school. For me too. I had never been to school and was so happy to give my children something I had never had. We started off early and made a detour to the temple first. On that cool morning we placed their schoolbooks on the floor by the shrine to be blessed, Lakshmnan rang the bell and I smashed a coconut to ask for blessings.

I was twenty-six years old and Lalita six when a card arrived from my uncle the mango dealer. His daughter was getting married and we were all invited to the wedding. My husband had used up all his leave and he couldn't come. I packed my best saris, my jewels, my golden beaded slippers, my children and their best outfits.

That same polished black car that had picked up Ayah and me from Penang harbour came to collect us but Bilal had retired. Someone else in a khaki uniform grinned toothily, touched his skullcap politely and stashed our bags into the boot of the car. I climbed into its leather interior with a sense of nostalgia. I had arrived a child, but now small bodies full of excited chatter that I had made inside my belly rubbed and bumped against me. The past shimmered briefly in the cool morning air. I remembered the lady with the deformed feet and the procession of dulang-washers as if it was a lifetime ago. How life had changed. How generous had the gods been to me? Outside the thin bubble of my thoughts the children quarrelled and fought for window space. My hand automatically reached out to slap away Sevenese's fingers pinching Jeyan's dark flesh.

Anna was terribly carsick and Lakshmnan, royally ensconced in the front seat with the window wound down and the wind in his curly hair, twisted around in his seat with a mixture of curiosity and disgust. I caught the driver's eyes resting on Mohini in the rear-view mirror and stifled a spurt of annoyance. I must marry her off quickly. The responsibility of great beauty sits uneasily on a parent's head. She was ten and already she was attracting too many adult-sized looks. Sometimes I sat up on my many sleepless nights and worried about it. Friendly spirits stood in my kitchen and whispered caution in my ear. I should have listened to them. Taken more care. Left her white skin in the sun to bake. Taken her father's shaving blade to her tiny face with my own hands.

Real surprise awaited me at my uncle's residence. First because he lived on a hill, and hills were generally the preserve of Europeans, and secondly because he lived in a very large, in fact an enormous two-storey house with lofty rooms, colonnaded verandas and an impressive pitched roof. It was built, my uncle proudly explained later, in the English Regency style of John Nash. I listened with a peasant's awe as he grandly informed me that the Anglo–Indian Palladian architectural lines of his home were associated with humanism and ideals of rank, prestige and elegance.

The third, totally unexpected surprise, was the impression that my uncle's wife, who had never laid eyes on me before that day, hated me. I felt it from the moment she opened the door and smiled at me. It stopped me in my tracks but the moment passed when my uncle ran forward and enveloped me in a bear hug. He looked at Mohini in disbelieving admiration and shook his head from side to side in satisfied approval to see how tall and strong Lakshmnan was. But it was Anna that made him cry as she looked solemnly up at him. Anna was small for her age. She had eyes that begged you to pick her up and apple cheeks that made you want to bite her.

'Look at her face!' he cried, picking her up and pinching her cheeks. 'She is the living image of my mother.' He wiped tears that had collected in the corners of his eyes. Then he knelt on the floor, kissed Jeyan and Sevenese, and bade us all enter. He had no choice but to ignore Lalita as she had hidden herself inside the folds of my sari in an acute moment of shyness.

Inside, the stone floor, deep verandas and extended eaves worked harmoniously together to create a wonderfully cool interior. As I looked around, impressed by the sheer wealth in the room, my gaze met luxurious items from all over the world. Beautiful jade figurines in glass cabinets, fine English furniture, exquisite Persian rugs and gorgeous, gilded French mirrors and armchairs covered in brocade. The place looked like a thief's nest. My humble uncle was very rich indeed. I realised that he was not a lowly mango dealer after all and found out later that he had diversified into the lucrative rubber and tin business. No wonder there were so many lorries standing outside the house.

My aunt showed us to a large room with a shuttered door that led to a balcony. It overlooked a small, very pretty Minangkabau village. Although I suspected that my aunt secretly detested me and couldn't imagine a reason for it, I was excited about our stay and the grand wedding to follow. Five hundred guests had been invited and the local town hall booked. For two days, large-scale cooking had been going on in mammoth iron pots. When we eventually wandered into the kitchen, twenty-one cakes and sweets were lined in large trays along one wall. Many ladies in saris chatted and gossiped as they cut out and fried small cakes and cookies. In large iron cooking pots, all kinds of vegetarian curries bubbled and toiled. I looked down at my charges and was horrified to see Sevenese's chunky little hands quickly cramming dozens of sugary shells into his mouth.

The next day I dressed my children in their new outfits and felt pleased that all the hours borrowed from the night cutting and sewing tiny invisible stitches had come to such fine resting places. It was not often that I saw my children in such finery. I had dressed all my three girls in the same green and gold outfits. Anna looked adorable and Lalita cute, but Mohini was a gorgeous mermaid with luminous, excited eyes. When we went downstairs I caught the shudder of rage and damp envy in my aunt's decorated face and I was perversely proud that my shimmering children, innocent and chasing each other, had such power.

It was a great occasion, a fantastic display of wealth. The vast town-hall floor had been decorated with the intricate classical kolum designs painstakingly hand-drawn by women on their hands and knees using a thin rice flour and water mixture. Women in expensive gold and silk saris sat in colourful clusters and gossiped over the din of beating drums and blowing trumpets under a ceiling hung with hundreds of pale yellow coconut leaves woven into a pretty plait, and mango leaves that waved like small green flags. Fifty young banana trees, heavy with green fruit and cut at the base of their shiny stems, stood upright to flank the path that the shy bride would tread upon. The groom stood handsome and proud at the end of the banana-tree-guarded path. When the bride arrived at the doorway of the hall she glittered like a goddess carried in a procession on a holy day. That her father was wealthy was of no doubt. Chains dripped from her forehead, hung in thick gold ropes around her neck and drew together gleaming stones to encircle her waist. The groom sat high on his raised dais and looked mighty pleased with himself.

After the exchange of rings, garlands and the tying of the thick gold thali chain, preparation for the great feast began at the other end of the hall. Small boys carrying stacks of banana leaves made a quick job of lining the floor of the grand hall with long rows of green leaves. People drifted into the rows, sat cross-legged facing a banana leaf and waited. When the whole hall was filled with rows of people sitting back to back facing a banana leaf, the servers arrived with aluminium pails of food which they served out with ladles. The din of human voices died away and the hall filled with the sounds of eating. There was soured yellow rice, plain rice and all manner of vegetarian dishes to choose from. Afterwards there was sweet broth, kaseries and ladhus.

In a green tent outside the hall a special table with white tablecloths, flowers and plates had been set up for the European guests who wore identical expressions of regal but inaccessible benevolence. I looked at them closely. They looked like a proud race who acknowledged their presence as a favour. An act of charity even. And it was fascinating to watch them eat with knives and tiny hoe-like implements.

There had been many a sidelong glance thrown in Mohini's direction, some admiring, some envious, some speculative, with plans for their growing sons. It had been an exciting day filled with pomp and splendour but by late afternoon Mohini was sick. We hurried into my uncle's car but by the time we returned to his home she was hot with fever and groaning with stomach cramps.

My uncle wanted to call a doctor but my aunt, her damp face still unforgiving, clicked her tongue with irritation and sent the old servant Menachi to bring in some margosa oil. Menachi was a shrunken old woman with narrow shoulders and skeletal limbs. Her lasting beauty was her dark eyes, fringed by thick, sweeping eyelashes. I have always loved looking into the faces of very old people and hers was exceptional. A history book with a story to tell. Her wrinkles, fascinating pages to turn. She had to stand on tiptoe to pour the margosa oil into Mohini's open mouth for she was very nearly the same size as Mohini.

'She will be as good as new in the morning,' said my aunt. Menachi's extravagant lashes fanned downwards obediently but as soon as my aunt's purple-and-gold-swathed figure had waddled out of the room the old woman slid up to me. 'It is the evil eye, not indigestion,' she whispered fiercely. She explained that so many people had gazed at my daughter's beauty and entertained envious notions that their ill thoughts had actually affected her. Her sunken eyes urged me to believe her. The silky eyelashes fluttered as she added that some people's eyes were so evil that they could kill with a glance. If they admired a plant, the next day it would shrivel up and die. She had seen it happen before.

A hand like a claw fastened upon my hand. It was true that to absorb the evil eye, people painted a black dot on their babies' faces to mar their perfect beauty and protect the defenceless child from envious glances. But Mohini was no baby. Bewildered, I looked at the old lady. 'What shall I do?'

She went outside to the front of the house and picked in her hand a small clod of earth. Then she went to two different areas on the grounds of the house and collected another two clods of soil. Every time she plucked one up, she muttered prayers under her breath. When she returned to the house she added salt and dried chillies to the soil. Holding it in her cupped palms she made Mohini spit into the mixture three times. Mohini, not cured by the margosa oil, was holding her stomach with a pained expression on her face.

'These eyes, and those eyes, and everybody's eyes, that have touched this person, let them go into the fire,' the old lady chanted as she lit the mixture.

We stood around in a circle and watched the mixture burn. The chillies and salt made hissing, crackling sounds, burned with a clear blue flame. When the fire burned itself out the old woman turned towards Mohini and asked simply, 'How do you feel?'

To my utter surprise, Mohini was without pain or fever. Gratefully I thanked the little old lady and she nodded modestly. 'Your daughter is a queen. Let not too many prying eyes fall upon her,' she advised, her shrivelled hand stroking Mohini's thick shiny hair reverently.

It was 13 December 1941 and I was packing to return home when my uncle came running into our room in a blind panic, his hair tousled and his eyes wild. In a shocked voice he told me that the Japanese had invaded Malaya. While we were feasting and celebrating they had landed in Penang. Apparently the big, burly British soldiers we had imagined invincible had fled, leaving us to an uncertain fate. Spittle blasted out of my uncle's mouth as he described the crowds that gathered in a market place in Penang just like a flock of dumb animals. How they had stared up into the skies at the metallic birds and watched with innocent awe as the shining beasts exploded bombs onto their upturned faces. All the while unsuspecting, believing the planes to be the mighty British come to save them. And their poor, crazed faces as they picked up severed, smashed limbs from the rubble around them.

War. What would it mean for my family? In my uncle's terrified, sweat-slicked face I saw all the horrible answers to my questions.

'They will be here soon. We have to start hiding the rice, the precious things . . .'

We heard a roar in the sky. It was only a plane flying low but my uncle shuddered and said in a voice cold with foreboding, 'They are here.'

The roads were blocked. Travel was impossible. The children and I had to stay.

My uncle's home was beautiful and there was always good food on the table but I was my aunt's unwanted guest. My uncle was hardly at home, rushing to one meeting after another with fellow businessmen who stood to lose a great deal. For two weeks my aunt supped silently on her mysterious hatred of me. Not knowing the origin of her hostility rendered me powerless, but as I walked into the kitchen one day I saw her glance at me and, turning, remark loudly to one of her servants, 'Some people pretend that they are coming to visit for two days and then conveniently end up staying for months.'

I had been packed and ready to leave when news came that the roads were blocked and no one could leave. She knew that. She had seen the packed bags. I didn't plan the Japanese invasion. I decided to confront her.

I walked up to her. 'Why do you hate me so much?' I asked quietly.

'Because you borrowed money from my husband and paid no interest,' she hissed viciously, pushing her damp face very close to mine. So close I saw the pores in her skin, the squelching dissatisfaction in the slant of her lips and smelt the odour of her greed.

My mouth opened and closed, dumbfounded. My disbelieving eyes swung away from her plain face made grotesque with bristling anger. Away from the eating mouth, outlandishly cerise, and the rabid eyes painted kingfisher-blue. Heat rushed into my face as if she had caught me stealing one of the exorbitant showpieces out of her locked showcases. My cart-wheeling eyes fell upon a full-sized wooden statue of a Balinese dancer. The delicate features of the smiling face were wonderfully crafted in solid ebony, her bejewelled and intricate headgear a delight to the eye and a witness to the carver's skill. I thought about the many lorries parked at the side of the house and the sacks of rice that piled on top of each other, reaching even the high ceiling of an Anglo–Indian Palladian house.

How could this woman live in this splendid house filled to the brim with riches that most people only dream about, be waited on hand and foot by so many servants and have her mind fixed on something as petty as the interest on a loan to a struggling relative from so many years ago? How greedy was the human soul?

'I offered to pay him interest but your husband refused,' I said finally.

The heat in my cheeks receded. I felt cold with anger

and deeply sorry for my poor uncle. I wouldn't have wished that mean creature on anyone let alone my favourite uncle. I resolved to leave that day, even if it meant walking all the way back to Kuantan carrying my children on my back. Perhaps it wasn't the money after all. Perhaps it was the obvious and genuine affection my uncle had for my children and me, but I was very proud in those days. I knew I couldn't stay another moment longer than absolutely necessary to make the arrangements for the return journey. When my uncle returned I informed him of my intention and as nothing he said or did could change my mind, he reluctantly made arrangements for us to travel by boat. It meant a long and arduous journey, perhaps even a dangerous one, but I was adamant. My mouth had settled into a thin, tight line.

The children squealed with delight, barely able to contain their excitement at the prospect of a boat trip. Their babble was filled with roaring tigers and tame elephants that used their gentle trunks to rescue us. My thin, tight mouth had no effect on their enthusiasm. When we left, my uncle's wife didn't come out to say goodbye and the only news I had from her was after the Japanese had taken away all the beautiful things from her house. By then my poor uncle had lost all his money. He had invested too heavily in rubber and the price of rubber plunged. Poverty-stricken, she wrote to me to ask for the interest. I sent the money immediately.

Menachi ran out with insect repellent home-made with burned cow dung. I dusted the children with the grey ash and we set off with a man hired by my uncle.

The journey started in the fetid, mouldy mouth of a forest.

It was not the romantic place I had pictured it to be. In the oppressive green gloom things curled, stretched and grew all around us. Hanging creepers, thick and tangled, brushed my shoulders lingeringly as if they longed to pierce their sharp little suckers into my flesh. Blood after all is the best fertiliser.

Trees grew straight and tall, like the columns in my uncle's home, for hundreds of feet without freeing a single branch until they reached light and air, then they launched into the skies.

Once we heard a deep roar. The jungle played with the sound, channelling it through its tangle of vines and creepers until it was deafening in our ears. The guide said it was the roar of a tiger, and a ripple of fear passed through my row of children like a gust of wind flying through a field of elephant grass. The man enjoyed our jerk into terror, our hiss of horror, before admitting that the tiger was too far away to be of any worry. He did not quicken his pace and slowly the dread of seeing black and orange stripes flashing between the green faded in its intensity.

The humid air stuck our clothes to our skins and caught the back of our throats. It was like breathing in steam. We trudged along wearily into the strong smell of earth and rotting leaves. Mosquitoes whined plaintively like a festering echo outside the scent circle of Menachi's insect repellent. Sometimes the guide hacked away at a branch or a hanging creeper but otherwise we made smooth progress.

Soon we reached the riverbank, where our boat awaited us.

The river was wide and fast flowing. I prayed fervently to Lord Ganesha, remover of all obstacles, 'Let not the river have any of us. Take us home safely, dear Elephant God.' Then we carefully boarded.

Our boatman was an aborigine. He had big untidy features and tight, honey-brown curls on his head. His skin was burned a deep mahogany by a lifetime in the sun. When he sat still inside his wooden boat he became a part of it, directing the noisy old thing almost as if it was an extension of himself. His body was lean and sinewy but he was even-tempered and full of good humour. Once, while he was trying to reach for and cut a large comb of ripening bananas that hung over the water's edge along the bank, the boat ground into sticky mud. After settling the yellowing fruit at the bottom of the boat he eased himself into soft ooze up to his chest, pulling and tugging at the boat until it was free. Then he flipped himself into the boat smoothly like a dolphin and grinned widely, showing purple gums.

He was caretaker to many fascinating tales about a submerged ancient Khemer city that lay ahead deep within the Cini Lake, buried under layers and layers of silt. He recounted in a melodious voice the legend of how the inhabitants of Khemer had flooded their own city to ward off attack but perished in the last encounter, leaving their Cambodian city buried ever since.

From his thick rubbery lips came mysterious tales about a legendary monster living at the bottom of Lake Cini and possessing a horned head as big as a tiger's and a giant undulating body that created waves which could easily overturn a boat. He told his wide-eyed audience that the monster supposedly travelled up the Cini River and into the Pahang River along the route on which we were travelling. The tales were greeted eagerly but later, when we reached choppy waters that rocked the boat, the children screamed with real fear, convinced that the monster was indeed underneath us and trying to secure a meal.

Once, an iridescent orange bird of stunning beauty sat on an overhanging branch and looked at its own reflection in the water. We passed a large tree with mighty branches full of small monkeys. The boatman cut the engine. In the sudden silence came an answering silence. The colony of small monkeys the size and the grey-brown colour of rats froze into stillness, watching us watching them, their many eyes shining like wet marbles. Then one monkey dropped into the water with a soft splash and began to swim towards us. Others followed more soft splashes. The water was soon filled with them.

The children were dumb with fascination and secret fear. Would they bite? Would they snatch, scratch? I looked at the boatman worriedly and he smiled back reassuringly. Obviously he had done this before. He took a small knife out of his pocket and cut a bunch of yellow bananas from his large comb, quickly covering the rest of the bananas with a brown sack. He handed the children a banana each.

First to arrive at the helm of the boat was presumably the leader of the tribe. His wet fur clung to his thin lithe body. Big round eyes scanned us quickly and with interest. He was a delight to behold. Tiny black hands flashed out to grab the banana that Lakshmnan held out, peeling it with astonishing agility. The skin he flung into the water. The sinking skin looked for a moment like a pale yellow flower. The banana vanished into his mouth in three bites, the small mouth chewing quickly. The miniature hand stretched out for more, his clever round eyes never leaving our faces. Mohini held out her banana and another monkey closer to her grabbed it quickly. More monkeys began to climb aboard the boat. Soon all the bananas were gone. They began to chatter and quarrel among themselves as they lined the helm of the boat, wet and curious. Their sweet faces considered our empty hands greedily. In the leader's eyes I was sure I saw speculation. As if he knew there was more under the sack. More monkeys were swimming across. They swam in groups of grey-brown. In the water they were silent and fast. Suddenly there seemed to be hundreds of them swimming towards us. And suddenly the harmless furry things took on plague-like proportions. I was a mother with very small children in the boat and none of them knew how to swim.

'Let's go!' I shouted to the boatman.

With neither fear nor hurry he turned on the engine and all the little creatures fell simultaneously and gracefully into the liver-coloured water. We watched them swim back to land. Soon they disappeared from sight, hidden by the green foliage until they reappeared again as brown flowers on the large tree's outstretched branches. I realised then the harmless nature of the beautiful monkeys and I felt privileged to have seen them.

About a mile after we passed the monkeys we sat back amazed. Unexpectedly, the river became an avenue of blooming lianas. Flowering vines draped down to the water's edge and spread themselves into the dense trees overhanging the river in a shamelessly promiscuous manner, smothering them in bright lilac hues and creating the most amazing tunnel-like effect. Like a magic cave in a dream. And everywhere the most beautiful orange and black butterflies with fringed wings, disturbed by our presence, flapped and rose up in clouds of wondrous colour.

At last the journey was over. Kuantan was so silent it was eerie. War had arrived. Ayah was standing at the doorway. He had his hands in the pockets of his trousers. From his nervous face I knew that something was wrong.

'What's the matter?' I asked, disentangling Lalita's monkey-like grip from around my neck and setting her down on the ground.

'The house has been looted,' he said gloomily.

I walked past him and stepped into our house. Not a single thing remained. Pots, pans, clothes, tables, chairs, money, the children's beds, with even their old stuffed mattresses, the framed pictures of embroidered flowers that I had sat up at nights sewing – everything was gone. Even the worn curtains that I was waiting to replace. All we had left were the things I had taken with me to the wedding. I had taken all my jewellery, thank God, four of my best saris and the children's best clothes. Our house was bare save for our heavy iron bed and my bench; too troublesome to carry away.

It wasn't the Japanese soldiers who were responsible. No, they came a little bit later and they were choosy about what they took. It was coolie workers from over the main road. An Indian settlement of very poor labourers brought over from India to do the back-breaking work of laying railway lines and tapping rubber trees. In India they were the untouchables or the very lowest castes, the Christian converts. Over the years, our expressions askance, protected by our cloak of superiority, we had watched them get drunk, curse and swear, beat their wives on a regular basis and at least once a year make a new barefoot little hooligan to run into our clean, safe world. Now they had their revenge. They must have watched our house and noticed that Ayah was out all day so they had helped themselves. My savings were buried in a tin outside. I rushed out, and was greatly relieved to note the ground was undisturbed.

Anna

Memories? Yes, I have memories but they are precious and far away, like butterflies. Tiny magic pieces of flying colour that the curious little boy of time has played with. No one dares tell him, 'Don't touch them or the dust comes off their wings and they will blur and fly no more.'

I even have memories of peculiar events that I think couldn't possibly have happened. Perhaps I dreamed it but in my memory banks is a clear picture of myself curled up in Mui Tsai's lap and suckling from her breasts. Tears roll down her sad face and drip onto my hair. Of course no such thing ever happened but the vividness of the image has often confused me.

The butterfly with the biggest, best wings I call Mother. When I was young she was a big bright shining light in our house. Undoubtedly the strongest influence in all our lives. From the moment I walked into our house from school I felt her in the air. I smelt her in the food she had cooked, saw her in the windows she had opened and heard her in the sweet, old-fashioned Tamil songs that she listened to on the radio. Before I was old enough to go to school I trailed her silently around the house, troubled by the sight of her moving, restless back. As soon as Father left the house in the morning she fiddled with the largest knob on the radio, making the little red dial on its dull yellow face move. And as it moved it made spooky, desolate sounds, sawing in half voices it met along the way until she found the right home for the red dial and happy music and dulcet voices filled the house. Then she began her endless chores for the day.

I can never forget the time when she went away for two days to visit a friend. It was as if she took with her the very essence that made our family. The house stood deserted and empty in the afternoon sun. Coming home from school I stood at the threshold and knew then what it would feel like if she died suddenly. Like a blow in the stomach of my blue uniform I realised that in her strong, sure hands were love, laughter, fine clothes, praise, food, money and the power to make the sun shine brightly into all our lives. But after that terrible thing happened, her powerful will reached out and pulled out not bright skies and sunny days, but dark clouds, blue thunder and angry storms to lash in on us.

The truth is that she stood in the middle like an enormous English oak tree and from her mighty branches we whirled round and round soundlessly like painted figurines on a ghostly merry-go-round. All of us. Dad, Lakshmnan, Mohini, Sevenese, Jeyan, Lalita and me. All the decisions big and small were put into a large platter and placed at her feet, and that incredibly quick, clever brain of hers made choices based on what she felt was best for us. And she wanted the very, very best. Nothing else would do.

At fifteen, Mother gave up her life for us and she took that as the right to live through us. She channelled her furious energy into us. Pushing us towards unattainable limits. Wanting for us what she never had or could be. And there was so much she had never had, so much she couldn't be. Her barrier was my father. She was often angry with him.

I suppose it was because he seemed satisfied with his dead-end job while all around him his colleagues got promoted and took home more money. She could never forgive him his kind, pardoning heart that refused to recognise human beings as the corrupt, mean and greedy creatures who unfailingly cheated their fellow beings. He wanted to help every soul that crossed his path.

Once he brought home yet another friend who needed to borrow some money. They came with signed IOUs ready to explain to Mother the repayment terms. She was so sick of the same scenario that she didn't even bother listening. She took the IOUs from Father's large hands and as they watched in open-mouthed amazement she tore the carefully signed slips of paper into tiny pieces and threw them up into the air. 'My husband's money is for his children. Whatever money we have is for our children,' she told the gaping man, and with a beaming smile disappeared into the kitchen.

That was the same smile that she presented to our headmaster, Mr Vellupilai. He didn't know it but it hid an almost obsessive streak that wanted the best so desperately that she was willing to sacrifice us all in the process. Our happiness seemed unimportant in the grand scheme of things. Mr Vellupilai had come to say that Lakshmnan was bright enough to skip Standard Two and move straight into Standard Three if Mother was willing. She watched the moustached man eat her shell-shaped biscuits, nodded politely and agreed with his suggestion, but as soon as his correct figure had turned into the main road she shed her skin and became a different beast altogether. Picking me up off the ground by my armpits, she swung me round and round in uncontrollable excitement. Unable to contain herself she threw me up into the air and caught me, her eyes merry and her lips curved into an inverted, laughing rainbow.

Being better, brighter and bolder was everything. Failure was a badly trained dog that lived in other people's houses. And when we did fail, which happened often, she took it as a personal affront. The sad undeniable fact was that all of us put together didn't quite come up to the ability or the intelligence that sat in one of her little fingers. We were none of us favoured with her talents. A fact that was very quickly apparent to us and eventually also to her. As the years went by she became an inconsolably unhappy woman and in turn she made us all unhappy.

But first let me tell you about the happy time. Let me tell you about the time before the blue sky broke into two. Before that thing that nobody talks about happened. When people used to admire the wonderful way Mother curled herself over her family and made us all look perfect. It was such a long time ago that I sometimes wonder if it existed at all, but it did. It was before the Japanese Occupation, when Lakshmnan used to come home with chocolates wrapped in plain green paper from the British Army camps near our house. Today the best Swiss chocolate cannot equal those simple slabs of confection that my brother brought home like prize trophies for Mother to divide equally among us. I took so long savouring the warm smell of my piece of chocolate that it half melted in my fingers before I finally consented to let it end its life as a smooth paste in my mouth.

'Come here, lad,' the big, burly British soldiers used to

call out to Lakshmnan. They tousled his hair affectionately and taught him to speak the kind of English we were never taught at school.

'Bloody fool,' he used to come home and say.

'Bloody pool,' Mother would repeat.

'Noooo, bloody fool.'

'Bloody pool,' Mother said earnestly.

'BLOODY FOOL,' Lakshmnan would say very clearly and very loudly.

'Bloody pool,' Mother would say, and listening quietly in the background we would begin to hear the irritation creeping into her voice.

'Yes, very good,' my brother would agree.

And those I remember as the happiest times of my childhood. When my mother was happiest. When she used to laugh with her mouth open and her eyes twinkling like bright stars in a night sky. Lakshmnan was my big, handsome brother and still the wonderfully clever apple of my mother's eye. Those days, everything he did and said brought a smile of pride and joy to her heart.

I remember the mad panic one afternoon when clumps of Lakshmnan's hair came loose in Mother's hands as she was oiling it. She swept her hand through his hair and many more strands clung to her disbelieving fingers. Bald patches stared defiantly into Mother's formidable eyes.

'*Aiyoo*, what is this?' she asked in a horrified voice.

Lakshmnan looked at the clumps of hair in confusion. He too was frightened. Was it some terrible disease?

'Am I dying?' he whispered with the uncanny ability all males have to exaggerate any kind of physical affliction or illness.

Mohini stood with her worried arms crossed in front of her, Jeyan stared mutely and Lalita sucked her thumb. Mother bombarded him with fast-flying questions. A few short answers later, she found out that he had carried home the sack of ragi flour on his head. Mother grew ragi in our backyard, harvested the seeds and Lakshmnan took it to the mill to have it ground. When my brother had gone to pick it up, the ground ragi was still hot. The heat from the sack was what had made his hair fall out in tufts. Once the culprit reason had been hounded out peals of relieved laughter flew into the afternoon sun. Mother alternately scolded, laughed and kissed my brother's bald spots as he smiled uncertainly, not sure if he had done right or wrong. Then Mother made us all little steamed cakes filled with brown sugar and green beans. We had three cakes instead of two and Lakshmnan had five instead of three. Those were the sunny afternoons I remember, before my brother became a cruel, sadistic failure in life.

Every evening we prayed as a family. We stood in front of the altar, a shelf built at Mother's eye level, clasped our hands and prayed earnestly. All I could see were the heads of the gods in the brightly coloured pictures. We all had our favourite ones.

Mother and I always prayed to the Elephant God, Ganesha. Mohini's prayers were to Goddess Saraswathy because she wanted to be clever and Goddess Saraswathy ruled education. Mohini wanted to be a doctor.

Lakshmnan prayed reverently to Goddess Lakshmi for great riches when he grew up. Goddess Lakshmi was responsible for bestowing wealth on her devotees. In those days moneylenders used to keep a garlanded picture of her very close to their hearts. Inside a blue frame on our altar she stood in a red sari, raining gold coins from the palm of one of her many hands.

Sevenese prayed to Lord Shiva because he was the destroyer who had fashioned a necklace out of a black cobra. He was also the most powerful of all the gods. If one were to pray hard enough, he could grant a boon of one's choice, and once granted it could never be revoked by anyone – not even Lord Shiva himself. Impressed by this information Sevenese began to pray for his boon. He was always very strange compared to the rest of us. I will never forget the day he walked into the house holding a long smooth stick in his hand.

'Look everybody,' he said, and right before our eyes he loosened his grip and the rigid stick he grasped upright in his hands moved and transformed back into a curling brown snake. When he was satisfied with the commotion he had caused he coolly wrapped the thing around his hand like a scarf and wandered off towards the snake-charmer's house. He was bloody lucky Mother didn't see him.

Little Jeyan prayed to Lord Krishna because kind-hearted Mohini had whispered in his small ears that he was as dark and as beautiful as Lord Krishna himself.

I don't know who Lalita prayed to. Perhaps she didn't have a favourite deity. I don't think I took too much notice of her. It was only Mohini who made a great fuss over Lalita.

Every evening we each sang one devotional song to our chosen deity and then Mother rang the little bronze bell, lit the camphor for the gods and rubbed holy ash and dotted fresh sandalwood paste on our foreheads. Father never joined us in our prayer. He sat outside in his wicker chair smoking his cheroot. 'God is within,' he claimed.

Sometimes when I think back I can cry for the innocent days when Father was a giant of a figure who could fit our little bottoms into the large palm of his hand and lift us into the air high above his head. And high up there was the safest, best place in the whole wide world. But that was before I began to feel sorry for him. Those were the days when a dark fire burned brightly in his eyes as he watched Mother smile with pride and joy. It was when he was still turning a lump of wood into the most beautiful carving I have ever seen.

For years I sat cross-legged on the floor beside him, watching him studying his bust for many minutes before he was finally ready to carefully coax one tiny shaving out of it. And when it was finally finished, everybody who saw it agreed it was indeed a work of art. It was more than genius. It was love.

Father had captured Mother as none of us had seen her, as only he knew her. A young girl drenched in sunshine from a small village called Sangra, before life had touched her. Then one day Mother turned years, hundreds of hours, of careful, loving labour, into sharp splinters in minutes. I have a memory of that day when her furious body destroyed the bust. When she was done, spiteful splinters of sharp wood lay everywhere. Angrily.

Now when I think back about Father I feel only regret. Deep regret. For he was the nicest person that ever walked the earth and surely the unhappiest. When I was very young, before Mother had made me feel ashamed of him, I used to love him a great deal. I remember he used to come home with small bunches of bananas that he bought with his pitiful monthly allowance. It was our little ritual. He sat in his chair on the veranda peeling the bananas one by one with his long, dark fingers. All the stringy yellow strands that could be pulled away from the inside skin he put into his mouth.

'It's the best bit,' he insisted nobly, giving us the rich, pale-yellow fruit. Mohini, Lalita and I sat solemnly at his feet as he shared it out.

I was only a child then but I clearly understood that my large silent father loved my elder sister more, so much more that he would have gladly held his hand inside a flame if only she had asked. He loved us all but he loved her best. I used to wonder if there was some measure of ugly sibling rivalry in my heart, but I honestly don't think so because it was not winning Father's love that was important. The prize always belonged to the object of Mother's attention.

In identical dresses we stood in front of Mother waiting for her approval. She would adjust a bow, sweep back a strand of hair and smile at both of us with the same level of satisfaction, and that was enough to reassure me that she loved me the same as my sister. Needless to say Mohini looked totally different in the same dress. People used to stare at her a lot, mostly men, uncomfortable stares. Nobody believed that we were sisters. They would look into the warm green of her eyes with amazement and sometimes a touch of envy.

I remember standing by the mirror as Mother did her hair and watching as she oiled and combed it until it turned into a shiny black serpent that undulated right down to the soft swell of her bottom. My own hair was always thin and fine, and when the Japanese came, to my greatest horror Mother reached for her scissors. She made me stand outside in the yard and went to work, and when she was finished long thin strands of hair lay in black patches on the ground. I ran to the mirror, tears streaming down my face. She had left no more than two inches of hair on my head. Attired in a pair of boy's shorts and a shirt I was sent to school. In the next few days I was somewhat mollified as more than half the girls in school turned into boys.

Mr Vellupilai dutifully redid the class registers to reflect the changes. In my class, the only girl who remained a girl was Mei Ling. Her mother had permitted her to remain a girl and she became our Japanese teacher's favourite. Then one day during recess he called her into an empty classroom and raped her. I can see her now, lips trembling in her white, dazed face as she stumbled out. Her belt, made from the same material as her uniform, was slightly askew. I knew, of course, that being raped was the ultimate catastrophe but I had no idea then what it entailed. I remember thinking that it had something to do with one's eyes. Because it was her eyes that were huge and bruised that morning. And for a long time I thought being raped was having your eyes hurt. No wonder Mother hid Mohini and her wonderful eyes. In fact, the headmaster himself came to our house to advise Mother to keep my sister from school.

'Too beautiful,' he said, coughing into a large brown and white handkerchief. Mr Vellupilai said he couldn't guarantee her safety with so many Japanese around. In between mouthfuls of Mother's fried banana cakes he told her that Japanese teachers were going to be sent to the school. 'They are coarse and vulgar,' he said. He would have no control over them; one must never forget that they did after all rape their way through half of China. With Mohini being at that age, he concluded delicately, he could not guarantee her safety. In fact his exact words were: 'I wouldn't like to put a cat and a saucer of milk in the same room and close the door.'

Mother needed no second warning. So Mohini got to keep her thick serpent of hair but she became a prisoner at home. Mohini was our secret. Outside our front door she stopped existing. We never spoke about her. She was like the chest of gold ingots buried under the house that the whole family lies to protect. No one saw the beauty that she was turning into. She could not even stand outside on the veranda or walk in the backyard to breathe some fresh air. For almost three years she remained so hidden away that even the neighbours forgot what she looked like. Mother's fear was that somebody might reveal her existence to the Japanese soldiers for a favour or out of jealousy. Times were hard and friends were few.

One day Mohini sat on the steps of our back door while Mother combed her hair. Like waves of the purest black silk her hair lay down her back. As Mother twisted the black silk in both her hands I spotted in the blazing sun the snake-charmer's eldest son. The lad had obviously been hunting for live mice or small snakes for his cobras to eat but had instead stumbled upon our luxurious secret. He stood frozen in the terrible heat, caught in the net of his discovery. His tattered, stained clothes were falling off his sinewy, bronzed body and in his muscled hand he carried a closed basket. He had no shoes and his hair was unwashed, but in the glare of the sun his eyes were like dark fathomless pits in his stunned face. The sudden movement of my head attracted Mother's attention and her body turned instantly to shield Mohini.

'Go away,' she barked harshly at the boy.

For a moment he continued to stare, hypnotised by the glorious hair, the milky whiteness, and then as suddenly as he had appeared he vanished into the wavering yellow heat. I looked into Mother's face and saw fear. It was not fear of the strange magic of the snake-charmer or the awakening reptile of desire that had shimmered in the young man's eyes, but fear of the rare beauty that sat so simply in my sister's face. Indeed, Mohini was like a magnificent quetzal, which flies straight up from the crowns of hundred-foot-tall trees, circles in song, then free-falls, dropping through the air, her iridescent feathers streaming like a comet's tail. Mother was the chosen owner of this resplendent bird. What more could she do but cage her breathtaking beauty? And a prisoner Mother's bird remained until the day she flew away for ever.

In my mind I can still see the two of us walking home from school, dressed identically, side by side in the sun eating balls of ice shavings dipped in syrup. We had to eat it fast or it would melt in our hands. We could never ever tell Mother when we had one because Mohini suffered from horrible attacks of asthma and was not supposed to consume anything cold. So we sneaked in the ice balls only when the weather sizzled. It was very serious, Mohini's asthma. Whenever it rained or even just drizzled, Mother would come to fetch us from school with a large black umbrella and the three of us walked home together, Mohini under the big black umbrella, me under a small waxed brown-paper umbrella that smelt strongly of varnish and Mother under the rain. I think she secretly enjoyed the feel of the big warm drops falling on her head. Always when we got home, freshly pressed, horribly pungent ginger juice would be waiting in a cup. Mother then boiled some water and poured it into the juice, filling the whole kitchen with biting fumes. After a spoonful of dark brown, wild honey was dissolved into the vile mixture. Mother handed over the cup and waited until it was completely empty. I watched almost in awe as Mohini drank it all down. On the roof the rain tapped and drummed insistently. I think I loved her a great deal then.

And I remember Mui Tsai too. Sweet, downtrodden little Mui Tsai. I think she was really attached to Mother but Mother was so determined that her imaginary gravestone would read, *Beloved Mother* that she couldn't see her friend begging for a little love. Her eyes were set far away on the horizon, where all her children were brilliant examples of good upbringing. Poor Mui Tsai. She often looked sad but that was when she was not yet broken. They broke her like a toy, her mistresses and the master. And after that she was no longer sad. I think her mind snapped. She went to a place where she had many babies and got to keep them all.

My best memories of Mui Tsai are her elongated shadows on Mother's kitchen wall far into the night. A secret rendezvous in the flickering, mysterious light of Mother's oil lamp. Whenever a nightmare jerked me awake in the middle of the night I crept into the kitchen, into the friendly glow of the kerosene lamp. There I found Mui Tsai and Mother cross-legged and talking in whispers or playing Chinese chequers on the bench. I would walk smiling into Mui Tsai's outstretched hands and fall asleep in her lap, but she aroused in me the same concealed pity that I harboured for my younger sister, Lalita.

I remember the birth of my little sister. A waif in a tightly wrapped bundle. She had small eyes set very close together in a broad face. And she was darker than all of us. My father had to nibble her ears to make her laugh. She was very quiet. She was like him, you see. She even looked like Father. Mother frankly admitted she didn't want any of her children to take after our father. She said his children from his first marriage were the sorriest creatures she ever saw. When she first looked into Lalita's dull eyes, she thought that through sheer will-power alone she could change her. Change the course of nature. She was only a baby. Babies could be changed.

But the older my sister became the more she resembled Father. In despair Mother took to rocking my quiet sister on her outstretched legs, singing, 'Who will marry my poor, poor daughter?' If you had heard the anguish in those simple words you too would have come to the conclusion that beautiful children inspire pride in their parents and ugly children inspire a tremendous surge of protective love. A need to compensate for society's neglect. Nature denied my sister beauty but it was my mother who carried protective love so far she unwittingly denied my sister the opportunity of marriage. I know it's wrong of me but I cannot be rid of the notion that it was *because* of Mother that my sister never married. The strength of Mother's will as she sang that sad line over and over again. If Mother heard me say this she would be very angry. She would say she tried her very best. Nobody could have tried harder to find my sister a suitable husband. Perhaps she should just be flattered that I think her so powerful as to change the course of my sister's fate with her little songs.

My earliest complete memory is when we went to my aunt's wedding party in Seremban. During our stay my great-aunt and my mother fell out over something trivial but it upset Mother so much that we had to travel back by boat along the treacherous River Pahang so she wouldn't have to spend another minute under the same roof as her uncle's wife. The only thing my mother told us for many years was that her uncle's wife hated her. She never told us why.

When we returned to our empty, looted home Mother had to use more than half of her savings to replace everything that had been stolen. To her credit she took the disaster in her stride. By mid-morning she had been to the markets and managed to stock up on some provisions and later replaced most of our furniture by buying pieces looted from others. By the end of that year the rest of my mother's savings had become just useless paper. The Japanese made us all very resourceful but Mother was an undefeatable force. Realising that her money was useless she sent Lakshmnan, more dextrous than a monkey, up the highest coconut tree in our compound where he tied her tin of money and jewels securely among the branches. Every so often he scampered up to check that her hoard was still safe. Covered in bird droppings, Mother's little fortune remained untouched for years. The advent of the Japanese made Mother an enterpreneur and she had quite a knack for it too. She noted that condensed milk was no more and the coffee stall on the way to Father's workplace sold only sugarless, black coffee. There was a market for cow's milk. So she sold her largest ruby and bought some cows and goats. Every morning before the sun was up she milked them and Lakshmnan took the milk to the coffee shops in town. During the day she left the milk to set into yoghurt and in the evening the ladies from the temple visited with empty containers to collect Mother's yoghurt thinned with water. They called it 'mour'.

I was nine years old then and I remember our cows as huge beasts with lumbering bodies and ponderous udders. They looked at me with liquid mournful eyes that made me guiltily try to make friends with them but they were really too stupid to befriend. There was never the light of recognition, nor any expression to be gleaned from their eyes except sad acceptance. Resigned to lead dreadful lives in smelly conditions. Always under their tails was dried dung.

Strangely enough, when I think of the Japanese Occupation I think of our cows. The way they came into our lives with the start of the Occupation and were all sold when the Japanese left. While it is true that Mother also kept goats, turkeys and geese, they left no impact on me. Lalita fed the turkeys and geese bean curd and spinach until they were big enough to sell and then cried when Mother sold them to a Chinese trader at the market.

Most of all I equate the Japanese Occupation with fear. The type of acute fear that has a taste and a smell all of its own. Metallic and oddly sweet. Lakshmnan and I saw our first decapitated head on our way to the market. The head was spiked on a stick by the roadside, attached to it a page torn from a school exercise book with the message *Traitor*. We laughed at the head. It was funny while we thought it wasn't real. How could it be real when there was no blood dripping from the severed neck or the large gash on the man's left cheek? When we got closer we realised that it was indeed real. The flies were real. So was the persistent sweetish, stale odour around it. Fear of a kind I had never experienced before hit me in the stomach. Instantly I feared for my father's life even though my brother assured me that they only beheaded Chinesemen whom they suspected to be Communists.

A few yards in front not just a head but a whole body had been skewered onto a stick and spiked into the ground. I felt my brother's steps falter. His grip on my hand tightened painfully but my brother is like my mother – he doesn't say die easily. We pressed on. I wish we hadn't. The Chineseman had looked like a fake dummy and not a very good one at that, but the second figure gave me nightmares for many years to come.

It was a woman. My brother's reassurance that they only chopped off the heads of Chinese Communist men showed itself a lie. Not only was the corpse a woman, she had also been heavily pregnant. They had ripped her belly open and a perfectly formed blackened foetus hung obscenely from the gaping hole. Her face was a terrible thing to behold. Her eyes bulged as if horrified to see us looking at her open belly and her mouth hung open as if getting ready to scream insanely. Big blue flies buzzed around her open, stinking belly. She carried in her limp hand a placard that read, *And this is how Communist families are treated*. The Japanese, it seemed, had a special hatred for the Chinese that went beyond the war. We walked on in silence.

After they stole Mui Tsai's fifth child she shuffled around like a bitter ghost. Inside she was cut and bleeding but to the outside world she was young and pretty. To the Japanese soldiers she was perfect. They found their comfort woman in our little neighbourhood. How they used her! They queued. One by one they took her on the kitchen floor, in the master's bed, on the rosewood dining table where the master and mistress ate every day. Every time they came they expected to have their food on the table and their sex wherever they happened to be standing. Our Mohini and Ah Moi next door owed their virginity to her. When General Ito and his men drove into the neighbourhood, the first mad rush was to Old Soong's house. At Old Soong's they found everything necessary to satisfy their basic needs. There was always the food that they were not only familiar with but also thoroughly enjoyed, and then there was always a young fair girl for them to do with as they pleased. Nobody's wife and nobody's daughter. Because they had Mui Tsai they didn't bother to look too hard for the other carefully hidden daughters. They might have guessed there were girls of usable age hidden somewhere in the neighbourhood, but Mui Tsai did for the time being.

Mother and Lakshmnan had built a secret hole in the ground for Mohini and to a lesser extent, if the Occupation lasted for many years, for me too. As a boy I should have been safe for a few more years but with the Japanese you never could tell. Mother said war brings out the animal inside a man. He leaves his compassion at home. Meeting him in enemy land is like turning a corner and looking into the yellow eyes of a large lion. There is never a chance to plead or reason. He will surely jump on you. The hiding place was a hole that had been cleverly cut out of the floorboards of the house. It dropped you onto the ground under the elevated floor of our house and ran straight into a hole with enough space for Mohini, me and maybe one day even Lalita.

Mother had dismantled the old chicken coop, run chicken wire around the legs of our house and herded our chickens into their new home under our house. She was gambling on the hope that the prospect of soiling themselves with chicken dung would put off even the Empire's most dedicated servant from investigating that small crawl space under our house. The trapdoor was covered with a huge wooden chest that Grandma had sent from Sangra. When the wooden chest was pushed over the trapdoor, the entrance was completely concealed. It was an ingenious hiding place and the Japanese, though they opened cupboards and peered into corners, never found it. Perhaps they didn't try too hard. Mui Tsai had already blunted the edge of their needs before they came around.

Once Mother tried to please them by giving them food. The first time they put the offered food in their mouths they spat it out immediately, looking at her with murderous rage as if she had offered them spicy food in order to mock them. She bowed low and begged for mercy. They slapped her bowed head. Sometimes they looked at Mother with strange expressions and asked where she had hidden her daughters. Standing beside her in my boy's clothes I felt her trembling against me. Once General Ito came very close and asked her again with such a knowing smile that it seemed as if one of the neighbours had betrayed us. But they were only testing and we sighed with relief when their truck turned away into the main road.

Mohini filled her secret room with small embroidered pillows and books. She made it pretty but we were forbidden conversation inside. We cuddled each other and listened in silence to the thumping of heavy boots on the floorboards. At the beginning we were very frightened in our secret cavity but as time went by we relaxed and learned to giggle very, very softly into our cupped hands thinking of the soldiers searching uselessly over our heads for our hiding place. I was so proud of our clever hiding place for I knew they would never find it, and I was right.

It was Father they came to take away.

Little Sevenese dreamed that he saw Father fall into a huge hole in the ground, his lips bleeding profusely. Mother didn't know the significance of his dream but she went to the temple to donate some money and say some prayers.

Two nights after we had forgotten about the dream they came. It was a dark night. The moon was a slender shape in the sky and the gods had flung only a handful of stars into the black void. I know because for many hours afterwards I sat in a daze covered by darkness and watched the sky. The neighbourhood was asleep, only Mother was still awake. She was sitting in the kitchen sewing. At the first sound of tyres crunching over the road she pricked her finger. For a second she stared at the dot of red that appeared on her finger but even before they had stopped their trucks and jumped out she had dragged Mohini and me out of bed and stashed us into our secret hiding place. Then she blew out the kerosene lamp and stood behind the living-room curtains. They had come with torchlight and bayonets. She watched them disappear into the lorry driver's house.

Minutes later they were out, the lorry driver at bayonet point. In the truck's headlamps he looked bewildered. They dragged his half-dressed body into the truck. From inside the poor man's house came the sounds of loud sobs and wailing. His children's terrified screams tore into the night. The soldiers stood for a while loudly discussing something in their guttural language. It was not Ito and his men. Ito and his soldiers were predictable.

We hated them but they were familiar figures of manageable terror now. These men looked far more menacing. They were not looking for free food or a pair of open legs. They were looking for something far more important than that. As Mother watched the group broke up and two of them began striding towards our house. Our front door thundered with their hard rapping. Mother rushed to open the door. Their flashlights shone briefly in her face before they pushed her aside roughly. Their beam fell on Father standing stockstill by the bedroom door. Immediately they grabbed him and marched him out of the house. They were stony faced in the wake of my mother's pitiful cries.

My father turned around to look at us but he didn't wave. There was no emotion on his face. He was still too dazed.

They drove into the night for about forty-five minutes. The lorry driver seated opposite Father began to sob and my father, who was wearing only a white singlet and his pyjama bottoms, began to shiver in the open-top truck. Eventually they were driven into a rubber plantation, up to an elegant, colonial-style stone house. In the moonlight, the unlit house was silver and ghostly. From the one open window on the first floor through billowing white curtains, floated hauntingly beautiful classical music.

They pushed him at sword point down some stairs into an underground chamber. Water dripped from the ceiling and ran down the dungeon walls. When his hand brushed against the walls they were velvety with green moss. The corridors echoed harshly with their footsteps and their breathing. The prisoners stumbled down a long corridor and were pushed into tiny cells. The door shut with a clang behind my father. Without the dull yellow light from his captor's lantern the room plunged into clouds of black ink. Two pinpoints of orange appeared on his eyelids. There was no relief in the sound of heavy boots receding. It was cold and damp in the room and he shivered and listened. Boots approaching. Rhythmic and hard. They passed. A dog barked outside. From somewhere nearby, water dripping.

My father felt his way around the room on his hands and knees. The walls were rough-hewn and crumbling and the floor solid stone. The room was bare, save for him and a sudden scuttling movement. He pushed himself quickly into a corner and with his back pressed into the wall he stared terrified into the blackness. It was a rat. He heard its claws clicking on the cold cement. A small sound. The hairs at the back of his neck rose. He hated rats. He could stand snakes, tolerate spiders, understand the need for slimy frogs and even condone the existence of cockroaches – but he hated rats. Oh God, and that terrible, smooth tail. He swallowed with nervous fear. He heard the scuttling sound again and bunched his fist. In the dark the rat's teeth became longer and sharper. He would bring down his bunched fist hard on the soft warm body. Yes, disgusting blood would squirt but he would then be safe. He remembered that his feet were bare. Once more he heard boots marching down the corridor. The sound terrified him. He felt his mouth dry.

He did not fear the Japanese. There was nothing to fear. He had done nothing wrong. He of all people had nothing to be afraid of. He had not even succumbed to his wife's scolding and bought the black market white sugar that she so wanted. HE WAS NOT AFRAID.

It was the rat he was afraid of. He told himself this over and over again. He had nothing to fear. He must concentrate on the rat that might try to nibble at his toes. He thought he felt a sword whizzing in the air just by his neck and he jerked his head. He saw his head fly apart, away from the shining sword. Blood flew out of his neck like red rain. 'Stop it,' he told himself in the intolerable darkness. He put the yellow face that had wielded the invisible sword away from his fevered brain.

Then he heard quite clearly the sound of screaming. A hoarse, ear-splitting scream. He froze, listening intently in the dark. The sound was not repeated. His mouth was so parched that his tongue stuck to the roof of it. He worked his throat but no saliva would come. Suddenly he felt the brush of bristly fur against his left leg. His hand came crashing down and hit the hard cement floor. The rat was fast. The scuttling was further away. The rat was mocking him.

The door opened and a bright light shone into his face. He lifted his hands and covered his eyes with a scream. The sudden glare was intolerable, like knives in his eyes. He felt fear. There had been no sound of boots.

From the darkness behind the bright light two shadows detached themselves and appeared by his sides. Two young Malay boys. They helped him to his feet with soft hands. Their eyes were blank, there was no use pleading with them. They led him down the dank, dark corridor that smelt strongly of urine. He realised this time around that there were many closed doors on either side of the corridor. Mostly he heard nothing, but once a deep sigh came from behind one of the doors. It was the despairing sound of someone who has no fight left, no hope left at all.

And then he was standing in a small rather bare room, all alone. In the room, lit by a naked light bulb, was a wooden table and two chairs. On the table stood a large jug of water and an empty glass. He stared mesmerised by the sight of the water. It looked clear, sweet and beautifully cool, with thick, gleaming ice cubes gently gloating on the surface. There was something so bizarre about finding the very thing he needed most in that bare room with the naked electric bulb that he felt uneasy. He looked at the single glass on the table. Surely he could just take a quick sip and no one would know? He looked around the room. The walls were solid and thick. He waited another five minutes. Still no one came.

He picked up the jug and took a mouthful. The liquid rested but a second on his parched tongue and then he was spitting it out. The water was so salty it was undrinkable. Now he felt real fear as he saw the mess on the floor. What had he done? It was a trick of some kind and he had fallen for it. There was probably someone watching him now through the keyhole. He began to shake from head to toe. Clumsily, hurriedly, he took off his white singlet and wiped the floor with it. When the floor was dry, with shaking hands he put his singlet back on. The key in the door turned. The door opened and a man in a remarkable mask walked into the room. Father was so startled by the incredible sight that he gasped and took an involuntary step back. He didn't know it at that time but he was looking into the perfection of a Japanese *Noh* mask. The man was wearing a loose robe much too long at the sleeves. He bowed politely in the Japanese way. Father quickly bowed back. When the man moved his head, the mask seemed to come to life. Under the overhead light, the skin on the mask was smooth and lustrous like that of a girl. Father stared at the mask blankly. A beautiful young girl/boy was smiling at him, warm, clean and innocent. Under the gently arched eyebrows in the empty sockets the stranger's eyes were shadowed but alive. Black and alive. My father stood in the middle of the room, intimidated and confused by the mask.

'The Imperial Army is pleased to have you here as our very honoured guest,' the masked stranger said very softly and for one heady, perfectly happy moment my father felt certain that it was all a terrible mistake. The Japanese Army had no reason to welcome him as a guest. He was a little nobody clerk without the brains to be promoted even once in his lifetime. Why, he had failed every exam he had ever taken! They could ask his wife, his children, the neighbours. They would tell him straightaway. It was simply a case of mistaken identity. The man wanted by the Imperial Army was obviously someone important who could help with their cause. My father opened his mouth to speak but the polite stranger gestured to the jug of water on the table and asked with a slightly petulant twist in his voice, 'Would you like a drink?'

And that was when my father knew that it was not a mistake.

The stranger carefully poured a glass full of water and held it out for my father. 'Sit,' he invited, pulling out one of the chairs. The long silken sleeve rode up his arm revealing hands that were unnaturally white, like the skin on the underbelly of a house lizard, and terribly misshapen. The ends of the fingers were strangely spongy. My father suppressed a shudder. He had never seen anything like it before. He felt a sudden fear clutch at his heart and understood the reason for the very long sleeves. He began to wonder with horror about the need for the mask.

This couldn't be happening to him. He was just a normal ordinary person who had no political affiliations or ambitions of any sort. He was a man content to sit on his veranda with a cheroot or hold his children on his lap while he listened to the radio.

The mask watched him with a pleasant expression. My father felt confused. A mask didn't have expressions. Then the mask floated towards him until it was only three or four inches away. The empty shadowed sockets were suddenly pits of terrible cruelty. Opaque and coldly amused, they were riveting. The dull glint in the masked man's eyes told Father that he had done this many, many times before and he had enjoyed it every time. Father stared disbelieving, almost intoxicated by the exquisite beauty of the mask and the evil that lay in the eyelets. The swelling red lips, sensuously moist, were almost upon him when the spell was suddenly broken and catching his breath Father jerked back, horrified. The man was evil.

'Drink, drink,' the mask cried expansively, but cold reptilian eyes considered the wet singlet with delicate amusement. My father felt the hairs at the back of his neck rise with revulsion.

'Drink,' the *Noh* mask urged, more insistently this time.

So my father took a large gulp of salty water. The water burned his sore throat. Immediately the man moved forward and refilled his glass. Then he began to speak. He spoke softly and sometimes my dazed father, in his damp, white singlet and the half-full glass in his hands had to strain to listen. What the man in the loose robes said immediately became an indistinct blur in his memory. All he remembered was the incredible impression that the mask appeared to change. Sometimes it was melancholy and sometimes it appeared bright and happy. Once angry. And he also remembered the voice. By the virtue of its very softness it inspired terror in my poor father, and of course he remembered the softly whispered urgings, 'Drink, drink.'

By the time their conversation was over my father had drunk the entire jug of salt water. His stomach cramped painfully and he was burning with an all-consuming thirst. The two Malay boys returned him to his room. In his room he found more salt water and a cold, tasteless gruel of discarded vegetables and rice. A day or perhaps more had passed. His lips had begun to crack. Somewhere there was the sound of a dripping tap. He could feel the coolness of it in his mouth. In the dark room he contemplated the blood of the rat. That was liquid, wasn't it?

More time passed and when they sent for him again two soldiers asked him repeatedly about a Communist he had never heard of before. Ah Peng . . . Ah Tong . . . it was all a blur. 'I don't know those men.' They slapped him hard. 'Not they, *him*,' they corrected angrily. 'Don't play games.'

'Yes, yes, him. *Him* not they,' Father screamed in pain.

'Are you denying that he ran into your neighbourhood?'

'He might have but he didn't come to me.'

'Who then?'

'I don't know.'

'Try to guess . . . You know who we are looking for.'

And so the questions went on and on, never-ending in their assumption that my father had indeed given shelter to a wanted Communist and was now obviously lying. The two soldiers beat him.

'Confess!' a voice screamed so close to his ear he felt it like an explosion deep inside his head, deafening and vibrating uncontrollably. With his screaming head in his hands he tried many answers but they were all unsatisfactory. With a perfectly innocuous looking wooden tool they tore the flesh between his fingers. Father fainted with the intolerable pain. They threw a bucket of cold water in his face. When he came around they pulled out one of his fingernails. How well cruelty suited them. The pink fingernail came out with a squirt of blood and a tiny chunk of flesh attached. They had done it so fast that it took my father some seconds to realise what had happened. His wild eyes stared at the freshly bleeding finger in amazement. Yes, he was slow on the uptake but could this be a sort of joke? Could all this really be happening to *him*?

The two soldiers smiled scornfully at the big, stupid beast writhing on the floor. Slowly the intense flash of agony blurred into a throbbing pain. Father took a deep breath and risked another look at his damaged finger. The wound looked worse than it felt. The pain was bearable. He looked up at the rough, sunburned faces of the soldiers.

'Pain nearly gone?' the one closest to him asked before snatching Father's hand in a vice-like grip and plunging it into the waiting jar of salt. That was when he began to scream like a madman. The torture was like nothing he had ever experienced. Like flames, pain shot up his arm, exploding in his nerves like a crack of lightning.

'I don't know him. I don't know him. Oh God, I swear I don't know him. Oh Lord Ganesha, protect me. *Pleeease*. Take me away from here. Take me away. Take me now.'

He lost consciousness and when he came around, two Malay lads were dragging him down the corridor. Hazily he saw two more local boys coming out of one of the many doors along the corridor. A Chinesewoman stumbled between them. She was naked from the waist down. Her shoulder-length hair was wild and matted and her eyes were glazed and blank. In the dim light of the corridor her face was chalk white. He couldn't help himself, his eyes travelled downwards. Suddenly he realised what he was seeing. She was bleeding copiously. The blood ran down the insides of her legs and dotted the floor. His first thought was that they had hurt her in her private parts but then he realised that she was menstruating. Strangely enough, her lack of shame in her own blood frightened him more than anything else he had seen so far. He snapped then.

'Oh, no, no, no, what have they done to you,' he sobbed like a child, crying for her as if she was a close family member; but as if his sorrow for her was invisible, she walked on, her face empty, a robot, or someone already dead, towards the room where the man with the mask waited.

They threw my father on the cold stone floor with his burning pain, a jar of salt water and the rat for company. He pulled himself into his corner, defeated and spent. His head spun in tight dizzy circles. He finally understood why the corpses posted around town, sagging inside their bonds, had blackened fingers. The afternoon sun scorched the flesh and burned the salt in the wounds.

He awoke with a scream. His finger was on fire. The harsh sound of his own scream was unrecognisable to him. Something was eating his finger. The rat was eating his flesh. He jerked his hand. There was a flash of pain in the dark but the rat was so hungry that it boldly refused to let go of its meal. My father thrashed frantically in an almost hysterical frenzy, slamming his hand on the hard floor until his hand was free and the scuttling sound moved away. His hand throbbed wildly. He began to sob softly. The room smelt of his own urine.

Days passed. He lost track of time. Everything had been reduced to a blur. He felt worse than any animal in a cage. His hand had begun to twitch uncontrollably. The salt water had made his lips crack open and bleed. His fingers moved on the huge, rough scabs on his lips with the horror of someone who finds leeches on his body. He lay many hours in the pitch black listening to the rat scuttling in the dark. When it sounded nearer he would stamp, bang and kick the floor until the sound receded to the edges of the room. He felt ashamed that his captors could have reduced him to such an inhuman state so quickly. He had always thought of himself as a dignified man and yet . . .

Finally, one day the door opened once more and he was taken back to the room of the first encounter with the *Noh* mask and the pure evil behind it.

There was a jug of water waiting for him. The sight of it made his knees buckle with horror and his hand moved instinctively to his mouth. The scabs were large and the bleeding was constant now. Every movement his lips made was excruciatingly painful. He shivered deep inside his being.

The robed man entered the room and walking towards the table poured some water into a glass. He held it out to my father.

The mask was truly a work of art. It now began to look like someone my father knew. Perhaps he was going mad. His eyes dropped to the offered water. Ice clinked inside the glass. It looked beautifully cool. He felt like gagging. My father shook his head and knew that his eyes were full of abject begging.

'Please no more,' he muttered through lips stiff and tight. The words made them bleed afresh. Was it his imagination? How was it possible for a mask to look disappointed?

'The Imperial Army has no further use of you,' the familiar mask said before it took a lingering sip of water. 'You shall die before dawn,' the masked tormentor announced quietly and left. The water must be unsalted. My father pounced on the jug and two soldiers slammed the butts of their rifles into his lunging body.

Later that night, four soldiers heralded ten men into a lorry. Loud classical music filled the cool night air. My father had no doubt it was the man with the lizard skin who listened to such beautiful music. He was a connoisseur of beautiful things, you could tell from the way he turned his brutality into an art. The men climbed into the lorry one by one. They all wore bleeding lips on their parched, dehydrated faces. Their hands trembled and their eyes bulged with terror. The lorry of beaten men drove away from the elegant house with its resident rats, its masked host of exquisite cruelty and noiseless Malay boys who appeared and disappeared like ghosts. The lorry driver sat beside my father. Dazed, he stared into nothing. They drove the men deep into a jungle and stopped in a clearing. The prisoners looked at each other with fresh fear. They recognised the smell of rotting corpses. The soldiers ordered them off the lorry, stuffed shovels into the men's shaking hands and commanded them not to dig but to fill a long deep hole. The hole was deep and so black that they could not see the twisted faces of horror or the worm-infested flesh inside but they could smell it. Rotting man.

Father looked around him. The light from the lorry's headlamps made them all look crazed and desperate. The smell, the ugly thoughts, the muttered prayers and the occasional wild laugh. They looked like men who had felt the soft cold breath of death at their necks. They covered the hole. Then they were instructed to dig another, same length and width as before. In the light from the headlamps he could see that there were other places of the same length and breadth, covered with fresh earth. It didn't bear thinking about. For two hours, maybe more, they dug. It was slow, back-breaking work yet no one wished for it to end. More than anything else in the heat of that night was the dread of the words, 'Stop. That's enough.'

Soon I will be dead, he thought, suddenly calm.

My father said he saw Death and Death was so close and such an adorable young child that he pulled him close and kissed the pretty child on the lips. 'Come and play with me,' the little child invited.

'STOP! That's enough. Stand facing the hole,' a loud voice ordered.

Soon he would be no more and the thought was strangely pleasing. He was aware that he was a failure in life and death had invited him so prettily. He made his calculations. Mohini would soon be married and I was bright enough to negotiate a good life. The boys would be fine, of course. He felt a little stab of pain for poor Lalita but her mother, that admirable paragon his wife, would take care of the little girl.

Wearily the men stood in a line. Some of them began to sob and others to plead through lips that bled copiously as they spoke. Blood ran down their chins. The pitiful sounds they made sounded like they came from very far away. The soldiers were unmoved. My father looked at the little black mouths of the Japanese machine-guns.

And indeed at that moment the young child called Death was starry-eyed and so full of sleep-tousled charm that my father was captivated. The child smiled at Father.

A small smile curved Father's spellbound mouth. He was ready.

The air was suddenly filled with machine-gun blast and light. His shoulder burned red raw as he slumped forward. The man next to him clutched his stomach and fell on my father. Together they collapsed in a tangle of stinking arms and legs into the pit. Inches away from Father's face, in the cold white light of the moonlight, he saw the face of our neighbour, a ghastly staring mask, and knew that Death was a cruel, heartless child. Others fell on top of them. Twitching and convulsing they played the game of Death to amuse the child. He made no sound when warm blood dripped on his face. All his screams of terror he held deep in his locked throat. From beneath the corpses he heard the soldiers talk in their guttural aggressive way. They stood over the hole looking in. They fired a few stray shots. Some bodies jerked inside the hole. My father opened his mouth wide but it was only to fill his burning lungs with air. He may not have been a clever man but he knew the value of silence.

First the headlights moved away and then the noise of the lorry lumbering off died into the night. It was dark, so dark in the pit of death that my father thought he would never see light again. He waited until the twitching stopped for he couldn't have stepped over a suffering body. The other bodies were heavy with the sleep of death. Arms, legs and heads pressed upon him. It seemed as if they wanted him to stay inside that dark pit with them. That night, he climbed over the nine other bodies. It was horrible. Finally he managed to pull himself out of the grave. Tiredly he sat for a while beside the pit he had dug himself. Vacantly he looked around. The moon smiled sadly at him and then he heard the sounds of the forest for the first time since they had driven out here. The incessant buzz of insects. A mosquito stung him. He slapped his neck and began to laugh madly. He was still alive. The sky was soft with grey clouds and a light breeze was blowing. He was torn and bleeding but he had cheated the charming child. Father had not missed the flash of thwarted anger in its soft liquid eyes. Never mind, he told the pretty pouting mouth now, 'Nine out of ten is still very good work.'

Father fell back into the pit for a pair of shoes from a dead man, then began moving into the night, staying within the jungle but keeping very close to the tyre tracks. Perhaps in a day or two it would lead him back into town but in the grey light of dawn he was horrified to realise that he was utterly lost.

My father returned home nearly two weeks after he

had been taken. One third of his bulk was gone. He smelt like the neighbour's cat that had crept under the firewood to die and not been discovered for a week. The skin on his body was covered in festering sores and bites. Like elastic his dark skin stuck to his big frame. He had been crawling in the jungle in circles, climbing over enormous felled trunks covered with slimy mosses and fungus, slipping and sliding in black mud and inhaling the sour smell of rotting leaves lying feet deep. And all the while feeding his blood to the swarms of giant mosquitoes, leeches, flies, fleas, winged ants and heaven only knows what other creatures God had seen fit to put into the blackest nights imaginable.

Father told me that at night, chemicals released by the process of rotting turn decaying leaves and dark lengths of whole, uprooted trees full of fungus and lichen on the jungle floor into a strange and never-ending pattern of phosphorescent and luminous shapes. He sat surrounded by the beautiful display of glowing light at his feet, frozen rigid with fear, keenly listening for the footfall of a tiger, knowing that a tiger's padded feet could tiptoe in the undergrowth without disturbing a single frond of a fern. It would simply appear before him, its lips tar-black and its teeth glowing.

My poor father. In the damp heat his shoulder burned day and night like red-hot coals on bare flesh. The wound was beginning to stink. He covered it with leaves. Every day at dawn he licked the dew off as many smooth leaves as he could find before stumbling on for as long as his legs would carry him. Once, in the dappled light, he just missed stepping on an enormous midnight-blue scorpion as it walked sedately across his path, its poisoned tail held high above its head.

He hardly ever stopped.

One day it rained in sheets, turning the paths he followed into rivers of red mud; another day it was so hot steam rose from the decomposing leaves on the jungle floor. Once he was startled and filled with wonder to discover giant potholes in the mud and to see the nearby tree trunks splashed ear high with black slime – elephant tracks. For a while he followed it but it led nowhere.

It took him some time but he realised without doubt that he was stumbling around in circles. Paranoia gripped him immediately. The indelible impression that the jungle *wanted* him grew inside his discouraged body. Its collective hunger appeared in every shape and form; even the creepers that hung from tree branches caressed him with such longing that they left damp, green trails on his face.

He was sitting on a fallen log watching a hairy-legged spider as big as his palm crawling up a fleshy creeper when he felt a tickling on his bare forearm. A maggot danced. As he looked at it in surprise another fell beside it. He simply stared at the two shiny white grubs frolicking on his flesh until a third joined them. Slowly he turned his head and even though he had guessed at once that his pus-filled shoulder wound was a mass of writhing, twisting maggots, the sight of them made him rear back and hiss with revulsion and horror. He realised that his hand had become quite numb. They are eating me alive, he thought, diving into the blackest despair.

He thought the golden, vindictive child of death was playing with him in the sweltering heat but he was wrong, the pretty child had lost interest in him. The maggots only ate the pus and the dead skin after which they all vanished, leaving a gaping clean hole in his shoulder. An Argus pheasant flitted in the giant ferns but so close to his hands that Father lunged for it. What he would have done with it had he caught it has always been a mystery to me, as Father could not kill a fly that flew into his mouth. The question never arose as he only managed to land face-down in rich black soil. Overhead, a brilliantly blue kingfisher with a gaudy orange breast flashed but Father saw it only as a blur of blue and orange, for he was becoming dangerously weak and faint.

Where the umbrella of leaves was thinner, butterflies as big as his face sailed around his head in graceful circles and sometimes he walked through mists of fruit flies, flapping his hands around his face listlessly. His shoulder still throbbed, his mouth was covered in sores and the skin on his body was painfully alive with hundreds of bites and brushes with poisonous leaves. He knew he could not continue for much longer. He dragged himself on, feebly.

Finally he found tracks, human tracks. The trees were marked. Overjoyed, he followed the marks. They led to a luscious clump of banana trees. As he tore hungrily into the grove heavy with fruit, dozens of leeches fell onto his skin from under the gorgeous green leaves. He didn't know they were on his body until he watched them, engorged with his blood and as thick as his middle finger, spring off his skin of their own accord. When his supply of bananas ran out he starved until he became aware of the scent of mangoes. He followed the strong odour until he stood before an amazing carpet of ripe fruit under a colony of wild mango trees.

Sitting on the yellow carpet he tore off the skins with

his teeth and ate ten, fifteen, maybe even twenty fruit. They were delicious beyond compare. He turned his singlet into a bag and carried on his journey as many mangoes as he could fit into it.

Then magically, unbelievably, the jungle gave way to symmetrical rows of rubber trees. He crept forward like a hunting cat, pausing behind each tree, his scalp prickling, expecting a Japanese soldier to leap out at any moment. An inscrutable yellow face, a bayonet deep inside his shrivelled stomach. But he met no bayonet. After the incessant buzz of millions of insects and the loud screams of birds and monkeys the rubber estate was deadly silent. He walked until he came upon an old dirt road, then he followed it to a tiny shack where two Indian men were manually processing crude sheets of rubber from latex using toddy, an alcoholic drink made from the sap of coconut palm. Father shouted out to them but only a weak moan came from his lungs. He opened his mouth to shout louder but his legs simply gave way beneath him and the darkness swallowed him.

They were good men. They brought my father home to us. I have never seen anyone as coldly professional as Mother. She was neither afraid of nor disgusted by her husband's condition. The smells, the wounds, the cuts, the bruises, the torn flesh, the shine of swollen skin. She burned bits of old cloth over the stove and used the snuffed out charred ends to rub over his entire body. Father groaned with relief as the carbon soaked into his sores. His swollen face she bathed with the liquid from boiled groundnut leaves. His wounds she cleaned and dressed and then she set about mending the broken man who had not recognised her at the doorway.

For weeks he lay in the large iron bed, a shrivelled, iodine-covered shape. His skin was muddy with sickness and clammy with perspiration. He called for water constantly, even in his sleep. The only name that came to his lips was my mother's and the only person he recognised when he half opened his eyes was her. Sometimes his hand reached out to touch Mohini's face and silent tears rolled down his face. His lips that had looked irreparable healed very fast but his body, ravaged by malaria, tossed and turned as if no cessation of the war inside his mind was ever possible.

'Take off his mask. Don't give him my quinine,' he shouted deliriously. 'Quick – close the doors. Hide the children,' he babbled. 'Can't you see? They're dead in the mud,' he screamed, shivering so violently the big bed shook.

On the first Saturday of his return, Mother came back from the market and on the chopping block outside the kitchen she unwrapped a dark green papaya-leaf package. Inside was a garishly red piece of crocodile meat. 'Good for healing wounds,' she said. 'He is such a long man and needs so much to fill him up again.' She cooked the meat with herbs. I watched as she spoonfed Father with that puce-coloured broth. The bits that dribbled down his chin she caught with her spoon. Every day, for many days, she untied papaya-leaf packages and cooked the bright red meat inside.

Day and night my mother sat by his bedside. Sometimes she scolded him and sometimes she sang to him, songs I had never heard her sing before. Maybe she did love him, after all. Perhaps she was only thorny of nature. I can see her now, a light figure sitting by the bed with my father's dark shape in it, surrounded by evening shadows. Leaning at the doorway, the sole of my left foot resting on the calf of my right leg, listening with awe to her sing songs that I had not known nested inside her, I remember thinking that Mother was like the ocean. So deep and so full of unknown things that I feared I'd never get to the bottom of her. I wished I were a stream that would grow into a river that could one day rush into her.

Then one day my father sat up and asked for a banana. We swarmed around him, fascinated, watching him eat on his own. Our purple father was a hero. He could manage only the feeblest of smiles that disappeared the instant they arrived. He bade Lakshmnan to bring to his bedside that special block of wood he had been saving for so many years. Then he began to carve a mask. Slowly, very slowly, a beautiful face took shape, with arching eyebrows and full sensuous lips. The mask, smooth and gently smiling, lay by the bed and Father stared at it a lot. Then one night we all awoke to the sound of banging and angry roaring. We rushed to his room and found him standing in the middle of it leaning limply against Mother's heavy wooden pestle. The mask, smashed to smithereens, lay in fragments on the floor. For a few seconds he looked at us almost as if he didn't recognise us before falling into a sobbing heap.

The next day I was standing at the doorway watching him eat alligator soup when he called me in. He patted the space beside his hips and I wriggled onto the bed, laying my head gently on his tummy. He began the story of his ordeal. Every word burned into my memory. After all, he had chosen *me* to tell his incredible story to. After that he improved fast, and soon he was walking around the house, but very quickly he began to forget the details that he had carved into my memory for ever. As the years went by he could only remember the mask or the pretty child of death in the haziest manner.

Jeyan

To strengthen my puny legs, Mohini was assigned the task of walking me through the woods behind our home, up along the stream and even occasionally as far as the Chinese graveyard on the other side of the main road. Hand in hand we walked, my sister clumping noisily along in a pair of those ridiculously uncomfortable, red, wooden clogs favoured by Chinesewomen in those days, and me in my sturdy shoes that Mother had paid good money for. On one of those walks a glinting piece of blue light in the flowing water caught my sister's eyes. She waded in, red wooden clogs and all, and returned, eyes shining, with a fabulously blue crystal clutched tightly in her hand. That was the beginning of the happiest time of my life. When the ground became a crystalline womb of infinite fertility. We found stones of stunning beauty everywhere – in the mud, along the roadside, under people's houses, by the riverbanks when Mother went to buy fish, and along the rocks near the market. We cleaned them carefully and once a week we took them to Professor Rao.

Professor Rao was an acquaintance of Father's, a gemmologist of some note. He had shown us yellowed, printed manuscripts, important papers he had written for the Gemmological Society of London. He was a courtly man and a scholar of Indian history. On his head grew hair of the purest white. His son, of whom he was very proud, was studying medicine in England. At every possible opportunity Professor Rao devotedly sent his son combs of unripe green bananas through friends and acquaintances. He often read us letters from a bright, cheerful lad, thanking him for the lovely, yellow bananas. They were perfectly ripe, the young man would enthuse.

It was Professor Rao who first taught us to walk around with a piece of flint in our pockets. Whenever we found a stone or a rock we struck it first with the flint and if the rock gave, it meant it could be polished to a high shine with steel wool. In this manner Mohini and I filled, almost to the brim, an old wooden orange packing case with beautifully polished, colourful stones and rocks. To my child's eyes the closed box under our house seemed like the most extravagant treasure equal even to Professor Rao's professional collection of rocks, crystals, fossils and gems.

Equal to his sawn and polished half-sections of geodes, unassuming rock eggs, the thick outer shells consisting of layers of swirling patterns made by rapid cooling in the earth's crust and inside, glorious cavities filled with the deepest purple crystals. Equal even to his three-foot amethyst cave which easily housed my whole head. Equal, I was certain, to his uncommonly large lingam, a phallus-shaped black tourmaline embraced by Hindus as the symbol of Lord Shiva. And equal, I thought, to his amber rock with its trapped live insect inside. I had not forgotten to take into account the morbid fascination factor in the dramatic blurring produced around the insect by its dying struggles.

I lay on a carpet of green and yellow leaves in our back garden unenvious of his Paua shells, his giant conches and his tree of coral with its precious beads still attached.

But now when I look at the contents of our box it makes me want to weep. All I can see is a box full of dusty rocks. A sad reminder of an innocent time, a happy time when hours could be spent under the house carefully polishing a stone to discover its deep orange innards. A time as fleeting and as delicate as a butterfly's wings, when stones of improbable cerulean blue, deepest topaz, and soft rose rested a while in my delighted palm.

Every week we left our slippers outside Professor Rao's home and went up the short flight of steps into his Aladdin's cave. At the threshold he greeted us in his white *dhoti*, his hands joined together like a lotus bud in the noblest form of greeting, his eyes rich with a thousand virtues and the footprint of god, holy ash drawn in the form of a U, on his high forehead.

'Come in, come in,' he bade us, clearly pleased to see his audience.

Inside his cool home we opened our tightly clenched fists and offered him warm stones for his perusal. Gravely he captured our stones in his tweezers and examined them one by one with a hand lens. Though it is certain that Mohini and I handed over junk more often than not, Professor Rao placed our stones with meticulous care on a special tray before delving into his spare room where the dark bottles of poisons he used to identify rocks and minerals were kept. He carried out the bottles, excitingly labelled with crossbones and skulls and purchased from specialist overseas suppliers, and carefully released a drop of colourless liquid on our offerings. Unblinking we stared. And sure enough for a few spellbinding moments our stones would sizzle, smoke and often turn freckled or flash with the most lustrous colours.

Afterwards his wife, a sullen woman, served us very sweet tea and her excellent marble cake. In her kitchen she listened to frivolous Tamil love songs but in the living room Professor Rao allowed nothing but the classical dour music of Thiagaraja to fill the air. While we nibbled at thinly sliced cake the Professor opened his silver box with its little compartments. Pan, betel leaf, slaked lime, areca nut, scented coconut, cardamom, cloves, aniseed and saffron rested inside. It was pure yoga, the exquisite way he pinched exact amounts of every ingredient, his long pianist's fingers folding the bright green leaf into a pyramid shape, piercing it shut with a single clove.

With the pan inside his mouth he brought alive the plight of an irritated oyster or the bubbling life of magma hundreds of miles beneath our feet, taking us under the earth's crust where diamonds have lived for millions of years. Softly his cultured voice carried us into great halls decorated with green marble from Sparta, yellow marble from Namibia and frescos by Meleager and Antimenes. On the grand walls hang perfumed oil lamps and wreaths of sweet-smelling leaves and violets. There Professor Rao will point to a decadent Roman host who has purposely chosen a bizarre collection of foods simply because they are rare and expensive and he is a rich gourmet. Slaves arrange upon a long banqueting table silver platters of warblers, parrots, turtle doves, flamingos, sea urchins, porpoises, larks' tongues, sterile sows' wombs, camels' hooves, cockerel combs, stewed kid, barbecued oysters and thrushes with an egg yolk poured over them.

'Look,' Professor Rao said, 'they eat with their fingers. Just like us.'

In awe we watch musicians, poets, fire eaters and dancing girls come and go until finally the second course is over and the proud host holds up an amethyst-encrusted goblet, shouting, 'Let the drinking symposium begin.' As he declares thus, his slaves drop a piece of amethyst into every guest's silver cup, for *amethystos* in Greek means 'not intoxicated'.

It was through Professor Rao's eyes that we observed court eunuchs of the ancient Chinese dynasties give equal attention to the job of finding a constant stream of young girls as concubines as preparing their Emperor's food in jade bowls to keep up their master's vigour.

After cake we followed the Professor to his glass case. He slid open the doors and another world opened before our eyes.

'Now let me see. Have I shown you my stone crab yet?' he would ask, putting into our childish hands the considerable weight of a large fossilised crab. Every detail preserved for ever. One by one all the treasures inside his glass case came out to pirouette before us. Wonderingly we ran our fingers along petrified wood, pieces of jet and rosaries made out of Shiva's tears, brownish-red rudraksh beads. We admired clear yellow tortoiseshell and at other times the tusk of a fossilised mammoth or the wild untreated ivory of hippopotamus and walrus.

Carefully he unwrapped round black stones that had been cracked open like a nut to reveal in their black interior sea ammonite fossils curled up and closed like a secret. He had found them on the Himalayan slopes. 'There was no range of mountains until India tore itself from a super continent called Gondawana and collided into Tibet, pushing the sea bed up higher and higher,' he said, explaining away the mystery of the sea ammonites' existence so high up a mountain slope.

To me, though, the crowing glory of Professor Rao's

crystal collection was always a Cherokee Indian crystal skull. Professor Rao told us that the Cherokee Indians believed their skulls sang and spoke and regularly washed them with deer blood before using them to heal or as an oracle. It was quite a beautiful thing with colour prisms deep inside it. Sporadically, when the colours in the skull dulled, the Professor buried it in the earth overnight or left it out during thunderstorms or a full moon.

With every visit he put a different chunk of crystal in our right hand and instructed us to place our left hand lightly over it. 'Close your eyes and let your heart whisper, "I love you," to the crystal,' he advised.

I held the crystal in the manner requested, closed my eyes and my monkey mind instantly scampered to the last slice of marble cake that still remained uneaten as I waited impatiently for the moment when he would say, 'Open your eyes now.'

'What did you see?' he would ask us excitedly.

I would have seen nothing more than green blobs on the orange screen of my eyelids but, thrilled by the experience, Mohini would report flashes of light, joy rushing through her veins like rainwater and slimy seaweed growing on her body. Sometimes she thought the stone in her hand pulsated, breathed and moved.

'They are the memories locked in the crystal,' Professor Rao would cry triumphantly.

One week, he had a surprise for us. The quartz crystal cluster that Mohini had held in her hands the week before had grown a rainbow on the tip of one of its crystals. We stared at the perfectly formed rainbow in wonder. Was it possible that Mohini had made it happen?

'Yes, absolutely,' Professor Rao beamed. 'The stone is sometimes like a shocked child. You have soothed it and it has responded to you.'

Subsequently he would ask her to touch and play with the crystal every time we came for a visit. It was the only crystal he had that had flowered a rainbow.

On our last trip to the Professor's house, just weeks before the Japanese invaded Malaysia, he slid open a match box and inside, nestled on a bed of cotton wool, was what looked like a huge drop of clear, very green oil. Professor Rao took out the solid drop in his hands, held it up against the light and swore it to be the most perfect emerald he had ever seen. It was priceless. Even raw its size and beauty were so obvious that the worker who had mined the stone swallowed it to smuggle it out.

'It is my life,' Professor Rao said proudly, but as he put it back into its unassuming home his voice was uncommonly gentle. 'It always reminds me of your eyes, Mohini, my dear child, and it will be yours when you marry my son.'

He was right about the emerald. It did look like my sister's eyes. Even from when I was a baby I have memories of her eyes. Sparkling gems. Laughing gems. How she used to laugh!

I remember her dancing.

I used to sit and watch her dance in the moonlight. I sat on Mother's milking stool as the cows slept in the shed and watched her, so different under the moon's silver stare, so beautiful. Her magnificent eyes, strange and long inside the thick, black rims made by lavish use of Mother's kohl.

'*Tai tai, Taka Taka tei, tei, Taka, Taka.*' Her clear voice used to ring out like the clapping of small children.

She arched her body, moving quickly, her hands sweeping out in the dark like the pale undersides of river trout jumping out of a black stream, her heels striking the ground, keeping rhythm with the clapping voice. Her anklets singing into the silver night.

'*Tai, tai, Taka Taka tei, tei,*' she sings, her fingers unfurling like fans. Her hands flying into the night to pluck enchanted fruit. She brushes them lightly, arranges them in a basket made of spun gold and offers them to the Great Goddess in the sky. Then the tips of her fingers reach down to touch her own feet and her feet, like the finest squirrel tail-brush, skip and rush forward, painting a picture on the ground. A proud peacock, a roaring tiger, a shy deer. It is always too dark to see. Her eyes dart sideways, left, right and left again. A look of wonder comes into her face. The picture is complete. Her feet move, the heels hitting the ground, rapidly moving in a graceful circle around the picture she has drawn. And when the circle is complete I know that her journey will be over.

'*Ta Dor, Ta Dor, Ta Dor, Ta, Ta.*' I watch her raise both her arms to the moon and spin faster and faster, the bells on her ankles ringing madly until she falls dizzy and breathless to the ground. She tilts her glowing face towards me, the rest of her body soft curves on the ground, and demands, 'Well? Am I getting any better?'

And for some strange reason she would remind me of Siddhi, that wonderful female who embodies the lure of mystical powers – so beautiful, so extravagantly eyed and yet spurned by the gods.

For those unreal seconds, fooled by the moonlight and the ecstasy of her dance, I would forget that it was not a mysterious celestial being that lay panting in our backyard but my sister, the most courageous person I knew. She was courageous in a way that other people were not, in a way that Mother thought was a weakness and Father thought bespoke a soft heart. How can I explain the fire that burned inside my sister when she saw an injustice done? Perhaps you will understand if I tell you about Mother's birthday dinner. That time Father saved for a whole year from his pathetic allowance to buy his wife a meal fit for a queen and her children.

Mother would have refused such an extravagance had she known of it in advance, but Father had made his plans secretly. He had ordered it all beforehand, paying for the meal in pitifully small instalments long before Mother's birthday. The whole family sat around a huge, circular table. First to appear were the chilli crabs, afterwards the mutton cooked in goats' milk, the creamy laksa noodles, the spicy seafood *char kueh teow*, the squid sambal pungent with the smell of belacan, the pomfret in ginger paste, the sugar-cane sticks wrapped with prawn paste, and on and on until the entire table was covered in steaming food.

'Happy birthday, Lakshmi,' Father whispered. There was a smile on his face.

Mother only nodded. Perhaps she was pleased for she smiled at us but as she began to fill a bowl with fried rice for Lalita a wail pierced the air. An old beggarwoman lamented loudly as a shopkeeper tried to chase her away by beating her legs with a broom. That was the way it was in those days. You had to beat beggars to keep them away.

Everybody stared, some sadly, some relieved that the smelly old woman would not be coming to their table to ruin their delicate appetites. Not Mohini, no. Her eyes brimming with tears, she shot up suddenly and charged towards the shopkeeper.

'Don't you dare beat the grandmother,' she shouted out.

Shocked by the sight of the girl flying towards him in such anger, the man's broom stopped in mid-air. The old woman, perfectly used to being beaten, stopped crying, her loose jaw hanging open. Mohini put her arms around the beggarwoman's waist and brought her to our table. To eat with us. My sister was not even ten years old then.

Even my earliest memories are tinged by her presence. I looked up from the hole in the ground that Mother stood me in daily to strengthen my legs and saw her in a myriad of poses. Acting out stories in which she alone played all the characters. Running this way and that way, pulling faces and changing voices she fluttered around me like a gay butterfly. Then, it seemed, only she had time for me. She must have looked into my small, begging eyes and known without being told that there would be no love forthcoming for the poor, ugly creature before her. That in my mouth were none of the adorable things that all children are endowed with to endear themselves but a lazy slug of a tongue. My sister took it upon herself to cherish me as best she could.

She did it every morning when the house emptied of people. After Father had left for work, Anna and my brothers for school and Mother for the market with Lalita in tow. Mother had to take Lalita with her or she would simply disintegrate into a heap on the floor and shed bitter tears until Mother returned as if it was far, far more than a trip to the market that she had lost. So every morning I found myself sitting cross-legged in a patch of weak sunlight by the kitchen window while

Mohini tugged and twisted all my hair into curly ringlets and told me stories about Lord Krishna, the blue
god.

'When he was a baby sitting outside, his mother saw
him eat a handful of sand so she rushed out to open his
mouth and clean away the sand, but when she opened it
she found the whole world inside his mouth.'

I sat with her fingers in my hair and her breath warm
on my head and envied a well-loved, mischievous child
who stole buttermilk, hid the garments of maiden
bathers for a fancy, killed a huge cobra with his bare
hands and held up Mount Govardhan to shelter a herd
of cows from a terrible storm sent by a jealous Indra. I
dreamed of looking out of a palace window onto a generation of *gophis*, fair milkmaids gathering lotus buds in a
green pool, each one secretly praying that they might
marry me. I dreamed of an eventual wedding to the
fairest *gophi* of them all called Ratha.

'One day your Ratha, soft as a mustard flower, will
come and I will place the sandalwood paste and kum
kum on her forehead,' Mohini teased. I always produced
the required sickened face but I believed her with all my
heart.

Those are my happiest memories. What else is left to
remember? Years spent at the mercy of cruel teachers.
They pinned my exercise books to my back during recess
so the extent of my simple-mindedness could be shared
with the entire school. They rapped my knuckles and
flung my work out of the door as worthless. It seemed
the extent of my stupidity was unimaginable to them.
They called me names and banished me to a corner of the
classroom. In the playing fields children I had never seen
before chanted out, '*Kayu balak*, *Kayu balak*, Timber,

Timber,' when they saw me. 'Thick as a piece of wood.'

Oh, I cried for my poor ears that had no lids.

I was so desperate that I humiliated myself to earn the right to a kind word, a greeting, or a conversation during break. I carried the school bags of others willingly, walked backwards around the field for their cruel amusement and barked like dog. But in time I discovered that friendship cannot be acquired thus so I learned to sit alone at the end of the playing field, my back to the laughing children, my small eyes facing the road, my slow mouth chewing my food.

'*Kayu balak, Kayu balak*,' the happy children sang to my back.

The teachers continued to berate and abuse my handwriting but I could not control my hand that had turned to wood. Tears escaped out of my carved eyelids but their furious faces refused to soften. How could I tell them that when I opened a book to read, inky blue fishes swam on the white waters of my page so I could not make out the words clearly? How could I add the numbers properly if they frolicked and played like spider monkeys across my page? By the same token, how could I even begin to tell them about my wooden hand?

Many years after the Japanese had wrecked our lives and left I wondered if I had fallen asleep on a mat of glossy leaves in the back garden and dreamed a Basohli painting studded with fragments of beetle wings that glittered like emeralds. Could it be that such a glorious, civilised time had really existed in my history? I went to visit Professor Rao. He came to the door, almost bald, two hands joined together to make a wrinkled lotus flower, and frail, so frail. I had remembered him more resplendent, bigger and smiling rapturously.

'Papa Rao,' I said, reverting unconsciously to my childish memory.

He smiled sadly. His hand reached out to touch my hair, oiled and streaked back from my forehead. 'The curls,' he lamented.

'They were ridiculous. Mohini's doing . . .' I trailed off.

His cheeks sagged. 'Of course,' he agreed dully, leading me into the house. The place was silent, smaller and strangely dead. There was not even the sound of Mrs Rao's sickly sweet love songs floating out of the kitchen. I could hear her moving about in another part of the house, her movements heavy and laboured.

'Where is the crystal cave, the geodes, the skull, the paintings?' I asked suddenly.

He lifted his right hand and dropped it uselessly back to the side of his body. 'The Japanese . . . they stole everything. It took three of them to carry my crystal cave.'

'Even your stone crab?'

'Even my stone crab, but look – they did not touch my lingam. The brutes didn't realise its value.' He walked over to stroke the curving dense black stone.

Something occurred to me. 'Has your son returned?' I asked.

'No,' he said, so abruptly that I knew an unimaginable ruin had come to pass. 'Shall we listen to some Thiagaraja?' he suggested, turning away quickly so I would not see the raw pain that seized his old face.

At the first pure sound of the veena's string Professor Rao dropped his head into his hands. Silent tears fell onto his white *dhoti* turning the cloth transparent so his poor, brown skin showed through.

'Papa Rao,' I cried, distressed by the sight of his tears.

'Sshh, listen,' he choked.

There was no marble cake or sweet tea. I sat frozen in my seat until every note of Bhairav's raga was finished and Professor Rao had recovered himself sufficiently to raise his head and smile tremulously at me. When I stood to leave he put his prized lingam in my hand.

'No,' I said.

'Soon I will be dead,' he said. 'No one else will love it like you will.'

Sadly, I carried the black stone home. The Japanese had not wanted it. They had not seen the beauty of it. It was a rejected thing, like me. I went under our house and sat on the box full of lovingly polished worthless stones and thought of Papa Rao's quivering mouth; and tears arrived. I held the black lingam in the palm of my right hand, my left lightly covering the smooth, rounded tip. Then I closed my eyes and for the first time my heart earnestly whispered, 'I love you, crystal.'

For a little while there was just the orange screen of my eyelids with the familiar green blobs until quite without warning there was a flash, like sunlight on water at the corners of my eyelids. And then I felt my struggling heart take a deep breath and still a little. Suddenly someone who understood my very essence held me in his arms and rocked me. A sense of peace stole over me. The stone comforted me and, by and by, I understood that I was never meant to be born a human being. I could have been happy as a rock. I could have been contented as a huge rockface on a mountain peak or a simple cluster of crystals luminous in the cold sunlight. On Mount Everest.

I would have perched high up over the world, unshakeable and secure in my worth, year in year out watching the pointless comings and goings of the deluded human race. On my granite hand I would wear a wooden watch, days and nights passing while the frozen hands on my watch sat motionless. But I am not a sparkling crystal or a craggy rock overlooking a handsome cliff. I see that instantly in my mother's face. It is not my fate to be so admired by mankind that they throw their lives at my feet so they may know me, so they may rest a while on my peak. I am a dullard with a square face carved out of immobile granite. The laughter and passions in other people a source of envy in my lonely heart.

I stare studiously at my wooden watch face and people zoom around me at great speed. When I look up the soul collector has been around and people I love have disappeared for ever and new little people have sprung up like seeds from the ground. When you look at me you only see a man trapped in a menial job – but be careful not to pity me for like the earth I will live beyond the pointless comings and goings of man. You'll see.

Sevenese

It was only when I found out about the snake-charmer's eldest son Raja's secret love for my sister that I first realised how beautiful she was. It was 1944 and I was eleven years old. I ran home so fast that the wind whistled by my ears and my white shirt-tails flapped madly in the wind. I dashed past Father dozing with his mouth half open on the veranda and made for the kitchen. She looked up from a bowl of brown chapatti dough and smiled at me. I stared at the starburst happening in her eyes. Indeed, Mohini was a spectacular creature. It was a revelation to realise that she was not simply the hand that arranged neat piles of curries around a mound of rice on my plate or the considerably gentler touch (the other, of course, being Mother's strong, rough hand) that ministered the hated weekly oil-bath ritual.

I looked into the green and brown flecks inside her lovely eyes and felt a warm glow spread inside me at the thought of how well this totally unexpected romantic twist fitted in with my plans. I can actually remember clasping my hands together and saying a prayer to God, thanking him for making my sister beautiful enough to attract the attention of Raja, for Raja was someone whom I had, for as long as I could remember, idolised and longed to befriend.

To others his sullen face and his striding figure embodied the strange inexplicable sounds and cries that came from the snake-charmer's house in the middle of the night. There was talk of evil and black magic. There was even talk of ghosts and spirits come back from the dead. People feared him and his father, but I didn't. From the day I found out that the grinning skull inside their house belonged to him I was obsessed with the need to know more. For years I had played with his younger brother, Ramesh, while gazing at the unreachable, tall figure of Raja in the distance. Everything about him was a source of intense curiosity and mystery. His powerful clay-coloured limbs, his dirt-encrusted clothes, his unwashed bronze locks and that peculiar but not unpleasant wild, animal smell that emanated from his body in tangible waves. Of course, Mother's vividly recalled bloody story about him as a little boy with curly hair munching bits of glass in the market place elevated him to unimaginable heights of dark powers.

I watched full of awe from afar as he tended to the beehives at the back of their home. I have no love of bees and can never forget the day when Ah Kow from next door threw a stone at one of the hives and the entire swarm rose up in a dark, angry cloud and roared like a waterfall. Even the Japanese soldiers with their long guns waited outside the house for their bottles of free honey. Raja though was unhesitating and fearless when he dipped his hand into the droning hives and softly stole their precious honey. Sometimes they stung him but unperturbed he casually plucked out their black stingers from his swelling face. Once he even wore a whole swarm like the most repulsive black and yellow beard on his face.

All for my pleasure.

Before Raja came into my life I was a Boy Scout by

day, a fruit thief by evening and a chain-gang terrorist on chosen weekends. Raja's brother, Ramesh, Ah Kow and I used to belong to a gang of boys that ran wild in other people's fruit orchards and staged fierce fights with rival gangs. It seems incredible to think back now that we actually fought these battles armed with bicycle chains, sticks and stones. We gathered in the outskirts of the old market place and charged at the enemy screaming frenziedly, hurling stones and swinging bicycle chains. Quite a lot of blood used to spill too, until Chinese housewives with bad hairdos and ill-fitting *samfus* rushed out of their homes cursing and brandishing brooms. They hit us over the head and occasionally managed to catch by the ear those of us too engrossed in the fight. Being caught by the ear was far worse than a hundred lashes on the head with someone's bicycle chain. The ultimate insult was when they bent very close to our ears and swore at the top of their coarse, uneducated voices, 'Devils, devils, little trouble-making devils. Wait till I tell your mother.' The rest of us had no choice but to instantly drop our murderous scowls and menacing stances and scamper away in all directions as quickly as possible. They were good fun, those fights, even if they were few and far between.

Mostly we were content to simply steal into watermelon patches and cart away their biggest and best. We lugged the massive dark-green fruit to a safe place and pigged out on red flesh until we couldn't move. Then we lay flat on the ground, arms and legs thrown far apart like stranded starfishes, and groaned at the blue skies. Once while we were stealing watermelons from a field a half-dressed man came running out of a dirty unused shed. He shook his fist at us angrily and shouted, 'Hey, you greedy pigs. Come back here.' One of the boys in our group yelped in horror, realising for the first time that it was his uncle's watermelon patch that we were raiding. His uncle chased us for a long way, cursing and swearing in Chinese.

Sometimes we climbed into fruit orchards and sat among the branches eating sweet mangoes and rambutans until we were literally sick. It wasn't long before one of the orchard owners bought a big, black guard dog. I must say that animal carried a ferocious bark in his mouth but we hurled such a rain of unripe fruit on his soft nose that he ran with his tail tucked tight between his legs and his red tongue flying behind him like the tip of a woman's scarf. After that one time he never came around any more. Only when we heard that someone had poisoned the unfortunate dog did it dawn on us that others were on to the same good thing as us.

At least once a week we hid behind the big old Chinese Bakery in the middle of town hoping to steal sticky buns filled with grated coconut cooked in molasses. As the van drivers loaded their vans with supplies for all the coffee shops in town we made a quick job of swiping huge handfuls. The buns were still wonderfully hot when we crammed them into our mouths. It was during those daring heists that we came to realise why the coffee shop beside the bakery sold the cheapest chicken rice in all of Kuantan. You could actually eat a satisfying meal for only twenty cents. Day and night there were people sitting at round tables stuffing their faces. Hidden away behind the dustbins we saw cage after cage of diseased and dead chickens arriving from all the different farms outside town. Unhappy chickens with half-closed eyes and undernourished, scantily feathered chickens swayed and lurched drunkenly over the dead carcasses on the floor of the cages. A young Chinese boy with a harelip slaughtered them, dipped them into a large vat of boiling water, plucked them bald and chucked them into a square tin container. Every once in a while a bad-tempered cook in dirty black shorts and a white singlet came out scratching and swearing. He smoked a cigarette then grabbed a handful of cleanly scrubbed chickens by their dimpled necks and went back into his cooking cubicle. From the restaurant proper came the sound of loud laughter and the call of people ordering more of that delicious chicken rice.

At other times we hung about in the back lanes trying to catch one of the cheap, painted prostitutes in action. Most of them were ugly and sour-faced. They stood in colourful clusters in the alleyways with bitter, knowing eyes and greedy, unnaturally pouting mouths. They leaned back against the dirty walls of the narrow back streets smoking endless cigarettes, and threw stones at us with surprising viciousness if they spotted us peeping.

Sex was a real curiosity but only once did Ramesh and I manage to witness the act itself. It was late in the evening and she was very young. Her mouth was deeply red and her hair raven black. We hid behind the smelly green dustbins full to overflowing with decaying rubbish and gazed pop-eyed at the man and the girl. It looked like he was bargaining and he even made as if to walk away but she smiled, stretched out a very white hand and looked coyly at him. He fished money out of his shirt pocket and put it into her outstretched hand. Suddenly they were in the middle of the act itself. It was all rather sordid and far from the intriguing thing I had imagined it to be. The man dropped his trousers and bent his knees in such a way that his bunched trousers remained trapped in the backs of his legs. His hard hands gripped the soft white flesh of her buttocks. Unconcerned that his wrinkled, thin butt was hanging out for all the world to see he buried his face in her left shoulder and pumped energetically. Every time he jerked into her she shouted out ecstatically, 'Wah, wah, wah!' But in her powdered, rouged face her glassy eyes had rolled upwards. Up and away from the smelly gutters and the rusty green weeds that struggled to grow in the cracks by the drain. Away from the edges of the broken stone steps, past the peeling paint on the walls, past the firmly shut windows that told her she was a slut and past even the roof-tiles full of moss, onto a patch of evening sky coloured orgasmic tangerine. On her face there was no pleasure, no boredom, no emotion. Just a very red mouth shouting, 'Wah, wah, wah!'

Inside my shorts a small snake shed its skin and grew thick and hard. As soon as the grunting man had finished he retrieved his grey trousers from the back of his knees, stuffed himself back into them with surprising speed and disappeared in the opposite direction. The girl brought out a crumpled, dirty handkerchief from her handbag and wiped herself quickly. There was skill in the flick of her wrist. She wore no underwear. Her private part was white, flat, triangular and covered in curly black hair. She smoothed down her short Western-style clothing, flicked her black hair over her shoulder and tottered away on very high heels. We listened to the tapping of them echo loudly in the deserted alleyway until she was swallowed by one of the anonymous back doors.

I am sure that first encounter with sex had a profound effect on me. It has imbued my idea of sex with the wrong flavour. That young girl's blank boredom and red lips shimmer before my eyes like a mirage in the desert. I crawl towards it on my hands and knees only to find myself in the wrong alleyway, wrong hotel room, wrong prostitute. I recognise that it is the prostitute's ennui that draws and excites me. The prize is the ability to bring animation into a bored face. It has driven me on for years. Even after I realised the truth about their tired souls I lived for the fantasy that red mouth in the alleyway created all those years ago, paying double if they managed an appearance of enjoyment, if they didn't ask, 'How much longer?' And they, that inexhaustible army of short skirts and smooth thighs, they never missed a beat, laying on a truly admirable repertoire of convincing groans, deep throat moans, dying gasps. Yes, I have wasted my life in bordellos looking for the girl in the alleyway – but isn't it strange that after all these years I can still see her so clearly? The spikes of her stilettos for ever buried in rotting papaya skin, a cloud of disturbed fruit flies rising up to her ankles and her knees buckling slightly. 'Wah, wah, wah!' she cries once more, her eyes rolling up to meet the evening sky. And then in my fantasy she looks directly into my eyes and moans with surprised pleasure.

Every other week in the afternoon Ramesh and I put on our mauve Boy Scout uniform with its distinctive scarf and walked to school. There we were taught obedience, helpfulness, the importance of being earnest, and good, upright behaviour. Afterwards we were issued with rectangular blue work cards, the front printed with the school's crest. We were then split into groups of twos and despatched off to the different affluent neighbourhoods around the school. We called at their gates, knocked at their front door and with shining smiles chorused, 'Aunty, do you have any odd jobs for us to do?' Invariably they had. We washed cars, cleaned out garages, mowed lawns, cut hedges, swept drains, collected rubbish into piles and burned them. Then we presented our cards, had them signed and got paid either fifty cents or one ringgit. The money we were supposed to hand over at the end of the day to the Scoutmaster, but Ramesh and I had double cards so for every ringgit we turned in we kept one.

You could buy cigarettes singly in those days. The shopkeeper looked you up and down but ultimately tended to mind his own business. As long as money was handed over he kept his opinions to himself and his abacus busy. At the beginning we sneaked into the clearing in the woods behind Ramesh's house, blowing hundreds of smoke rings into the humid air, listening for the crash of small wild boar as they hurtled along in the bushes, but as we grew braver we migrated into town. In the late evenings we sat in a row by the side of the road near the cinema with our legs dangling inside the enormous monsoon drain that ran right through the town, smoking and watching the girls go by. When the monsoon winds blew and the heavy rains poured for days on end, strange things rushed by in the water. A dead water buffalo bobbing stiffly, a large, wildly struggling snake being swept away, a smashed rattan rocking chair, furiously dog-paddling rats with calm faces, bottles, excrement and, one day, what became Lalita's favourite doll. It was a foot tall with curly yellow hair, pretty blue eyes and a small plastic mouth painted a pale pink. Some spoilt European child must have tossed it into the water in a fit of temper. The December rains were yet to arrive so when it floated by with its round staring eyes in the gently moving water I scooped it out and took it home, where Lalita, with shining, incredulous eyes, opened her arms wide.

I should say though that smoking by the drains carried far more danger than the gatherings in the woods. Mother had spies everywhere. Any woman in a sari could be counted upon to efficiently broadcast any incident with a great deal of embellishments added. I had seen the effect of one of Jeyan's escapades. Poor kid. By the time he got home Mother was already seething. But the sorry part was he was hardly ever bad. Once in a blue moon sums up the frequency of his stunts but the unlucky little chap always got caught.

Occasionally we faked illness and skipped school to end up in the cinema. Once, standing in the queue to see a new risqué movie, we were surprised to see our headmaster hiding behind a pillar, his bulging eyes darting about suspiciously. He was a man of such excruciating fastidiousness that one imagined him to be sickened by his own bodily secretions. We would have run or ducked or something but for the sight of a light-green ticket for the matinee performance of *Vimochanam (The Evils of High Drinking)* nodding limply between his sweaty fingers. He was not there to pounce on us after all. Locked uncomfortably into his stiffly starched white shirt and old-fashioned black trousers he was positively bleeding embarrassment from every strict, law-abiding pore. The dreadful, hilarious moment when our glances must meet arrived. He froze, but for a frightened tic at the side of his face which made his moustache twitch madly. Clutching his ticket he suddenly scuttled into the darkened hall. For days I wondered if he would tell

Mother, but apparently shame has a way with outrage.

But some days, nothing could dispel the wind of boredom that blew listlessly in and out of our tiny little town where it seemed nothing ever happened. When simply going to the river on the other side of town to watch the bare-bodied men catch alligators and turtles was not enough, we turned bloodthirsty and used our slingshots to hunt lizards. The best slingshot among us was Ismail, Minah's youngest son. He had a passion for killing the pale grey lizards that was legendary. He took it upon himself as a good Muslim to kill as many as his skill allowed. It was a lizard that had betrayed the hiding place of the prophet Nabi Muhammad to his enemies; it destroyed the webs that a faithful spider had carefully spun over the mouth of a cave to conceal the prophet's entry into it. At the end of a killing session when Ismail stopped to light a cigarette he would have amassed a grotesque pile of no fewer than fifteen lizards beside him. Stretched out in the shade of the angsana tree and staring at pieces of blue sky through the leaves I was secretly envious of Ismail's pile and engrossed with thoughts of how to increase my own. It never crossed my mind that thousands of miles away, Nazi soldiers were equally engrossed with thoughts of enlarging their horrific mountains of dead Jews, famished and naked Jews, their skin like polished bone. Lying in the shade on those sultry afternoons war felt so far away, but when it came it came so suddenly there was really no time to prepare for it at all.

The Japanese landed in Penang on 7 December 1941. After watching movies about 'Made in Japan' bombs falling apart with a soft plop and making jokes about bow-legged soldiers too cross-eyed to shoot straight, we were stunned by their sudden complete control. Who were these Asian dwarfs who could make the mighty British flee in the night? And then they arrived in Kuantan. In the wake of the deep gravelly voice, the resplendent uniform and the polished boots of the white man, the first Japanese soldier was unattractive and uncouth in ill-fitting clothes. He had a yellow peasant face, wore a cheap, peaked cloth cap with flaps hanging over his neck, and had a flask and a tin container of rice, salt fish and soya beans secured to his belt. At the end of his short legs he wore rubber-soled canvas boots split-toed so the big toe was in a separate section from the other toes and into this cleverly adapted footwear the bottoms of his trousers were pushed. Thus ready for the muddy horror of tropical conditions he stood as the conquering hero. In our foolish, romantic youth we credited his one and only redeeming feature as his rifle and long bayonet.

'But they look like you,' I whispered incredulously to Ah Kow the first time we saw a group of them in town. Ramesh nodded in agreement but Ah Kow stared at the soldiers with hatred in his small eyes. How right he was to feel hate, for they tore apart his family. We watched them march up the road until they disappeared from sight. Expendable men in expendable uniforms who spoke rough guttural sounds and shamelessly unbuttoned their trousers in public places to let fly streams of yellow urine. How could these men have vanquished the British? People who lived in superior houses with servants and drivers to serve them, eating only choice food made up of hunks of red meat bought from the Cold Storage. And their children, naturally too superior for the local educational system, had to be sent back to the motherland after they had burned themselves brown under our sun. How many times had I stood head bent, humbly raking leaves in their backyards while surreptitiously listening to their privileged children laughing and talking in that peculiar but superior accent of theirs.

'What your name, then?' they demanded curiously, with murky-coloured eyelashes and eyes bluer than the sky. There had never been any doubt that they were the children of the greatest people in the world, with the biggest empire history had ever known. To the colonised mind it was an honour to serve such a race and it seemed downright impossible to imagine them malleted by an Asiatic people with a mission as narrowly feudal as the Japanese invaders'. Nothing more elaborate than the desire to bestow Singapore on their Emperor as a present for his birthday on 15 February 1942. And Malaya was a basket of raw material on the way.

The war, it seemed, was over before it began, but it was only the beginning of the daily grind, the misery, the unspeakable cruelty of the Japanese Occupation that lasted for the next three and a half years.

We returned from Seremban to a home looted empty except for my parents' big iron bed and the heavy bench in the kitchen. Everything else was gone. There was not even a mat to sleep on. The eight of us spent an uncomfortable night on the big bed. We awakened at dawn and I can remember running in the dark to the market with Lakshmnan and Mother, the mouths of empty sacks in our clenched hands.

The market was unrecognisable. Far from being a scene of war it was crammed full of goods as if it was a Sunday market. Locals who were used to haggling loudly over puppies, cats and poultry scrambled to grab bottles of jams, marmalades and pickles. Old Chinese-woman fought for tins of sardines, pilchards, luncheon meat and canned potatoes, and argued over canned beet-root, bags of sugar, tinned apples and pears, boxed fruit juices, medical drug supplies and clothing stolen from abandoned British homes and warehouses. We filled our sacks to the full. Where we buried our ginger to keep it fresh we deepened the hole in the ground to hide our new stockpile.

This was before the first wave of soldiers arrived in open trucks, threatening the loss of heads as a punishment befitting the serious crime of looting. It was harsh but instantly effective. Heads on poles is difficult to beat as an effective deterrent. With the new decree a problem arose. How to hide things that obviously didn't belong to you yet were piled right up to your roof? Day and night for more than a week, large bonfires of pure panic burned. The looters of the big European houses piled fridges, electric fans, toasters, gleaming pianos and whole sets of large furniture into a big heap in front of their attap houses that were not even fitted for electricity, and set a match to it. We watched chairs, cupboards, tables, rolled Persian carpets and beds burn with a bright, tall orange blaze spitting thousands of sparks. For Mother it was a blessing in disguise. She and Lakshmnan traversed the areas where the servants of the big European houses lived and picked out the furniture she wanted from unlit bonfires.

Things in our neighbourhood changed drastically with the Japanese Occupation. Girls turned into boys overnight and girls of a certain age vanished into thin air. Father lost his job, Ismail lost his father, and Ah Kow lost his brother to the Malayan Communist Party. He went off to live with the hill people, as they were known, in some camp called Plantation Six near Sungai Lembing, where their main effort seemed to be small-scale ambushes on Japanese patrols.

The Japanese wasted no time. They set about making us walk a mile in their culture, their morality and their very foreign method of living. As if standing to attention and singing their national anthem every day before morning exercise, or forcing children to learn the Japanese language, could instil love in us for their ugly flag (that we instantly dubbed a soiled sanitary towel) or their distant Emperor. It is amazing to think that they did not comprehend that we bowed low at the sight of a Japanese uniform in the street not with respect but from the fear of being slapped across the face. Every day on our way to school we passed a sentry guard who stared at us sternly, his unsmiling face puffed up with self-importance. It was obvious there was nothing he enjoyed more than punishing someone who failed to bow satis-factorily before the symbol of the Emperor. Long live the Emperor. In the streets, moving buses with a soldier standing on the roof rained propaganda leaflets on people's heads.

Hiding behind the dustbins we no longer heard the idle chatter of prostitutes but the frightening thud of feet as panting people were chased in broad daylight down the back lanes in the worst parts of town.

A few times while at school we would hear the planes flying low and the siren going off. All of us would throw ourselves to the ground and remain so until the siren stopped and the lights came back on. I remember seeing a cow blasted away by a bomb once. It had glassy staring eyes and a huge chunk missing from its torn bloated body. We held our noses and went very close to it, close enough to see the massive raw wound that left its entire stomach exposed. Flies buzzed and Ismail vomited near the cow but the rest of us were quite fascinated by its destruction.

There are moments in our lives that live for ever. The first time Raja deigned to talk to me was one of those moments. In the bright sunlight a black shadow fell over me. When I looked up he was looking down on me sprawled on the ground nursing my scraped knees and bleeding palms. With the sun behind him he looked like someone from a superior race of warriors. His large straight fingers dripped with yellow ink. He knelt beside me, brushed his magic liquid on my raw knees and hands and the stinging pain disappeared. His strong hands hauled me up. 'So you are the boy who lives in number three.'

I had never heard him speak before. His voice was deep but soft. I nodded bemused, unable to speak. This was the boy who swam fearlessly in the river on the other side of town where the large, smiling alligators with jaws full of ivory teeth hunted. During the dry spells when the river turned brown and the mud dried on his skin, he would stride home wearing map-like dusty yellow patterns on his skin almost like the skin of a snake.

He smiled slowly. I remember thinking then that he was wild, wild like the black cobras he tamed and charmed into dance. When you looked into his young eyes they were like cool mirrors, but if you dared to look really deep you could see the ancient fires burning inside. I thought I had looked close enough. I imagined that I had seen all there was to be seen. I am still sorry I didn't look closer. What others took to be powerful bonfires of great destruction stoked by dark, unmentionable things I only saw as a small friendly flame creeping towards me. Like water desires to be horizontal I coveted his dangerous world. An exciting world where a second chance was a glamorous illusion created by a long black enemy in the grass. Raja was a sorcerer of black magic and the very animal I longed to emulate.

I asked him once, 'Is a snake-charmer ever bitten by his own snakes?'

'Yes,' he said. 'When he wants to be bitten.'

I used to sit and watch Raja eat. He ate like a wolf, his shoulders hunched, a hard sheen of suspicion in his eyes, and sharp teeth tearing into his food. Soon, to my mother's intense irritation, I began to eat like that as well. That was always her biggest weakness – no sense of humour. As soon as I got home from school I wolfed down my food and rushed over to his house. Raja never went to school, never had and never wanted to. He was wild through and through. There were no soft edges to him at all, except his forbidden and secret love for my sister. That he was utterly besotted was patently obvious. He spent hours like the deadly snakes he charmed crawling silently on his underbelly in the bushes at the back of our home hoping for a glimpse of her, he yearned avidly for the smallest scrap of information about her. What she ate, what she did, what she said, when she slept, what made her laugh, her favourite colour. Inside my little person nodding to sleep was all the information that he longed for. Every word I uttered was devoured with embarrassing greed. And the more I spoke, the deeper he fell into the well of love. His face would melt right before my eyes like the bees' wax candles that his mother made and burned in their house. A small smile would blunder onto his uncultured face and his straight, bronze eyebrows would droop slightly over his dark eyes. He couldn't read or write and he wore rags, but inside the hard shell of his body a red-hot passion bubbled dangerously.

I was young then and unwise to the ways of love. His passion was no more than my stepping stone to get closer to him. I saw no harm in encouraging what I thought was a rather endearing tenderness for my sister. All I could see was the increase in my own stature. Fate, I thought, had presented me with an interesting hold on him. Somewhere inside me I must have known that no marriage was possible between my mother's Mohini and my hero in rags, but in my defence how could a child have known that love could be so dangerous? I had no idea that it could kill.

Raja made the daily grind, the sheer boredom of the Japanese Occupation go away. He changed the grain of my childhood. Sitting on logs under the towering moss-laden neem tree we traded stories. He leaned forward and listened to mine carefully and then he told me his. And the stories that lived inside his curly head were of the most surprising kind. African stories. Old men with crinkly hair announcing at the door of the witch doctor's hut, 'I have come to eat black goat.' Old women who could splash sand into their open eyes and chickens that absorbed the evil spirits living inside a man.

'*De'wo'afokpa. Me le bubu de tefea n'u oh!*' 'Take off your shoes you are desecrating the magic area.'

I would stare into his face, caught up in the magic power of a foreign language. For hours I sat barefoot, staring into his glowing eyes, listening to his deep, softly lethal voice. From the still afternoon air he plucked out fearful djins who stood so tall their heads disappeared into the clouds and on another day he would smile gently and weave a world where a stick given by a praying mantis and placed in an earthenware pot could turn into a beautiful baby girl. Sometimes I closed my eyes and his voice made shining ebony bodies run into the burning African sunshine or gleam midnight-blue among the silver trees in the moonlight. I looked at his dusty bare-foot feet in the sand and when my eyes travelled back up I saw many fierce faces dipping in unison into a wooden trough and drinking deeply of milk made rosy with bulls' blood. Out of his reddish-brown lips came the spectacle of public circumcision and strange initiation rights where nubile virgins and young men danced, whirling faster and faster around an orange voodoo fire until they came out of their own bodies and watched themselves take and be taken by everybody else.

Like an empty cupboard accepts other people's belongings I gladly received ancient stories about lions that turned into men, sacred snakes sent out into the dreams of the sick to lick their wounds and heal them and Musakalala the talking skull, but I think my favourite story has always been the story of Chibindi and the lions. Let me think for a moment so I may once more taste the flavour of a very long time ago, a flavour that I have forgotten since and long for.

Many years ago, under a neem tree that no longer exists, felled to grow a big international hotel with a swimming pool, restaurants and in the basement a night-club with a rather luscious breed of prostitutes lining the bar, Raja stood as Chibindi, the Great One, a hunter whose magic song could tame wild lions.

'*Siinyaama, Oomu kuli masoonso, Siinyama.*' 'Oh you

who eat meat, There is only dry grass in this bag, Oh you who eat meat.'

Under the neem tree all around us growling lions stopped and began to dance to his magic tune. Backwards and forwards they pranced on their hind legs, their tails swishing from side to side, twisting and turning their bodies, nodding and wagging their heads. The great cats purring with sheer pleasure. They would have torn him to bits but for the fine, strong voice with which he sang his song. Louder and louder climbed his voice and faster and faster the big cats twisted and turned their tawny bodies.

Chibindi stamped his feet as he chanted; holding his hands in front of him at shoulder level he moved them up and down as if encouraging a whole pride of lions dancing on their hind legs to dance faster and faster. Soon the terrible lions forgot their greed for the flesh of man.

Just remembering Chibindi brings back memories. Sad memories. Yet I can see Raja now, standing under the neem tree, thumping his bare feet on the dry ground, his arms waving madly, and he has forgiven me.

One day, to my greatest excitement, Raja agreed to teach me snake-charmer secrets. Secrets only passed on through the generations from father to son. It was like a dream come true. Suddenly I was wrapping snakes around my neck like Lord Shiva. Venom, I learned, was the most precious thing man had, and fear the most precious thing a snake had. Fear is the smell the snake looks for when it flicks and darts its tongue about. Only when it smells fear will it attack. Raja said that it was a long time ago that he had taken out the fear inside him, given it sharp teeth and fine, long claws, rubbed swiftness into its thick limbs and made it wait beside him.

'Tonight the moon will be full,' he told me one afternoon. 'Moonlight excites snakes. They come out to dance. Tonight at the Chinese cemetery?' His young, old eyes watched me, questioning, testing.

The first few times I shook my head regretfully, wishing with all my yearning heart that I could go. Even once, I told myself, would be enough. He had much to teach me, so much to show me – but always there was the spectre of Mother's elongated shadow waiting in the kitchen like a crouched tiger until the early morning light slowly crept in through the open windows. It never ceased to amaze me the way she hardly slept. I don't think she ever slept for more than two or three hours a night. However one afternoon under the neem tree I simply nodded, and the words, 'OK, tonight at the Chinese cemetery,' appeared on my tongue.

As it happened it turned out to be surprisingly easy to slip out of my bedroom window, climb down onto a strategically placed drum and slither away noiselessly. At the snake-charmer's house Raja was waiting in the shadows. As I passed, a hand shot out suddenly and pulled me into the darkness. He put his forefinger to his lips.

He was my taboo but I was his secret.

A pungent smell of crushed onions came from his dark form. He moved without even the whisper of air against his clothes for he wore no shirt. Chibindi's skin gleamed like varnished red clay in the pale moonlight. Around his neck on a yellow string was a gold amulet shaped like a horn. It glinted in the night. The amulet I knew was meant for the spitting cobra. The spitting cobra searches for the glimmer of its enemy's eye so it may aim its deadly poison right into it and blind him while keeping a safe distance. A sparkling amulet distracts the attention of the cobra and he will spit at the amulet instead.

In his hand Raja held a forked stick and a gunnysack. I was thrilled. Blood throbbed in my neck. What adventures lay before me?

'Take off your shirt and trousers,' he whispered very close to my ear.

From a rusty tin he scooped out a pungent mixture, the horrible reek that I had noticed earlier. Swiftly he coated my naked limbs with his puree that had the consistency of yoghurt and was cool on my bare skin. His hands were hard and sure. I remember thinking that the only soft thing about him was his love. Like the soft centre of a boiled sweet.

'Snakes hate this smell,' he explained his breath warm against my skin.

I stood quietly under his ministrations. 'The cemetery is the best place to catch them,' he told me in a hushed voice. Many snakes came to the cemetery for the fowl and small piglets that Chinese people left on the graves as offerings to appease their ancestors. Because it was an ill omen to eat food offered to the dead, not even the drunks or the very poor came to steal the rich banquet available. The snakes feasted and became large and plentiful. He talked in a low excited voice about a beautiful cobra that he had almost caught the last time. It was the largest one he had ever seen. It must have been a truly remarkable specimen because it made his eyes glitter hotly that night. I put my clothes back on hurriedly and worried about Mother and the incredibly strong smell that now covered me from head to toe.

'How come you don't have to rub this smelly stuff on

your body?' I whispered, wrinkling my nose with disgust.

He laughed softly, rubbing his hands vigorously with some crushed leaves. 'Because I *want* them to come to me.'

We took a short cut through the back of his house, past the field, through the small jungle where I had spent hours practising blowing perfect smoke rings and past the row of shop-houses. The cemetery lay on a few sleeping hills. Even from afar, the sight of the grassy mounds illuminated pale green against the night sky and dotted with white gravestones filled me with foreboding but I followed Raja's confidently striding body silently through the tall grass.

Under the full moon round pomelos looked like ghostly orbs amongst the gravestones. The air was filled with the smell of fresh flowers on the graves but the fragrant air was thick and unnaturally still. Nothing moved. I have thought since then that a Malay or a Christian graveyard can be a peaceful place at night but a Chinese graveyard is an altogether different matter. Far from being a place of rest, it is a place where spirits still hungry with earthly desires wait for their relatives to come by and burn them paper houses complete with furniture, servants and big cars with number plates parked outside. Sometimes they even burn paper images of a favourite wife or a bejewelled, richly robed concubine holding stacks of fake spending money. That night I was conscious of them everywhere, the impatient, hungry spirits, their restless eyes following me with jealous yearning. The hairs at the back of my neck sprang away from my skin and a small, sleeping spider called fear jerked awake and began crawling slowly inside my stomach.

Tablets engrossed with Chinese writing and black and white photos of the dead seemed unnaturally white against the dark foliage. A small boy with liquid eyes looked at me sadly as we passed his grave. A young woman with thin, cruel lips smiled invitingly and a horribly old man seemed to scream soundlessly at me to leave him to sleep in peace. Everywhere I looked unsmiling faces stared sullenly at me. Our footsteps were quiet in the still, sibilant air. I looked at Raja.

His shoulders were taut with tension but his eyes were alert and bright. His pronged staff probed the ground in front of him, whispering through the shrubs. Once or twice he pointed to a slithering body or a disappearing tail in the undergrowth. Dear God, the place was crawling with serpents. Near a very large tree he stopped suddenly.

'There he is,' he whispered.

Fearfully I swung my eyes in the direction of his gaze. On the ground a monster of a cobra was curled around the exposed roots of a big tree. Its thick body glistened in the silver night like a polished, extremely expensive belt. The wide belt hissed and uncoiled slowly.

'I can catch it now, but I want to show you something first.' Slowly Raja lowered himself to his knees. Behind him I swallowed and took a cowardly step back, ready to flee.

The snake was aware of us. It began to move its lustrous body away from us slowly, scales brushing scales, soundless in its precision, the muscles under its skin strong and sure. Suddenly, amongst the moving black scales I saw its cold eyes watching us. The urge to run was so strong I had to clench my teeth and bunch my fist to stop me disgracing myself.

From his trouser pocket Raja brought out a tiny vial. Very slowly he rubbed the contents onto his hands. The smell was sweetly aromatic. Then he began to chant slowly. The cobra reared suddenly as if it had only now sensed mortal danger.

I froze.

In front of me, Raja's fine full limbs gleamed. Every atom that lived inside his body had become still. He was listening. And all of him, even his skin, became an extension of his ear. A deadly silence seemed to descend on the cemetery. After a while there was just Raja, the snake and me, and the only thing that moved was Raja's mouth. The cobra fanned its hood open, raised its head high into the air and stood so stock-still that it could have been a freakishly good wooden carving. Out of the shadows of the tree its eyes were very, very shiny. Ominous and watchful it pinned its unblinking gaze on Raja. Raja ceased chanting and stood up very, very slowly. He walked toward the cobra and held out his hand.

I stood transfixed, holding my breath. The shiny black hood came closer to his bare outstretched hand. He has gone completely mad, I thought, but to my astonishment the cobra flicked out its forked tongue then rubbed its head like a sleepy kitten might and slowly curled its thick body up Raja's hand. The snake moved up his outstretched hand in a sensuous dance until it was at eye level with him. They stared at each other. Raja had become a wooden carving himself. Seconds, perhaps minutes passed. Not a muscle moved. Time ground to a halt. The world stopped spinning so Raja could have his prize snake. I have lived many years since that night but it remains the most amazing thing I have ever seen. He was truly the master that night.

Like a dark flash Raja made a lightning-fast movement and the stunned cobra swayed back and opened a dark-red mouth but Raja was already gripping the sides of its head immovably in his hand. I could see its glossy fangs and the colourless liquid that dripped from them. All at once the tricked creature was writhing furiously. Raja held the head high above his head like a trophy as he surveyed his long catch. Its thick body curled and slapped uselessly against his lean tall frame. Then the struggling snake went into the sack whereupon it calmed down instantly.

'I shall keep this cobra for my own. He is too long to fit into a basket and too heavy to carry to the market place,' Raja said with great satisfaction in his voice. His voice was full of justified bravery. How I envied him that night.

'Come we must get you back in bed.'

We walked quickly through the jungle. With the woods behind us he turned to face me. 'Will you tell her? Will you tell her that I tamed the king of all serpents?' he asked, a quiet pride quivering in his voice.

'Yes,' I lied, knowing I would never ever tell anyone in my family about my adventure. I would instantly be imprisoned at home for ever. I'd be made to peel potatoes or chop onions in the kitchen all day.

But now I was hooked. I was past afternoons under the neem tree listening to stories, that was for babies. The adrenalin rush that had flooded into my body watching Raja and the monster snake staring at each other in the moonlight was addictive. I wanted more. Surely Mohini's brother deserved more. I begged, I cajoled, I bribed.

'Show me something more,' I implored. I was relentless in my efforts. 'Soon the Japanese will be gone and Mohini will walk to the temple. I can arrange an accidental meeting,' I promised untruthfully, watching the black in his eyes turn to burning embers. 'My father listens to the BBC and he says that the Germans have already lost the war. The Japanese will be gone soon. They have almost lost the war.'

He looked at me carefully and something flickered across his closed face and for a moment it seemed as if he knew my promises were false and my friendship hollow, but then his eyes became blank. 'Yes,' he conceded. 'I will show you more.'

He took me to the dilapidated, deserted house at the other edge of the jungle. The rotting door opened wide at his touch. Inside it was dark and cool but quiet, very quiet. There was the impression that the jungle was taking over, slowly creeping in. Sand-coloured roots had broken through the cement floor and wild plants were growing in the cracks in the walls. There were gaping holes in the roof and in the broken corners of the ceiling pale pink roots spiralled downward, but in the middle of the room a single light bulb hung from the wooden rafters in a perfectly eerie manner. I shivered inside my shirt. I was glad Raja was with me.

We sat cross-legged on the cracked floor among the large roots. Out of a cloth pouch tied around his waist he produced a little bottle. He pulled out the stopper. Immediately a pungent smell wafted out. I crinkled my nose with disgust but he assured me it was only the juice of roots and tree barks and that a sip would show me another world. He began to build an uneven pyramid of wood and grass on the cement floor of the deserted house. When he had coaxed a small yellow fire into the dry branches he turned to me and offered me the bottle. There was no expression on his face. I was sure it was a test of some kind and to hesitate would have revealed my doubt and fear. I took the bottle from his hand and took a good gulp. The brown mixture was thick and oily in my mouth. The hair on my arms stood on end.

'Look into the fire,' he ordered. 'Look into the fire until it talks to you.'

'OK.' I stared at the flames until my eyes burned. The fire steadfastly remained mute. 'How much longer?' I asked, tears starting to cloud my vision.

'Look into the fire,' he said, very close to my ears. I could smell him, that peculiar animal smell, the scent of something that lives in the wild by its wits.

I was starting to feel giddy with staring at the dancing tongues of yellow and orange but every time I wanted to look away, a firm voice instructed, 'Look into the fire.'

Just when the backs of my eyes began to burn, the fire turned blue. The edges burned green and the middle burned turquoise like the uniform secondary school girls wear. 'The fire is blue and green,' I said. My voice sounded far away and quite unlike my own, and my tongue felt thick and heavy inside my mouth. I blinked rapidly a few times. The fire burned a bright blue.

'Look at me now,' Raja instructed. His voice sounded like a whisper or a hiss. My head lolled around on my neck and my heavy eyes fell on my hands. With something approaching detached wonder I noticed that the skin on my hands had turned transparent. I could actually see the blood pounding and rushing through my veins. I stared at my hands in shock and then I noticed the floor. It was moving. 'Hey,' I said thickly, turning to look at Raja.

'Great, isn't it?' he grinned.

I nodded, grinning back. I was eleven years old and as high as a kite on secret roots and tree bark. It was then that I noticed Raja was changing. I peered into his face.

'What? What do I look like?' Raja asked eagerly. His eyes were feverish in the flames of the small fire. He looked like a wild animal.

I blinked and shook my head, unsure of what my eyes were seeing. I looked at the fire. It was burning yellow again but I had the strongest urge to reach out and touch it, hold it and enter it. If only it was bigger, I thought, I could stand in it. The thought frightened me, and in frustratingly slow motion I focused on Raja once more. It took some time to get the blur out of the edges of my vision. Thoughts formed in my brain and words appeared out of nowhere. They were mine and yet how could I have spoken them? 'Can I touch the fire?' I astonished myself by asking.

'Don't look at the fire any more. Tell me what I look like,' Raja persisted. 'Do I look like a snake?' he asked. Had he sounded hopeful? I felt confused. Were there points for agreeing? I shook my head weakly and my head swung on my neck like a balloon filled with water. My whole body was alive with strange sensations. Inside my skin my blood pounded in a not-unpleasant way. When I shut my eyes a burst of colour appeared across my closed eyelids. Beautiful rainbow colours appeared and merged again in countless patterns.

Smiling I opened my eyes and Raja stood before me. His eyes glittered fiercely and his teeth seemed long and ferocious. There was something wild and unfamiliar in his face. For a while I could do nothing more than stare in shock at the transformation, then I quickly shut my eyes. I was no longer excited but full of deep foreboding. Water lapped against the walls of the balloon. I needed to think but my head was heavy with the water that swished around inside. Raja was turning into a frightening creature. Inside him was not Chibindi the dancing lion-tamer but something evil and ugly that I didn't recognise. Something I had never suspected. Poor sweet Mohini.

'*What do I look like?*' he asked again. His voice had changed too. I had heard it before in the cemetery. I had heard it among the gnarled feet of a large tree in the silence of white stone tablets. It was a very low hiss.

'No, you do not look like a snake,' I slurred with a tongue gone fat and lazy. I was too frightened to look at him directly. 'I want to go home.' My heart was pounding in my chest.

'No not yet. The effect will wear off soon and then you can go home.'

I began to shiver with fear. Raja and I did not speak. I dared not. I could feel him breathing beside me but I kept my eyes downcast on the moving floor. It was as if the cement was a thin cotton cloth and underneath it a million ants moved, milled and teemed. Beside me I felt the heat that came from Raja but I refused to turn my head and see what beast sat beside me. Whatever drug gripped me it was all powerful. What a trip! No other reality existed but what I could feel and see at that moment. Too young to recognise that I was hallucinating, I stared at the floor terrified. A lifetime passed sitting there not moving, my heart pounding wildly like an African drum just waiting for the dangerous creature to pounce on me at any moment.

Finally Raja said, 'Let's go.' His voice was flat. He sounded disappointed. 'Come on.'

I looked into his face, into the flat, dead eyes in his slightly triangular face and shot back in alarm. Yes, he did look like a snake. He had turned into a snake. The potion we had consumed had turned him into a snake. I felt my face to see if I too had turned into one. My face under my hands moved and I cried out in horror. Inside my numb mouth my teeth began to chatter. I was turning into a snake too. Crazy thoughts jumped into my head. He had brought me here to turn me into a snake so he could keep me in a basket and make me dance to his stupid little flute. I sobbed helplessly in slow motion. The sound long and drawn out.

When his face came very close I shut my eyes and began to pray to Ganesha. Then Raja's voice was in my ear. 'The magic is too strong for you. Don't worry, in a few more minutes everything will return to normal. Come, we will walk together. It is getting dark outside.'

I opened my eyes, surprised. He had not hurt me. I watched him in a daze as he put out the fire and came to help me up. We walked together with me leaning heavily on his arm. I refused to look at him. 'The fresh air will do you good.' His voice still sounded like the rasp of sandpaper but now that we were outside I felt better. Safer. It was evening and there were people taking slow strolls, laughing and talking in low voices. Their voices seemed very far away.

'Don't worry, all will be normal in a little while. Stand straight and walk like a man. Keep your head up.'

Finally we turned into our little neighbourhood. The thought of Mother waiting at home was frightening.

Right away she would see that I was not normal. She would see the moving skin and be livid.

Inside the walled garden of Old Soong, Mui Tsai was building a fire. She was burning all the dead leaves and grasses and Old Soong was standing by with his heavy hands on his hips watching her like a grinning crocodile, his large mouth open and full of teeth. I looked at the fire that was as large as a funeral pyre and suddenly without conscious thought I began to run towards it. I ran like the wind. I was an iron filing rushing towards a giant magnet. Mui Tsai stared, open-mouthed and confounded. I thought she looked like a frightened rabbit. Laughing, I ran towards the beautiful fire, my hands outstretched, and the fire reached out and called me to it. Within the orange tongues eating dead leaves was an attraction greater than I.

The first blast of purifying heat hit my body as I leaped into the fire but instead of being in the middle of my master I was lying on the ground with Raja on top of me, his heart knocking on my breastbone. I looked into the glittering eyes, into the unfamiliar mutant triangular face and knew that I had done the impossible. I had scared him.

'Stop it,' he hissed. 'Try to behave like a normal person.'

There was nothing to say. I had not reached my master's feet.

Raja led me to the steps of my home and strode away. Mother came out and I stared astonished at her. She was beautiful. A most dangerous female tiger, her eyes polished yellow amber and indescribable. And she was furious. Not with me. Just generally furious. I saw it in her burning eyes.

'What happened?' she growled, coming down the steps as fast as a springing cat. When she touched me I wanted to flinch so strong was the energy that emanated from her body. I could hear Mui Tsai's nearly hysterical voice in the background telling her about my leap into the flames. I felt Mother's eyes looking at me, at my moving skin. Inside the house, Mohini was hiding behind the curtains. Like a cat. Beautiful soft and perfectly white with large green eyes. There was something so benign and so beguiling about her that I wanted to reach out and stroke her. It was clear now why Raja loved her so deeply. I frowned as I realised the implication of Raja's transformation. A snake and a cat in the same room. I should never have encouraged him. I opened my mouth to warn Mother but Lalita's distressed face pushed itself close to mine. In her hand, held very close to her head, was the doll I had saved from the monsoon drain. I stared at the doll curiously. It appeared strangely lifelike. Suddenly it winked slyly at me, opened its mouth and bleated like a goat. A horrified scream gathered in my windpipe but a great gush of air rushed into my throat instead and black spots appeared in my view. Like the kind of ink spots you see in old photographs or the way an old mirror goes cloudy and gets badly speckled. Slowly the spots grew bigger and bigger. More spots appeared like spreading ink until my world became black. After that I don't remember anything else but Mother tells me that I screamed like one possessed for a mirror. Thrashed wildly with the strength of a full-grown man to get into the house so I could look at a mirror.

I was ill for two days. Mother was told to rub a paste of spices and chillies on my head to clear my thoughts. When I was better I couldn't bear to see Lalita's staring doll any more. I felt that its eyes, far from being sight-less, hid old evil. Every time I looked at it I saw it alive and staring at me, its mouth curving to bleat like a goat. I reached out my hand to touch it, so I would be re-assured that it was only a doll, only to recoil in disgust. Its skin had the texture of the dead people the Japanese had stuck on poles or left hanging upside-down at the roundabouts. I know because once, goaded beyond endurance, I accepted a dare to touch one of them. The dead man's skin was cold and slightly pliant. It made me sick to think of my innocent sister sleeping next to the monstrous thing. When I was better I threw the doll into a monsoon drain on the other side of town and watched the fast-flowing water carry it away until it was a pink and yellow speck in the distance. I returned home to a distraught Lalita and pretended to help her to search for the doll for hours. Then I blamed Blackie, the dog next door.

After that incident I was very careful. I had seen Raja once in such a way that there was no going back and no forgetting. There could be no more pretending that the people who came to see his father, their mouths twisted with thwarted intentions, and who left clutching cloth packages and hopeful expressions didn't exist. No more pretending that the red and black lumpy cloth packages they carried away were filled with the essence of apple or pink pomegranates instead of the horrible bits from all those midnight trips to the unmarked graves so a lover might be punished or an enemy destroyed. I began to avoid Raja.

Then came the day Raja approached me and asked for a lock of her hair. For precious seconds I could only stare blankly at his closed face then I shook my head dumbly and ran away. I already knew what charms these people could do with a lock of hair. I began to fear Raja. I couldn't forget the glittering eyes in the triangular face watching me, watching me, and watching me.

So I began to watch Mohini. Every day I rushed home from school and examined her carefully. Her smile, her words, her limbs, everything had to be minutely observed to be certain that no subtle changes had occurred in my absence. I was going crazy with guilt and worry. In the mirror a stranger with haunted, feverish eyes stared back. At school I had even stopped noticing the foul taste of the castor oil they poured down my throat. I had no wish to go crawling back to my old gang so I sat on my hard wooden chair in school and stared blankly as one teacher after another finished his class and walked out. When the last bell for the day rang I charged out of the classroom. Once I had finished examining Mohini for signs of I don't know what I sat down and waited for the evening to arrive.

Every day at dusk when the sun had sunk over the shop-houses and the threat of the Japanese soldiers had been laid to rest for the night, Mother let Mohini walk in the back garden. It was my sister's favourite time of the day. Sunset, when the sky was still tinged with unreal purples and moody mauves just before the mosquitoes got too avaricious on her skin. She walked along Mother's rows of vegetables and sometimes picked a plate full of jasmine flowers for the prayer altar from the steadily growing jasmine bush at the end of the garden. It was her much cherished walk into the world outside but this I knew to be the most fearful time of all. For lying flat on his belly in the bushes and trees was Raja, watching me, watching her, watching us. So I learned to stand guard over her. I learned to stand by the back door and worry, watching her in the gloom until she came back in and closed the back door. Sometimes I would even walk beside her, keeping so close to her and peering so worriedly into the bushes that touched by my concern she tousled my hair and smoothed the frown on my forehead.

'What's this?' she used to ask tenderly as her fingers brushed the deep creases in my forehead.

But of course I could never explain to her. I knew Mother had plans, big plans for the jewel of our family. A great marriage to a great family. So 'this' became my secret shackle. I had fixed it to my own leg and I had to bear it. 'This' was what I knew lay motionless behind the still bushes.

I wanted to tell her about cobras. Tell her what I knew, what I had seen. Warn her that though they are fascinating creatures she must fear them for a cobra recognises no master. It will dance for you if your song pleases it and it will drink the milk you leave by its basket every day but it owes you no allegiance. You must never forget that, ultimately, a cobra never betrays its own nature and for reasons known only to it, it may turn around any day and sink its poisoned fangs into your flesh. In my child's head Raja was a big black cobra. I wanted to tell her about Raja. I thought constantly about his eyes glittering coldly in his face. He meant to have her or harm us. I felt certain of that.

One day, dashing home from school, I found him leaning against the wall of Old Soong's house waiting for me. He unwrapped a black cloth package and took out a small red stone. It sparkled in the sunlight. When he put it into the palm of my hand it was neither light nor cool, it was strangely heavy and as hot as a newly laid chicken egg.

'I have a present for your sister. Put it under her pillow as a lovely surprise,' he said in that velvety voice that I had learned to hate.

I threw the strangely hot stone on the sand and ran away as fast as I could. He didn't follow me. I could feel his burning eyes on my back. When I reached the steps of our home I turned around and he was still standing by the red-brick wall watching me. There was no anger on his face. He raised his hand and waved at me. I was full of fear that day. How I longed for the days when he was a brave warrior called Chibindi.

That evening I saw Mohini bend to pick something up from the grass. Something that looked shiny in the dark. Petrified I screamed and pretended to fall. My sister came running. As if in great pain I asked her to help me into the house. She forgot about the bright, shiny thing on the ground. Later that night I tiptoed out of the house. It was moonless and I could barely make out the object in the grass. I bent to pick it up and Raja's bare feet came into my vision. I straightened slowly, dreading what I would find before me.

'Give her to me,' he ordered. His voice was hard and emotionless.

The blood ran cold in my body. 'Never,' I said, but to my disgust my voice sounded small and weak.

'I will have her,' he promised and, turning away, melted into the darkness. I peered anxiously into the inky night but he was gone like the wind, taking his despair with him.

That night I dreamed that I was hiding behind some bushes watching Mohini walking by a river. There were colourful birds singing in the trees and she was laughing at the antics of some cheeky monkeys with silver-rimmed faces. I saw her drop to her hands and knees on the bank and, holding her heavy hair away from her face with one hand, drink like a small cat. A few feet away was a shape in the water, a pair of terrible watching eyes, unblinking and full of menace. A crocodile. I fear crocodiles. The most frightening thing about them is that you can never tell by looking at their eyes if they are dead or alive. They have the same blank expression. It makes you wonder if they come into this world through a different door.

The crocodile, pretending to be a harmless log, glided silently towards her until without the slightest warning it intended to snap its powerful jaws over her head. Pull her in with a sickening splash. I wanted to warn her like I wanted to tell her about the black cobras but I couldn't remember her name. The monster opened its massive mouth. I ran to the edge of the water screaming but it had already fitted her head easily between its yellow teeth. In my baggy shorts I stood at the edge of the river paralysed with a mixture of horror and disbelief and stared at the wild thrashing in the river. The brute disappeared into the water taking her with him. She was no more. The water turned calm. The river had fed. From the bank on the other side Raja's distorted face screamed out words as he ran into the crocodile-infested water but he spoke in that dream language that I cannot understand while I am sleeping and cannot hear when I am awake.

I woke up with a jerk, sweating and so frightened that my heart thumped hard in my chest and my throat was tight and painful. Beside me my brothers slept peacefully. They had not been playing with the devil himself.

Disturbed and uneasy I crept up to the girls' bed to look down at Mohini sleeping. Lightly I ran my fingers along her smooth arm. She was warm.

Mother's slightly exasperated voice filled my head: 'Once when Mohini was about eight years old your father and I quarrelled and because we weren't speaking he asked her to make him some coffee. I stood in the kitchen and watched her put nine teaspoons of coffee to one teaspoon of sugar. Then I stood hidden behind the cupboard and watched him drink every last drop of that coffee without changing his expression. That is how much your father loves your sister.'

Regret and shame came upon me. I had betrayed her. Passed on her secrets and made a mess of everything. All my guilt was reserved for my sleeping sister. Raja's hopeless despair didn't touch me. I made myself a bed beside her on the floor. From now on I was determined to guard her with my life. Something horrible was about to happen but I wouldn't allow it. I lay absolutely still, gazing at the dark ceiling and listening to my sister's breathing. Somewhere far away some animal called. The sound was remarkably human. It was a very long time before the rhythmic breathing of all my sisters lulled me back to sleep. My last thought was, I should tell someone.

Lakshmi

The first thing the Japanese soldiers did when they came to our sleepy neighbourhood was to shoot Old Soong's dogs dead. One moment they were in a frenzy of ferocious barking and the next firecracker-loud moment, their huge bodies collapsed. Red blood seeping quickly onto the black and white gravel.

'*Kore, Kore,*' the soldiers barked, fiercely rattling and banging the locked gates with the butts of their rifles. I watched from behind our curtains with my stomach in knots. Mohini's hiding place was clever but I was still petrified that they would find her. Their savagery was beyond comprehension. We had seen the bodies skewered right from the groin through to the mouth, like pigs ready for roasting, lining the streets. And we knew about the execution grounds in Teluk Sisek on the way to the beach where they killed people in pieces. A trembling hand, then a frantically jerking foot, perhaps the rest of a shocked arm, a bleeding leg and finally the condemned head. We even knew about the wife of the owner of the cold storage shop in town who alone by moonlight went to collect up the pieces of her husband so she could give him a proper burial. It was the way of the Japanese. Cruel and barbarous.

Crouched under the window, my husband, Lakshmnan and I saw Mui Tsai's timid figure appear at the front door.

'*Kore, kore,*' they shouted at her. She ran out to unlock the gates. They pushed them open roughly and eyed her narrowly. That look. I felt her shiver from where I stood. She bowed low. They talked in an aggressively loud and ugly language. They strode inside, carelessly stepping over the dead dogs. They were hungry, very hungry. They roamed the house consuming whatever they fancied and taking anything small that they could carry on their person. They knew in a few days they would probably be fighting in the jungles of Java or the poisonous swamps of Sumatra.

They looked for jewellery, pens and watches. The master was not at home but his expensive watches lying by the bedside they strapped onto wrists already lined with watches. They put the point of their long sword in the mistress's soft belly and pointed at the empty showcases. At first she pretended not to know what they meant but then they gently nudged the point of the sword a little deeper into her pampered flesh. Sobbing she screamed to the cook to dig up the jade figurines from under the rose bush. They seemed happy with their find. They pointed at the rosewood box. The servants rushed to open it. The soldiers seemed especially pleased with the ivory chopsticks.

The strangers wished for sugar. They made signs and guttural noises. The mistress frowned, the servants looked back helplessly. The unshaven, unkempt beings grabbed the terrified cook by the hair, soundly cursed and slapped her. They began overturning all the containers. What extraordinary impatience! Finally pure white grains flooded out of a falling jar. 'Aaah, the sugar.' They stopped upending containers.

They came very close to the mistress. She held her

breath. They bore the nauseating stench of unwashed bodies in combat. A foulness impossible to forget. They stank like people with no souls. They made their rough signs once more. Ghastly white, she stared at them but they only desired an open fire in the back garden. They wanted to cook their own food. 'Firewood.' The servants rushed to find firewood. The strangers lolled on the ground outside, their guns lying casually beside them, waiting for their outdoor feast to cook while Old Soong's terrified household stood in a row and watched. The strangers ate like hungry dogs. Then they left.

We saw them walk towards Minah's house.

We saw her open the door of her house muttering, 'Ya Allah, Ya Allah,' wearing the loose, white, shroud-like prayer costume of her religion. It was not prayer time but a shroud to hide her magnificent curves. Only her frightened face showed. A small, frightened circle. Her five children gathered around her and stared at the men as they searched the poor house. They made a circling motion with their fingers around their wrists and necks. Minah understood. She was prepared. She handed over a handkerchief tied into a knot. Inside was an old chain, an even older ring and two bangles bent slightly out of shape. They threw it back in her face in disgust. They did not stay long. You see, I have not told you that before they left Old Soong's house they threw poor, unloved Mui Tsai on the kitchen table, queued up in an unexpectedly orderly fashion and used her until they were all satiated.

At the Chineseman's house next door they broke a mirror and carried away three suckling pigs. The two older boys had run out through the back door. They climbed into our backyard and streaked past the open fields disappearing into the small jungle.

My heart was in my throat when their hard boots climbed our wooden steps. I felt it flutter in fear. They burst through the door like a hurricane. Why, up close they were tiny and yellow. No higher than my husband's chest. They stared up into his black, ugly face. What hard mean eyes they had! Like the elephants trained to make obeisance to the Sultan in the glorious days of the Moghul Empire we all bowed respectfully, deeply, in unison. They stomped around the house till the floorboards shook. They opened cupboards, lifted the lids of boxes, looked under tables and beds but they did not find my daughter. In the backyard they opened the chicken coop, snapped the necks of the squawking creatures and, grabbing three to four chickens by the neck in each hand, they pointed to the coconut tree. Lakshmnan ran to climb up the tree. They drank the sweet water and discarded the coconut skull where they stood. On their way out of our neighbourhood they pulled Old Soong's impressive black iron gates out of their hinges and carried them away. The Japanese were greedy for iron in those days. Most houses stood without gates or any fear of thieves for the Japanese punished the smallest crimes with torture and beheadings. Crime fell to an all-time low. In fact, nobody bothered to lock their doors any more when they went out during the entire period of the Japanese Occupation. No, do not envy us our crime-free lives because in the end those dogs made us pay in blood. They were arrogant, uncouth, cruel and unforgivable, and as long as I live I shall hate them with a mother's wrath. I spit in their ugly faces. My hate is such that I will not forget, even in my next life. I will remember what they have done to my family and I will curse them again and again so that they will one day taste the bitterness of my pain.

As soon as they arrived, the Japanese banned the locals from any sort of looting. Two men accused of it were blindfolded with their hands tied behind their backs and brought to the square where the night market was held every Thursday. The soldiers diverted passers-by into the square like sheep until an appropriate number of onlookers had been gathered. The accused men were forced to kneel. A Japanese officer cut off their heads one by one, carefully wiping his blade with a piece of cloth after each execution. He spared not even a glance for the rolling head, its mouth open in a silent scream, spraying blood on the sand or the truly frightening sight of the severed body jerking on the ground, gushing fountains of blood from the neck, its legs kicking spasmodically. The officer only looked at the hushed crowd of shocked onlookers and nodded his own head in silent warning.

Their message quickly established, the Japanese indulged themselves on a grand scale. They not only looted but also desecrated the homes they visited. They never asked, they never compensated, they simply reached out and took whatever they wanted. Land, cars, buildings, business, bicycles, chickens, crops, food, clothing, medical supplies, daughters, wives, lives.

At first I didn't curse them. Their brutality didn't actually touch me. The heads on the roundabout I learned to ignore very quickly. Their Imperialist propaganda did not even rate as a nuisance. Did I care that they had forbidden wearing a necktie in public? I understood war made for horrible atrocities. I simply decided that I would not let such a foul and ugly race beat me at a game

I knew so well. I was arrogant in those days. I knew how to produce food for my children from thin air if necessary. I will survive this too, I told myself confidently. My husband had lost his job as soon as the Japanese regime started so we lost our entitlement to the precious ration cards. Ration cards meant rice and sugar. We were considered useless people. People the regime would rather not waste their limited resources on. Suddenly I had eight mouths to feed and no income. I had no time to moan and groan or to appreciate the pitying looks from the ladies in the temple whose husbands had managed to retain their jobs.

I sold some jewellery and bought the cows. They made my life hard but we would never have survived without them. Every morning come rain or shine while it was still dark I sat on a low stool in the cool air and milked them. The coffee stalls and shops paid us in Japanese currency bills with pictures of coconut and banana trees on them. They passed nervously from hand to hand for these banana notes as they were called had no serial numbers and were worth less and less every month. Tobacco was worth more than Japanese currency. Some people converted their money into land and jewellery as soon as possible but as I had barely enough to keep the children going it was hardly an issue in our household.

Without the ration cards rice could only be purchased on the black market at exorbitant prices. Rice had become rare and precious. Vendors took to moistening the rice to increase its weight and return a better price. People hoarded it by the grain and kept it for special occasions. Birthdays or religious celebrations. We had tapioca most of the week. Those were the days when tapioca ruled. You saw it everywhere. Baked into bread, processed into noodles. Even the leaves could be boiled and eaten. The daily job of shredding, boiling, cooking it saved our lives but I hated it. Hated it with a vengeance. For years I had tried to persuade myself that I really liked it but I hated its slimy taste. The bread was like rubber. It bounced on the table and when it was between your teeth it stretched. The noodles were terrible. But eat it we all did.

I tried growing whatever I could lay my hands on. Even turmeric that for some strange reason bore only shrivelled, oddly malformed fruit. Towards the end of the first year of Occupation, though, I had made friends with Mrs Anand. Her husband worked in the Food Control Department and he managed to smuggle rice from the north of Malaya from the Japanese Army rations. I hid our illegal rations of rice in the rafters of our roof. Our cows and my garden shielded us from the severe food shortage that attacked the whole state of Pahang. So severe was it that finally the Governor suggested that people eat two meals a day instead of three. Perhaps he didn't know that people were already consuming only two meals a day.

Anything imported became like gold dust. Before the Occupation I had always washed the children's hair with a special seedpod from India. It came tied in bunches. You soaked the bone-hard dark brown pods before boiling and mashing them. The resulting dark brown mush was the perfect shampoo. It cleaned the hair until it squeaked. I improvised and washed all my children's hair with ground green beans. During the Japanese time I made my own soap with leaves, tree bark, cinnamon and flowers. We brushed our teeth with our index finger dipped into finely ground charcoal or occasionally salt.

We used the soft branches of neem leaves as tooth-brushes. I made my own coconut oil, for the price of a tin of coconut oil had shot up from six ringgit to three hundred and fifteen ringgit by 1945. People were selling ten small eggs for ninety ringgit. But what is that compared to the price of a sarong, which increased from one ringgit and eight cents to a thousand ringgit? I did try to make cloth from pineapple leaves and tree bark but it was rough and could only be used as sacking material.

Razor blades became so precious that everyone used to sharpen and resharpen old blunt blades by carefully pressing and rubbing them back and forth against the inside walls of a glass. Motor cars disappeared, except those used by the military and important Japanese civilians. Some Japanese wearing blue ribbons had long since purloined Old Soong's car. Taxis were running on charcoal and firewood. The Japanese Army reserved almost all medicines and hospital supplies for its own use and we were left to traditional medicine. Next door the Chineseman's second wife almost lost her leg by trying to cure a deep cut with a poultice of pineapple and over-ripe banana. The wound turned blue and began to give off a rotten smell. Gangrene almost set in.

The water in the pipes became steadily worse as the water-treatment chemicals were reduced. Minute cream-coloured worms sometimes writhed as if in mortal pain inside our drinking water.

After Minah's husband was shot I had to be the bearer of bad tidings. In her doorway she crumpled into a heap. I felt very sorry for her so I crouched down beside her and stroked her fine blue-black hair. The smooth curve of her cheek brushed my hand. She might have had the admirable skin of a baby but she was totally without savings. Some chickens, a vegetable garden and the odd piece of old-fashioned jewellery were all she had.

'Don't cry, it's going to be all right,' I lied.

She only shook her head and sobbed softly.

Minah was almost not managing when one evening a green Army jeep parked outside her door. A rather smart Japanese man in civilian clothes sprang out and walked into her house. After that he was often parked outside her house. One day Minah sent her five children to her sister's in Pekan. She told Mui Tsai that there was better schooling over there. Then the Japanese man with the jeep began to stay overnight. A few weeks later he moved in. I stopped visiting her and she stopped talking to us. Perhaps she was ashamed to be the kept woman of a Japanese official. A few times I saw her outside her house. She had started wearing Western-style dresses and Chinese *cheongsams* when they went out together in the evenings. She wore cosmetics and painted her nails. Actually she looked like a movie star. Her fair calves flashed inside the slit of her silk *cheongsam* as she climbed daintily into his jeep. I had a problem. What if she sacrificed Mohini for a piece of land, a better house, a diamond ring or a bag of sugar?

One day we came face to face. It was unavoidable that it should happen but that it should happen in his presence was unexpected. As I rounded the corner they both climbed out of his jeep. I slowed my steps hoping that they would enter the house before I reached them, but she stopped and waited for me and he waited with her. I smiled. Friendly. I feared both of them now. She was also the enemy. My secret depended on the weakest link and I was looking at it.

'Hello,' she called. She was as beautiful as ever.

'Hello. How are you?'

'Fine,' she said, smiling. Her lips were red and her cheeks rouged but her eyes were still sad. On her arms exquisitely carved dark-green jade bracelets jangled like a polished warning.

'How are your children?' I queried, stumped for conversation.

'They are very naughty and they refuse to learn at school,' she replied modestly. 'How are your five wonderful children doing?'

I smiled slowly. Gratefully. My secret was safe with her. For now. She knew I had six children. She had just counted Mohini out for his benefit. I realised that she had engineered this meeting so that I could sleep in peace.

'They are all fine. Thank you for asking,' I said and moved on. We understood each other. When I turned back to look they were going into the house. His arm was around her waist.

A year of the Japanese Occupation passed. While swimming and swinging just like Tarzan on the vines that grew along the river Kuantan, Lakshmnan made friends with an aborigine lad. The aborigines are the best trackers and hunters you could possibly find. Their jungle craft is second to none; they can watch and track you for days without you ever knowing of their presence. The boy taught Lakshmnan how to make and hunt with a blowpipe. Lakshmnan soon introduced us to a whole new range of cuisine.

He returned home with long ugly lizards that, in fact, once cooked, had a rather delicate flavour. We ate wild boar, deer, squirrel, tapir, tortoise, freshly killed python, strong-tasting tiger meat and once even elephant. Lakshmnan told us of the tribesmen's return from the hunt, a gory procession straining under huge hunks of meat dripping blood on their shoulders. Neither my husband nor I could bring ourselves to eat the elephant meat – I put too much faith in my Elephant God; but I asked him for forgiveness and gave it to the children. The meat was coarse with thick grey-brown skin attached, but the children said it was not too bad. One day Lakshmnan came home with a baby monkey slung over his shoulder and Old Soong, who had been by his window watching, sent his cook to ask if we would sell him the head with the brains intact.

He cracked the skull, poured black-market cognac inside it and then slurped off the contents with chopsticks. That very evening he called Lakshmnan to his house and told him that he would reward him handsomely for the genitals of a tiger or a bear. A month's rent, he said. Eating them conferred immortality.

At school the children were made to learn Japanese and from them I learned to say '*Domo Arigato*'. Whatever the soldiers asked for I nodded immediately and said my thank you readily in their unbearably guttural language. I could see that it pleased them that I had taken the trouble to learn their sounds. They thought me docile. They did not see my fear. Even when they were holding on to a squawking chicken with a cloud of feathers flying around them I feared them. I remembered that they had taken my husband, shot him and left him for dead. Not even Mui Tsai's assertion that they favoured boiled insipid white rice and sugar as a dish worth sitting down for could lessen my instinctive distrust of their mean eyes.

They must not be provoked.

I knew that in my heart. One bowed instantly and

lowered one's eyes in their presence. Sometimes General Ito, who was always the first inside Mui Tsai and could speak bad English, asked me where my daughters were hidden. I knew he had no idea but he had such sly eyes that I trembled like a leaf thinking of Mohini's soft skin right under his feet.

I told myself again and again, 'When they are all gone I will celebrate. Now I will lower my eyes and give them the youngest, tenderest coconuts from my tree.' I had heard the stories of them cutting down whole trees because there was no one available in the house to cut them some coconuts. For this reason alone I had Lakshmnan cut down the best coconuts before he went to school each day. As soon as they came to our house and pointed to the tree I immediately rushed out with the green fruit. They slashed them open with their bayonets. I watched them covertly, the way they drank, juice gurgling out of their mouths, down the strong columns of their hateful throats, staining their uniforms a darker shade of brown. I wished them harm. I hated them but my real fear lay deeper. Deeper than a cut coconut tree or the discovery of my jewellery hidden high among the swaying leaves. I feared they would brave the clucking chickens and the ground thick with chicken droppings and search under the house. Take my daughter away.

The thought used to keep me awake at night. Every time I saw the Chinese girl next door running free, her hair shorn to military length and her breast bound so tightly that her chest in her boy's shirts looked as flat as a board, I worried about Mohini. I thought my daughter's hair simply too beautiful to cut and I knew that even if I bound her burgeoning breasts and cut her wonderful hair her face was impossible to ignore. The cheekbones,

the eyes, the luscious mouth, they would all give her
away.

My only option was to hide her.

I was sitting alone watching the stars so far away when
Mui Tsai lifted the mosquito screen and climbed into my
kitchen. It had been so long since she had come to visit
and I had missed her terribly. She collapsed childlike and
ungainly on the bench beside me. In her hand she carried
a small, sticky brown cake. It was the festival of the
Chinese gods. A time when the minor gods and spirits
visited all the Chinese houses on earth and carried tales
of wrongdoing up to the heavens with them. To bribe
them Chinese householders baked the sticky sweet cakes
that made it impossible for them to tell unpleasant things
about the homes they had visited.

Mui Tsai knew that I enjoyed eating the hard crust on
top of the cake.

Resting her chin in her hands, she considered me
gravely. It was then that I realised with shock how many
shadows hid in her eyes.

'How are you?' she asked. She was still the best friend
I had.

'I'm fine. How are you?'

'I'm pregnant,' she announced bluntly.

My eyes widened. 'The master's?'

'No, the master never visits any more. Not since the
Japanese soldiers. He is afraid of disease. My body
disgusts him. He is rude and cold but I prefer it so.'

'Oh God,' I said, shocked. Her misfortunes never
seemed to end. She must have indeed been born under an
unlucky star.

'Yes, it belongs to one of them,' she stated calmly. All
the shadows in her eyes moved like old ghosts in a

haunted house. I watched them crouch then lengthen again.

'What are you going to do?'

'The mistress wants me to get rid of it,' she said very simply. She shrugged in an oddly casual way. 'Anyway, how can I keep it? What if it is the son of the one who urinates inside me after he has finished planting his seed?'

'What?'

She looked at me with a twisted smile. Something strange happened inside her eyes. 'Do you know where I can have an abortion?'

'No, of course not.' The full extent of what they did to her she had never told me and I had never asked.

'Oh well, I'm sure the mistress will know.'

I could not help her at all. Badom, my midwife, had died two years ago. 'Oh, Mui Tsai, please be very, very careful. These things are so dangerous.'

She laughed carelessly. 'I don't care. Do you know the strangest thing ever? Lately I keep hearing the sound of a newborn baby crying in the next room. And when I go there the crying baby is gone.'

I looked at her with worried eyes but she laughed once more. It was a hard sound. She said that she was not frightened because it was only the ghost of her first baby calling to her. Then we played a few games of Chinese chequers. I won all of them and I didn't even need to cheat. Her mind was elsewhere.

A few days later an ambulance came screaming into our neighbourhood. It stopped outside Old Soong's house and two attendants dressed in white rushed out. At first I thought it was Old Soong but it was Mui Tsai. I ran towards the ambulance and saw a sight I will never forget. Her pale face was twisted with pain and her eyes glazed as if she was going to pass out. On the stretcher her hand kept moving spasmodically as if she was trying to push her stomach away from her body. Thick blackish blood had stained her *sam foo* and her small feet were covered with spongy bits of purplish blood. The mistress was running behind the stretcher declaring to the attendants in Malay that she had found Mui Tsai in that state and had had no idea the girl was even pregnant.

Mui Tsai looked right through me, so torn with pain that she didn't even recognise me. Big drops of sweat beaded her forehead and she rolled from side to side in agony. I touched her hand. It was ice cold. Frightened, I tried to hold it but it jerked out of mine. The white-coated men pushed me aside impatiently and she was lifted into the antiseptic interior of the van. It looked very serious. It looked as if she was dying. The ambulance doors slammed shut. I looked at Mui Tsai's mistress as she stood by the ambulance, her eyes uncaring in her flabby face. The mouth that had once been intriguingly sulky was now simply sour and bad-tempered. I wanted to walk up to her and push her to the ground but that would mean she would see me. I would then stop being one of the invisible tenants. We could lose our home, my garden. I turned away woodenly and walked back to my house.

Mui Tsai returned a week later. Many hours in the day she used to sit under the Assam tree all by herself. Sometimes I saw her carefully trace the patterns on the stone table with her finger and other times she simply stared vacantly into space. When I went out to stand by the gate to talk to her, she looked at me from her shaded seat as if I was a stranger. Defeated even by the effort of getting up and walking over to meet me, silent tears ran down her face. I realised that my presence upset her. But when Anna went to stand by the gate, she hobbled over and, linking her fingers with my daughter's, crooned to her in Chinese, a language Anna didn't understand.

Before I carry on with my story I must first tell you what a wandering old soothsayer, who stopped for some refreshment in Sangra, told my mother about me. I was but a baby then, crawling in the dust. He picked me up, and for a long time he studied my innocent face. He watched me gurgle and blow bubbles at him. As everybody waited for the future to come tumbling out of his mouth he stroked a long, grey beard with a hand that looked more like a gnarled tree branch than a human limb and pronounced that God put a jungle into every human's head. Some He filled with gentle creatures, doe-eyed deer and graceful impala, some with chattering monkeys then others with wise, nodding owls – and sometimes with cunning, running foxes. But in mine He had in His wisdom put fierce, marauding tigers.

People who have led saintly lives have no reason to tell their story, but people who have clawed at their loved ones have to justify themselves. Hence I tell you everything. Everything so you may learn to do differently.

The war was almost over and by May 1945 news came of Germany's defeat and surrender. On 6 August, the Americans bombed Hiroshima. The BBC spread the news that Japan had been hit with a powerful new radiation weapon. The entire city had been wiped out with a beautiful mushroom cloud. On 15 August, the Emperor announced to his subjects their surrender. We heard the news almost immediately on the Allied nations' broadcasts. Stories abounded of Japanese soldiers turning on themselves in despair and committing *hara kiri* with daggers. Sometimes they appeared despondent and confused but it didn't stop others gate-crashing the parties of elated locals, slapping and humiliating the merrymakers. The war was over, yet in the streets Japanese soldiers were still very much in charge. We were quiet people and determined to keep our heads down until the British arrived. I still dried Mohini's washing over the fire in the kitchen as I had done for the last three years. No one must know she existed until the yellow bastards were all gone. I had been to the temple that morning to thank Ganesha for the grace he had shown my family. We had escaped intact – even stronger for the experience. I looked beyond the window and marvelled at my children. Lakshmnan and Mohini were pounding flour. Anna was skinning a chicken with a frozen expression on her face. It was that sort of unusually peaceful day when I can even remember my thoughts. She will turn vegetarian one day, I thought. Jeyan was playing with Lalita inside Mohini's secret hiding place and geese squabbled in the yard. Sevenese was at a Boy Scout meeting that he had been forced to attend by his Scout-master. I was frying spinach in curry powder and garlic.

Droplets of water in the washed spinach leaves spat furiously in the hot oil and I clearly remember feeling contented. Happy with my lot. The Japanese would soon be gone and things could go back to what they were. My husband could return to work, the children to school, to be taught proper subjects once more, and I to the task of saving money for my girls' dowries. I would need less for Mohini but Lalita was doubtless going to need more. I planned good marriages for my daughters. A dazzling life stretched ahead for my children. The first thing I would do was sell the bloody pool cows. Too much hard work.

I left the spinach to fry a little longer. As I sliced an aubergine lengthwise, lost in my own thoughts, I heard the squeal of tyres. A squeal that I had learned to dread and a squeal that could mean only one thing. My knife hovered in the air for an instant, freed from my slack grip, before I sprang up and ran to the front window. Two jeeps full of silent Japanese soldiers were turning into our dirt road. My heart began to pound like a mad thing inside my chest. I screamed in a panic at the children. I opened the trapdoor and Anna, who was closest, ran in. 'Japanese! Quickly, Mohini!' I shouted running back to the window. The soldiers were already splitting up into twos and walking up the path to our house. I turned away from their grim yellow faces and saw Mohini and Lakshmnan run breathlessly into the living room. She was going to make it into the hole in time and Lakshmnan could close the trapdoor behind Anna and her. I turned back and saw two soldiers begin to walk up our stairs. The one with the blue ribbon I knew was General Ito.

'Come on, Mohini,' I heard Lakshmnan hiss urgently. I could hear the raw fear in his voice and that same fear I suppose was responsible for what happened next. As he pulled her he lost his footing and fell through the trapdoor instead. The heavy black boots were just outside the door. They never knocked, they kicked. In that split second Mohini made a terrible decision. She decided it was too late to pull him out and there was not enough space for her to crawl in too. So the stupid girl did the unthinkable. She pulled the trapdoor shut and pushed back the chest over the hole. When I turned around from the window I saw her standing in front of the chest.

I had kept my daughter indoors for so long that I had stopped really seeing her and had forgotten the way other people used to react to her. Now my eyes widened with sheer horror, for suddenly I saw her with the lustful eyes of a Japanese soldier. She was a delightful nymph, the enchantress Mohini reincarnated. Her shabby surroundings served only to magnify her beauty. Caught in the sunlight, her green eyes were huge and luminous. The years spent indoors had turned her caramel complexion into a creamy, pink-tinged magnolia. Her shocked mouth, slightly open, was like a pink, plump fruit, its skin thin and defenceless. Her pearly white teeth gleamed. The old blouse she was wearing was really too tight around the chest, but unimaginable sums of banana dollars were needed for cloth and since the only eyes that laid on her were her family . . . every time she panted in fear the material rose and fell against her budding breasts with such a suggestive thrust that it hurt my eyes. My eyes dropped to the narrow waist and lingered at a midriff exposed by two buttons lost so long ago. The old skirt, its slip rotted away, was transparent in the light that streamed in from the window behind her. Her thighs drew my eyes. Smooth and rounded. Childish but, oh, so appealing. The truth was she was a fourteen-year-old goddess. And to them she would be a prize hole. I shook my head with disbelief. No, no, no. It was my worst nightmare come true. I couldn't believe it was happening. How could this happen now? The war was over. We had almost made it. Locked in a trance of sheer terror I could only stare.

The door burst open and four black boots thundered into the dead silence. Time slowed as my eyes swung in slow motion towards the brown-clad animals. Yes I knew what I would see. They stared riveted and dis-believing at my baby. I shall never forget their small black eyes usually opaque with mean hardness turning shiny with greed. Like the jackal that comes across a whole buffalo when he has spent his entire life believing that the eyes, entrails and testicles rejected by the lion was a feast. Even if I close my eyes now I can remember that pinprick of light that shone in their eyes as they took in the sight of fresh meat.

Then one of them was striding across the room. General Ito. He took my gentle flower with the crushed rose for a mouth by the chin in his hard hand and turned her face this way and that as though checking to see if his eyes had deceived him. He made a greedy guttural sound in his throat. His hand dropped to her neck, the thick hand encircling it and one finger gently caressing the skin at the base of her throat. With a quick movement, his hand like a yellow snake reached behind her head and snapped the rubber band that held her hair. Silky glorious hair sprang around her face and I heard his hiss of in-drawn breath. His awe at the unexpected treasure in his hands was terrifying. Mohini stood paralysed with shock. I saw his neck stiffen and, putting his hand on the small of her back, he urged her forward.

'Come,' he ordered harshly.

I sprang forward. 'Wait, wait! Please wait,' I cried. Without the slightest warning the point of his knife was resting in that tiny intimate space between my breasts. He had moved so fast. I gaped.

'Move,' he ordered coldly.

'Wait, you don't understand. She's only a child.'

He glanced at me with superior amusement.

'She's Indian. She's not Chinese. Japanese soldiers only take Chinese girls. Please, please don't take her,' I babbled incoherently, desperately, to the fiercely moustached face.

'Move,' he repeated and I saw his eyes stray to the point of his knife. A bright red stain was spreading on my blouse; his knife was embedded in my flesh. I stared at the blank face. Yet, I knew the man. I had known him for three years. I have given him my best chickens and my youngest coconuts.

'Please, honourable General, let me cook for the Imperial Army. I have good food. Very good food.' Suddenly I could smell the choking fumes of spinach burning in the pan. I saw his lips twitch. I dropped to my knees. Crying. Begging. I knew that man. So many times he had asked me with cold black humour, 'Where do you hide your daughters?' I hugged his legs tightly with both my arms.

There was disgust on his yellow face as he kicked me hard in the stomach. The pain was like an explosion. I fell, clutching my murdered stomach. Roughly he pulled Mohini towards the door. On my hands and knees I howled, like a wolf on a moonlit night. He must not leave my house with my daughter. Suddenly, nothing was more important than stopping him from getting through the door. My mouth opened and words dropped out. Words that I wish with all my heart I had never uttered.

'I know where you can get a Chinese virgin. Flesh that has never tasted a man's hands,' I gasped wildly, horrified beyond belief at what I was doing and yet unable to stop.

His shoulders stiffened but he carried on towards the door. He was interested.

'She is exotic and beautiful,' I added. 'Please,' I sobbed. 'Please.' I could not let him walk out.

He paused. The fish took the silvery bait in its jaws. The yellow face turned. Two mean eyes stared at me unfathomably. He let go his grip on Mohini. A strange smile slashed itself across his hard face. He was waiting for me. I beckoned to Mohini and she stumbled blindly towards me. I stood up and gripped her hands tightly, holding her close to me. She trembled inside my grasp like a small dying mynah bird. *It is wrong!* screamed the blood that pumped into my temples.

'Next door,' I sobbed. 'They have a girl next door behind the cupboard.'

He bowed stiffly. A mocking bow. I swallowed a tight knot of fear in my throat. A look evil and cold crossed his small almond-shaped eyes. I shuddered with fear and knew instantly that I had sacrificed poor Ah Moi in vain. He walked forward and pushed me so hard that I slammed into the wall. I crumpled into a stunned heap and saw him grab Mohini by the hand and stride out into the bright sunshine. I heard their heavy boots loud on the veranda. The whole house was vibrating and crashing from their hob-nailed boots, a dreadful sound that has haunted my nightmares ever since. For an instant I was poised on my hands and knees, frozen into immobility by sheer horror – he had taken her after all. Then I picked myself up and ran. I ran out onto the veranda and down the wooden steps, now full of muddy boot marks, that I had just that morning washed. I ran, arms outstretched, in my bare feet on the stone-filled path. The bastards were there within my reach. She was climbing in. I reached the truck. I even touched it but as soon as my grasping palms touched the hot metal of the jeep it roared into life and those laughing bastards pulled away in a cloud of dust, their tyres screeching. Her small oval face turned back to look at me. She never uttered a sound, not a single word had crossed those lips of hers. Not, 'Save me, Mother,' not, 'Help me!' Nothing.

I chased them, you know. I chased them until they disappeared out of sight and then I didn't stop or fall to the ground and cry. I just turned around like a Taiwanese wind-up toy and walked back.

On my wooden steps I left bloody footprints. The torn soles of my feet walked through my house and into the kitchen towards the cooker. I removed the blackened, smoking spinach from the fire. It is a disagreeable smell, burning chilli and spinach. Inside me, I heard the sound of deep sighing. Ah, the bamboo in my heart. For a long while I must have stood in front of the stove just listening to it. 'When will you sing for me? When will I hear your song?' I whispered to it but it only sighed the more.

Then I made a decision to have tea. I would treat myself to tea with real sugar. I had bought a tiny precious amount from a friend who worked at the Water Works Department just a week ago and I decided I would have some now. Tea with molasses was simply not the same. For three years I had hankered for tea with beautiful white sugar but I had always denied myself. Put the children first. Yes the children had always come first.

I put some water into a kettle to boil and spooned tea leaves into a large blue mug. As I stood staring at the tea leaves it occurred to me that they looked like swarming black ants. And when I poured the hot water in they looked like dead ants, dead ants. I put a lid on the mug and I heard tiny sounds, desperate sounds but very tiny. Someone was calling me. Actually more than one voice was calling out to me. There was also the muffled sound of banging. I decided to ignore them. I looked for the sugar and couldn't remember where I had hidden it. Confused, I sat on my bench. Outside it began to rain. 'The child's surely going to get wet. In a while I'll pound some ginger for her. Her chest is so bad,' I murmured softly to myself. I pulled my knees up to my chin until I must have looked like a tight little ball and I rocked myself to and fro, to and fro, singing an old nursery rhyme that my mother used to sing to me. I shouldn't have left her all by herself in Ceylon. Poor Mother. It is unbearable to lose a daughter. No, I would not think about the lost sugar. It was easiest to simply sing and rock. I sang the same four lines again and again.

Time must have passed, and now and then I thought I heard that same insistent sound of children knocking, calling out to me and crying. It seemed too as if the calls were becoming desperate, begging and terrified screaming, but they were so faint, these strange sounds, and so far away that I stuck to my earlier decision to ignore them and concentrate on the pain in my head instead. My head pounded as if a hammer was at my temples. It seemed I was swimming in a sea of pain and only the continuous rocking motion could steady it a little.

A very long time later a sound nearby penetrated my cocoon of pain. Squinting my eyes from the afternoon light I turned and my husband was standing in the kitchen doorway. His wide, black face looked hideous and instantly I felt hatred and a rage such as I have never known before. How dare he leave us to fend for ourselves against Japanese soldiers while he sat gossiping with that doddering old Sikh security guard outside the Chartered Bank building? It was all his fault. Black fury rose up and swamped me until I saw nothing. Unthinkingly I had unfurled myself and was flying towards him, screaming wildly at the stupid, shocked expression on his ugly face. The drumming in my head had become so loud that though I saw his lips moving I heard not the sounds that must surely have come out of them. My fingers connected with his high cheekbones and I dug my short nails into his flesh, shiny with a layer of sweat, and pulled them as viciously as I could down his face. At first he was too shocked to react but when I howled and brought my hands up again he caught them in a vice-like grip. 'Lakshmi, stop it,' he said, and I watched his gouged cheeks, the blood flowing down his face into his collar, with unreal fascination. 'Where are the children?' he asked, so quietly that I had to raise my eyes from his collar and look into those small, frightened eyes.

'They have taken Mohini away,' I said dully and as suddenly as my anger had come, it dissipated. I felt lost and longed for a husband who would take my burdens away for one hour. Someone who would make things right again. His nostrils flared like some huge beast in pain. Suddenly he was on his knees. 'No, no, no,' he gasped, staring into my eyes in disbelief. I looked down at him and felt no pain and no pity. No, he would not take over, not even for one hour. He got up slowly like a very old sick man and went to push away the chest. The children tumbled out, sobbing, into his large arms. He gathered them all close to his large body and sobbed with them. I saw them, my children, as they stole fear-filled looks at me and snuggled up to him. Even Lakshmnan. Children are such traitors.

'I told them about Ah Moi next door,' I said, and I saw my husband's back stiffen.

'Why?' he asked in a shocked whisper. There was a look of such betrayed horror in his eyes it was as if I had stabbed him in the back. So he didn't know me after all. Blood ran down his dark cheeks and dripped onto his collar.

'Because I thought I could save Mohini,' I answered slowly. A tear escaped and rolled down my face. Yes, only then I understood what I had done. Yet, given the chance would I do differently? Maybe if I had been cleverer in the way I had bartered. If only she had run into the fields and hidden in the bushes. If only Lakshmnan hadn't fallen. If only . . .

'Oh God, oh dear God what have you done?' my husband said quietly. He hugged our clinging children once more and said, 'I shall go next door and if it is not too late, try to warn them – but if it is too late then I don't ever want to hear anybody mention this ever again.'

The children nodded vigorously. They wore such huge frightened eyes. He ran out of the house. We waited in the kitchen. None of us moving, eyeing each other like strangers in two separate camps. Sevenese ran into the kitchen. Boy Scout meeting obviously over. His eyes were ferocious. He must have seen my bloody footprints. 'Has the crocodile got Mohini?' he panted.

'Yes,' I said. My son had called a spade a spade.

'I have to find Chibindi. Only he can help her now,' he cried wildly before dashing out of the house.

Ayah came back very quickly. He was too late. The soldiers had already come back for Ah Moi. That night, Lakshmnan ran away from home. I saw him make for the jungle where Sevenese usually disappeared with the disgusting snake-charmer boy. Lakshmnan returned the next night, bedraggled and bruised. He didn't ask about her. He knew from my face that they hadn't brought her back. He wouldn't let me hold him. I didn't know it then, but that was the day I lost him for ever. I put a plate of food in front of him. For the longest time he stared at it as if there was a war going on inside him. Then he pounced on it and ate as if he hadn't seen food for weeks. Like a starving animal. Then suddenly he vomited violently into his own plate. He looked up at me, his mouth and chin stained with lumps of partly digested food and howled, 'I can taste the food she is eating. Sour. So sour. She wants to die. Ama, she just wants to die. Help her, somebody, please, please.'

And as I watched, horrified, he crumpled into a ball on the floor at my feet whimpering in a thin high voice. I never realised until then what my twins really shared inside their perfectly still pauses where no words were necessary. What sounds, what smells, what thoughts, what emotions, what pain, what joy? Time passed, my beautiful son whimpering at my feet and I, I was frozen into immobility.

For so long now Lakshmnan had shed the skin of childhood and worn the mantle of manhood so willingly that I had stopped seeing him as a child. He would rise before the sun appeared on the horizon to take the covered pails of fresh milk over to the coffee shops in town and return with the stacks of banana notes. He herded the cows out to the fields to graze, cut long grasses for their evening fodder, took them to the small river to be bathed and cleaned out their living quarters twice a week. He hunted game for his family and washed the clothes I had soaked the night before in ash and the water strained from boiled rice when there was no more soap to be had. He had done a man's job but he was only a boy. I couldn't bear to see him like that. I squatted beside him.

'It's not your fault,' I said, stroking his hair, but in his head a thousand accusing voices hissed, *'Lakshmnan did it. Lakshmnan did it. He let the Japanese dogs take her.'* I tried to hold him but he didn't see me squatting there with tears running down my face. He didn't feel my hand. He pushed his bunched fists into his cheeks until his face looked like an agonised mask and he screamed, but still the pointing voices wouldn't go away. *'Lakshmnan did it. Lakshmnan did it.'*

I could feel the shocked eyes of my other children in the doorway, safe and clean in their grief and their understandable sadness, but he was trapped in his terrible guilt. He had loved her the best and yet he was the one responsible for her shame. If only he had not been so clumsy. If only he had sprung out as soon as he had fallen. If only . . .

Who would marry her now? Nobody. She was irretrievably scarred. Damaged goods. Would they leave her pregnant? Our pride and joy would be scorned and whispered about. The flower that we had tended so carefully, destroyed. The eyes I had washed in a tea solution to bring out their true translucence, hurt for ever. Had she really spent the last three years a prisoner in her own home for this? In Lakshmnan's tormented mind she was frozen in that moment of panic and choice. The fault, he knew was his.

'They will bring her back,' I said gently into his face, so close to his lips I smelt his sour breath. 'She is not dead. They will bring her back.'

He stopped suddenly. His bunched fists came away from his cheeks and he looked into my eyes for the first time. What I saw inside his glittering eyes haunts me to this day. I saw a land blackened, windswept and desolate. She was gone and she had taken with her the fruit trees, the flowers, the birds, the butterflies, the rainbow, the streams . . . Without her the wind howled through gaunt tree stumps. When they snatched her away, they snatched away a part of him too. The better part. By far the better part. He became a stranger in my house, a stranger with something cruel and adult lurking in his barren eyes. In fact, what I saw in his eyes he saw in mine. A mean snake of terrible might. It urged us to do the unthinkable. When you hear what I have done you will think less of me, but I was powerless to resist its will.

For the next three days my husband sat transfixed by the radio hoping for news. He moved his chair a little so he could watch the road through the living-room window. And for those three days I ate nothing. I looked at plate after plate of boiled tapioca, cream-coloured and slightly shiny, in a daze. Lakshmnan woke up earlier than usual, rushed through his chores and then sat on the steps outside staring at the main road, his broad shoulders tense with waiting. He spoke to no one and no one dared speak to him. The children stared at me with large frightened eyes as I pretended to be busy. Only when the child of night ran into my day, its feet blackened by the sins of day, could I close the kitchen door and lie on my bench staring helplessly into the inky Malayan night. I refused to consider my daughter's fate. Refused thoughts of sun-darkened, sinewy hands tainted with the metallic taste of guns, of those voracious mouths and those covetous tongues. And the stench of them. Oh God, how hard I tried not to think of that man who urinated inside Mui Tsai. I lay instead listening to the night sounds, the crickets, the buzzing mosquitoes, the call of small wild animals, the whispering of the leaves in the wind. Listening for my Mohini.

On the afternoon of the third day they returned Ah Moi. She was bruised, bleeding and barely able to walk but she was alive. I know because I stood three feet away from the window just inside the shadows and watched her grief-mad mother run out of the house shrieking at the sight of the frail figure wilted over the supporting hands of two soldiers. They dropped the girl at her mother's feet and left. The family carried the girl in. I was filled with dread. Where was Mohini? Why had they not returned her? I should have run out and demanded to know.

Perhaps they will return her tomorrow, I told myself meekly.

That night, although I tried to keep awake I was overcome by a strange lethargy and fell asleep in the kitchen. It was a restless sleep filled with strange dreams and I awoke many times hot and thirsty. Disturbed and ill at ease I roamed the house relentlessly, moving from room to room, my mouth mumbling, my eyes restless. I opened a window and looked out into the night. Everything looked and sounded normal. There were crickets in the bushes and the sad notes of the flute from the snake-charmer's house. Mosquitoes hummed. I closed the window and went to check on the children. They looked like strangers to me. It was too hot.

Cool water cascaded down my body and crashed loudly on the cement floor, flooding the entire bathroom, making dwarf waves that slopped over the small ledge built at the doorway and ran down the corridor. I stood in the flooded corridor and, feeling slightly better, decided to brew myself a strong mug of tea. If my husband was awake I would make him one too. I walked into the bedroom, a wet sarong pulled up to my armpits and tied above my breasts.

Ayah was sitting on the bed with his head in his hands. When he heard my steps he looked up. On the bed was a tiny green dress. I walked closer and touched the silky material. It was cool between my fingers. I had cut up one of my good saris to sew that dress yet I had forgotten making it. It was another lifetime ago, Divali, the festival of lights, when I had dressed her in green to match her eyes. I remembered then the oil lamps that I had surrounded the house with and I remembered her wearing the dress. God, she was so small then. Even the priest in the temple had pinched her cheek admiringly. I looked at the hunched defeated figure sitting on the bed in a daze.

'Where did you find this?' I asked. I was conscious that my voice was accusing. There was not a thing inside my house that I didn't know existed. From top to bottom I knew where everything was and yet he had carefully hidden away this dress all these years.

'I was saving it for her daughter,' he whispered.

Somewhere inside me was a feeling of such vast emptiness that I simply couldn't acknowledge it. To validate the vacuum would shrivel me into nothing. Silently I took some clothes out of the cupboard and walked out. The well-being that my energetic bath had imbued in me disappeared. He had opened his pain out like a giant fan. So raw with discordant splashes of red and menacing blacks that I took a step back, shocked. I should have held his grieving body in my arms but it was not in my nature, instead I nursed a growing jealousy. His love appeared in my eyes to be purer, higher than mine.

I brewed the tea and sat watching it until it grew cold. I yearned to run out of the house, storm the Japanese Garrison and demand her release but I could only sit like a powerless old woman remembering the past. Remembering the time I took my children to a Chinese temple on Kuan Yin's birthday. There, among life-size paper horses, a huge statue of the Goddess of Mercy in her customary flowing robes, and shining bronze urns full of thick red Chinese joss sticks, we burned thin grey incense sticks, reams of coloured paper and little flags meant to symbolise wealth and prosperity. It seemed like yesterday that my children had stood in a curious, hushed line of shining black heads, their chubby hands clutching small flags scribbled with Chinese characters that spelled their names. One by one I watched them solemnly burn their flag in a corrugated zinc container. Above them fat red lanterns swayed and nodded in the early morning breeze. Afterwards we each released a caged bird that a temple attendant in white had painted with a small red dot on its tiny body so no one would dare to catch or eat it. I had stood there and prayed for my children as they watched the birds flying free with beautiful, entranced expressions of sheer delight. Keep them safe, protect them, and bless them, dear, dear Goddess Kuan Yin, I begged but when we were leaving I remember looking into the goddess's cool, serene face and thinking that she had not heard me.

Outside in the darkness I could hear Ah Moi's brothers crawling about in the drains looking for cockroaches. Carrying candles they combed the neighbourhood drains every night looking for cockroaches to bottle and feed to their chickens in the morning. I was diverted by their hushed whispers in Chinese.

'Wah, look how big that devil is.'

'Where? Where?'

'Near your leg, you corpse head. Quick, catch it before it runs into that hole.'

'How many have you got now?'

'Nine. You?'

Their voices and their squelching slippers in the wet drains faded away. I tried to feel outraged by the thought of their young hands cupping over those disgusting creatures in the filth but it was the way during the Japanese Occupation. Grain was scarce and chickens fed on a diet of juicy cockroaches grow bigger faster.

I was hot again. I splashed icy cold water on my face and reheated the cold tea. Sometime afterwards I must have fallen asleep on my bench for I woke up suddenly. I had left the lamp on. The kitchen clock said it was 3 a.m. The first thing I remember was a feeling of peace. That constant throbbing in my head was gone. I had lived with it day and night for so many years that its sudden total absence felt strange. I put my hands to my temples in sheer amazement. As I sat there marvelling at what everyone else takes for granted, my husband walked into the kitchen. His broad shoulders were slumped with defeat and the whites of his eyes glimmered wetly in the dark.

'She's gone. She's finally gone. They can't hurt her any more,' he said in a broken voice. Such a gentle man. He couldn't begrudge her the white peace that surely awaited her innocent little soul. There was sadness in the giant leather-backed turtle's eyes. Then he turned away quietly and left. My throbbing headache rushed upon me once more with merciless vengeance as I stared at his retreating back.

I understood. She had been in my house. She had awakened me and spoken to her father. She had come to say goodbye. I didn't need to wait any more. I knew what had happened. I suppose I had known from the time I saw the bastards return Ah Moi to her family. That was why I had not rushed out to ask for her. I already knew. She was lost to me. Inside me I felt that monster serpent, black and horribly vindictive, that I told you about earlier, stretch and hiss boldly.

Mrs Metha from the Ceylonese Association came to sit in my living room and offer her condolences. For a long time I sat locked into stillness, looking at her ugly mouth and the dull nose stud that perched on the right side of her hooked nose.

'Only the good die young,' she proclaimed piously, and suddenly I was overtaken by the strongest desire to slap her. I could actually see myself get up and slap her so hard that her face swung all the way back on her scrawny neck. The impulse was so strong that I had to rise. I offered her some tea.

'No, no, don't bother yourself,' she said quickly, her eyes alert, but I had already turned my back on her. I thought I hated her. I also thought I recognised her. She was the envious crow that Mother had warned me about. The one who drank other people's tears to keep its own feathers black and shiny. The crow that sits on the highest tree so it may be the first to see the funeral procession.

In the kitchen I made tea. I spooned in the last precious stock of sugar. When the tea was ready I tasted a little from a small teaspoon and judged it perfect. I knew she'd drink every last drop. I put the mug of tea on the bench and I thought about that little green dress lying on the bed. For a little while I permitted myself the luxury of being weak and instantly the waiting tears burned painfully into my eyes, running down my cheeks and splashing into the mug of tea. You see, the only tears the envious crow must never drink are the tears of a grieving mother. A mother's tears are so sacred they are forbidden or its feathers will become dull with disease and it will perish slowly and excruciatingly. I was right about my tea – she finished it all – but I was wrong about her. I made a mistake that day. Mrs Metha wasn't the crow Mother had warned me about for she came back many times with many offers of help. She died recently and as she lay on her deathbed, as ugly as ever, I felt sorry for what I had done. I bent my head and whispered my sin into her ear. It seemed as if her shrivelled body shuddered slightly, but her eyes when I met them smiled. She died without saying another word.

Ah Moi I thought was not to be on my conscience but it was not to be so, for less than a week later the hunched figure of her father was driving the bullock cart past our house with her body wrapped in a mat woven from coconut palm. I stood behind the curtain and watched like the black cobra that hides in a secret nook in the jungle, observing the grieving mother beat her head on the stone pillars after she places her dead son before the shrine of Lord Shiva. Poor Ah Moi had hanged herself from the rafters of her house. She had died of shame.

Her father buried her in an unmarked grave some-where not far away. After their strange and poor burial Ayah went to offer condolences but I couldn't face First

Wife. Even from our house I could hear her blood-curdling howls of grief, thin and shrill like a dog in mortal pain.

I had lost a daughter too. Put in the same situation, I knew that she would have done exactly as I did. A mother's love recognises no laws, no bounds and bows to no masters but itself. It dares all. At that time I couldn't see that I had done wrong. I refused to mourn Mohini properly. Instead I let myself believe that my greatest regret was that it was not I who had saved that little green dress. I should have thought to save that green dress. Every now and again I searched for it as if it were the secret key to everything. Even now I search for it and though I can't find it I know he keeps it because he believes that she will return. One day. He hides it in some very secret place away from my prying eyes, my jealous heart and my soiled thoughts.

Part Two

The Scent of Jasmine

Lalita

Our family history can be divided into two distinct ages: before and after Mohini died. With her death Mother, Father and Lakshmnan changed into unrecognisable people. They even looked different. I would never have thought it possible for people to change so drastically in one afternoon. People, I thought, were solid objects . . . and yet they did. My entire family changed beyond recognition one hot afternoon a long time ago.

The strangest thing is, I can't even remember that momentous day. In fact, I can't even remember Mohini. Maybe I am angry with her, that unlucky spirit who changed all our lives by simply going away. That is unfair, I know. She was dragged away at gunpoint; but still another part of me wants to accuse her for not being ordinary like everyone else. And that too I know is unfair. She didn't choose her looks.

Sometimes I remember her as the scent of jasmine on Mother's hand. Don't look so confused. There is an explanation. Mohini died at the end of the Japanese Occupation. During the Occupation Mother kept cows. She got up at four in the morning to milk them before she came to awaken us, smelling of the wholesome aroma of cow's milk. As soon as the Japanese were sent packing, Mother sold all the cows. She didn't arise at four in the morning any more, she arose later – and the only thing she did before she woke us up was to fill a tray with jasmine flowers for the prayer altar. My childish perception remembers the scent of the jasmine flowers on her fingers like an aftertaste of Mohini's passing. How I hate the smell of jasmine! It reeks of death.

When I try really hard to picture my sister I remember her only as she is in the one precious photograph that we have of her. For many years Mother kept it in a little silk purse until one day Sevenese took it to old Chin Teck's shop in Jalan Gambut and had it framed in a black and gold wooden frame. Mother took down from the living-room wall Anna's best needlework effort, an embroidered peacock cavorting in a green field of orange flowers, and hung the photograph in its place. The photograph was from just before the Japanese war, the entire family captured in their best finery although I can't remember the trip to the studio or ever posing for the photograph. A black and white testament to my flawed memory.

Mother is wearing the thick gold thali chain she got married in and the famous ruby pendant that she sold at the beginning of the Japanese Occupation. She sits and stares into the camera's eye, boldly refusing to smile. There is handsome pride in her face. She is no raving beauty but she is aware of her good fortune. Father is standing, big and tall in a short-sleeved shirt that is a masterpiece of meticulous ironing. Slightly hunched, he smiles self-consciously into the camera and yet you feel that he hasn't quite met your eye. Lakshmnan's chin juts forward and his chest is puffed out like a robin. There is the same bold quality in his gaze that Mother has in hers. He understands that he is destined for great things. Anna has clasped her chubby hands in front of her in an endearing gesture and is wearing her favourite red shoes.

I think I remember those shoes. They had shining buckles on the sides.

Jeyan's hair has been painstakingly curled by Mohini but he is narrow-shouldered and his dark eyes are already dull with defeat. Sevenese grins toothily, his hands deep inside his baggy hand-me-down shorts. There is a devil-may-care glint in his eyes. He resembles a street urchin dressed up to look like one of Mother's children for the day. Then I see myself. I sit on Mother's lap with a dazed look in my small sleepy eyes. I scrutinise my own image for eyelashes and can find none. Then I look at my mouth, slightly agape, and it is instantly apparent that I have been denied even the fleeting beauty of childhood.

The eye searching for a resting place, is drawn to Mohini. The ultimate resting place. But she refuses to meet the onlooker's stare and has turned her head to gaze instead at Lakshmnan. Even in profile it is patently obvious that she is beautiful and different. Caught in motion and by the very act of not looking straight at the camera she becomes somehow more alive, more real than all the other frozen people in the picture. It is strange to think that we are all alive and she is not. She is alive only in our motionless picture.

Before the time when I was awakened every morning by the smell of jasmine, Lakshmnan was my hero. The foreign soldiers had taught him to say, 'Hey kid.' And that is what he used to call me. In English. Always with a smile in his voice. He always seemed so big and broad. I remember him shirtless and barefoot, his young, strong muscles rippling in the sunlight as he energetically beat all our washing clean. Drops of sparkling water used to fly around him as if he were some sort of Water God. In my mind he is caught for ever beating our dirty clothes on the smooth stone in our backyard. Young, vibrant and terribly handsome with a brilliant rainbow-coloured future waiting for him in the distance. Water droplets full of the sun are for ever flying around him. I sit in Mother's vegetable patch and can't take my eyes off the mythical Water God. Watching the clever way he made the sun colour the soapsuds. Green, red, yellow, blue . . .

Then I remember him on the heavy grinding stone. Every morning my brother ground the spices that offered taste to our meals for the day. He turned handfuls of dried spices into small warm-coloured mounds of chilli, cumin, fenugreek, coriander, fennel, cardamom, and turmeric on a little silver tray for Mother, like a gift. Little wet piles of yellows, greens, oranges, deep reds and shades of earth.

Why can't I remember anything else? Why don't I remember the things that Anna and Sevenese can remember?

Mother gets intolerant of me but I can't help it. The past for me is not big events but everyday things like coming home from school and seeing her sitting cross-legged on the bench in the kitchen stringing garlands of colourful flowers to adorn the pictures of all the gods on our altar. No incident stands out on its own merit. Just things I saw every day. The colourful garlands coiled on a silver tray beside her. The S-shaped Siamese mangoes she used to keep in the rice so they would ripen faster. Or the delightful hours I spent lost inside the contents of her wooden chest. Made of solid black wood with chunky bronze handles, it was the most intriguing thing of my childhood. A box abundant with Mother's treasures. Inside were her brilliantly coloured silk saris that she had always said would one day belong to my sisters and me. I ran my fingers over the cool, silky material and tried to imagine which ones would be mine one day. The green ones I knew were meant for Mohini. Mother said that green was happiest on Mohini's skin. Inside the box were also Mother's important papers, and bunches of raffia-string-tied letters from Grandma. After the Japanese left, Mother's chocolate box of jewellery came down from the top of the coconut tree and found its rightful place inside the wooden chest. The chocolate box once opened was bewitching. Rubies, sapphires and green stones twinkled and winked as if happy to see the daylight and to reach for human skin.

I have surprisingly crystal clear memories of plants, insects and animals. Beautiful purple leaves that can hold a drop of rain like a sparkling diamond on their surfaces, or sitting outside in the sun for hours mesmerised by ants. What amazing creatures they are. Back and forth, back and forth with loads many times larger than their own enchanting bodies. And if I sat very, very still for long enough a dragonfly might descend on me. They are beautiful things, with diaphanous wings that carry the rainbow within them. I am humbled by their big, warm, crystal-ball eyes with the dot of black deep inside. I wondered what I looked like to them as I watched them eating dozens of mosquitoes and gnats. Their legs were ticklish on my skin. And most surprisingly they can take off backwards. Sometimes big beetles with hard black wings and little curved horns landed suddenly on my hands, but of all the insects that rested on my outstretched hands and looked up at me foolishly, grasshoppers were my favourite. I looked into their still faces and thought them thoughtful and even a little sad. Sometimes delightful millipedes with unnecessary feet would wander up my hands, or drunken daddy-long-legs would blow onto my skirts and lurch crazily in the wind. Once I sat and stared at a bat that had flown into the mango tree at dusk. He hung upside down from a thin branch and crunched the utterly naked head of a baby bird.

But of all the creatures in the world my favourites were the chickens that lived under our house. I loved them when they were small, fluffy and yellow and I was proud of them when they became cooing, clucking beady-eyed hens. Only I was small enough to bend at the neck and enter their home under the house. It was always musty and dim but wonderfully cool with the feathery smell of chickens hiding inside the ammonia odour of their droppings. They crowded around me clucking, making it impossible for me to take another step without squashing them with my rubber flip-flops. As soon as I stopped they mobbed around fluttering their wings, hopping into the air and sometimes yelping impatiently, waiting for me to scatter their feed so that they could peck at the ground in a mad, greedy panic. I watched them feed, endlessly entertained until I had to rummage through their boxes and find the eggs that sometimes had double yolks in them. Mother would never allow the girls in our family to eat those curiously deformed eggs because it was believed that eating them might cause twins in future.

It was the rooster I had to be careful of. He was a magnificent creature but incurably mad. He tossed his head to one side and allowed his one peculiarly dazzling yellow eye to follow the journey of my bright-blue rubber slippers. And sometimes he chased me and attacked me, banishing me from under the house for no good reason at all. Sometimes I used to sit on a stone by the legs of the house and wonder what could have made him so permanently outraged. Yet I loved him.

A few days after Mohini died, Mother slumped sideways slowly until her head lay on Anna's lap as they sat on the bench in the kitchen. I remember watching her with surprise. Mother never leaned on anybody. Anna stared straight ahead and her small plump hands lay limply on Mother's head.

'Now that she is gone I must get rid of all the smelly chickens from under the house,' Mother said, her voice flat and blank.

I stared at her, horrified, but true to her word the chickens were slaughtered one by one until they were no more. The chicken wire was removed from around the legs of the house and the ground cleaned. It wasn't dim and musty under there any more. All the smelly chickens with the shiny feathers were gone.

Of course I have lovely memories of Father. I used to sit and watch him eat watermelons on the veranda. He could make a slice last so long that I could fall asleep watching him. One by one the seeds slipped out noiselessly from the corner of his mouth into his left hand. All this of course was before Father lost the taste for life and began wandering aimlessly around the house shuffling from room to room looking as if he had lost something.

In his time my father was a true artist. He carved a beautiful bust of Mother, which I imagined was what she must have looked like before – before him, before us, and before the multitude of disappointments that dropped without fail into her life. My father captured eyes bright with laughing intelligence and a smile full of carefree cheek. He caught her in a moment before we all caged her with our stupidity, our slow ways and our lack of her easy ability. It was all our fault. We turned her into a restless tiger who paced her cage day and night, growling furiously at her captors, us. When our home was looted while we were at that wedding in Seremban the bust disappeared with everything else until the snake-charmer's wife saw it in the market. A man took it out of a sack and was selling it for just one ringgit. She bought it and brought it back for Mother. The rescued bust returned into Mother's showcase until Mohini died. Then Mother took the bust out of the cupboard and smashed the beautiful thing into splinters. Even then she wasn't satisfied. She heaped the pieces into a pile and burned them in the backyard. The sun was setting and in the evening light she stood with her back to us all, her hands on her hips, watching black smoke curling from the pile of wood splinters. When her bust was but a pile of ashes she returned to the house. None of us dared to ask her why she had done it.

When I was little, Mother and I used to walk to the market every morning. To mask the boredom she started a game. She became Kunti, an ancient storyteller in a small village in Ceylon, and I was magically transformed into Mirabai, a beautiful little girl who lived in a secret forest with a gentle family of deer.

'Ah, there you are, dear Mirabai,' she crooned thoughtfully, as if she really was terribly ancient. Then she held me by the hand and told me the most wonderful stories about turbaned conch-shell blowers from a different time. About Rama, his magic bows, and Sita crying inside her enchanted circle. How I held my breath, dreading the moment when Sita, unable to resist the deer, steps out and into the evil arms of Ravana, the demon

King of Lanka. And the Monkey God's tail growing and growing and growing. There were miraculous stories about a sacred, five-headed statue of the Elephant God that a temple priest found on a shrinking riverbed in Mother's village in Ceylon.

Of all the stories she told, my favourites were always the ones about the Naga Babas – naked, ash-caked ascetics who roam the barren Himalayan slopes hoping to stumble upon Lord Shiva deep in meditation. I could never ever tire of the Naga Babas in Mother's world. Their immense powers and their terrible rites of initiation. The years spent in cold caves staring at blank stone walls and dismal months in the burning deserts. Sometimes I think Mother's stories are what I remember best of my childhood.

In the afternoons I sat by her legs as she turned lengths of material into clothes for us all on her Singer sewing machine. I remember watching her legs go up and down as she pumped the pedal. The wheel turning faster and faster as the ravenous machine ate yard after yard of cloth. When I was older I used to rest my chin on the smooth metal surface of the sewing machine and worry that it might accidentally eat Mother's fingers. For a very long while I was nervous of its obvious greed and malicious teeth but eventually I learned that Mother was really too clever to be outdone by it.

I remember too the caramelly smell of sugar melting in clarified butter inside our big, black iron pot. Those were the good old days when Mother settled me on the bench with a few raisins by my crossed legs and set about making yellow kaseri for teatime. She made the best kaseri ever, with plump raisins and sweet cashew nuts hidden within. I loved watching Mother make alvas too.

The way she held the black iron pot firmly by its ears and stirred the mixture until the oil came out of it and it became as transparent as coloured glass. Then she spread out the orange glass mixture on a tray and cut it with a sharp knife into diamond shapes. While it was still hot she dug out and let me have all the edges that didn't quite make it into a perfect diamond shape. So even now that I am all grown up I have a strange liking for alva, still hot. For the not quite perfect edges. Like a time machine it takes me back to those afternoons when it was just Mother and me happy in the kitchen. Father was at work and everyone else was at school. I suppose Mohini was at home too. Of course she was. She spent the entire time the Japanese were in this country hidden away inside the house.

Sometimes, after she became less than a memory, I used to imagine that I had seen her fair feet disappearing beyond a doorway. I felt certain that I had heard the pretty sounds of the bells she always wore on her ankles, but when I ran around the corner there was never anyone there. It used to disturb me terribly that I didn't have memories of her. I strain and struggle with my memory. Did she wash my hair? Stand me on the kitchen step outside and oil my body on Friday afternoons? Didn't she pick me up and tickle me until I cried with laughter? Didn't she also help stir the sugar mixture to make the alvas? Didn't her fair hand smuggle more raisins from the mixing bowl and scatter them at my feet when Mother's strict back was turned? Yet I can only see Mother bent over the hot stove stirring the sugar and ghee mixture with her wooden spoon. Anxious that it should be perfect.

Even when I think of us standing in a row in front of

the prayer altar I can't really remember Mohini. I can picture Mother praying with such intense devotion that tears slipped out of her closed eyelids, her voice quivering, as she sang her songs of praise. Mother believed that if she lit the oil lamp, burned the camphor, prayed every day without fail and rubbed ash on our foreheads, she could protect us all and keep us out of harm's way. I can even hear in my head Lakshmnan singing in that strong, firm voice of his, Anna's little babyish voice and Sevenese's beautiful, high voice that sounded more like a small bird singing in the morning than a little boy's voice. I can even recall Jeyan's tuneless songs that Lakshmnan couldn't help sniggering at. But I can't remember Mohini's voice, if she was there at all. Of course she was there! She stood there next to Lakshmnan with wet hair all the way down her back.

They tell me I should at least remember helping Mohini to make pickles. Stuffing fifty green limes until they were bursting with rock salt and storing them in a tightly shut glazed pot under the bench for three days until they looked like cut open hearts. Then taking them all out and arranging them carefully on large curving areca nut leaves to dry in the sun until they were yellow-brown and as hard as stone.

'Don't you remember us all sitting together on the kitchen doorstep and squeezing fifty fresh limes into the pot filled with the hardened brown limes until even our fingers hurt?' they ask incredulously. 'Can't you remember how Ama used to add in a mixture of ground chillies and fennel into the pot? And didn't we all watch while Mohini replaced the cover on the pot and tied it as tightly as she could?' I stare at them stupidly. In the beginning, when her departure was still razor sharp, I used to take down her photograph and stare at her avoiding my gaze. Could I have just erased her from my memory? No, it is impossible. I am not that powerful, surely. Then why can't I remember her like everyone else does? That afternoon when they found her and took her away, I have no memory of at all. I can't even remember those three hellish days when no one knew if she was dead or alive.

Maybe I was too young. Or maybe that twisted dream of Father coming all by himself into the zinc-roofed lean-to, built to house the cows, his shoulders hunched and his face contorted with monstrous pain, is not a dream after all. Maybe it was simply too complex for a child to remember herself, frozen with helpless shock, afraid even to breathe under the house, her hands full of soft yellow chicks.

How absolutely motionless she had sat when she saw him lean his forehead against Rukumani the cow and sob so hard that she knew in her little child's heart that he would never mend again. She should have died instead. She knew without being told that nobody wanted her all that much anyway. Surely her father would never have cried so. She felt rejected by and implicated in his suffering that appeared to her dumbfounded eyes far, far too enormous to manage. It was after all her fault. She had no business taking up space inside Mohini's hiding place. Silently she watched him crying so hard that even the cows moved restlessly in the shed, their bells clanging, and still he cried like a baby.

I was ten years old when Mohini died. And it seems it was for many years that Father sat hunched in his chair for hours staring at nothing. At first I thought that if I brought my cuts, bruises and injuries to him he would sing to my hurt limbs in his truly horrible voice as he had always done before. Then I would giggle and both our pains would slip away quietly by the back door, for he had always joked that even the worst pain could never bear his bad singing. But when I stood beside him holding my hurt limb, he would stroke my thin, frizzy hair absently and his eyes would remain focused in the distance. Maybe, far away on the horizon, Mohini stood and called to him. And then I became too old to sing to and he never sang again.

My brother Sevenese was only a boy then but already all his strange powers were inside him. On the night that Mohini died he saw her. He awoke hearing the sound of bells. He sat up in bed shaken out of a sound sleep. There among mirrors and other small objects that gleamed here and there in the moonlit night her apparition stood as solid and as real as he was. Surprised, he stared at her. She looked very white and very beautiful. Dressed in the same clothes that she had left the house in she was instantly familiar and dear. Everything about her looked warm, real and ordinary. She was just standing there, watching him. There was not a mark on her face or body that he could see. Even her hair was shining and combed. Then she smiled gently.

'Oh, good,' he cried, with relief and joy. 'They didn't hurt you.'

He watched her walk with that soft tinkling sound to the other bed where Anna and I were asleep. He said she stroked our hair softly and bent to kiss our sleeping faces. We neither awakened nor stirred. He watched with growing confusion. There was something odd going on that he could not understand. Then she moved to the other side of his bed and kissed Jeyan, breathing softly, and stood looking down for the longest time at Lakshmnan, so exhausted with worry and waiting that he was dead to the world. With an expression of deep pity she bent down and kissed her twin brother gently, her lips lingering on his cheek as if reluctant to let go.

'He has such a hard life ahead of him. You must try to guide him though I fear he may not listen,' she whispered strangely. Then she looked straight into Sevenese's bewildered face. 'Listen carefully for my voice, my little watchman, and perhaps you will hear me.' Then she turned and walked away with the sound of soft tinkling bells.

'Wait!' he cried, his arm outstretched, but she carried on walking into the dark, not turning back. In the corridor on the way to the kitchen the soft tinkling of bells died away. Thinking he had dreamed it all, Sevenese got out of bed and went into the lamplit kitchen where our mother was staring out into the night, her shoulders hunched and defeated. For once her hands were empty. They lay upturned helplessly in her lap. That in itself confused and disturbed my brother. Mother's hands were always busy, sewing, mending, cleaning the anchovies, picking the little black insects out of our rice, writing letters to her mother, crushing dahl or doing something.

'Has Mohini come home, Mother?' he asked her.

'Yes,' she said sadly, staring out into the night sky. Suddenly she turned her head to look at him curiously. Her eyes were just black holes in her slack face. 'Why, have you seen her?'

He stared at her. 'Yes,' he said, suddenly frightened. A small voice inside his head whispered that he never need worry about Raja abducting Mohini again. Never again need worry about his selfish part in turning a teenage crush into an uncontrollable obsession. The Japanese had solved his problem for him.

A curious thing happened just after the Occupation. The departing Japanese had to abandon their warehouses full of treasures and confiscated property. During the Occupation they had not had the spare ships to carry non-war essentials back to their motherland, and once vanquished they were forced to leave our country empty-handed. The snake-charmer's wife came running to our house to tell us about a large warehouse by the market place that had been broken into.

'Quick!' she cried. 'The whole warehouse is crammed full of things and everybody is helping themselves to bags of sugar, rice and all sorts of things.'

'Go now,' Mother told Father. 'Everybody is looting the warehouse by the market. See if you can get something too.' He changed from his sarong into a pair of trousers while Mother fidgeted and muttered impatiently under her breath.

'Hurry,' she shouted to his disappearing figure on the bicycle.

Father cycled as fast as he could, but by the time he reached the warehouse he was too late and everything was gone. He had passed a procession of people carrying aloft big boxes and bulky sacks, but inside the gaping doors of the store there was only litter on the floor and a vast sense of emptiness. He rode his bicycle right into the middle of the empty storehouse and surveyed the scene. He thought dispiritedly about Mother's expectant hands and sharp tongue, but as he was cycling out he saw an oblong box half-hidden behind the door. It had obviously fallen out of someone else's sack. He picked up the box and was surprised to find it rather light. Quickly he climbed onto his bicycle and rode home.

'That's it?' Mother exclaimed, looking with disappointment at the box in his hands. The snake-charmer and his son had been lucky enough to come home with a large bag of sugar and a gunnysack full of rice. She shook the wooden box and we heard a dull thudding sound. Whatever was in it, was well packed. The wooden box had been nailed shut. Its meticulous packaging hinted that it was something out of the ordinary. Mother prised open the box with a knife while we crowded around her curiously. She pulled the lid away and removed the straw that had been used as padding. First her hand touched cold smoothness. A jade doll, so beautifully made that I heard Mother gasp, was in her hands. She held it up. The translucent stone glowed a gorgeous dark green. The doll was only six inches high. She had very long hair swirling about her hips and a peaceful expression on her face. None of us had ever seen such exquisite beauty. On the small gold stand she stood upon was a carved inscription in Chinese. There was silence in our house. Mother had gone a strange colour.

'It looks like Mohini,' Sevenese said in a too-loud voice.

'Yes, she does,' Mother agreed in a terrible voice. At that time I thought it was because the horrid Japanese had taken away our Mohini and given us a little toy instead. Mother let us all touch it before she placed it into the family showcase where the bust of herself had once rested. The doll dwelt inside our showcase with my collection of cheerful pipe-cleaner birds and the intricate coral pieces that Lakshmnan had picked up from the beach. It would be many, many years before I learned that the inscription described the doll as Kuan Yin, the Goddess of Mercy, a Ching Dynasty piece, more than two hundred years old. A piece of information that was unimportant to Mother, for she had known what it was and what it meant to her the moment she laid eyes upon it. She felt the vapour of horror and saw the disappearing hem of all her hopes.

Inside her head she saw crystal clear the dreaded old Chinese fortune-teller and recalled the words she had fought so hard to forget. 'Beware your eldest son. He is your enemy from another life returned to punish you. You will know the pain of burying a child. You will attract an ancestral object of great value into your hands. Do not keep it and do not try to gain from it. It belongs in a temple.' But if she gave the statue away to a temple it would mean she believed the cursed man and his wild predictions. Yes, she had lost a child, but so had thousands of people. It was the war. That's what war did. It killed your children. The fortune-teller could not, *must not* be believed. Her favourite first-born was *not* an enemy. She simply refused to believe it even when she held the green jade doll very close and it whispered, 'Beware your eldest son.' If she put the statue deep into the showcase behind the corals and behind the colourful pipe-cleaner birds, she thought she could will the fortune-teller wrong. But her will consumed her and her eldest son's destroyed her.

I remember Mother saying that Lakshmnan had begun to grind his teeth in his sleep after Mohini died. Suddenly I begin to fear Lakshmnan. I don't know where the fear comes from, but I am terrified of him. It is not that he has hit me or hurt me, or that I have seen him punch a hole in the wall in a temper or do some of the other things that Anna and Mother grumble about. But suddenly in my mind he is no longer beating the clothes on the stone with the sparkling water droplets flying like diamonds around him, but an angry Asura, one of the cruel giants that rule the Underworld. I feel his anger under his skin so close to the surface that the smallest, slightest scratch could make it come rushing out as red-faced and uncontrollable. I don't even remember when he stopped calling me, 'Hey, kid,' in that stylish way of his.

After the Japanese left I was sent to school but I was only an average student. My best friend was Nalini. We found each other when the Chinese girls in our class refused to sit beside us, complaining to the teachers that we were dark because we were filthy. When the teachers forced them to sit with us they complained to their mothers, who arrived in school and demanded that their daughters be allowed to sit apart from the Indian girls. 'Indian girls have lice in their hair,' they claimed haughtily, untruthfully. So Nalini and I ended up sitting together. We were both dark and plain but she was a great deal poorer because I had something she had not. I had Mother.

To me, Mother is a fine woman. Without her, none of us would be here today. I am deeply sorry for my inability to make her proud of me. I would gladly become the successful extension of her that she worked so hard to mould us all into. How I wish I could have been in the picture that Mother had in her mind. I can imagine that picture; it is a perfect birthday-party scene in a beautiful house. Perhaps it is the birthday of one of Lakshmnan's children and all of us are driving into his grand driveway in our expensive cars. We are all wearing nice clothes, with our husbands and wives smiling beside us and our children running forward to fling themselves joyfully at their smiling grandmother. Her arms are open to receive the many tiny bodies in their beautiful clothes. Then Lakshmnan bends his six-foot-two-long body and kisses Mother gently on the cheek. Lakshmnan's wife smiles indulgently in the background. Beside her there is a table full of gaily wrapped presents and a delicious spread of food.

Why, I sometimes wonder, does Anna not want this picture? Why does she have such carefully concealed contempt towards Mother for wanting it? I long for it. Anna behaves as if Mother has ruined this whole family. That is perfectly untrue.

Lakshmnan's wife accuses Mother of being a tan-coloured female spider. She says that to avoid being devoured our poor father brings home a brown envelope full of money every month. Yes, perhaps Mother is a tan-coloured spider. All her life she has spun from nothing food, the most exquisite clothes, love, education and shelter for us all. I am the daughter of the spider. I can't but think her beautiful. I have spent my whole life trying to make Mother happy. For when she is happy, the entire house rejoices, the walls smile broadly, the curtains flutter with joy, the light blue cushion covers laugh in the sunshine that pours through the open windows and the flame in the cooker dances with delight. As I look to her, inside me strange feeler-like things are unfurling in the wish to be like her even though I know that it is Father that I resemble.

I can't think of a problem that has ever defeated Mother. She takes them in her hand easily, fearlessly, as if they are only handkerchiefs needing to be folded. Occasionally there are tears to be shed but they too can be tidied away. When the Japanese left Father was fifty-three years old. There were still seven mouths to feed in the house and so Mother and I got on a bus and headed for Mr Murugesu's office at the hospital. He had a bright, roomy office with whitewashed walls and large bay windows behind his paper-filled desk. He ushered us in as if we were important guests that he felt honoured to have in his presence.

'Come in, come in,' he invited earnestly. You could tell straightaway that he was the decent type. His windows opened out into a pretty square garden, a covered corridor ran through the middle of it joining two buildings. Nurses and doctors chatted and walked along the corridor. Mynah birds rested in the trees and two boys played conkers. Outside it looked rather fun but, inside, Mother was crying. Mr Murugesu visibly shrank in his chair. Mother dabbed her eyes with one of Father's large handkerchiefs and begged Mr Murugesu to offer Father a job.

'Look how small my youngest is,' she implored, her face turning to me. 'How will I feed and clothe all of them?' she asked the bewildered Mr Murugesu. A few more minutes of this and he shot up from his chair as if his seat had suddenly become too hot to sit on. 'Don't worry, don't worry,' he assured her gruffly, adjusting his glasses and opening a drawer on his left. 'Ask your husband to come and see me. I'm sure we will find something in the accounts department for him. We can talk about his salary when he gets here.'

Mother stopped crying and thanked him profusely. Gratitude came out of her in big, warm waves to envelop the discomfited man. 'Pleasure, pleasure,' Mr Murugesu mumbled. From inside his drawer he produced a square tin. With the tin in his hands his eyes were losing that bewildered helpless look. He opened it and offered the contents to me. Inside was a selection of Indian cakes, glazed with sugar and shiny with temptation. I picked out a ladhu. 'Thank you,' I said shyly. It was big and substantial in my hand. The aroma of sugar and cardamom wafted tantalisingly up into my face. By now Mr Murugesu had completely recovered himself and was wearing a delighted smile upon his benevolent expression.

'Don't eat it here. You will make a mess of Mr Murugesu's office,' Mother advised in her 'don't you dare show me up in front of strangers' voice.

'No, no, let the child eat it now,' Mr Murugesu insisted in his high, happy voice.

I bit into the bright yellow-and-red round ball. Instantly, soft round crumbs fell on my nice 'going out' clothes and rolled onto Mr Murugesu's polished grey floor. I remember looking up surreptitiously at Mother and finding her glaring at me angrily. Her eyelashes were still wet, but by then all her tears were already neatly folded into Father's white handkerchief.

The war was over and there was much to rejoice about. Old Soong was turning sixty. Third Wife had decided to throw him a gala birthday party. A fortune-teller had predicted that this might be the last birthday for Old Soong. So it had been decided that it would be a celebration to rival all celebrations. All the wives and children would be there. For days the cook had soaked, stuffed, tied, marinated, baked, fried and stored in airtight tins all sorts of delicacies. Mui Tsai cleaned, polished, washed and helped in the kitchen. The whole house had been decorated with red banners painted with special writing for even more prosperity.

Even Third Wife spent a great deal of time in the kitchen tasting, advising and scolding. Cook had prepared the master's favourite dish, dog meat, in three different guises. In one she had dropped powdered tiger's tooth for continued vigour, in another powdered rhinoceros horn for sexual vitality, and in the last aromatic roots for good health. Special long noodles had arrived to bestow the master with longevity. There was a suckling pig shiny with glaze grasping in its mouth a gaudy orange. There was even a dish of bearded wild boar. To start the meal there were two types of soup – shark's fin and bird's nest.

Everything was ready. Even Mui Tsai had been given a new plum-coloured outfit for the special occasion.

On the appointed day the guests began to arrive. In large shiny cars they poured out, their prosperity evident in their corpulence. In beautiful clothes they entered laughing into Old Soong's house. Mui Tsai had passed by our house in the morning and in her tired eyes there had been excitement that Mother said she had not seen for a very long time.

'My sons will be here today. I will see all of them,' Mui Tsai whispered to Mother.

It was a very big occasion so the whole neighbourhood came out onto their verandas to watch. From our veranda I could see Mui Tsai flitting in and out of the kitchen, keeping an eye on the arriving guests, waiting impatiently for a look at her sons. Eventually, First Wife arrived. She had grown bigger with time and walking on either side of her plump body were two boys. Mui Tsai's sons. They were dressed in identical flame-red Chinese costumes embroidered with colourful birds of paradise. Standing erect and proud beside First Wife, they looked around them curiously. I could see Mui Tsai standing by the kitchen door, transfixed by the sight of her second and third born. Then came Second Wife and she had the other two boys. They wore blue silk and pushed each other boisterously.

At the sound of crashing cymbals the lion dance began. Six men inside a colourful lion costume pranced and danced to an enchanted audience.

After the children were fed they were allowed out to play. While everybody was inside eating I saw Mui Tsai slip out to watch her children playing, going as close to them as she dared. She stood very still watching her sons. They rushed about with sticks, meant to be guns. Perhaps they were the victorious British, for spotting Mui Tsai staring at them they pointed at her and, shouting in Chinese, began picking up handfuls of sand and small pebbles from the driveway and bombarding their Japanese enemy, Mui Tsai. I saw her go rigid with shock.

'Hey!' Mother screamed from our veranda. Putting on her slippers, she ran towards Old Soong's house. 'Hey, stop that!' she called out angrily but in the throes of their cruel game and their own whoops and shouts of victory, Mother's voice was lost. Second Wife appeared at the doorway and said something in such a stern voice that the boys hung their heads in shame. Mother stopped running. The boys ran to Second Wife and kissed her hand in apology. She said something else in a gentler voice and they ran to the other side of the house where a selection of sweet Nyonya cakes specially ordered from Penang waited. Second Wife went back into the house without looking at the stone figure of Mui Tsai.

At the fence I saw Mother call to Mui Tsai gently.

She walked towards Mother in a daze. There was a small cut in her forehead and blood was trickling out slowly.

'When I was young I used to throw stones at the pregnant stray dog at the market place. Sometimes we even threw stones at the beggars who came to our houses. This is my punishment,' she said softly.

'Oh, Mui Tsai, I'm so sorry. They don't know,' Mother consoled the poor girl.

'And they will never know. But they look good, don't they, my children? Their eyes are bright and one day they will inherit all that is my master's.'

'Yes, they will.'

She turned away sadly and entered the house through the back door. That was the last time Mother saw Mui Tsai. Suddenly she was no more and in her place was another Mui Tsai who went about her business without a smile or the slightest inclination to befriend the neighbours. For a time no one knew what had happened to our Mui Tsai or where she was. Then one day, Old Soong's cook answered Mother's query by making a circling motion with her index finger against her temple.

Ayah

It all happened such a long, long time ago and to return to that time so full of hope is horrendously painful now. I was a young man then and it didn't seem wrong to gain a bride with a bouquet of lies, but I have paid dearly for it and yet I wouldn't change one moment of my life with your grandmother.

Not one moment.

I wasn't allowed to see the bride until the day of the wedding. When I heard the drummers quicken their beat I knew it meant she was approaching. Unable to wait another moment, I looked up to see the face of my new bride and I couldn't believe my good fortune when I saw your grandmother. The only secret aspiration that I had ever harboured was to see a cave of ice. But here in my grasp was far better than my wildest dream. Here was a girl of unimaginable wild beauty.

As I stared at her she looked up, but because I was so big and ugly, the first emotion that came into her face when our eyes met was horror. For a moment she looked around desperately like a small, frightened deer that a hunter's net had snared in the night.

She looked defenceless and if she had remained so I would have cared for her dearly and tenderly like I did my first wife, but as I watched a wonderful transformation occurred. Her spine straightened and her eyes became fierce and bold. It was like watching a deer turn into a large and beautiful tiger. And quite without warning my drab little world turned upside down. Inside me I felt my stomach slip, slide and softly sink right down to the bottom of my body. 'Who are you?' my shocked heart whispered inside my body. Then and there I fell in love. So deeply that the organs inside my body moved.

I knew straightaway that she would never be just someone to bring up my two children or the companion in my old age but the woman who would turn me into a puppet on a string. With one fair hand she had jerked my motionless limbs into life. Ah, and what exquisite movements my limbs made under her bold hand. I thought I had grasped the moon that day and it was many, many years later that I realised it was only the reflection of the moon in a blue plastic pail that I had touched. The moon is beyond my grasp. Always has been and always will be. It was time that finally revealed that to me.

I can remember my wedding night like the most beautiful dream. Like a pair of wings. Suddenly having something so precious in your hands that your pathetic life changes for ever. Not with happiness but with fear. The fear of losing it. And because I knew I was undeserving. Those wings had been gained through deceit. Soon even the gold watch, that much-admired thing of beauty and status, would be no more. It was only borrowed from the same friend who had lent me the car and Bilal the driver. In my guilty heart I loved her already. Deeply. I would have done anything, gone anywhere for her. My soul bled to think of that day when she would come to despise me. The old witch Pani had deceived her mother with tales of riches only a good woman would believe – and yet how could I condemn her, when her net of lies had caught such a rare butterfly?

I fooled myself that one day my rare butterfly might be persuaded to love me. The years, I thought, would wash away my disgrace. The years passed and no, she did not learn to love me but I pretended to myself that the special butterfly cared in its own special way.

She was so small I could span her hips with my hands. My child bride. There was no way to love the girl without hurting her. When she was sure I was asleep that dark night she sneaked out to bathe in a neighbour's well. When she returned I could see she had been crying. Through the black slit between my eyelashes I watched her watching me. In the emotions that crossed her young face I saw a child's hope and a woman's fears. Slowly, slowly, as if against her will but pushed nevertheless by an innocent curiosity, she brushed my forehead with a tentative hand. Her hand was cold and damp. She turned away from me and fell asleep quickly, like a child. I remember the wedge of her back, sleeping. I watched its gentle rise and fall, gazing at skin so smooth as if woven from the finest silk thread, my mind wandering to the stories the old women in my village used to tell when I was a young boy. About the lonely old man on the moon who enters the rooms of beautiful women and lies down to sleep beside them. She was so beautiful, my wife. That night I saw the moonlight shine through the open windows and lie softly on her sleeping face. In the pale light she was a goddess. Beautiful as a pearl.

My first wife had been the gentlest soul alive. She was so gentle and so tender-hearted that a fortune-teller had predicted that she didn't have long to live on this earth. I had cared for her dearly but from the moment Lakshmi's eyes had challenged mine at the wedding ceremony I was passionately and deeply in love with her. Her clever, dark eyes had flashed with a fire that burned the pit of my stomach, but they took me for a fool and I suppose that is what I am. Even as a child I was slow-witted. They called me the slow mule back home. I wanted more than anything else to protect her and shower her with all the riches that her mother had been promised, but I was only a clerk. A clerk with no prospects, no savings and nothing of value. Even the money I had earned before my first marriage had gone to make up my sisters' dowries.

When we first returned to Malaysia, she used to weep late into the night when she thought I was asleep. I would wake up in the early hours of the morning and hear her crying softly in the kitchen. I knew she longed for her mother. During the day she could keep busy with her vegetable patch and household chores, but at night the loneliness swelled inside her.

One night I could bear it no longer. I got out of bed and made my way into the kitchen. Like a child was was lying on her belly, her forehead resting on her crossed forearms. I watched the curve of her neck and I was suddenly filled with aching desire. I wanted to take her in my arms and feel her soft skin lying against mine. I walked up to her and put my hand on her head but she reared up with a hiss of terror, clasping her right hand to her heart. 'Oh, how you scared me!' she accused. She leaned further back and looked at me expectantly. Her eyes gleamed wetly but she had closed her face like a drawer. For a while I stood looking at her unyielding figure and her cold, tense face and then I turned away and went back to bed. She didn't want my love or me. Both she considered abhorrent.

Dreaming in the night I sometimes reached out for her

and even in sleep she moaned and turned away. And I knew again that I loved in vain. She would never come to love me. I gave up my children for her and yet even now, after everything that has happened and everything that I have lost, I know there is not a single thing I would change.

The day my Mohini was born was the biggest day of my life. When I first looked at her I actually felt a pain, as if someone had reached into my body and squeezed my heart. I stared at her in disbelief. One word rushed into my brain. 'Nefertiti,' I whispered.

Nefertiti – the beautiful one is come.

She was so perfect that incredulous happy tears gathered in my eyes that I, of all people, had been responsible for producing this marvel. I looked into her tiny sleeping face, touched the straight, black hair and knew her to be mine. Now as a present for thee . . . one human heart . . . mine. Your grandmother called her Mohini but to me she was always Nefertiti. It was how I thought of her. In my mind Mohini was an illustration in an old Sanskrit book of my father's. Standing as slinky as a Snake Goddess, her hair long and black, her sidelong glance inspiring equal measures of fear and pleasure. Her reckless feet dancing gaily atop the hearts of many men. Boldly, proudly, she enjoys her corruption. No, no, my Nefertiti was like the most innocent angel. An opening flower.

I was thirty-nine and I looked at my useless life full of one failure after another and knew that if I never passed another office exam, never did another thing, that precious moment when the midwife handed me my Nefertiti, tightly bundled in an old sarong smelling of myrrh, would be enough.

As the years went by I found it easy to bear the

supercilious looks of my juniors as they passed their exams and became my seniors. One by one they passed me, unvarying in their slightly contemptuous, slightly pitying look and yet I was happy. The children had begun to appear – each one something special. I would cycle home, the wind in my hair, as fast as I could with a bunch of bananas or a quarter of a jackfruit tied to the handle-bars and as soon as I turned into our cul-de-sac something would happen inside me. I would slow down so I could look again at the house where my family lived. Inside that small, uninspired house was everything I had ever wanted in life. Inside was an amazing woman and children who made me catch my breath. A part of Lakshmi and, to my unending joy, a part of me.

And then without any warning they came to take her away. Just like that they killed her, the child we had so carefully tended for years. Oh, these stupid tears. After all this time. That unbearable night when she came to me. Look at these stupid tears, they refuse to stop. I am like an old woman. Wait, let me get my handkerchief out. Give me a minute – I am just an old fool.

I recall sitting in my bedroom with the lights off, my body on fire with fever. The shock of her abduction had brought on a bout of malaria. There was only a little light from the half moon in the sky. It was a hot night and earlier I had heard Lakshmi bathing. I remember I was praying, my breath burning hot. I never used to pray. I accused the holy of pure greed. 'It is a fact,' I pontificated grandly, 'that we pray for more.' I argued that even at the highest level a request for self-enlightenment was still a selfish want, but the truth was I was too lazy to offer my thanks for the good fortune that had fallen into my lap. 'God is inside the heart,' I said grandly. I thought I was a good man, and that was enough. After her birth I took it for granted that I had been born with a garland of good things, but that night I was restless and full of foreboding. I raised my hands and cried out to God just like all the other despicable, needy human beings. 'Help me, dear God,' I prayed. 'Give me back my Nefertiti.'

Inside my head there was no peace. A million visions desired entry, twisting and turning with grotesque grins and mean eyes. They were all unfinished and raw. I closed my eyes to chase the burning visions away and, quite suddenly, I saw Mohini escape through a door with a faulty lock. Perhaps I was hallucinating but I saw her run down a long corridor, her bare feet noiseless but the asthmatic rattling loud inside her chest. She ran gasping past tall windows with closed shutters. There was a turn in the wide corridor that ended in a door left tantalisingly ajar. I saw it all, her face convoluted with fear and then the hope that illuminated it as she raced towards the open door. Then I saw the guards. How they laughed!

They laughed in her pale wheezing face. It was all a trick.

I grabbed a blanket and huddled into it. I was cold. Cold. So cold.

I saw a hand, thick and meaty, squeeze her chin and a brutal, red tongue appear from nowhere to lick her eyelids. I saw her fall to the ground gasping desperately for breath. She called for me then, 'Papa, Papa.' But I couldn't help her. Shivering in my bed I watched her turn blue and I saw them try to pour water down her throat. She choked and gasped. They stood back confused and helpless and watched her die. Ah, the cold in my heart.

I saw her in a hole with her eyes closed but then she opened them and looked directly at me. I saw her wearing her mother's sari and standing in the middle of a jungle waiting to be married but her unadorned hair was spread out over her shoulders like a grieving widow's. It was like being in a nightmare.

'It is the fever. It is only the fever,' I whispered wildly into my wet pillow, my teeth chattering wildly. I held my head in my hands and rocked so the pictures in my head would all blur and slowly fall out and in their place would only be soft darkness. I rocked and I rocked until the pictures blurred and ran into each other like blood.

'Oh Nefertiti,' I whispered brokenly. 'It's only the malaria. It's the shock. It's only the shock.' I was going mad with cold. My own helplessness angered me. I hated myself. She was alone and scared. If only I had been home instead of sitting outside the Chartered Bank with the old Sikh guard, sharing a cheroot . . .

The guilt. I cannot tell you how it pressed upon me that night. Why, why, *why* on that day of all days did I leave the house? Hopelessly I banged my forehead against the wall. I wanted to die.

It was the beautiful, spoilt child of death from the moonlit night outside the death pit from years ago. He was annoyed that I had refused to play his little game. 'Have me. Go on take me now,' I pleaded with the vindictive child. 'But return her, return her, return her.'

I chanted vaguely remembered mantras from my childhood. If I wished hard enough . . . If I prayed hard enough . . . If I went to the temple and made a vow to fast for thirty days, shaved my head and carried a *kavadi* on my head on Thaipusam Day would she come back?

Lost in my black despair it took some moments for me to realise that my head had cleared. I didn't feel cold and the terrible pain inside my heart had suddenly disappeared. I lifted my head. The room was still lit by bluish moonlight, but something had changed. Confused, I looked around and a feeling of peace and calm flowed over me. All my cares, fears and petty insecurities dropped away. So beautiful was the feeling that I thought I was dying. Then I understood. It was her. She was free at last. I told her to be happy. I told her I would take care of her mother and I told her I would love her for ever.

Then the feeling was gone as suddenly as it had come. All the pain of her loss came crashing back. And what a blinding loss it was. I clutched at my chest and the room pressed down on my freezing body like a wooden coffin.

My poor life stretched out long, dull and profitless in front of me. Inside my chest my heart was not a whole thing any more but a mass of red shreds. The red ribbons flew inside my body and caught on the other organs inside me. They fluttered there helplessly. Even now they are there, caught between the branches of my ribs or lying crushed between my liver and my kidney or even curled around my intestines. They flutter like red flags of defeat and pain. She was only a dream.

At first I could see the same raw pain in my wife and eldest son's eyes, but then their pain turned into something else. Something unwholesome. Something I couldn't understand. I would look into Lakshmi's eyes and something like hate would slither in the depths of them. She became ill-tempered and cruel, and he became a nightmare. Fresh hate used to shine in his face when his mother asked him to help Jeyan with his maths. He gritted his teeth and stared murderously at his younger brother, waiting for that poor boy to make a mistake so he could have the pleasure of hitting his head with a wooden ruler or pinching him until his dark-brown skin turned grey. His venom remained unsatisfied. Once he started you could actually see him war with himself to stop.

One day I tried to talk to him. I motioned for him to sit beside me but he stood before me tall and strong, his limbs powerful and full of life. He was not a reflection of me. All my sons are a rejection of me. If poor Jeyan is like me then it is certainly not through choice. In my slow way I talked for too long. He looked down at me from his contemptuous height and stared at me sullenly. Not a word passed his lips. No explanations, no excuses. No sense of regret.

Then I said, 'Son, she is gone.'

And suddenly a look of such shame and such pain crossed his face that he looked like a trapped, injured animal. He opened his mouth as if to draw breath and instead drew in a passing spirit. It was a furious, turbulent spirit that he swallowed. It caused the most shocking transformation. *He was getting ready to lash out at me, his father.* His shoulders clenched and his hands bunched into hard balls but before the animal could turn on me Lakshmi walked into the room. Another astonishing transformation occurred, the uncontrollable rage escaped out of his open mouth. He dropped his head, his shoulders hunched and his fists opened like a dead man's. He feared her. He understood instinctively her power. The uncontrollable monster had a master. His master was his mother.

The past is like an armless, legless cripple with crafty eyes, a vindictive tongue and a long memory. He wakes me up in the morning with dreadful taunting in my ear. 'Look,' he hisses, 'look at what you have done to my future.' And yet I wait behind doors expecting her to burst through. 'Papa,' she cries, holding a useless green pebble in her hand 'I think I found a green malachite.' My shredded heart has done this for twenty-three years. And every evening when she doesn't rush through the doors the sunset will seem that little bit duller, the house that little bit stranger, the children that little bit further away and Lakshmi that little bit angrier. It was the war. It took so much away from everyone. Not just me.

I am not a brave man and everybody knows that I am not a clever man. In fact, I am not even an interesting man. I sit on my veranda all day long dozing, dreaming and staring into nothing, but by God, how I hate the Japanese. The mean yellow faces, the cold black slits through which they watched her die. Even the sound of their language can turn me cold with murderous rage. How could God have made such a cruel people? How could He have let them take the one thing of value that I had ever had? Sometimes I can't sleep for all the thoughts of the different tortures I would inflict on them. Piece by piece, their limbs I hang from trees, or a mouthful of needles I feed to them, or perhaps I offer a small friendly fire at the soles of their feet. The smell of their toes burning. Yes, they keep me awake, these fiendish thoughts. I toss and turn in my big bed and my rare butterfly mutters under her breath with irritation. It is what the war did to us. It made us hungry for what is not ours.

Lakshmi

Anna got wet in the rain on Friday evening. By Saturday she had a mild cold. I put her to bed, rubbed her chest with Tiger Balm, gave her a drink of hot coffee with an egg beaten into it and wrapped her up in blankets, but by Sunday her chest was tight with phlegm. When I heard the beginnings of that terrible rattle I was filled with fear. Anna was showing the first signs of the disease that made Mohini unable to bear her ordeal with the Japanese brutes, otherwise they would have returned her broken body as they had Ah Moi's. I ran to Old Soong's house.

'The red-eyed rat,' I cried breathlessly to his cook. 'Where can I get it?'

The pregnant red-eyed rat arrived in a cage. Ayah refused to even look at it. He tried to persuade me but my mind was made up. 'She is going to swallow that animal,' I said tightly, my eyes flinty.

Anna looked at the rat with perfect fear in her eyes.

'Ama, actually I think I am much better today,' she announced, smiling brightly.

'Really? Well, come here then,' I said coolly. I put my head to her chest and heard the horrible rattle. 'Sevenese, pound some ginger for your sister,' I called out.

Anna walked back to the bedroom, her shoulders slumped. Why did everybody behave as though I was doing something that would hurt them? I wanted my daughter well again. I regret with all my heart that I did not give the newborn rat to Mohini. If I had not listened to my husband's paranoid arguments she might still be alive now. The rat was almost due to give birth. The main thing was to swallow the baby in the first few moments of birth, just after removing the sac. I watched the mother rat very closely. Often she regarded me with clever, shining eyes as she scuttled about in her cage. I wondered if she knew that I wanted her babies. I kept the floor of the cage very clean.

The rat gave birth. Before she could even begin licking her babies with her disease-carrying tongue I pulled one tiny, reddish-pink rat no bigger than my thumb out of the cage. It made a tiny, tiny movement with its legs. Quickly I wiped it on a clean cloth. Anna was looking at me with an alarmed, incredulous expression. She began to shake her head and walk backwards. I followed her until she stood with the bed behind her.

'I can't, Ama. Please,' she whispered.

I dipped the head of the tiny rat in honey. 'Open your mouth,' I ordered.

'No, I can't.'

'Lakshmnan, bring the cane.' The cane arrived very quickly.

She opened her mouth. Her face was pale and her eyes were glazed in horror. 'Ama, it's moving,' she cried suddenly. 'It's legs are moving.' Her mouth closed with a snap.

'Open your mouth now,' I ordered. 'It has to be swallowed immediately.'

She shook her head and began to cry. 'I can't,' she sobbed. 'It's still alive.'

'Why do I have such disobedient children? All the Chinese people cure themselves like this. Why are you making such a fuss? This is all your father's fault. The way he spoils you all. OK, bring the cane, Lakshmnan.' Lakshmnan came forward. He raised his right hand and his sister half opened her mouth with a whimper. I grasped her chin.

'Wider,' I commanded.

Her mouth widened fractionally and I lowered the tiny rat inside. I thought that if I put it as far down her throat as I could, it would be easier for her, but I saw its legs scratch her tongue and the next minute her eyes closed and the face under my grasping hand became a dead weight. She had fainted. I was still holding the rat by the tail when she fell back onto the pillows. My husband, who had been watching at the doorway, pushed forward, grabbed the rat from my hand and, walking to the window, flung it as far away as he could. He looked at me with great sadness then held Anna in his arms and fanned her gently with an exercise book that was lying by the bedside.

'Lakshmi, you have turned into a monster,' he said quietly as he rocked her. 'Bring some warm water for your sister,' he said to no one in particular. Lalita ran into the kitchen and came back with the water.

I returned the rat the next day and Anna has suffered from asthma ever since.

You are shocked but there is worse to come. The monster I missed in the mirror.

Lalita wanted a coconut bun when the bread man came around one afternoon. Fifteen cents a coconut bun cost in those days. I opened my purse and could tell at a glance that some money was missing. I counted it carefully and mentally calculated every single thing I had bought in the market that morning then I counted it all again. Yes, one ringgit was definitely missing. I had 39,346 ringgit in the bank, 100 ringgit under the mattress, 50 ringgit in an envelope tied together with mother's letters and 15 ringgit and perhaps 80 or 90 cents in my purse. I asked my children one by one if they had taken the ringgit. 'No,' they all said, shaking their heads. The bread man and his buns left our neighbourhood. No one was having anything until I got to the bottom of the disappearing ringgit mystery.

Only Jeyan was still not home. I knew it was him. It had to be. How dare he help himself to the contents of my purse! Did he imagine I wouldn't notice? I began a slow boil.

'It must be Jeyan,' Lakshmnan echoed my thoughts.

'Could you have made a mistake, Ama?' asked Anna.

'Of course not,' I answered, greatly irritated. I looked at the wall clock. It was three in the afternoon. 'Bring me some tea.' I walked outside and sat down to wait. From the veranda I could see the clock inside. The tea arrived and I drank it. I looked at the clock. Thirty minutes had passed. The rage grew. The monster serpent that lived inside me awakened in the terrible heat. I shifted tensely in my chair. My own son, stealing money from me. I had to teach him a lesson that he would never forget. I looked at the time. It was four o'clock. I stood up and paced the veranda restlessly. From the corner of my eyes I saw the children sitting nervously upright in their chairs. I leaned against a wooden post and saw my dear Jeyan hurrying down the path, his guilt written all over his square, stupid face. I watched him come up to the house. He slowed his walk into a sort of shuffle. Didn't he know that prolonging the inevitable confrontation would only make me angrier still? As dumb as a lumbering beast. Everybody knows you have to brand a bull to teach it anything. I would brand him.

'Where have you been?' my voice was deadly calm.

'To the pictures.' It was to his credit that he didn't lie.

'How did you pay for the entry?'

'I found a ringgit by the roadside.' His voice trembled and shook with fear but what an effect it had on me. I lost myself in my fury. The bubbling pit erupted and the monster in me took over. There is no other way to explain it. The last thing I remember myself saying was, 'How did you pay for the entry?' That was me, beloved mother, but after that the monster took over, said and did the things I could never have said or done. I stood silently by and watched everything the monster's cold fury did. It wanted to see him suffer and beg. I saw it take a deep, controlled breath. It was incredible how calm the monster was.

'Lakshmnan,' the monster called coldly.

'Yes, Ama,' my eldest son answered eagerly.

'Take your brother and tie him to the post in the back-yard and beat him until he tells us where he got the money from,' it instructed.

'Lakshmnan moved quickly. He was a big, strong boy and in minutes Jeyan's skinny limbs were firmly tied. The serpent stood at the kitchen door and watched Lakshmnan take off his brother's shirt. That eldest boy of mine showed a whole lot of unexpected initiative. Dark skin gleamed in the sunlight. I stood at the kitchen window and watched Lakshmnan run to fetch the cane. I watched from afar as the cane vengefully struck the skinny back. Very clearly, in between frenzied screams, came the confession.

'I took the money from your purse, Ama. I'm sorry. I'm so sorry. I'll never do it again.'

The monster turned away. The confession was not enough. Deadly calm, it walked to the bottle with the orange top. It shook some of the fine, red powder into its cupped palm and then it went outside. It stood before Jeyan's writhing body. His upturned face twisted with pain and fear begged, 'I'm so sorry, Ama. I'm so sorry.' Tears ran down his face in little rivulets.

The monster stared at him emotionlessly.

'I promise I'll never do it again,' he whined frantically.

While I was gone the raging monster looked deep into my little boy's pained, frightened eyes and was suddenly livid once more. It bent down and, without warning, blew hard into the palm of its hands. A cloud of red powder rose into the air. He closed his eyes but not fast enough. The effect of the chilli powder was instantaneous. It made him scream hysterically, his whole body jerking convulsively, his fingers clawing the air around the post uselessly.

Stunned, Lakshmnan stared at me dumbstruck then he returned to his appointed task of whipping his writhing brother mercilessly. I walked back into the house and out to the veranda. The screams became almost delirious.

'*Ama!*' Jeyan shrieked for me.

On the veranda of the snake-charmer's house stood his thin wife looking at me.

'Ama!' Jeyan screamed again.

All the other verandas were deserted but curtains twitched.

The monster sat down. A gentle breeze was blowing.

'Ama, help me!' Jeyan yelled and suddenly, as if shaken out of a dream, I woke up. The monster was gone. I turned my head and a tearful, terrified Anna was staring at me.

'Tell your brother to stop,' I cried.

She dashed out to the back shouting, 'Stop! Ama said to stop! Stop, now. Stop beating him. You're going to kill him.'

Lakshmnan came in dripping with sweat. His hands were shaking but his eyes were wild with a savage excitement. I saw the footmarks the devil had left on his wet forehead.

'Go and have a bath,' I told him, avoiding his eyes. His glittering eyes saddened me. With the monster gone I felt strangely hollow.

Then Lalita came out from under the table, the missing ringgit resting in the middle of her palm. It was I, I who had dropped the money under the table. My heart hurt. He hadn't taken the money. I had got carried away. I had gone too far. Where had I learned such cruelty? What had I done?

Outside I saw Anna washing her brother's eyes and cutting him down. Like a limp rag doll, he fell to the ground. A dark mess on the sand. I picked up a bottle of sesame seed oil and went outside to give it to Anna.

'Rub some on his back,' I instructed. There was a catch in my voice. Anna's hands were shaking. I turned my eyes to the trembling body slumped on the ground. Jeyan's skin had peeled off in places and strips of raw flesh were visible. I took his chin in my hand and looked into his badly swollen, red-rimmed eyes. His face felt wet and feverish. Angry red veins had flowered all over the whites of his eyes but he would survive.

'I'm sorry,' I said, and saw in the narrowed, purple blackness of his eyes, very clearly hate.

The evening sun was setting and the orange glow looked near enough to reach out and touch. The sky was the most delightful pink. Like a baby's bottom slapped hard. Mother used to say that a pink sky meant a good prawn catch for the fishermen. I closed my eyes and in the sky were Mother's long, beautiful eyes. They were wet and sad. What have you done? I felt my own tears prick the back of my closed lids. I heard her voice say from far, far away, 'Have you forgotten everything I taught you, my wilful, rebellious child? Have you forgotten the beautiful pregnant queen with the cruel heart?' No, I had not forgotten. I remembered every word.

'She was so evil that after she had eaten her fill of the sweet, honey mangoes she rubbed sand into the flesh she did not eat so that the stray pregnant dog watching her could not even eat her leftovers. She sniggered into her cupped palms but her cruelty did not go unnoticed. You see, my darling Lakshmi, no cruelty ever goes unnoticed. God is watching. When the black-hearted queen's delivery date arrived she gave birth to a litter of puppies, and the mongrel dog to a prince and a princess in the palace gardens. The king instantly understood what had happened. He was so furious he banished his queen from the palace and adopted the children as his own.'

I walked back into my wooden palace. My husband would be home soon and I prepared myself for the silent censure in his small, sad eyes. I promised to guard the ferocious monster inside me better. And for while he stayed silent but we both knew he was waiting to get out, take over. Sometimes I felt him pounding in my veins, thirsting for blood.

Anna

My brother Sevenese said that sometimes animals spoke to him in his dreams. Once in the middle of the night he dreamed of a cat that stood outside our door and said quite clearly, 'It's so cold. Please let me in.'

Startled, he woke up. Outside, a storm bellowed inconsolably. Flying winds lashed at the window shutters and screamed at our front door. Huge drops of rain drummed loudly on the corrugated zinc roof over the extension. Inside the house, the air was damp and heavy.

My brother got out of bed, propelled by a force greater than him: fearless curiosity. Flashes of lightning filled the corridor with white light and a clap of the thunder made him jump and clasp his hands to his ears. On such a troubled night, who knew what treacherous spirit, what insane demons waited on the other side of our closed front door, but open the door he must. At the other end of the corridor in the flickering light of the oil lamp, he saw Mother's shadow on the kitchen wall, bent over her sewing. He pulled back the bolt on the front door and opened it fearlessly.

On the doorstep, patiently waiting, was a bedraggled mother cat and five shivering little kittens. The cat looked up and stared unblinkingly at him, her eyes bright sapphires in the grey of the stormy night. He stared back speechless but, as if he had invited her in, she gently grasped in her mouth her shivering babies by the loose skin on their necks and carried them one by one into the warmth of our kitchen. Sevenese and Mother made a bed with rags on the kitchen floor, watered down some condensed milk in a shallow plate and watched with satisfaction as it disappeared underneath her little pink tongue.

According to my brother that is the only time he can ever remember feeling close to Mother. He forgot about the thin cane hanging on its hook on the kitchen wall and was aware only of the sweet smell of banana jam on Mother's breath when she held him close to her and kissed the top of his head. He felt warm and loved and was glad to be indoors with her while the night raged outside.

Mother allowed him to keep the cat. The kittens she found homes for.

For a stray, the cat was strangely regal. Tall, with a small triangular face and a coat of the lightest, most luxurious grey you could possibly imagine, she stalked about the house, her nose high in the air. My brother grandly named her Kutub Minar and made her a basket beside him. Some nights when he awoke sweating and terrified by one of his wretched nightmares, he turned towards her basket and never failed to see the reassuring sight of her head raised, two blue pools of light regarding him steadily. When she stared at him with those moonlight-washed eyes my brother swore a silent energy passed through him until his heart stopped pounding madly in his chest. And only when he was calm once more did she yawn widely, lay down her head, close her eyes and fall back into a patch of yellow sunlight in a field of glorious flowers.

Kutub Minar made certain to keep out of Mother's

way. She rested her small, sharp chin on her paws while her alert, beautiful eyes followed Mother's every move warily. Mother was like a caged panther. It is no wonder she made the cat nervous. Animals are attracted to still, peaceful people. People like my father and Lalita. The first time Sevenese came home from the snake-charmer's house the cat arched her spine, hackles quivering, ears flat against the sides of her beautiful face and swore at him. Her long tail lashed from side to side. Sevenese stared at her distended claws in astonishment. She was surely getting ready to spring at his throat. Then all at once she realised that it was her beloved master that she spat at and with a strangled cry she dropped her tail and streaked into the fields at the back of our house, disappearing into the woods. It was either the smell of the snakes or the hunger of the malignant spirits that the snake-charmer consorted with that spooked her so. She remained a good companion all through my brother's childhood, dying suddenly when he turned seventeen. One morning we woke up and found her dead in her basket, curled up as if deeply asleep.

For many years after Mohini died I used to wake up in the night and see Sevenese sitting up in the dark of our bedroom waiting for her ghost to appear. He sat so silently and so still it was freaky to watch. Last time he had been caught off guard. This time he had questions for her and things to tell her. He had not dreamed her. 'Listen carefully for my voice, my little watchman,' she had said. He listened very carefully but the years passed without another word from her. Divalis came and went. Every year we surrounded the house with clay lamps the night before, as we had always done, awakened at dawn, bathed and wore the bright new clothes that Mother had sat up late into the nights making and ate a big lunch full of choice food. Everyone's favourite dish was on the table. Lalita and I still scrupulously carried trays of festive cakes and trembling bits of colourful jelly over to our neighbours' homes but Divali had lost something. It had become hollow. Divali in an unhappy household is like a smile from a dead child. The smile so brittle that none of us dared speak about it even though we all saw it. It was there in all our eyes as we smiled cautiously at one another and watched our family members become distant strangers.

Lakshmnan, the strangest of all. It seemed to our confused eyes as if he hated us and openly enjoyed any spectacle of our humiliation or pain. And there were many. Cannily he redeemed himself in Mother's eyes with the exceptional grades he brought home. He was so clever he was able to sell his class notes to his friends on a weekly basis. Lakshmnan studied like a fiend. He poured himself into his work. Every day he studied late into the night. He had the shrewd idea that he might meet the Goddess of Riches in the house of the Goddess of Education. He was in a labyrinth but at the end of his labyrinth was a pot of gold, wondrous riches and precious stones. He wanted that which he could touch proudly and use carelessly. He wanted long cars and big houses. He wanted to handle money with his left hand. If education was the tasteless bread he must eat in exchange for his shining cold dream then eat it fiercely he would. Top place in his class was a savagely fought battle between him and another boy called Ramachandran. If Lakshmnan returned home with a black face it meant Ramachandran had pulled first place out from under his feet.

We had all missed three years of proper education under the Japanese so when they left we were returned to the same level we had been at before the war began. So it was only when Lakshmnan turned nineteen that his senior exams sailed out of the horizon and loomed closer. In those days, senior papers were marked overseas in England, and afterwards you could use your School Certificate to attend college or even go straight to university. Lakshmnan did nothing but study. His curly head bent over a book, his brow furrowed with concentration, consuming endless cups of Mother's steaming hot coffee. She was very proud of him.

Success seemed assured.

On the day of the exam Lakshmnan left confidently, but even before the sun had cleared the tops of the coconut trees Mother saw him return, escorted by Mr Vellupilai himself.

'What's the matter?' she asked worriedly, walking around the side of the house to meet them.

'I don't know, Ama, but I couldn't even see the paper for the pain inside my head,' Lakshmnan said. There were dark shadows under his eyes and dazzled even by the weak morning sunlight they squinted at Mother from his bemused face.

'The teacher found him slumped over his paper on his desk. I think you had better take your son to a doctor,' Mr Vellupilai advised gravely.

Immediately Mother took Lakshmnan to the hospital. They couldn't tell her what the matter was. Perhaps it was strain or pressure. However they said Lakshmnan needed glasses. He was short-sighted. Mother ordered the spectacles at an optician in town. Lakshmnan walked beside her dazed, disbelieving. What had happened was a tragedy. It showed in Mother's face when we came back from school. They had both set great store by his success at the exams. Now he would have to wait a whole year to re-sit them.

One evening I looked out of the kitchen window and saw Lakshmnan sitting under the jasmine tree smoking. He was smoking with jerky, nervous puffs and I realised instantly that he wanted Mother to see him. Some part of him wanted to goad her, test her. My brother was bored.

When all is lost there is only the Devil and the god he reveres, Money. Lakshmnan had always burned to be rich but now he wanted it easy. His greedy heart led him to a crowd of wealthy Chinese boys. They had cars, girl-friends with the kind of names you would give to a fluffy kitten, a collection of bad habits that they were oddly proud of, and they talked of business deals worth thousands and thousands of ringgit. They boasted carelessly of their losses at the gambling tables. 'Easy come, easy go,' they crowed. My brother recognised in their loosely fisted hands the seeds of the secret trees that bore the fruit of money. How he admired them! He did not see that inside them beat cold hearts the size of a clenched fist. From them he learned to say, '*Sup sup sui*' – no problem, piece of cake, and '*Mo siong korn*' – don't worry about it, it doesn't matter.

He never brought these new friends around to the house but I saw him with them on my way back from school. I didn't like the look of their sly, narrow eyes but I never told Mother about them. I was too frightened to tell on him. Also I guessed that they only wanted his notes. No, not the ones that were for sale but the ones that made him the top of his class. Come this time next year I knew they would be gone, their bald heads and hooked beaks deep inside another carcass.

Lakshmnan and I sat for the senior exams together. This time around he didn't study. 'I can still remember what I learned last year,' he announced arrogantly as he put on his shoes to go out for the night. When the results came he had only managed a Grade Two. Ramachandran the year before had picked up a Grade One and was studying at Sandhurst Military College in England. He sat in a shoeshine's chair, had his photograph taken and sent it home with the caption: *Look how far I've come. The colonial masters are cleaning my shoes now.*

With a Grade Two, Lakshmnan's highest opening was as Labour Officer in a Government office, but even that option was closed to him as there were no jobs around at that time. I had attained a Grade Three and my head-master offered me a teaching post. Mother was pleased and I became a teacher.

Lakshmnan was furious and frustrated. I can remember him nervously hurrying to and fro in the living room like a caged ape for hours on end. Other times he sat in the living room smoking endlessly, his fingers tapping the wooden table distractedly, staring at nothing, with a pile of empty cigarette packets strewn carelessly on the table and an ashtray full of dead stubs. For many weeks he ranted and raved about his bad luck then finally, gritting his teeth with rage, he joined me in the teaching profession. That was not the plan. How he hated teaching! Walking along the corridor I have passed his class and seen him teaching with his fists clenched.

The way the teaching system worked in my day was that you were trained for three months on the job. Every weekend you went away to a different location where you received your training. Lakshmnan wanted to do his training in Singapore. It was not the 'superior level of training' that he was really after but the bright city lights. He was truly excited by the idea and for the first time he became almost human in his interactions with us. Our house radiated with the sunshine of his altered self and Mother's happiness. He had been so difficult and so unhappy for so long that Mother thought it must be a good idea to send him to Singapore. It had grieved her to see him sit in the living room impatient and restless, smoking box after box of cigarettes. That afternoon they sat in the living room discussing the logistics of the idea.

My brother Sevenese was reading a comic book in the bedroom when a voice popped into his head. The comic book fell out of his suddenly nerveless fingers. It was the voice he had been waiting for, for so many years that he had nearly forgotten it. *She* had spoken to him. He jumped out of bed.

'Don't let him go,' the voice said.

Immediately he ran into the living room and announced in a rush that Mohini had told him that Lakshmnan must not go. First there was shock on Lakshmnan's face, then pain, monstrous pain. He still would not talk about her death. In fact, the mere mention of her name made him leave the room.

'What utter nonsense!' he shouted, springing out of his chair.

'What are you talking about?' Mother asked Sevenese, blanching like an almond.

'I just heard Mohini's voice say very clearly, "Don't let him go,"' Sevenese said.

'Are you sure?' Mother asked. A worried frown buried itself into her forehead.

'I don't believe this. Mohini has come back from the dead with advice about how I should run my life. This is absolutely ridiculous and I can't believe that you're entertaining such rubbish,' Lakshmnan spluttered at Mother. He exploded childishly, 'I can never do anything I want to in this madhouse.'

'Why are you so angry? Just wait a minute,' Mother said, but Lakshmnan did what he usually did. He stamped off, slamming his clenched fist into a pile of bricks outside in uncontrollable temper.

Of course Lakshmnan left for Singapore. Mother was unhappy but to stand in the way of his fist pounding and teeth grinding took a much harder heart than that soft spot she had reserved for him. She sent him off with a suitcase full of new clothes and his favourite savoury snacks. At first he wrote home quite often, cheerful letters that were full of his comings and goings, and it seemed as if Mother had made the right decision to let him go after all. But Mohini was soon proved right. Without any warning the letters dried up. An uninformative postcard arrived after two months and then nothing at all. Mother began to worry and fret. She should never have let him go. In her perpetual bad temper everything irritated her. Poor Father, for many weeks I don't think he even dared speak.

Then came the day Mother could wait no longer. She sent a friend's son to find out what was happening to her first-born. He returned with the news that Lakshmnan had become a gambler. He was to be found at mah-jong clubs in the worst parts of Chinatown. In those seedy halls he had quickly cultivated a passion for gambling that was so strong you could almost see him salivate at the sound of mah-jong pieces clicking. He spent all his wages and forgot to attend his teaching classes. The headmistress, mindful of his height, glaring eyes and fist-punching ways, quickly transferred him to a tiny school in a little fishing island off mainland Singapore so she would not have to deal with his poor attendance record personally. The tiny village barely had electricity.

To think he had run away from Kuantan to end up there.

He hated it and left immediately, but without funds he could only sleep on a friend's floor. By then he had accumulated large debts. There was disbelief in the family as those incredible words issued from the polite stranger's mouth, in between sips of Mother's tea.

In her usual efficient way Mother settled Lakshmnan's debts and sent him a return ticket. He came back, to our utter amazement, not with his tail between his legs but like a conquering hero. Mother cooked his favourite dahl curry and the chapattis he favoured. She bought him a Wolsley car in return for the promise that he would find a job and settle down. He looked grand behind the wheel of his new car. He found himself a teaching position but the call to gamble was in his blood. It would not be silent. It coaxed, gnawed, nagged, sang and whispered, 'Mah-jong!' like satin against silk inside his veins until he could bear it no more. It was a relief to quieten the relentless whispering even if he lost all. We listened blankly as he explained, with his forefinger and thumb millimetres apart from each other, how close he had come to winning. So close that he must try again.

The terrible battle in my family began. He demanded money and threatened to break open Mother's chest and help himself to the money and jewellery inside. His eyes flashed angrily behind his thick glasses.

'See if you dare,' Mother challenged, eyes glittering dangerously. Roaring, he stormed out of the house, kicking the doorpost as he went out. As soon as his salary laced his hand he would disappear for the weekend and return unkempt and broke. The black threats would resume once more. One pay day I saw Mother stand in the living room and stare sadly at the mess of cigarette butts. I knew what she was thinking: 'Where is he?'

She decided she would find him and see for herself the new mistress that emptied her son's pockets so thoroughly and held him so tightly in her steely embrace. Mother took a rickshaw into town, entering the area she had never set foot in before. She walked up a set of stone steps towards a coffee shop, she asked an old man perched like a scavenging crow over a till for directions and he silently pointed towards the back of the shop. She went through a dirty curtain and down a narrow corridor. There were the sounds of children talking and laughing coming from the curtained doorways along the hallway. A small Chinese girl with a thick fringe that nearly covered her eyes poked her head through one curtained doorway and smiled shyly at Mother.

Finally Mother found herself standing in front of a tattered red curtain. Another world lived behind that curtain. A world so shabby and shameful that her hands shook as she pushed the unclean strips of cloth apart and looked into a surprisingly large, very dirty room. The walls were thin planks nailed together, the roof a mesh of zinc sheets, and the grey concrete floor dirty. A sideboard was stacked high with unwashed plates, bowls and chopsticks. Not even for the purpose of dining could the gambling be stopped. An ancient woman, hunched and almost bald, was slowly clearing away the mountain of dirty dishes. There were five round tables where men and women with glazed, obsessed faces sat. The air was uneasy with the stale smell of cigarettes and the sweet aroma of roasting pork from a kitchen somewhere close by. And in that filthy gambling hall, Mother's unhappy eyes alighted on her beloved son, bespectacled, erect and handsome. For a moment there was searing pain, the knife of betrayal. As she watched in disbelief he shouted out, 'Mah-jong!' and laughed greedily, a gambler's laugh. Look at the unholy light in his eyes. Look at the concentration.

Shocked she took a step towards him. She would change him yet. But then he made a quick, almost vicious movement with his hands that was so bafflingly foreign to her that it chilled and stilled her. The gesture was understood and quickly copied by another player and she knew he was lost to her. He lived in a world denied to her. She stood there frozen, staring at the hell her beautiful, wonderful, errant son had fallen into, and an image from the past so sharp that it actually hurt, flashed before her. Ah, she had been so young then. Humming to herself, swirling her hand in a blue basin of hibiscus petals waltzing softly in hot water. It must have been that moment when the water had turned the right colour of magic rust, for she picked up her gurgling, bright-eyed baby boy and gently lowered his kicking legs into the carefully prepared bathwater. How he laughed and splashed. How wet he made her! How curly the hair on his little head. How very long ago that was, and how many hopes had painfully crashed on the rocks of life since then. She stepped back through the dirty curtain and, in mortal pain, made her way down the filthy corridor.

She could not forget the greedy laugh. It haunted her nights. He had smiles only for the pale chips that lay on his side of the table. She felt lost and afraid. If she had relented before and given him money for the sake of peace, she refused point blank now to lend him even a single ringgit. She hid her own money and jewellery and confiscated my bank book so I could not be persuaded or bullied into parting with any of my savings.

The house became a war zone. Petty things exploded in your face. Once the thorny side of a durian skin came flying through the air straight towards my surprised face. Thank God I had the presence of mind to duck. The holes that the durian skin made in the kitchen wall are still there. Then, unexpectedly and suddenly, things calmed down when Lakshmnan began to help Mother in her efforts to marry me off. It was during this time that he became familiar with the practice of dowry.

It was like a blast into his brain. *Marriage equals dowry.*

Mother had set aside ten thousand ringgit for me. Surely he could command at least that as a bridegroom. He began to make his calculations but custom dictated that he could not be married before me. An impatience grew in him but custom had to prevail. The eldest daughter must be married first. Diligently he went on all the husband-finding journeys and eagerly sang the young men's praises. He saw the good in all of them and Mother saw only the bad until a proposal from a surveyor from Klang fell into her lap.

The prospective suitor who had managed to impress Mother with his qualifications set a date to 'see' me. There were set rules to such an occasion. The parents and their son visit the bride and while they are talking with her parents, she will bring in a tray of tea and cakes. All polite conversation will cease and they will look her over, often very critically. The poor girl will then nervously pour the tea and coyly hand out the cakes before leaving, saying as little as possible. She is allowed to smile shyly at the prospective in-laws.

I was not nervous about that day. I had played the game a few times before as Mother had already turned down a few hopefuls. I had liked one of them but I trusted Mother's judgement implicitly. She is like a bear. She can smell from miles away the smallest token of rot, even if it is carefully hidden away in the deepest recesses of a person. At that point I didn't really know what a surveyor actually did because it was not as grand a profession as that of a doctor or lawyer, but I had neither the qualifications nor a dowry large enough to attract one of those. However, my far-sighted mother believed Malaya was a growing country and it was only a matter of time before good surveyors would be in great demand. One day she hoped a small fortune for my husband and me. More than anything else she wanted a clever man for me. She said that she knew life with a stupid man and wanted different for us.

I hoped my suitor's standards would not be too high. I sat in front of the mirror and saw nothing remarkable. Beauty had been defined by Mohini. I only had to remember her magnolia skin and bottle-green eyes for my own looks to pale into mediocrity. I never wore make-up in those days because Mother didn't think it suitable, although both Lalita and I wore copious amounts of powder. Sometimes Lalita splashed so much onto her skin that she emerged from the bedroom looking very much like a white-faced cappuchin monkey.

Poor Lalita was the epitome of all Mother's fears. If Mother had sat down and made a list of all the things she didn't want in a daughter she would have come up with a picture of Lalita. Father's wide hips, flat bottom, chicken legs from God knows which side of the family, a pair of wide-set small eyes and a fleshy nose.

'Anna!' Mother called.

'Coming,' I replied, and ran off to the kitchen to help to cut out the coconut cookies that I would later serve to our guests. It was a very simple recipe but it had a secret ingredient that made it taste better than normal coconut cookies. Ginger flowers. It was a hot afternoon and Lalita was sitting outside on the grinder drinking coconut water straight from a green coconut. I thought to myself that it was time she stopped spending so much time in the sun. Her skin was already too dark. I called to her and she ambled in obediently.

'Stop sitting in the sun so much or nobody will want to marry you,' I admonished gently.

'Mother says nobody will marry me anyway. I wish I was as good-looking as you.'

'Don't be so silly. You know very well that she only said that when she was in a temper. Of course you'll get married when you're older. There's someone for everyone. Now cut the cookies and I'll arrange them on the tray.'

We worked quietly while I tried to imagine my husband-to-be. I hoped he was fair. When we were finished I showered and changed into a pretty blue and green sari, which suited my colouring well. I plaited my hair and threaded a few jasmine flowers into it. Then I smoothed powder on my skin and painted my forehead with a small, perfectly round black dot. My friend

Meena assured me that if only I would wear a touch of lipstick and drop of kohl in my eyes I would be very attractive indeed but I was too frightened of what Mother would say if she caught me with carmine lips and elongated eyes. I wondered what she would say if she knew my nickname in school was MM, short for Marilyn Monroe. It was the sway in my hips that was responsible for the insulting nickname. In our old-fashioned town nice girls didn't become actresses. To start with, the job desired a girl of easy morals, and such a one as Marilyn. Why, she was surely a slut.

I twisted around in front of the mirror to check that my sari was well tucked into place at the back and then I sat down to wait. Mother came in. In her hand she had a stick of kohl. Wordlessly she knelt before me, gently pulled my lower lid away from my eyes and applied the kohl. She did the same to the other eye. I sat very still and stunned. I had no idea she even knew how to use a stick of kohl. Then from the palm of her hand she unscrewed a soft pink lipstick.

'Open your mouth,' she instructed. I opened my mouth obediently and holding my chin with her left hand she applied a layer carefully onto my lips. Then she critically examined her handiwork and nodded with satisfaction. 'Don't lick your lips,' she advised. She stood up and left. She must really want me to marry the surveyor, for she had never done that with any of the others. I turned back to the mirror and stared at myself with amazement. Mother had transformed my face. My eyes looked large and beautiful, and my lips interesting and soft. Meena was right.

Soon there was the sound of polite voices in the living room. Suddenly I was nervous. Pouring tea under the eagle eyes of strangers was a tricky business but what made the butterflies inside my stomach flutter madly was the tension in Mother. She really wanted the match. What if they didn't like the way I looked? What if they turned me down? She would surely be annoyed with me. Then from the living room came her voice. 'Anna,' she called sweetly.

I stood up, smoothed my sari carefully and went into the kitchen.

'There you go,' Lalita said, thrusting the tray into my hands. There was a giggle in her voice.

I walked into the living room, head bent, the way a proper unmarried girl should do and, putting the tray on the coffee table, I poured the tea, handing cups to the parents first and only then to the prospective bridegroom. I did it all with eyes downcast. I saw trouser legs, two men's feet (dark), a sumptuous lime-green sari and a pair of small ladies' feet (fair). I lifted my head and passed the tray of cookies around. The parents were the usual Ceylonese type. The father reclined back and the mother assessed and calculated. She had an imposing face with high cheekbones, very large eyes and a straight nose. She smiled at me and I smiled back.

'You are a teacher,' she commented.

'Yes,' I agreed softly.

She nodded. There was much skill in the way she had tied her sari. Even while she was sitting down, the pleats of her sari remained sharp and distinct. I moved on to the dark hands that had taken the saucer and cup from my hands before. He was thin, and judging by the length of his awkwardly folded legs, tall. He had the curving lips of someone who laughed often but his deep-set eyes burned enigmatically, staring into mine with an intensity that made blood rush into my cheeks. They reminded me of the way my mother's eyes could burn. I looked away quickly. He was so black he was blue. My children are all going to be black, I thought, walking away from the living room, trying hard not to let my hips sway, knowing every eye was on my retreating back.

Lalita was grinning widely at me from the safety of the kitchen. 'Well?' she asked, eyebrows raised. I shrugged.

Together we stood by the kitchen door listening to Mother and the prospective in-laws in conversation. I hoped that she wouldn't like the boy. He made me uncomfortable. The way he stared at me confused me. Also, he was far too dark.

The guests left and Mother came into the kitchen. 'I like that boy,' she announced, her eyes shining. 'He has real fire in his eyes. Real ambition. He will go far, mark my words.'

'He's a bit dark, isn't he?' I ventured carefully.

'Dark?' she queried. And that solitary word she cast like a net of disapproval. Struggle was pointless. 'Of course he's dark. He's a surveyor. He spends all his time in the jungles.' And so the matter was decided. I was to marry the man with the burning eyes. Mother and brother began to make plans. Lakshmnan fell upon the brilliant idea of a double wedding. 'Eliminate an unnecessary expense,' he said, talking Mother's language. Finally they agreed. Now he could seek his bride.

When news reached my prospective in-laws that Lakshmnan was seeking a bride they immediately sent word. What luck, they said, they had a daughter of marriageable age! They proposed an intermarriage. Although Mother was not keen on the idea Lakshmnan insisted that they at least look at the girl. So Father,

Mother and Lakshmnan travelled all the way up to Klang to see the prospective bride. Mother said her heart literally dropped when they arrived at the address. A tiny house in a slum area that for some peculiar reason had been draped with chicken wire so it resembled a giant chicken coop. She believed in the future potential of the surveyor but the prospect of giving away her precious son to people who lived in that sort of house was impossible for her to digest. In fact, she wanted to turn around and leave straightaway, but Lakshmnan argued reasonably enough that they had after all come this far. 'What is the harm?' he asked. Words he lived to regret.

When the bride's mother came out to greet them Mother saw her look past them towards the Wolsley before turning to assess my brother. Mother looked at Lakshmnan and saw what the bride's mother saw. If not for his thick glasses he would have been perfect. With broad shoulders and a handsome moustache he was quite a catch. Until one chanced upon his gambling habits, of course. They entered the chicken coop.

The furniture was poor. The chair under Mother rocked unsteadily. A girl walked into the room with a tray of tea. Mother swallowed her surprise. A matchmaker friend had given the impression that the girl was good-looking. In fact, the girl was tall and angular with broad shoulders and a disproportionately large chest. Her face was not soft and kind but fierce, with her mother's high cheekbones, a large mouth and eyes that were daring and sensuous. They boldly assessed Lakshmnan before turning to rest on his parents, softening into a shy maidenly gaze.

Oh, but Mother was not buying. The girl was a

madam. Mother saw instantly that she was trouble. Big trouble. It was in every line of her face.

Mother sipped her tea and into her conversation she slipped the fact that her son was a terrible, actually a compulsive, gambler. She told them that she didn't want the responsibility of hiding that fact and ruining both marriages, and frankly told them that she did not believe in intermarriages.

After Mother dropped her bombshell there was a moment's silence but the bride's mother had seen the car and the upright beauty in Lakshmnan's face. Her daughter couldn't do better. In fact, she probably didn't believe Mother at all. She must have thought that Mother was lying because she didn't want to give her son in marriage to their daughter. 'Oh, don't worry about that,' she assured Mother, her sharp eyes flashing. 'My husband used to be an appalling gambler. Addicted to horse racing for years and yet I had a happy life. I went short for nothing. My daughter is a clever girl and I have confidence in her ability to handle the situation.'

They were pushy and thick-skinned as well. Mother sat there fuming but unable to leave because she didn't want to jeopardise my match. She could well understand their eagerness for her son. Their daughter was no beauty. She thought the girl hideous, with rashes that disappeared into the sleeves of her sari blouse and ended God only knew where. Little did she know then that what in her time was angular and unattractive would today be universally considered good-looking. Height, good straight shoulders, large breasts, long legs, slim hips and wonderfully high cheekbones. But she was certainly no soft, round-faced Indian beauty and, sitting there viewing the bride critically, Mother could never have guessed in a million years that waiting quietly inside the bride's tummy was her favourite grandchild. That one day her son would rush home and announce with tears in his eyes, 'Ama, Mohini has come back to us. She has come back as your granddaughter.'

No, she will not marry my son, Mother thought to herself that day.

The parents were shifty and their lodgings so poor that Mother found it hard to imagine they could have a dowry of ten thousand ringgit sitting in any bank. Besides, if the girl really was a qualified teacher as her parents claimed, why then was she not working? Either they were lying or the girl was unimaginably lazy. Either way it did not bode well for Mother's plans and hopes. The girl simply would not do.

Lakshmnan began grinding his teeth in the chicken coop. He had made great plans for the money and Mother was spoiling everything. In his fevered imagination he had already doubled and tripled his dowry at the gaming tables. For so long now he had nurtured the intoxicating illusion that if he sat at the tables with enough money behind him, his luck would have to change sometime.

They said their goodbyes politely.

In the car Lakshmnan announced abruptly, 'I want that girl.'

'But you've always wanted to marry a fair, working girl,' Mother said, surprised.

'No, I like this girl,' he insisted.

'As you wish,' Mother said. She sat in the car in a cold rage. Father looked out of the window in silence. He enjoyed looking at miles of green rubber trees. It calmed him. It made it easier to ignore the waves of rage pouring out of his wife and his eldest son.

That night, my brother Sevenese had a dream. He was sitting on a stretch of barren land. For miles as far as the eye could see was dry, red soil. In the distance a buffalo-driven cart was trundling towards him in a cloud of red dust. Around the buffalo's neck was a bell that tinkled softly. My brother had heard that sound somewhere before. The driver of the cart, who wore a long white beard, said, 'Tell him the money will be lost in one sitting.' In the cart behind him was a long black coffin. The bell tinkled in a gust of strong wind. Yes, my brother had heard that sound before. 'Look,' the old man said, pointing to the coffin, 'he never listens to me. Now it is dead. You tell him. The money will be lost in one sitting.' Then he hit the poor buffalo with a long stick and the cart continued its journey through the barren landscape.

'Wait!' my brother cried, but the cart moved on in a cloud of dust. Only the memory of the twinkling sound remained. Like the little bells Mohini had worn on her ankles. He woke up and his first thought was, 'He must not marry her. The marriage will be unhappy.' Until he had dreamed it nobody had realised that my brother's sudden interest in marriage had everything to do with the dowry. But of course, it all made sense. The burning compulsion to marry that unemployed, dark girl with the scary rashes had greed for a mother.

Lakshmnan and Mother looked up from their breakfast. Sevenese felt like a deer in a den of snarling tigers.

'The money will be lost in one sitting,' he told Lakshmnan. There was a dead silence in the room. Lakshmnan stared at Sevenese with a strange shocked expression.

'Don't marry her. It is a mistake,' Sevenese said. The same thought zigzagged round the room. Once before we had disregarded Sevenese's warning and had regretted it. Could we afford another mistake? This one could be colossal.

'I heard the bells that Mohini used to wear on her ankles,' Sevenese added.

Shock was replaced by cold, implacable anger. Lakshmnan did not grind his teeth or haul Sevenese up by the collar. 'You are all wrong,' he said, so quietly and so out of character that we were far more stunned than if he had ranted and raved. Then he walked out stiffly.

Mother sat down immediately to write a letter to the girl's parents. She explained that on our return she had found the oil lamps on the prayer altar had extinguished. It was an ill omen and she had been advised not to proceed further with the match. Sevenese took the letter into town and posted it.

A letter came back addressed to Lakshmnan. Lakshmnan tore it open and read it in the vegetable garden with his back turned to us. Then he crumpled it in his fist and threw it into a clump of banana trees. He turned around and came back into the house, a preoccupied expression on his face. He went to look for Sevenese. By then Sevenese was already a Health Inspector with the Malayan Railway, travelling up and down the country inspecting the cleanliness of facilities offered by the company. He was down for the weekend but was in the bedroom packing to leave in the morning.

Lakshmnan stood in the doorway. 'Did she actually say I would lose it all in one sitting?' he asked abruptly.

'Yes,' Sevenese said simply.

For perhaps an hour Lakshmnan prowled the house restlessly, deep in thought. Finally, it seemed his turmoil was over. He went to Mother and announced that he would marry Rani or no one. What his thoughts were with regards to the dowry he told no one. Perhaps he thought he wouldn't gamble it all away. Perhaps he had big plans of starting a business like his Chinese friends.

As soon as he left that evening to play a game of cricket in the school playing field, Mother rushed out to retrieve the crumpled letter from the banana grove. I think that letter still exists in her wooden chest.

Dear, dear man,

Please do not forsake me. I think I am already deeply in love with you. Ever since you left I have not been able to eat or sleep. Your beautiful face is constantly in my mind. We do not believe in such nonsense as extinguished lamps being ill omens. It is the nature of a lamp to extinguish when its wick shortens to nothing or the oil burns away. An act of carelessness surely cannot be an ill omen for our marriage.

I am a simple girl from a poor family. My father saved many years for my dowry and it will be the perfect downpayment for a house or you could use the money to start your own business. A talented man like you could do so much with the money. Your father told me that you were interested in business.

I have suffered greatly in my lifetime but by your side I will be happy even with plain rice and water. Please, my love, do not forsake me. I promise you will never regret the decision to marry me.

Yours for ever,
Rani

Mother was livid with anger. She was so angry her hands shook. She had disliked the girl on sight and she had been right to. The sneaky madam was waving the dowry money like a red rag to a bull. She turned on my father.

'It's all your fault,' she cried unreasonably. 'It was you giving her the idea by talking about Lakshmnan's good business sense. Why couldn't you just shut up? You knew that I had brought up Lakshmnan's gambling habit to put them off.'

Father was silent as he usually was. In his eyes was dumb acceptance. Didn't he know that that very look infuriated Mother all the more?

Lakshmnan had his own way. He had his double wedding. It was a horrible day. Mother was in a terrible mood. She refused to wear flowers in her hair and wore a dull grey sari with hardly any patterns on it. She stood to one side stiff and unhappy. Lakshmnan, too, far from being happy that he had got his own way, was sullen and unsmiling. He seemed impatient to get the ceremony over with. That night Lakshmnan's new mother-in-law came quietly up to him to delicately confide in him that they didn't have the ten thousand at that moment, only three. In the softly lit room her inky black eyes shimmered with cunning. The many years of being a compulsive gambler's wife, of playing hide and seek with the fishmonger, the butcher, the baker, the vegetable man and the coffee seller had taught her well.

'Obviously we will give you the other seven thousand when we get it. A cousin in financial trouble has borrowed the money. We couldn't say, "No." You don't mind do you?' Her intonation and diction were flawless. She must have come from a family of good breeding.

Of course Lakshmnan understood. He was not my mother's son for nothing. The rest he would get in Never-Never Land. She held the bulky envelope out. Take the cash, waive the rest. He was being cheated. He knew it.

Blood began to pound into his head. He had married their ugly daughter. He was due ten thousand. All his elaborate plans, of starting a new business, the deals he would cut . . . they hung in tatters. A justifiable rage was building inside him. 'No,' he wanted to say, 'take your ugly daughter and come back when you have the full dowry.' But the silken invisible vines that clung inside his being pulled and pressed against his chest. Cold alabaster chips lay waiting, their tongues clicking, whispering, 'Take it, take it. Oh, make haste.'

The outrage of being cheated allowed Lakshmnan to rush out of the house and lose all the money in one sitting. His wife, he soon found out, far from being happy with plain rice and water, expected to be able to dry-clean her saris. A notion that made my mother rigid with shock, and even Father choked on his hastily swallowed tea.

Part Three

A Sorrowing Moth

Rani

My mother named me Rani so I would live the luxurious life of a queen, but when I was just a baby a sorrowing moth landed on my cheek, and though my mother recognised it instantly and brushed it away with a howl of dread, the grieving dust on its downy wings had already settled into my skin. The dust was like a spell on my soul, outwitting happiness and embracing for my poor body the terrible rigours of existence. Even marriage, the one thing that had shone like a polished paradise of true love, everlasting happiness, has been just another disappointment in my life. Look at me, living in a small wooden house with creditors baying at the door day and night. I have only re-lived my poor mother's wretched life.

I curse the day that black widow spider, my mother-in-law, came into our house spinning her silken lies. Like strings of silver they flowed out of her terrible mouth and caught me struggling in their web. The truth is, between them all they forced me to marry Lakshmnan. Before he came into my life I had doctors, lawyers, engineers and even a London-trained brain surgeon who came to ask for my hand in marriage, but it was I who hesitated. Spoilt for choice I managed to find imperfection in all of them. A crooked nose, too short, too skinny, too something. In my polished paradise I saw a prince, tall, fair, good-looking and rich. I thought patience was a virtue. Finally – look what I got.

It is too late now to wish for one of them instead.

'Rani,' the spider said, 'my son is a good man. Upright, hard-working and kind. He is only a teacher now but one day with his keen business sense who can tell where he will stand in the world.'

Of course, there was no mention then of any gambling habit. In the end I was forced to marry Lakshmnan for the sake of my brother who was suddenly and mysteriously enamoured with the spider's daughter. If you ask me, it was very suspicious that he was suddenly adamant that he must marry that girl. Even in those days there was nothing even mildly approaching spectacular about her, with her down-trodden puppy dog eyes and an unexciting mouth. Yet my brother was seduced from indifference to steely determination in one encounter.

'I will have her and only her,' he declared, with fated eyes. It is impossible that she could have intoxicated him with her joyless eyes and that holier-than-thou mouth. No, no, living so close to the snake-charmer's they had availed themselves to his evil spirits. Together the mother and daughter put a charm on my brother. My father said that the first time they went to see the bride, they were offered a plate of coconut cookies that tasted nothing like any other coconut cookie he had ever eaten. Even Mother admitted that they were different. 'Like eating flowers,' she said. So delicious in fact that my brother ate *five*.

I know the old witch hid something in those cookies. A love potion to make my brother fall for her flat-faced daughter. He became strange, driving his motorbike all the way to Kuantan whenever he could. Not to spend time with the girl. Oh no, the spider would never allow that. He drove all the way there just to sit in a coffee shop across the road from the Sultan Abdullah School and gaze longingly at her while she took her students into the school playing field for their daily physical exercise. Now tell me if that doesn't sound like a gift from a snake-charmer to you.

'Marry him,' they all chorused. What could I do? Stand in the way? No, I sacrificed my shining dreams for my brother.

So I married Lakshmnan.

And what have I got to show for it? A fine mess, that's what I have. An ungrateful brother who doesn't even speak to me any more, a useless gambler for a husband, and children who are disrespectful to me. I have suffered greatly.

Do you know what Lakshmnan did with my dowry money? He gambled it all away on our wedding night. All of it. Ten thousand ringgit was gone before the night was through. I often travel back in time to that night. It is like a secret place protected by the ravages of time. Everything is mummified so beautifully it shocks me every time I visit it. Every thought, every emotion carefully preserved to fool me into thinking it's happening all over again. I see, feel and hear everything, everything. Bring some cushions to put under my poor, swollen knees and I will tell you exactly what my wonderful husband did to me.

I am a twenty-four-year-old bride again and have returned to mother-in-law's horrid little bedroom with the unpainted wooden walls. I am sitting on the edge of a strange silver bed facing the mirrored door of a dark wood wardrobe. In the mirror my face is shadowed but unmistakably young and my body firm and slender. I clearly see the yellowing mosquito net hanging like a soft cloud over me from the four posters of the big bed. The growing moon is luminous in the sky. Moonlight is a funny thing. It is not really a light at all but a mysterious silver glow that favours and caresses only the pale and the shiny. I watch it ignore a rolled decorative carpet and steal all the rich colours out of a matt embroidered picture on the wall, but highlight a gleaming glass jar with orange squares around the middle. I see that it is particularly kind to a collection of cheap chinaware, a wedding gift just out of its wrapping, for they stand out gleaming white and pearly pink. A silver tray shimmers.

The air is damp and heavy. The waistband into which all the folds of my elaborate sari are tucked is wet and uncomfortable against my skin. A small fan whirls heroically through the thick, oppressive air. I listen to the expensive rustle of my silk sari. It is like a whispered conversation that I cannot understand. The window is open and the noise of chirping night insects outside is unexpectedly loud in my city ears. I am used to the sound of people.

I lick my dry lips and the taste of lipstick mingles in my head with the smell of recently painted nail polish. There is clammy sweat in my tightly linked fingers. And there goes that nonsensical daddy-long-legs moving drunkenly across the wall. He hasn't changed at all. He looks exactly the same even though he is really fifteen years old now. I can hear the clamour inside my brain like a Chinese funeral, the gongs, the cymbals, the weeping, and the wailing and inexplicable sounds of shuffling feet, and then I hear the silence of everyone else in the house. Everyone knows I am here. I have been careful not to make a sound and yet they can all hear me. Hear the horror and smell the shame of my position.

I can smell it even now. The pungent smell of my shame coming from the small pot of jasmine flowers that I had presented to him as a token of my love. I had bowed my head and shyly, with both hands, held out the little pot to him. He took the offering from my hands but as I raised my eyes I witnessed him carelessly toss it on the table by the bed. It lost its balance and rolled onto its side, pretty flowers tumbling out, falling on the table, falling on the floor. He had not even looked at my gift in his haste to leave. He left me alone in our satin bridal bed strewn with flower petals and dashed off to some seedy joint in Chinatown.

Now that he is gone I hear the silence in the house but I know my new family is sniggering into the palms of their hands. Laughing at me. Alone I sit stiffly in my grand sari and wait for him. Quietly. Calmly. But inside me is an anger so terrible it is glowing white-hot. It eats my insides. He does not care for me. My position is unbearable.

I have been made a fool of.

If he imagined that I was going to play the shy, foolish bride he is much mistaken. I was born and bred in the tough city and brought up to be bold. I am no country bumpkin. Often I have been likened to a highly strung racehorse. The hours pass and in the mirror my beautifully made-up eyes glitter fiercely. My face has hardened in the mirror into the angry statue of Goddess Kali and my hands are slowly becoming clawed and stiff with clenching. My soft red lips have disappeared into my face and only a thin tight line is visible. I crave revenge. I want to fly at him and sink my freshly painted nails into his eyes.

Still he does not return.

But when he comes back at dawn, demented with a strange inward anger, I can only stare at him in shock. Wordlessly he falls on me and rapes me. I do not cry, I do not shout, I embrace him. I pull him towards me eagerly; envelop him so tightly inside my limbs that we move like one animal. Even in the midst of my white-hot anger I know this to be my power. His weakness will always be my power. In this bed I will be master. His need of this incredible coupling will always bring him running back again and again to me. Drugged by the discovery of my own power and sensuality I feel my own anger slip out of my eyes, burning the backs of them and bringing tears hurrying down my cheeks. I watch spellbound as his hard body strains into an arch and his mouth opens and closes with soundless screams in a parody of a mourning mother hippo standing over the stiff, dead body of her child. But suddenly he is vaulting away from my clinging body.

He sits hunched by the side of the bed, his head buried in his hands, and he cries like a thing broken. The moonlight favours my husband, stretching out his naked back so it seems curving and endless. Playing a game on his body. A little light here, a little shadow there. It makes him beautiful. I reach out my hand and softly, reverently, touch the smooth, exquisite planes of his body. My fingers are dark on his light skin. He is sorry. I feel humbled by the emotions I have unearthed.

This is my wedding night, I think. It is not at all what I had expected but the powerful emotions and the passion are far, far better than the silly romantic dreams I have childishly nurtured. He is mine, I think with pride, but the very moment the heady thought fills my head he makes a sound like a deer coughing and sobs, 'I shouldn't have married you. God, I should never have married you. What a terrible mistake I have made.'

I can see it now, my dark hands stilling suddenly on the curve of his hard flank as I listen in astonished wonder to him sob over and over again, 'I should never have married you.'

He had lost all our money, humiliated and hurt me deeply, and yet my body had quivered and trembled like a musical note under his. His unreachable despair was strangely addictive and his heartless rejection fired my blood. The challenge of taming such a man was irresistible. One day I would be the one to hold this beautiful hurting being in my arms and be the one to make all the pain go away. I will make you love me, I think. One day you will look at me with shining eyes, I promise myself.

I can still feel the scars of that night. It was a cruel unforgivable thing he did to me but he was so beautiful I was blinded by his radiance. You should have seen him then. He used to take off his shirt and carry weights in our backyard, and the Malay women who lived across the street used to stand hidden behind their curtains and watch him. When we walked in the streets together people stared at us and envied me such a man.

I know he would have come to love me if not for the spider that hung over our early life, dribbling poison into his ear and spinning lies about me. She hated me. She thought I was not good enough for her son – but who is she to talk? Even when she was young she was no beauty. I have seen photographs of her and all she could ever lay claim to is her fair skin. She was jealous of everything I had and always managed to find fault with everything I did, but the truth was she didn't want to lose the little influence she had left over her precious son. She wanted him for herself, and the way she did it was with money. She tried to control him with money. She could have helped us financially. That miser has slowly piled up an enormous stash in the bank – a sum that my husband helped to accumulate. She could have helped us but she thought she'd rather watch me fall flat on my face.

She puts on airs and graces but she doesn't fool me. Fancy telling my daughter that all the male ancestors in her family were burned like kings in funeral pyres built solely from sweet-smelling sandalwood, when in fact her father was nothing but the son of a servant! My mother is of a much, much purer descent. She comes from a family of very highly regarded merchants. In fact, my mother was betrothed to a very wealthy merchant in Malaya. He had chosen her from a large selection of photographs, and the preparations for a grand marriage ceremony were ready when she was sent for from Ceylon. She set sail with a maiden aunt as chaperone and a large iron box full of jewellery. She was sixteen and extremely beautiful, with gorgeous cheekbones and large, liquid eyes. A family friend had instructions to journey with them, protect them and make sure the innocents arrived safely. Little did my mother's people know that the person they had entrusted their daughter's safety to was a traitor. My mother's guide was a big, dark man who forced her into a hasty marriage to him on the ship during the voyage.

By the time she disembarked, the seed that grew into my eldest brother was already growing in her belly. Sometimes even now if I close my eyes I can hear Mother crying softly through the thin wall that separated their bedroom from the living room where we children slept on mats on the floor. From my position in the corridor I could hear her begging softly in the dark for a few more ringgit so she could buy some food for us. When I heard her cry like that I used to wonder what life would have been like if I had been born to Mother and her rich, waiting bridegroom. But then I think I would miss my father very much, for I love him dearly.

I loved him even when he was wrenching Mother's jewellery from her unyielding body and while there was no food in the house and we were all starving. In fact, I loved him even when he was dashing out of the house for the races clutching his week's wages in his big dark hands. I did not stop loving him when the man at the grocery store humiliated me, shouting rudely that I shouldn't expect a single loaf of bread until my father cleared the account. God, I even loved him when he sent my three brothers away to live at his cruel sister's chicken farm where the poor things had to clean rows of chicken coops every day and got beaten with a length of plank by their uncle.

When I think of Father I always remember him in the small provision shop that he sort of inherited during the Japanese regime, a one-storey wooden structure, its walls dark-brown planks that were rotten in some places but all ours. The shop was out front and we lived in the back behind a patterned curtain. The shop meant we had rice, sugar and provisions during the Occupation. I used to watch Father weighing things on his old scale using various lumps of metal for different weights.

Cataracts have made him blind now but in my mind I can see him sitting at his cramped table surrounded by gunnysacks rolled open at the top and filled with grains, beans, chillies, onions, sugar, flour and all kinds of dry things. When you walked into the shop the overriding smell was of dried chillies and then you caught the whiff of cumin and fenugreek and only then the slightly musty smell of the gunnysacks themselves. Lining the entrance was an intriguing array of biscuits in large jars with red plastic tops.

I loved that shop. It was Father's but when it was closed it was all mine. When the wooden front was locked shut I spent hours playing with the scales and going through Father's papers. I read aloud his order books that had pages jammed with his big, untidy writing, prices and large ticks in blue ink beside them. I made the till open its mouth and played with the money inside, pretending to sell things and give change, and before I left my shop I always slipped some coins into my pocket. I enjoyed the sound of their chatter in my pocket and Father never seemed to notice their absence inside the mouth of the till.

I think those were the happiest days of my life.

Then there was the boy who used to deliver the goods for the shop. He told me I was beautiful and once he tried to caress my face near the back of the shop but I only laughed at him scornfully and told him I could never marry anyone with such dirty hands. I was only twelve years old then but I had a dream. I wanted a rich man like the man promised to Mother. One day I would have servants and nice things, beautiful clothes, and only shop in Robinson's. I would have my holidays in England and America. When people met me they would be respectful and mindful of their words. They would not dream of speaking to me the way they spoke to my mother. One day I would be rich. One very fine day . . .

After the Japanese went away, Father lost the shop at the racecourse and we moved to Klang. The real hard times arrived, when Father forgot to come home for weeks. We were hungry for days. My brothers stole food from the shops across town but the shopkeepers there recognised them and came to our house to beat them. Poor Mother had to run out to the front door and fall at their feet begging and pleading. That was the time too when strange men used to simply stride into the house hoping to find something of value they could take away with them. They left empty handed, spitting disgustedly on our doorstep. Somehow we all survived.

The day came when I passed my Form Five exams and became a fully qualified teacher but I decided that I didn't want to work. Why should I? It was time to marry the rich man of my dreams. I didn't want to work, bring up children and supervise servants as well. But thanks to my splendid husband I have no servants to supervise.

When I first went to live in the spider's house I was very good and polite to her. I helped to cut the vegetables and sometimes I even swept the house, but I could see that she was dissatisfied with me. Every time she looked at me I felt the cold disapproval in her fierce eyes. Everything I did was wrong. She watched me with those swift, condemning eyes of hers as if I was a thief in her house.

It was many years before I realised that I had stolen her most precious thing. I had stolen her son. After a while I began to worry about her watching eyes. Such envy. It spewed out of her mouth as soon as she opened it. When I was pregnant for the first time with Nash, someone told me that if I ate saffron flowers brought specially from India, plenty of oranges and the petals of hibiscus flowers, the baby would be born fair. So I went out and bought these things secretly and ate them in our room with the door locked so she would not see and cast her evil eye on me. After three months in that blighted house I often felt ill and had to sit outside on the veranda away from her envious eyes. I am certain she must have seen the orange skins and the flower buds in the rubbish bin and cast her evil, for my son Nash was born dark. When I was pregnant with my two daughters I ate exactly the same things and yet both my Dimple and Bella are fair. And that is how malignant her eyes are.

I have always been wary of my husband's side. They deal in strange things. Look how strong their magic is on my brother. After all these years and even after he has made so much money and young girls throw themselves at his feet, he is still deeply devoted to his perfectly unremarkable wife. And then there is also this eerie thing all of them have about that dead girl, Mohini. Why, I can't even talk about her in Lakshmnan's presence. He leaves the room as soon as I mention her. Once he came upon me so angrily when I mentioned her in the middle of an argument that I think he actually wanted to kill me. His hands fell upon my neck and I felt how they itched to tighten their violent circle around my throat. When I was quite blue and nearly dead he pushed me away looking ill, his futile hands limp at his sides. The way the entire family keeps that dead girl's image glowing in their lives is downright unhealthy. When my husband was first presented with his daughter he went as white as a sheet.

'Mohini,' he whispered like a crazed fool.

'No, Dimple,' I said, for I had decided to name my eldest daughter after the famous Hindi movie star. I don't see any resemblance to my husband's family at all. In fact, Dimple looks exactly like my mother. She has the same bone structure. Gorgeous cheekbones in a heart-shaped face. The spider came to see Dimple and wanted to call her Nisha. It means new moon or something similar. She said that giving a child a meaningless name would make the child's life meaningless too, but I don't believe in such old-fashioned rubbish. I wanted a nice modern name, so I stuck with Dimple. Isn't the name Dimple so much better than Nisha? After I brought Dimple home from hospital that strange man Sevenese came to visit. He went to the cradle to look at Dimple and blanched. Right before my eyes he went ashen, his face twisting with horror. 'Oh no, not you too,' he cried.

'What? *What?*' I screamed, running towards the cradle, thinking the baby had stopped breathing or something equally dreadful had happened, but inside the pink and white cradle Dimple was sound asleep. Her little chest rising and falling in small even movements, a sweet pink tongue protruding out of her sleeping mouth. I touched her face and it was soft and warm. I looked up at Sevenese angrily for the unnecessary shock he had given me but he had composed his face again.

'What is it? Why did you say that?' I asked, irritated.

He smiled carelessly. 'Just someone walking over my grave.'

I wanted to slap him but I pestered him for an answer. He only laughed and pretended to talk about other things for a while but he never really liked me and conversation came hard to him. He stood up and left abruptly as if another second in my home would have been an unbearable ordeal. Sometimes I think he has only one foot in this world. I do not understand him.

Sevenese is not the only hard nut for me to crack. I find it difficult to understand people generally. Why is my kindness always repaid with envy and ill feeling? Even my own family has conveniently forgotten the good I have done them. Sometimes when my father and mother fought my mother became very depressed about her life. She went into her bedroom, closed the windows and lay in bed for days not doing anything. When I crept in there, not even her pupils would move. There was nothing in her face. It was blank. At times like that I alternated between incredible panic that she would never come out of her trance and the overpowering need to hit her as hard as I could just to see if I could raise a reaction from her. In those dark days it was I who used the money I had made from teaching Mrs Muthu next door to read and write Malay to buy food for the family. It was I who went out, bought the loaf of bread and shared it out among my brothers. Everybody else sneaked in, ate hurriedly and sneaked out again so they would not have to deal with Mother's comatose body. Now they refuse to acknowledge they owe me help.

I spent my last cent on them even though I was no more than a child myself, yet rich in their big mansions they now turn their backs on me. 'Cut your cloth to suit your means,' they crow, as if that alone will keep the wolves from the door. 'Other people live on less,' they cry scornfully. Then they screw their faces up disapprovingly and question self-righteously, 'What about the money I gave you the last time?'

As if a handout of two or five thousand will last a lifetime. They want me to live like the spider but I won't. Why should I live like a miser counting every penny when I have such rich relatives?

At the beginning when we moved into the new house Lakshmnan and I struggled to pay the bills but I was resourceful and went into marriage brokerage. Found some bridegrooms some brides. It was I who found Jeyan a bride, spending my own money to travel up to Seremban to hunt him a bride. Yes, I got a commission but it hardly covered my costs. And what a flower I found for him too. All right, she had no qualifications to speak of, but for such a man as him, she was a prize beyond compare. After their marriage I invited them to come and stay with us in our home and they stayed with us for three months, eating and living as if it was their own home. I even went to a Chinese *sinseh* to get him some medicinal roots and powders to increase his potency. He was a puny man. Believe me, it was only through my efforts that they have their two daughters now. And what did I get in return?

The strumpet started making eyes at my husband. I rescued her from spinsterhood and brought her into my own home so she wouldn't have to live under the long shadow of the spider – and how did she repay my kindness? By trying to entice away my husband! She was ungrateful but very clever. The scheming hussy hung about in the kitchen, decorated from head to toe in her Sunday best as if she was a paragon of domestic virtue. She insisted on cooking every meal. Silently I suffered tasteless bits of meat floating in watery curry. Then one day I saw my husband slapping meat on the table for her. She had dared to ask *my husband* to buy her meat. Even I do the marketing myself and there the coquette was, slyly getting under my man's skin. I saw the danger immediately. I know a woman's mind. Women are far more deadly than men. What is a man but an unsuspecting extension of that roll of flesh that hangs between his legs? No, it is the woman that is the predator.

A woman's heart is like a mouth full of long, inward-growing teeth. Each one filed to a sharp point and cleverly disguised by a beautifully made-up face, a soft glance, a lightly crossed leg, a silken thigh, a white wrist or an exposed, perfectly smooth nape. One by one she sinks her teeth into her unprepared prey and the harder he struggles the firmer her inward-curving grip becomes until he is stuck fast and paralysed into submission. My husband was very handsome and she wanted him for herself. He was unaware of the teeth but I was not. Then one evening she stole my best recipe and tried to pass it off as her own right in front of me. The cheek of the woman.

Enough was enough.

The foolish woman dreamed, my husband on a white horse. He is no hero. There is not an ounce of tenderness in that man. He is like a male lion, too selfish and too grand to be capable of love. Such a mouse as she was he would have chewed and spat out in minutes, still dissatisfied. She saw our violent fights and persuaded herself that my husband and I were enemies.

'No,' I told her slack-jawed face. 'We are like the two halves of a pair of garden shears my man and me, joined at the hip, for ever snipping at each other and yet slicing in half anybody that gets between us. Do you see where you are standing right this moment?' I asked her. 'In the middle,' I screamed. 'He is in my blood and I am in his. Sometimes he makes me so angry I want to pour boiling oil into his belly button while he sleeps or fling him to the crocodiles so they digest everything, bone, hair, horn, hoof, skin and even his spectacles. But another time I am jealous even of the air he breathes. Why, I am even insanely jealous of the women that he looks at on TV.'

No, she didn't know about my passion. She could not have imagined. She stood there shocked and gaping like a fish out of water. My love is like an insect-devouring plant that lives on the flesh of insects like her. Even when you see me flying towards him in a black rage aiming for his eyes or even when I set his own son Nash against him I love him deeply and will never let him go. He is mine. Yet, so secret is my love that not even my husband, the object of my uncontrollable passion, knows about it. Yes, I learned early on that my love was a whip which he could use against me, so he continues to live in the firm belief that I hate him. The very sight of him.

'Get out of my house,' I screeched at them. Both of them. Even the sight of Jeyan and his pathetic lovesick eyes had begun to irritate me. He hung around the scheming bitch, staring at her like a stupid dog. Sometimes I think he even panted like one. I gave them twenty-four hours to find new lodgings. Fortunately they needed less.

Once I had got rid of the two blood-sucking leeches from my skin good things began to happen. Lakshmnan managed to cut a land deal with some Chinese businessmen. Usually they cheated him blind. They used him to do all the legwork and when it was time to sign the papers they left him out, sharing the proceeds among themselves. He came home complaining bitterly that the only straight thing about a Chinaman was his hair. I always listened to his grievances, bathed his wounds but sent him right back out there again. 'You are a male lion, king of the jungle, roar like one,' I said. And finally, after many misses, he cut his first deal. He made six thousand ringgit. *He put six thousand ringgit in my hand.* You can't imagine what a sum like that feels like after scratching for cents all your life. Six thousand was an amazing amount of money in those days. You have to think that a teacher's salary was about four hundred ringgit a month to have an idea what a fortune that was. But I was not stingy like that loathsome spider and I absolutely refused to hoard money like her lest it grow too close to my heart. So I threw Nash the most splendid birthday party ever. Oh, it was brilliant. Kuantan had never seen anything like it. First I went out and bought myself the most amazing black and red outfit with a high collar and barely clothed arms. To match the outfit I splashed out on a divine pair of red shoes. Then I blew two thousand ringgit on the most perfect choker necklace ever dreamed up. Bristling with real diamonds and rubies the size of my toenails it was a real darling.

Then I planned and prepared.

The fridge I ordered from Kuala Lumpur arrived and then finally the day of the party came. I slipped on my new red shoes and could hardly believe that it was me in the mirror. The hairdressers had done a fantastic job. They were the most expensive in Kuantan but they certainly knew their business. At five o'clock the guests began to arrive. Little people dressed in flounces, ribbons and miniature bow ties.

We had the usual cake, jelly and lemonade in the garden but the real party was later, much later, when all the little people were gone and only the fashionable people, women with nipped-in waists and flaring hips and men with dark, narrowed eyes remained. I had hired outside caterers and a small band. Then there were fireworks and proper champagne. We took off our shoes and danced barefoot on the grass. It was absolutely brilliant. Everybody got drunk.

When we woke up in the morning there were people asleep on the steps of our front door. I even found a pair of knickers in the fridge. People still remember it to this day. But after my party things went wrong once more. Lakshmnan gambled away the remaining two thousand and suddenly we were left moneyless again. All the people who had come to the party and sent such profuse 'thank you' notes refused to help. One even pretended not to be at home when I went to call on her. Bella turned five and there was no money even for a cake.

To buy food for my children I pawned my new two-thousand-ringgit necklace for a measly three hundred and ninety ringgit. I can remember the eyes of the Chineseman behind the iron bars light up when I nudged my necklace over the barrier towards him. I remember him pretending to study it reluctantly under a cracked magnifying glass. Six months passed but I didn't have the money to redeem my necklace. Lakshmnan took the pawn ticket to the spider to see if she wanted to redeem it and keep it until we could afford to buy it back from her but the spiteful creature said, 'No, I want nothing to do with your wasteful ways.' And my beautiful necklace was thus gone to the Chineseman with the unholy light in his eyes. Lakshmnan and I began to row badly. How we fought! We could come to blows over the way the egg had been cooked that morning. Very quickly we learned the muffled music that flesh on flesh makes. I stopped cooking. Most of the time I just had a take-out for my children and me and I think I heard him cook some lentil curry and make a few chapattis for himself when he returned in the evening. He ate by himself downstairs. By the time he came upstairs I was already in bed. To irritate me he used to hold his mother up as a shining example. 'She has never had a take-out in her entire life.' There was less and less money for me. Food was so expensive and there was nobody left to borrow from any more.

Then suddenly when Nash was nine years old his father cut another deal. He came home with nine thousand ringgit. That night we started talking again. And that is when I said, 'Enough is enough. It's time we all moved to the big city. Tried our luck in Kuala Lumpur.' I was sick and tired of living in a backwater small town where everybody knew everybody else's business. I had no friends left in Kuantan anyway. Even the neighbours were giving me the cold shoulder. I was glad to leave. The only person I could bear was my father-in-law. He never stopped being nice to me. When I was really desperate I used to visit him at his workplace and he would slip me a few dollars for the children's food. When all our belongings were on the lorry I turned to look at the house once more. And I thought, God, how much I hate you.

Lakshmi

Aah, you want to know about the flying durian skin. Sit down beside me on the bed and we will travel back into the murky past together. It was during that beastly time when Lakshmnan's gambling habit had turned life into hell on earth for all us.

'Ama,' Anna called out to me.

I ignored her call. I had seen her arrive with the durians. I had just had an argument with Ayah because I had seen him slipping money into Lakshmnan's hands. Making me look like a monster and giving our son the impression that gambling was OK. I was hard on my children because I love them and wanted what was best for them. If it was an easier life I wanted I, too, could have slipped him a few notes now and again as a peace offering but I wanted to change Lakshmnan for the better. I wanted him to kick the habit and I deeply resented his father's weak stance.

'Ama!' Both Anna and Lalita were calling to me now. I snorted and ignored their calls. Footsteps approached my bed. I turned on my side and stared resolutely out of the window at the deserted neighbourhood. It was too hot outside. Everybody was indoors fanning themselves. I felt Anna lean against the bedpost.

'Ama, I've brought you durians,' she breathed softly. In her early twenties, Anna was not the raving beauty Mohini had been but she made that intriguing Malay expression, '*tahan tengok*', come alive. The longer you looked, the more you found to appreciate and enjoy. That day, the profile she saw was stiff and inflexible. I heard the slight fear in her voice and was somewhat mollified by it. Also, I could smell the durians. My favourite fruit. If she had waited one second longer I would have turned my head and smiled but instead I heard her turn and leave. I was disappointed and hurt that she hadn't insisted, hadn't tried harder to persuade me. They will bring it on a plate and that is when I will accept the offering, I thought to myself. I heard her footsteps head towards the veranda.

'Papa,' I heard her call her father. Her voice was noticeably happier and lighter.

No matter what I did or what sacrifices I suffered for my children, they always treated their father with a special regard and gentleness. Surely it was me who deserved the credit for everything that they were! The joy in her voice was especially irritating to me that day. They moved to the kitchen, laughing and happy. Without me. I could imagine the scene. Newspapers spread on the floor and the whole exciting ritual of opening the spitefully sharp fruits. Holding on to each one with the help of a thick pad of rags and striking it with a large knife. The dull crack and the anticipation . . . How soft the flesh? How creamy the fruit? How good the buy?

It must have been a good fruit for I heard a low murmur of approval. Someone laughed. Easy conversation flowed. I waited for a while but no one came bearing my share on a plate. Had they simply forgotten that I loved this fruit, that I even existed? Listening to their relaxed chatter, new, more deadly hostility filled my stomach. I shot out of bed. My chest was heaving with anger. I never know where the anger comes from but when it appears, it blots out everything. I forget reason, sanity, everything. It is an intolerable force inside me and I simply want to transfer it. Get rid of it. Panting with rage I rushed into the kitchen. The happy tableau turned their faces, mouths filled with creamy messes, and stared at me almost in horror as if I was an intruder. Perhaps I looked to them like a monster. I was so furious, my vision blurred. I didn't think. Something burning hot and ugly rushed up from my stomach and exploded at the base of my skull. Black. The world became black. The monster inside took over. Picking up a discarded durian skin full of vicious thorns, I slammed it straight at Anna. Thank God she ducked. It flew whizzing over her head like a cream and green bullet and crashed into the kitchen wall, its hard thorns embedding it in.

We stared at each other, she with incredible shock and I, the monster now gone, with confusion. Nobody moved. Nobody said a word when I turned away and walked back to bed. There were no words for the emotions that came into my heart. Nobody came to hold me or talk to me. The house just became silent. Then I heard them moving about, cleaning, opening doors, a broom sweeping the floor, durian skins being dropped into the dustbin, water flowing from the tap and the rustle of newspapers from the veranda. Nobody came to see the dejected old woman with the hunched shoulders and broken heart.

I hadn't meant it. I loved my daughter. Again and again I saw the durian skin whizzing inexorably through the air, heading for her shocked face. I could have killed her or certainly disfigured her for life if she hadn't ducked. I felt tired and drained. I could hardly bear myself. I cried for the woman that I was. I cried that I had not the courage to make the first move and I cried for my crippling inability to put my arms around my own daughter and say, 'Anna my life, I am so sorry. Deeply, deeply sorry.' Instead I could only wait. If only someone had come in to talk to me, I would have apologised. Said I was so very sorry. But no one came and nobody ever spoke about the incident again. Isn't it funny that after all these years, no one has ever mentioned it to me even in passing?

Anna got married and left with her husband, and my new daughter-in-law Rani came to live with us. I had not been wrong about her. She was a madam. In every way she could, she wanted to show us that she was 'city folk'. Impressed by nothing and blasé about everything. Far from the humble ways of a family that lived in a larger version of a chicken coop she surprised us with the expectations and behaviour more suited to the spoilt daughter of an extremely wealthy family or even minor royalty. Expensive saris were carelessly left bunched and hanging on the washing line outside for a good few days before being sent to the dry-cleaners. When she did it the first time we were shocked, as she had intended us to be. Beautiful saris are precious heirlooms that are handed down from mother to daughter. I still have the saris that my mother gave me, carefully folded in lining paper and stored away in my wooden chest.

Lalita asked, 'Shall I bring it in? Take it down from the clothes line?'

'No,' I said. 'Let's see what she does.' By the second day I could see that all the areas exposed to the direct afternoon sun had begun to fade. Even on the third day she did nothing. The exposed parts were turning powdery red. The deep red sari was already ruined for ever.

'Mother-in-law, do you know a good dry-cleaner somewhere around this area?' Rani asked doubtfully on the fourth day.

It was only then I understood that a beautiful sari had been unnecessarily ruined so she could appear sophisticated in our eyes. She had a good brain inside her head and a clever tongue but she was lazy. Lazy to an unexpected level. All she wanted to do was boast about the doctors, the lawyers, the businessmen and the brain surgeons who had come to ask for her hand in marriage. I didn't want to ruin our relationship at that time by asking her what had made her choose a gambling teacher instead. I just pretended I had never seen that letter she had sent to Lakshmnan begging him to marry her. Once she offered to cut vegetables. Horrified, I watched her washing sliced onions and grapple with potatoes as if they were alive in her hands.

At ten o'clock she locked her door, to reappear at lunchtime. After lunch she returned to her room to *sleep* until her husband came home. It was the most shocking thing I had ever seen. Never in my life had I encountered such sloth. When she became pregnant with Nash she refused even to enter the kitchen, claiming the smell of food made her feel ill. She tied a cloth around her nose and sat chatting in English with Ayah in the living room or on the veranda. She liked him because he was always slipping her money on the sly. She remained in bed and her food had to be taken to her in her bedroom. In the evening she wanted to go to the movies or to have dinner out. Is it any wonder that no amount of money was ever enough for her? Money ran through the gaps between her fingers like fine sand. She is the only person I know who once asked someone who was going on holiday to California to buy her two ready-made saris from a boutique in Bel Air. It is an extravagance that is still talked about by the ladies in the temple whenever her name is mentioned.

The years of milking cows in the cold, early morning hours had taken their toll on me and my asthma was quite severe by then. In the night, when I couldn't sleep with it, I heard her whispering fiercely to Lakshmnan. Instigating. Like matches to tinder.

Then one morning Lakshmnan came out of their room and said to me, 'Since I didn't get all my dowry money I think it's only fair that you give me some. After all, you have a lot in the bank that you don't need and it was mostly through my efforts that you managed to save that much.' The moment the words left his mouth I knew them to be hers. She wanted my money. The wasteful madam wanted me to finance her foray into the high life. She was staying in my home, eating my food and poisoning my son against me late into the night. I was livid, but even if it killed me I refused to fight with my son because of her. I knew she stood behind the door of her room, listening to her poison work.

'What do you want the money for?' I asked calmly.

'I want to start a business. There are deals going that I would like to invest in.'

'I see. Even though the dowry should be given by the wife's family, as I have given to Anna, I am prepared to help you – but first you must show me that you and your wife are capable of saving and can be trusted with a large amount of money. Since you and your wife live here paying for nothing, show me that you are able to save a sizeable amount of your wages for two months and I shall be glad to give you the money then.'

'No!' he shouted. 'Give me the money now. I need it now, not in two months' time. The deals will all be gone by then.'

'In two months there will be other deals. There will always be deals.'

'It is my money. I helped in its accumulation and I want it now.'

'No, it is my money at the moment, but I have no intention of using it and can't take it up with me. It is all for my children and I am happy for you to have the lion's share, but only when you show me that you can be trusted with it. That is not so unreasonable, is it?'

A rush of anger filled his face. He made a strangled sound in his throat and lunged blindly towards me in frustration. I saw his face, black and twisted, charge at me. He rammed me hard into the wall. I banged my head and hurt my back with the impact of his shove. With my back to the wall I stared at him in disbelief. I could hear Lalita crying useless tears in the background. He had raised his hand to the woman who had given birth to him. I had taught him this. I had created this monster, but it was my daughter-in-law who had breathed life into it. I cannot explain the grief in my heart. He stared back at me, dumbfounded and horrified by what he had done. My son had become my enemy. He dashed out of the house and she stayed in her room.

When I looked into the mirror that day I saw a sad, old woman. I did not recognise her. Like me she too wore a plain white blouse made of cheap cotton material and a faded old sarong. Her neck and hands were bare of jewellery. Her hair was already grey and pinned into a simple bun at the back of her head. She looked so old. Who would believe she was only forty? She stared at me with heavy, pain-filled eyes. As I watched her, her mute mouth opened. No sound came out of its black depths. I felt very sorry for her because I knew the black hole couldn't express her unimaginable loss even though every cell in her body screamed out with it. For a long time I stared at that defeated stranger standing in my clothes before I turned away. When I reached the doorway and looked back she too was gone.

They left the house two days later. Moved to a one-bedroom split-level house near the market. Rani didn't even bother to say goodbye and I did not see her again until Nash was born. Ayah, Lalita and I went to see her at the hospital. The baby was dark like her but with big, round eyes and bursting with health. She had named him Nash. She was very proud of him and not too happy when I tried to carry him. I brought him the usual gold rings, bangles and anklets that one gives to a grandchild. I put them all on his little body with my own hands and she took them all off and placed them in the pawnshop as soon as she left the hospital.

Then Dimple was born and Lakshmnan came running to the house. 'Mohini has come back as your granddaughter,' he babbled foolishly. Poor boy. He has never recovered. And yet in the hospital I stood and stared, for the child did look remarkably like my lost Mohini. I picked her up and suddenly the years fell away. I thought I was holding my own Mohini in my arms. I thought I would turn around and see her twin, curly haired and gurgling, in the other cot. That I would have another chance to do it right this time but I looked up and met my daughter-in-law's eyes. The black eyes were watching me very closely. 'She looks exactly like my mother,' she said.

And I knew then that there would be no second chance. She wanted no ties at all with us and she would have cut Dimple off completely from us as she did with Nash and Bella had Lakshmnan not loved the child so much that it made her jealous. That's why only Dimple and not the other two came to stay with us for the school holidays.

Oh, I was glad to have Dimple! I even purposely fanned the poisonous thoughts in Rani's head. She knew that her husband did not love her but she wanted to believe he was incapable of love. She could not bear that he could love someone else, even his own daughter. That possessive jealous streak in her refused to lie down even for motherhood. The older Dimple grew the more obvious it became that she looked nothing like her maternal grandmother and remarkably like Mohini. I saw Lakshmnan staring at Dimple with a mixture of wonder and surprise. As if he couldn't believe how very much like Mohini his daughter looked.

And we, we waited for the thrice-yearly school holidays. Two weeks in April, three weeks in August and then, best of all, the whole of December and part of January. The house seemed brighter, bigger and better when Dimple was here. She brought a smile into Ayah's face and put conversation into Sevenese's mouth and I, I finally found a place where all my hard-earned money could go. It wasn't that I didn't love Nash and Bella, but I loved Dimple the best. Nash and Bella had been taught to hate us anyway. I wished I could keep Dimple with me all the time but no, Rani would not allow that. She knew that would be letting me win. No, she thought she would torment us both, my son and me. From the time Dimple was only five years old she began to send the poor child back and forth like an incorrectly addressed package. Oh, what big, sad eyes the child had. I counted the days when she would come to live with us and cried when the time of her departure neared. And after we had waved her goodbye and Lakshmnan's car had turned the corner, the emptiness was indescribable. Then I would take out the calendar and map out her next visit.

Rani had her Western ways about her. She refused to teach her children their own mother tongue but I decided that I would teach Dimple our culture and teach her to speak Tamil. It was her heritage and her right. I began to tell her our family stories for there were many things I wanted to leave in her care. Then one day she walked in and announced that she wanted to save all my cherished stories like the aborigines in the red deserts of Australia do. 'I have decided to make a dream trail of our history and when you die I will take over and be the new custodian of our family dream trail,' she said importantly. From then on like a real custodian she walked around with her tape recorder recreating the past for her children's children. Finally there was a reason for my existence.

The years were passing but I just could not find a bridegroom for Lalita. She had failed her Form Three exam despite sitting for it three times. With no qualifications she wanted to train to become a nurse but I wouldn't hear of it. How could I let my daughter wash strange men in intimate places? No, no, such a dirty job was not for my daughter. I sent her to typing school but whenever she went for an interview she was so nervous she couldn't stop making mistakes. I was getting desperate. If she had been a working girl she might have found a husband, but with her looks and being unemployed even a dowry of twenty thousand only brought forth unsuitable men of suspect character – divorced, strangely old and irresponsible crooks out for the money. And, once, a man so fat I dreaded to think of poor Lalita suffocating beneath him.

The years were passing faster and my health was worsening. The dosage for the little pink pills had risen from a quarter to one and a half. They were so strong they made my body tremble but there was no other way to keep the asthma dog at bay. I stuffed folded newspapers into my chest and my back to keep out the cold night air. My aching bones told me I was getting old. The days flew like wind in the trees, one grey day no different from the next.

Sevenese took up the study of astrology and started telling fortunes. He practised on his friends and they dropped in with their charts clipped under their armpits. Before he left on his trips he gave me envelopes full of his interpretations for his friends to pick up. It turned out that he was so good at telling fortunes that strangers started to appear at our door with their charts in their right hand.

'Please,' they pleaded. 'My daughter is getting married. Will this boy be a good match?' The pile on his table grew and grew but I realised that the deeper he delved into that shadowy world the more he drank, the deeper his despair, the more cynical his disposition and the more savage his charm became. He did not want to marry and settle down. Women were sharp-eyed playthings and children perpetuators of a disgusting species. 'Man is worse than beast,' he said. 'Crocodiles will climb out of the water during severe droughts to share the lions' meal but man will poison his neighbour before he shares his.'

He drank far too much and returned home late, staggering and muttering to himself, his eyes red and his hair tousled. Sometimes he smelt of lingering perfume. Cheap perfume. I did not need to ask where he had been. There used to be a dark place called the Milk Bar in town. He had been spotted going through the swing doors by ladies from the temple. Gaudily painted women, not so young but still smooth of leg smoked outside the establishment. Too often he lost his keys and banged on the door well past midnight, singing in Malay for Lalita to open the door, '*Achi, achi buka pintu.*'

I feared he had become an alcoholic.

Jeyan had not even attempted to take his Form Three exams. He knew he couldn't pass. He became a meter reader with the Electricity Board. When the time arrived for him to marry, Rani, who had taken up the practice of a marriage broker of sorts, sent word that she had found him a wife. There were no takers for Lalita. She was already thirty years old. Almost too old to be married.

Lalita

When Rani found a bride for Jeyan, Mother took him to see the girl. She returned full of good humour and high spirits. The girl was fair and comely. Mother said in his last life Jeyan must have earned excellent karma to deserve such a girl in this life. Ratha was an orphan, brought up by a kindly spinster aunt who had managed to set aside a dowry of five thousand ringgit for the girl. It was a very paltry sum to negotiate with, but Mother was so determined to have the girl for Jeyan that she would have agreed even if there was no dowry on the table.

I watched Jeyan sit in a chair looking at Mother mutely, blankly, as is his way. He could have been listening to her but I know my brother too well. With the preoccupation of a child he took out once again and carefully examined the precious memory of a reckless sidelong glance all for him. He thought only of a pair of hennaed feet that took turns to delicately burst out of the pleats in the middle of a green and red sari, and a pair of small hands that had served him tea and shyly passed the soft cakes around.

Behind his inattentive expression blazed a kind of suppressed excitement. An awareness of the essence of the woman was already in his being. He was dreaming. Of gleaming musk on tumid breasts, skin covered with silky down and a body that moved beneath him like a gliding swan. He was dreaming of a sweet life with Ratha.

The date for the wedding was set. It was decided that it would be a small, simple temple wedding. It was really Mother who decided this. The girl had no relatives and Mother was not inclined towards showy displays of wealth. A small wedding seemed logical. We locked the house and went to stay at Mother's cousin's home in Kuala Lumpur. His house was small and filled with savage children. All day long they rushed about screaming and shouting, falling over adults as if they were pieces of furniture. They fought each other, cried then sang and tumbled down the stairs as if they were not flesh and bone but India rubber balls. From that house we were to leave for the simple ceremony planned in the temple.

On the big day my brother stood in the hall resplendent in a white *veshti* and his bridegroom's headgear. He stood straight and tall in front of Mother to get her blessing. For once his square face looked eager and animated. While Mother stood there savouring the pleasure of having secured such a lovely bride for her dull son, a small boy whooping like a Red Indian dashed into the hallway and promptly slipped on a patch of spilled oil. As we all stood and watched, he skidded across the floor like a bizarre giant eel. The eel crashed straight into my brother's ceremonial preparations. A large silver platter of kum kum went flying into the air, red powder rising like a red mist before it plunged to the ground, rolling noisily, scattering fine powder all over the floor. The noise of the platter falling and rolling endlessly on the tiled floor was deafening. Mother's smile fled, and her face became a mask of stunned disbelief.

For a few seconds nobody moved. Even the little boy

who had caused the big bang froze in fear. He lay on the floor and looked up at Mother's terrible expression with big, frightened eyes. Mother stared at the mess on the floor as if it was not cheap red kum kum that you could purchase in any provision shop but a pool of blood collected from the bodies of her slain children. I stared at Mother.

'Why, oh why did that stupid boy have to come here of all places?' she muttered, shaking her head. 'It is a bad omen but it has come too late. There is nothing to be done but what is already planned.' And with those words her face became like stone. She moved quickly. The gods had spoken but they had spoken too late: the wedding must go on. She helped the stunned child up, shooed him away sternly and instructed a girl hovering nearby to clear away the mess and then she stepped forward and blessed her son. 'Go with God,' she said clearly. Then Father stepped forward to bless Jeyan.

The bridegroom got into a car decorated with blue and silver ribbons and everybody else squeezed into any available vehicle. I walked beside Mother, her face like granite, her steps as determined as a marching soldier's. In the car she sat ramrod straight, saying nothing and staring blankly out of the window. Once she sighed softly, regretfully. It felt as if we were heading for a funeral house in inappropriate clothing, Mother in her mango-coloured sari and me in my royal-blue sari edged with the brightest fuchsia.

Secretly I thought Mother was overreacting although I didn't dare open my mouth to say as much. It was an accident pure and simple. That it didn't happen earlier was the miracle. Outside the temple the car slowed to a stop. Jeyan climbed out. In the midday sun his new white costume was blinding. Someone straightened his head-gear for him. He was King for the day. He nodded. He was nervous.

Inside the temple, Mother smiled at women drenched and layered in jewellery. They stopped gossiping about the bride to smile back. As she passed they resumed their talk, their lips alternately busy or pursed, but their dark eyes forever alert, roved and weaved through the crowd. They looked at me pityingly.

We stood by the dais and watched the bride, escorted out by her elderly aunt and friend. I thought she looked very beautiful in a dusky pink sari with small green and gold dots and an intensely embroidered gold border. She was slim and graceful. Indeed, Jeyan was extremely lucky. At the dais she folded her legs beneath her and slipped into place beside my brother. She did it with such natural grace that I wondered anew why someone so pretty would agree to marry my brother. She wore a lot of jewellery but I guessed a sizeable proportion was costume. We knew she was poor. As I contemplated her situation I suddenly realised that from her downcast eyes tears were rolling down unchecked and trickling onto the expensive sari that Mother had chosen and bought for her. A small dark patch was spreading steadily on her lap. Astonished by the sight of the salty stream, I quickly glanced at Mother who had not missed the tears. She seemed as mystified as I was.

'Why is the bride crying?' Low voices buzzed. For sure, those were not tears of joy. The girl was crying her heart out. Within the huge pillars of the temple the small crowd that had gathered to see an occasion of marriage began to whisper and twitter.

'Look, the bride is crying,' they whispered among

themselves. As we watched, baffled, the bride's elaborate, press-on nose stud slipped from her nostril and landed on the darkening stain in her lap. Silently she picked it up and refastened it on her wet nostril. Nobody missed that. The murmur in the small congregation became louder and a veil of red settled on Mother's cheeks. She was embarrassed by what looked like the bride's apparent distress or reluctance. But no one had forced her. Mother had spoken directly to the girl. She had been willing. 'Yes,' she had nodded, dropping her head.

The drums were loud when Jeyan turned towards his bride and tied the ceremonial thali around her neck. I saw him start when he noticed his bride's tears. Confused, he turned to seek out Mother's eyes. She nodded as a sign for him to carry on. Reassured that a bride's tears was another mystery that he was not privy to, he turned back and finished tying the all-important chain that would bind them as man and wife for ever. The ceremony was over.

At the reception Mother couldn't eat or drink anything. The sight of food made her feel sick. We left for Kuantan immediately. The journey was silent. Mother was morose and unhappy. Why was the bride crying? Why had the little boy come from nowhere to kick to smithereens the very things that symbolised a happy marriage?

The next day the newly married couple arrived at our home. They were to stay with us until they could afford to buy a house of their own. Mother had offered to contribute some money towards their new home. From the window I saw Jeyan's new wife alight gracefully from the car. She looked tranquil and composed. The tears were gone. Mother went out of the house to welcome the new bride with a tray of yellow sandalwood paste, kum kum, holy ash and a small pile of burning camphor. Ratha fell at Mother's feet, as the custom required. When she rose from the ground I saw for the first time my sister-in-law's eyes. They were blind with sorrow even as her mouth smiled politely and accepted Mother's blessings. No sooner had she been shown to her room than she was out once more.

She looked for detergent and began to clean.

She cleaned the kitchen, washed the bathroom, wiped down the kitchen shelves, dusted and mopped the living room, rearranged the contents of the spice cupboard, swept the backyard and cleared the weeds growing around the house. And when she was finished she began all over again. The moment she was free she volunteered to wash the clothes, clean the drains or do the cooking.

Her beautifully tragic face smiled away help. 'Oh, no, no.' She could manage. Not to worry, she liked cleaning. She was used to hard work. She spoke only when spoken to. In her cleaning rounds she found a dirty old basket under the house. I had once kept my doll in that old basket. Triumphantly, silently, she cleaned it and stood in the living room with it tucked into the crook of her elbow. 'I can do the marketing,' she offered hopefully.

'There's money inside the porcelain elephant in the showcase. Take fifty ringgit with you,' Mother called from the bedroom. Mother liked her, you see. She was pleased with her new daughter-in-law. Unlike Rani, Mother liked Ratha from the moment she met her.

Ratha took the money, did the marketing and returned with the exact change. Mother was pleased. 'See? I was right to trust her.'

In the kitchen Ratha set about turning the market produce into exotic meals. She was like an alchemist. She took some meat, some spices and some vegetables and turned them into sumptuous meals that clouded your senses and drugged you into hopefully asking, 'Is there any more?' Her genius was undeniable. She prepared jars of ginger marmalade and tomato chutney that followed you into tomorrow and next week. Unflinchingly she beheaded adorable wood pigeons and unsuspecting wild fowl, marinating the dark meat in papaya skins to tenderise them. They melted in the mouth like butter.

When we sat down, it was to little steamed Chinese dumplings filled with sweet pork or river fish stuffed with lime, cardamom and cumin seeds. She thought to scent rice with kewra essence before steaming it inside the whitened hollow of a bamboo stem, and to cook snake gourd with tamarind and star anise so it tasted like caramelised sugar. She knew how to bake chicken inside green coconuts and all about the secret taste of spicy banana flowers cooked with pomelo rind. For hours she gently boiled bamboo shoots until all the fine hairs fell off and she was left with the most delicious accompaniment to her glorious purple aubergine mash. She smoked mushrooms, sautéed orchids and served creamed, spicy durian paste with salt fish.

The marvel of the woman. She was too good to be true. How did she do it all?

How lucky Jeyan was!

Mother was beside herself with pride that such a daughter-in-law should enter her home. 'Look at her and learn,' she whispered harshly to me, looking critically at my uncombed hair. 'If only Lakshmnan could have acquired a wife such as this, he could have made something of himself,' she sighed wistfully.

At five o'clock every evening Ratha appeared bearing a platter filled with Rajastani cakes made with ground almonds, honey and butter, or succulent milk balls in rose syrup, and sometimes the most delicious deep violet cookies made from secret ingredients, or, my favourite, sweet and spicy sprig-like cakes made from nuts.

'Where did you learn all this?' Mother asked, truly impressed.

'A dear neighbour,' she said. As a child she had befriended an old woman who was the great-granddaughter of one of the sixteen celebrated cooks in the court kitchens of Emperor Dara Shukoh, Shah Jehan's eldest son. Emperor Dara Shukoh was a man proud of his sumptuous style, and only the most luxurious and refined could be sent from his kitchens for his approval. From torn pages and loose sheets, relics of the once great Mughal Empire, the old woman taught Ratha the secrets of Mughal cooking.

Ratha once fashioned a pomegranate for Mother made entirely from sugar, almonds and fruit juice and glazed with syrup. Mother broke it open and it was all there, the kernels, the seeds and the tissue between the seeds. It looked so real that I saw profound admiration and respect creep into Mother's eyes for the skill of the girl. For me she replicated a loaf of sweet bread with roasted almonds on the top. It was too beautiful to eat so I put it into the showcase. For Anna she made a mynah bird. So clever and so pretty. Of course it was too beautiful to eat.

'Come and sit beside me,' Mother invited once more.

'Just this one last thing,' Ratha replied, going to scrub

under the box where the coal was kept. No one had cleaned that spot for the last twenty years.

When finally there was truly nothing left to do, although I think she would have liked to clean the stove again, Mother said, 'Leave it. Have a little rest beside me.'

So she came reluctantly and sat, pulling her simple housecoat down low so that it almost covered her ankles. She kept her eyes downcast. Mother smiled encouragingly at her favourite daughter-in-law. Inside Mother's brain was the question, 'Why were you crying?' but from her lips came questions about Ratha's past. The girl answered dutifully, carefully. You couldn't accuse her of being cunning or obtuse, for she answered everything honestly and unhesitatingly and yet you had the impression that you were being meddlesome. From the slightly questioning look in her eyes one felt her demand again and again, 'And what business is it of yours?'

It was easy to see Mother's dissatisfaction, discomfort. She looked at Ratha and saw the picture of a pretty, neat, clean, smiling girl yet between her and the pretty picture was a remarkably polite but invisible barrier. There was something very wrong and Mother was determined to find out what it was. She never did.

Ratha had strange toilette habits about her. She disappeared into the bathroom with a wooden-handled brush with steel bristles and came out pink and glowing. Yes, she said surprised that we were surprised, she exfoliated her skin with it.

Jeyan skulked about watching her covertly as if she belonged to someone else. He slipped out of their shared room like a thief. His eyes caressed her, moved over her, rested on her and stroked her. All his private intentions stood tapping their feet impatiently. Sometimes you saw him try to catch her eyes, and you had to quickly avert yours in sheer embarrassment for the pleading in his. My brother was intoxicated with his new bride. Then on the fifteenth day came an invitation from Rani. The newly married couple were invited to dinner.

'See you soon,' they said to Mother on their way out.

'Return home safely, my children,' she bade.

Later that night Jeyan returned home alone.

'Where is your wife?' Mother queried anxiously.

'She's still at Rani's. In fact, Rani has invited us both to stay at her house for a while and she has sent me home to fetch Ratha's things.'

'Where will you both sleep?' Mother asked in a tone of bafflement, considering Lakshmnan and Rani's one-bedroom house and the surprising turn of events.

'In the living room on the floor, I suppose,' Jeyan said shrugging, impatient to take his wife's belongings and be gone.

'I see,' Mother said slowly. 'All right, take her things.'

Jeyan hurried into the spotless room he had shared with his wife for fifteen days. He threw all her belongings into a pathetically small bag and carried the bag onto the veranda where Mother sat silently. There he stood uncomfortably until she said, 'Well, go on then.'

He threw me a hasty look full of relief and shot down the stairs, the small bag banging against his thin legs. Mother sat on the veranda watching him leave with the strangest expression on her face. Even after he had turned into the main road and could no longer be seen, she sat staring hard at the horizon.

Ratha's wooden-backed brush with its hard steel bristles sat on the ledge outside the bathroom. In his haste Jeyan had missed it. I picked it up and ran the sharp bristles over my skin, recoiling with shock at how sharp and harsh they actually were on my bare skin and marvelling that someone could use such an object on their own body. Why, it could have been an instrument of torture.

Once I saw her in the market, a basket tucked into the crook of her elbow. Slender green beans and a bushy reddish-brown squirrel's tail leaned gently out of her basket. She was standing by the man who sold coconut water looking forlornly at the poor monkeys in their cages. She looked so tragic I squeezed back and let the tall stacks of gunnysacks full of rice at the side of a stall hide me. She was truly an intriguing creature. So full of sad secrets. All of a sudden she turned her head as if conscious of my scrutiny. Maybe she saw the shadow of me but she pretended she hadn't. I saw her hurry away from the monkeys who screamed and threw themselves angrily at the wire cage. I imagined her, lips slightly pursed, cleaning Rani's house from top to bottom and then starting all over again while Rani rested with her feet that she imagined swollen on a stool. Perhaps too she would replicate in sugar an aubergine or a bunch of green fingers for her new hostess.

Two months had passed since Ratha had gone for dinner and mysteriously not returned. Life went on as before. Jeyan came by in the evenings but he always seemed in a hurry to rejoin his wife. I know Mother was hurt that Ratha had left without even a proper goodbye but all she said was, 'I am happy as long as they are happy.'

Then one day Jeyan came bursting through the door in a frenzy of panic. His face was twisted with some unfamiliar emotion. It was nearly nine o'clock and Mother was waiting for the wrestling to start. She never missed it, got really involved, rooted loudly for her favourite wrestlers and even today still believes all those kicks and punches are for real. I don't have the heart to tell her otherwise. I know my mother; the match would lose most of its appeal. Anyway, that night when Jeyan came he was breathing heavily and almost incoherent with panic. 'Rani has given us twenty-four hours' notice to get out of her house!' he cried.

In those days when Government servants did something unpardonable or really terrible like stealing they were given twenty-four hours' notice to leave their quarters. And laughable as it seemed, Rani had taken it into her head to issue the same official-sounding notice to her brother-in-law and his wife.

Inside Mother's chest I could hear the sound of wheezing. 'Why?' she asked.

Jeyan threw his arms wildly into the air. 'I don't know. I think they argued. Lakshmnan has left the house in a rage and Rani is accusing Ratha of being unsatisfied by one man. I tell you, she is a madwoman. Can you believe that she is sitting outside on the steps of her house shouting loudly for all to hear that Ratha is trying to steal her husband? It's not true at all. Ratha loves me. Rani is crazy. She is crying, screaming and saying crude, vulgar things like Ratha wants both the brothers. In the kitchen Ratha is on her hands and knees washing the floor. I don't know what to do. What shall I do? Shall I bring Ratha back here?'

'No, not here because Ratha doesn't want to live here and I cannot have her back after the way she left but there are rooms available in the shop-houses over the road. Go and rent a room quickly. The shops are open until nine thirty at night.'

'But the rent, the deposit . . . ?'

'What happened to your dowry money?' Mother asked, her brows knitting.

'It's gone. Rani needed money badly so she asked Ratha for it. She promised to give it back in the next few months though.'

'When did all this happen?' Mother asked, in a very quiet voice.

Jeyan didn't have to think. 'Last Monday.'

'Didn't your wife want her husband before that, then?' Mother sneered angrily but poor Jeyan could only stare at her helplessly. He was only a man. No match for Rani, her dextrous tongue and her scheming ways.

'Find out how much the room costs and I will give you the money,' Mother told Jeyan. 'Now, go quickly. Otherwise I will surely end up paying for a hotel room.'

'All right, thank you.' Jeyan was already turning away, his face big with terrible worry. Mother's door was closed to him and his wife. Rani was ranting and raving on her doorstep and his wife was on her hands and knees brushing Rani's floor. And now it seemed clear that even his dowry was lost to a scheming woman. He had never faced such a multitude of problems in all his life.

'We should never have gone to stay in her house,' he muttered to himself. Jeyan was naturally obtuse to the ways of women. Once Mother asked him, 'Jeyan, do you know why your wife was crying on her wedding day?' He looked at her blankly, perplexed. Didn't all brides cry with joy during their wedding? Later he asked Ratha and came back to report. 'She won't tell me,' he complained almost petulantly. 'She says it's not important why.'

'Call it nerves if you want,' she said wearily, when he returned to insist.

So Jeyan and his bride moved to a cramped room on the first floor of a shop-house. They had to share a bathroom with ten other people and there was plenty to keep Ratha's cleaning instincts busy. She must have been very busy indeed for she never came to visit. Mother was sure that Rani had completely poisoned Ratha against us while she had the chance.

Late one afternoon Rani came to visit. She brought a small bag of grapes. The imported variety, she explained importantly. Mother thanked her and I hurried to relieve her of her package. She eased herself into a chair. I washed the grapes and, putting them on a plate, brought them into the living room. I offered them to her.

'How are you keeping?' Mother asked. You wouldn't think it to watch them but I knew that she hated Rani and was perfectly aware that the feeling was returned in equal measure.

'It's my joints,' she said, with an ache in her voice. She lifted her sari to show fleshy ankles. 'Look how swollen they are!' she cried. I stared at her healthy legs. Perhaps they did trouble her in the night but during the day they certainly looked healthy. Delicately she threw the green sari back over her legs and reached for a handful of grapes. 'I've come to explain to you about this whole mess with poor Jeyan and that terrible woman. I don't want you to get the wrong impression. I took that girl in purely from the goodness of my heart. Honestly, sometimes I think I am too good. I help people and they stab me in the back. I even bought her husband vitamins so he would be more vibrant with her. And what does she do? She tries to entice my husband as if I wouldn't notice. I've eaten more salt than she has eaten rice.'

She popped a couple of grapes into her mouth and chewed them reflectively. 'I knew straightaway what she was up to. Whenever Lakshmnan was in the backyard lifting weights she was in the kitchen pretending to clean. She doesn't know that I can see her when I am sitting on the sofa in the living room. I can see the looks she throws out of the kitchen window. I'm not blind. She wanted him to think she was hard-working. Trying to make me look bad. I borrowed a measly five thousand ringgit from her. A teacher's salary doesn't go far. The children were hungry. There was no food in the house and there were bills to be paid. Anyway I have since heard that she is running around saying that I, can you believe, *I*, who gave the ungrateful girl a roof over her head, have eaten her dowry.'

Rani stopped to draw breath and look outraged. 'In fact, you should give me that money, Mother-in-law, so I can have the pleasure of throwing that paltry sum in the little slut's face and stop her from pulling the good name of this family through the sewers.'

Mother's hand trembled harder but her smile stayed fixed.

Rani left later that afternoon without her money. For half an hour Mother paced the floors of our house, muttering, 'Amazing, just amazing!' She was so angry she couldn't sit still and then suddenly she laughed out loud. 'What a cheek my daughter-in-law has! Indeed, she must think me a fool. She expects me, me of all people to put not one, not two, but *five* thousand ringgit in her hand and hope that it will reach Ratha's hand. Hah, if I want Ratha to have the money I will give the girl the money myself and not try to pass it through this greedy crocodile's stomach first.'

Soon Ratha was pregnant. She suffered badly from morning sickness. Mother sent Marie biscuits, marinated ginger and three maternity dresses. She also offered to supply the down payment on a terrace house in a newly built development outside town but Ratha was too proud to accept and through Jeyan sent a polite refusal. I saw her once in the night market wearing one of the maternity dresses that Mother had sent. She had cut her hair to a more manageable length. Tendrils of hair curled around her thin neck, making her appear younger, more vulnerable. She was sad. Even amongst the busy, pushing throng of people I felt her sadness. This time she definitely saw me but she pretended not to, hurrying away into the colourful crowds.

A daughter was born to Jeyan. Mother and I went to the hospital to see Ratha and the baby. We took beautifully hand-stitched clothes with matching caps and miniature jewellery for the little girl. The baby was lovely, all pink and smelling of powder and milk. Mother said Anna had been the same colour when she was born. When Ratha saw us it seemed as if she held the baby tighter and closer to her breast. It is the only thing of value that she has ever had, I thought. Her knuckles shone white through her skin and the baby yelled in earnest.

'Come to your granny,' Mother crooned to the red-faced infant. Ratha frowned unhappily but in Mother's strong sure arms the baby unclenched its fists and stopped its tiny but furious cries. Mother gave the sleeping child back to Ratha and I saw her breathe a sigh of relief once the baby lay in her arms once more. A few days later Ratha and the newborn baby returned to the small room over the laundry shop.

'The fumes from the laundry are bad for the baby,' Mother said to Jeyan.

'Nonsense,' Ratha dismissed, when Jeyan told her what Mother had said.

She was pregnant again when I next saw her. She had on the same maternity dress that Mother had bought for her two years before. It was faded. Her hair had grown some. She had it in a ponytail. She looked unhappier than ever.

The second baby arrived. At the hospital she smiled politely at Mother and me. There was nothing behind that smile, neither hostility nor warmth. It was a stranger's smile. Her older child sat quietly on the bed. She stared at us curiously with large moist eyes. When Mother tried to carry her she covered her eyes with her hands and sobbed helplessly. She was frightened of this fierce woman whom she had never seen in all her life. As if scalded, Mother turned away. She busied herself pushing back the bedclothes to look at Jeyan's second child. Another girl. This time Mother didn't try to carry the child. Suddenly she seemed preoccupied and far away. After a few uncomfortable minutes we left. There was a sour taste at the back of my mouth.

Things were turning sour in the room on top of the shop-house too. Jeyan no longer rushed home to watch his wife with glazed eyes. He came to our house straight from work. He sat in the living room and stared at the television blankly, and after he had eaten his dinner he complained loudly to anyone who would listen about his wife. She was mean. She was turning the children against him. She refused to cook for him. She even refused to wash his clothes. Then things got even worse. She beat the children if they spoke to him. She emptied the contents of the dustpan onto his freshly laundered clothes that the Dhobi delivered outside the door. She had a special hatred for the first daughter. The girl was too much like her father. The child was becoming withdrawn and unreachable. She only spoke when spoken to and she was slow. 'Faster, eat faster,' Ratha would shout close to the child's ear and push food into her mouth faster and faster until the poor thing was choking and coughing. Then there would be tears, more angry words and smacks. It seemed that Ratha hated Jeyan with a vengeance. But how to be surprised? The kum kum had spilled before the marriage. The marriage had died then. This was only the stink of decomposition.

When the oldest girl was five years old Ratha asked Jeyan to move out. He found a room in a different shophouse along the same street. The truth was, he didn't know how to live without her. He had learned to live with the abuse and the hate, but he didn't know how to cope without her. She was in his blood for better or for worse. He wanted to remain close, to watch her and his children, but she refused even to look in his direction. She made it perfectly clear that she wanted nothing at all to do with her husband. She began divorce proceedings. Jeyan thought he would refuse to pay her maintenance and in that way he would bring her running back. From his shabby room a few doors away, he watched her, sure that she would never cope. No friends, no job, no caring family, no money, two babies to care for and all the bills to pay. She would have to come back, crawling on her hands and knees. I saw the vindictive light in his slow eyes. Teach her a lesson, it said.

But she vowed never to go back. She ignored the burning eyes that followed her as soon as she left her doorway. She drew an old unused blanket over the window at night so it was impossible to see even a shadow. Then she made a plan. She didn't want his money.

First she did odd jobs, went to work with her cowering children's small kitten faces attached to her skirts. That was hard. The women she worked for were heartless and exacting but they tolerated her children because she was such an impeccable cleaner. In the nights she began to sew sari blouses for the rich ladies she worked for and their pampered friends.

Slowly she saved up enough to go to cake baking lessons from an ex-policeman's wife. In a flat in the block of blue and white residences reserved for policemen and their families she learned to bake cakes. Then she used her precious hard-earned money to attend icing courses. From his window Jeyan jealously watched her, her progress, her freedom from him. He took to drinking in the evenings. In his blue meter-reader uniform he sat in the small sheds around town drinking the local samsoo.

I have seen him falsely merry in the company of other men. They are all bitter there, with failed marriages yapping at their heels and the weeping shadows of their abandoned children pulling at their ragged shirt-tails and begging for a little bit more love. How they dismiss women! Nags, sluts, good-for-nothings. Then they lewdly discuss the prostitutes that walk the streets by the newly built flats. It took Jeyan a long time to accept that Ratha was really lost to him, but by then he really didn't care about anything any more.

In her small room she practised until her gently piped

Happy Birthdays looked good enough to eat. Then she began to give lessons in the civic centre. She survived without a single cent from Jeyan. Her classes became well known in Kuantan. Not only Indian ladies attended, even Malays, well-known for their inborn sense of creativity and their patience for intricate artwork, began gracing her classes. They went home with bunches of rambutans and mangosteens fashioned from sugar. She moved out of that tiny room above the laundry that made her eldest daughter cough in the night. How she hated him! How she hated the woman who had spawned him! She wanted nothing more to do with us. We had cheated her of a life.

Thin and frightened, her children followed her into her new life. 'You have no father,' she told them. 'He is dead.' They nodded with large, believing eyes, like dumb angels, their tattered wings in their hands. Who knows what passed through their poor brains? Poor little things, their world so filled with cruel adults. Do they really not remember that stick-thin man who used to sometimes raise them high above his head? That man with the big, simple face and the slow mouth with only a few words inside it. Yes, they remember him as they remember the lost buttons on their blouses. Inside clothes, clean but worn they learned to tiptoe around their mother in their narrow room. Her temper was always so fierce and so nearby. She took them by the hand to school. Their teacher was a friend of Anna's.

'They are such good children,' the woman confided in Anna. 'But I wish they'd speak a little more.'

The last time I saw Ratha, she was getting onto a bus. They had moved to the other side of town as far away as possible from her drunken pathetic husband. I watched her carefully. The children were not with her. Even from the back I recognised her instantly. Perhaps it was the steel brush, or perhaps it was the hard life but something had altered her person to an almost unrecognisable degree. Her skin hung in small folds around her bones. At her elbows pleats of skin flapped as she adjusted the basket on her arm. Then she turned to pay the bus driver and collect her change I saw with shock that half of her mouth had twisted permanently downwards like a semi-paralysed stroke patient. Her hair had fallen out in patches and in some places I could see pure scalp. She reminded me of a Tamil movie I had once seen where the heroine runs away from the camera's eye into woods. It is wintertime and all the trees are bare and stark with sleep. All you see is her disappearing back. The disappearing back reminds me of her. The camera moves further and further away from her. She is becoming smaller and smaller until she is but a dot on the horizon. Goodbye Ratha.

I never know where the years go but I do not sit outside amongst the plump ladies fingers, the richly coloured aubergines watching insects any more or feeding the chickens in my magic cave under our house. The land outside is a barren wasteland. Weeds have taken over. I wake up in the morning and begin my household chores and then it is time for an afternoon nap. Then there is the TV, of course, till bedtime. Sometimes a movie at the cinema and on Fridays the evening prayers at the temple beckon. One morning I woke up and I was forty-five, unmarried, and Father was eighty-two years old. I looked at him, an old man on a rickety bicycle. For years I had watched him from the window as he climbed on the same rusty old bicycle and rode down the same path, and worried that one day he would fall and hurt himself. But I was at the market the day it finally happened. It was Mother, standing by the window watching, who saw him tumble to the ground, tripped by the bulging roots of the rambutan tree grown huge with the years.

She ran out of the house without her slippers to help my poor old father as he lay there on his back, too stunned to move. Mother was sixty-one years old. Her limbs were old and shrinking but there was still great strength in them. She crouched down beside him. His face was like a dried-up riverbed. Full of deep cracks. For years she had read him like a book. He was in terrible pain. She reached out and touched the cracks. Even through the pain he stared at her in surprise. The back wheel of his bicycle was still turning. She tried to help him up.

'No, no,' he groaned. 'I cannot move. My leg is broken. Call the ambulance.'

So Mother ran to Old Soong's house. A servant let her in. That was the first time she had been inside the place. She recognised the rosewood dining table where Mui Tsai had served dog stew to her master, and where the master had first run his fingers down her young thighs. Where the Japanese soldiers had thrown her on her back and raped her one by one. The terrazzo floor was cool under Mother's feet.

'Mistress Soong,' Mother called out in a thin, hoarse voice.

Finally Mistress Soong opened a dark, wooden door and walked out. She was ugly beyond description. All her beauty was gone. She was fat and going bald. In her eyes, made smaller by rolls of fat, there was no joy. In fact, Mother's presence seemed to make her uncomfortable.

Here was someone who knew her secrets. All her ugly secrets must lie inside this old hag. The hag opened its mouth and explained the necessity for a phone. Mistress Soong pointed to a phone near the hallway. After the call Mother thanked Mistress Soong and quickly walked out.

She passed Minah's house where a long time ago she and Mui Tsai had seen the big python. Minah was long gone. Her Japanese protector had left her with a piece of land and money and she had moved away. Mother quickly passed the Chinese house where poor Ah Moi had hanged herself all those years ago. Father was lying flat on his back. He had not moved at all. She felt like crying and didn't know why. It was obvious that the injury was not serious. Why did she feel suddenly so lost, so abandoned? As if he had left her when it was she who had left him to call an ambulance. Why, after all these years, did she suddenly feel a pain in her heart at the thought of his pain, at the thought of losing him? She tried hard to remember that he irritated her, annoyed her and frustrated her beyond endurance.

She looked down at him and he looked at her.

There was no expression on his face. He just looked at Mother as he had for all the years she had known him. Solid, dependable and as malleable as dough. She thought she should tell him something of what she was feeling. Perhaps he would be comforted by her confused thoughts, her strange longing for him to be well. Then I came running and the soppy words died in her throat. She felt embarrassed that an old woman like her had thought those silly things. She was grateful that she had not spoken those ridiculous, childish words. It might have shocked him into a heart attack.

She left me with Father and went into the house to get

ready. She wanted to accompany the old man to the hospital. Stand by his side. She certainly felt too restless to stay at home alone. Quickly she changed out of her faded brown and green sarong and put on a light blue sari with a small dark green border. Into her *choli* she tucked a purse that she had first filled with money. Who knows how much medicine could cost these days? She combed her hair and twisted it into a tight bun at the nape of her neck. All of this had taken her only a few minutes to accomplish.

The house was very quiet. It seemed to know that a tragedy had occurred outside. It seemed to know that old bones don't heal. Finally she met her own eyes in the mirror and stopped, startled. They were foreign. She looked closer. Some distrusted emotion swam inside. It made her feel uneasy so she quickly looked away and started to think practically. Her feet. Something had to be done quickly with her feet. She washed the blood off the soles and, slipping her feet into her slippers, went to wait by the old man. She stood over us regally, watching me huddled beside Father, smoothing the white hair around his head, while silent tears poured down my face. But my weakness gave her strength. She was glad then that she had not succumbed to those strange emotions. She is a proud woman. She did not want to look weak or foolish. It was a good thing that it was not her huddled in that undignified fashion on the ground, sobbing her heart out. She knew the neighbours were looking from behind their curtains. Once they might have all crowded around trying to help, like the time when the Japanese soldiers took away Minah's husband and shot him dead. But now the neighbourhood was full of new people. A whole generation of people who smiled and waved from afar. People who believed in a strange, Westernised concept called privacy.

The ambulance drove into our cul-de-sac. I waved wildly, calling out, 'Here, here! Over here!'

Two white-coated men transferred Father onto a stretcher. He winced with pain. For Mother there was a feeling of *déjà vu* seeing him on the narrow stretcher being ministered to by urgent hands clothed in white. She remembered the last time she had seen him stretched on a narrow bed. He had been grey and unconscious then. She had been only a baby herself then. She climbed into the ambulance and sat quietly as it sped along the streets of Kuantan.

Father closed his eyes tiredly. He seemed so far away. Strangely she longed to touch him, to feel that he was still there with her. Her own thoughts confused her. Perhaps she was getting old or perhaps she understood his tiredness. She had long known that his days dreamed and longed for nightfall, where forgetfulness would descend like a thick, soft blanket. Perhaps she feared the ultimate nightfall that he appeared to welcome, invite even. Once his eyelids fluttered open. They lingered on her wordlessly, and as if comforted by the sight of her anxious face they fluttered shut again. She was pleased to have been his rock. She felt regret melt and slowly fill all the little holes and crevices inside her being. She had been horrible to him. All his life he had done the best he could for her and she had been nothing but impatient, rude and overbearing. She had made sure that all the children knew that she was in charge. She hadn't given him face. She had even been jealous of all the little affections that they smuggled out into his bleak world. She had been selfish and petty.

It was only a hairline crack in his thighbone. They wrapped his leg in white plaster. He lay on the bed with his eyes closed. She realised that he was losing colour. He used to be so black and now he was fading. He was now grey-brown. They brought around a tray of food. He looked at the pale food and shook his head unhappily. Mother mixed some of the rice and the runny fish broth and fed Father the way she had fed us all when we were very young. Like a child, Father ate from her hand. From that day onwards he would not eat unless Mother fed him herself.

'I'll bring home-cooked food tomorrow,' she promised, glad to be able to contribute positively. When she left the ward she left with a heavy heart. She couldn't understand herself. After all, she had spoken at length to the doctor. It was only a hairline crack. And he had assured her that there was absolutely no reason to worry. In three weeks the cast could come off and he would be as good as new. She took the bus home. Taxis were so expensive. Anyway she always enjoyed sitting on a bus. By the time she got home it was already four and she hadn't eaten a thing all day nor taken her asthma pills. Quickly she swallowed some with water. She had no appetite but her stomach rumbled audibly so she ate some rice and curry.

For three weeks her life took on a pattern. She woke up with no thought for breakfast, quickly cooked some food and rushed to the hospital. She fed him with her own hand. Then she collected the empty tiffin carrier and returned home on the bus. At home she took her asthma pills and in about half an hour she steeled herself to eat her lunch. Of course she didn't know that swallowing the strong asthma pills on an empty stomach was damaging her stomach walls. Every day the acid inside her stomach was eating into the walls. She ignored the occasional twinge and cramp. There were more important things to do.

On the day the cast was supposed to come off, Mother went early. She waited by his bedside while they cut away the hard, yellowing cast.

'There you go,' said the doctor cheerfully to Father.

Father tried to move his leg but it was like a stone attached to his body.

'Go on,' urged the doctor. 'Move your leg. It will be a little bit stiff but it's as good as new now.'

Poor Father tried as hard as he could to move his leg.

'It won't move,' he said finally, exhausted with the effort of trying to shift his stone leg. The doctor frowned and the nurse made a face. These old men. Always fussing unnecessarily. Mother looked on. The twinge in her stomach bothered her. It had become a burning pain.

The doctor examined Father's leg again. Finally he declared that perhaps the cast had been too tight and what Father needed now was physiotherapy. He gave the impression that a little therapy would have Father running up and down the hospital corridors again. In fact, his leg was dead. All the nerves in it were dead. It was cold and hard. It was quite without doubt paralysed.

For three months Father endured therapy at the hands of unsympathetic nurses. They accused him of being lazy. One day he woke up to find a small piece of paper inside his mouth. He thought it was one of the nurses playing a joke on him. He was lonely and now the butt of their jokes. He knew that his inability to get better irritated them. They often behaved as if he was purposely not trying to walk. He asked to leave. He told the doctor he would do his exercises at home. He had big strong sons who could help him. An ambulance brought him home. They carefully transferred him to his big bed.

I heard him sigh with relief.

But now that he was home he stopped doing his exercises and slowly but surely his other leg became stiff. The paralysis stole up his legs and began to creep up his body. He became a strange figure bent at the knees. When we tried to straighten his legs they slowly inched their way up the bed until his knees were bent again. A month passed and Mother was diagnosed with chronic gastritis. There was nothing she could eat without causing her extreme pain. All day long she drank warm milk and ate balls of rice mixed with yoghurt. She couldn't even eat fruit any more. An apple or an orange could make her cough blood. A tomato might make her scream in pain and food with the smallest amount of spices or oil would make her throw her plate on the floor in pure frustration.

In the bedroom it was obvious that Father was dying. Mother sat by his bedside but even she was powerless to stop Death from claiming him inch by inch. Indeed that is how Death took him, day by day creeping up his body with casual unhurried ease. When Death claimed his hands, she put hot-water bottles on them as if she could warm up his flesh and stop it from dying. But the truth was the pretty child of death was making Father pay for eluding his clutches all those years ago when he had sat outside the hole in the jungle, laughed and said, 'Nine out of ten is still very good work.'

Mother made Lakshmnan or one of the boys come by once a day to lift him and change his position. He was full of bedsores. They picked Father's frail body up in their hands and washed him as if he were a child.

In seven months he was paralysed from his neck down. His entire body was so still and so oddly cold to the touch that it seemed as if he was already dead. Father did everything slowly. Now he was dying slowly, painfully. It was his way. His suffering breath was unpleasant. He no longer wanted food. Slowly his head grew cold too. Mother tried to pour milk down his throat but it only dribbled out of the corners of his mouth and down his chin. And still she refused to give up. She sat beside him all day.

One day he looked into Mother's face and whispered, 'I have been more fortunate than Thiruvallar.' After that he stopped speaking and the horrible stillness of death settled in on him. Through his half-closed eyelids only the whites of his eyes showed. His breath grew so shallow that only a mirror held to his face showed that there was still breath in his stiff body. His face and head were so cold and yet he was breathing. His eyes stared ahead into nothing. For four days he lay cold and yet breathing. Then on the fifth morning Mother woke up and he was cold all over. There was no longer warm breath coming out of his nostrils. His mouth was half open. All his children and grandchildren were at his bedside when Mother called Dr Chew. Dr Chew pronounced Father dead.

Mother didn't cry. She asked Lakshmnan to straighten his legs. From the kitchen she brought a thick piece of wood and then she left the room. Lakshmnan slammed the thick wood on my father's kneecaps. We heard a crack and my brother slowly pushed down the stiff legs until they were straight once more. Lakshmnan brought out Mother's bench into the living room and laid Father on it. The mattress from the big silver bed was taken outside into the backyard and burned. It made a large fire that evening. I saw Mother standing there all by herself watching the orange flames quickly eat into the cotton stuffing. She looked like a widow fearlessly contemplating suttee. I could imagine her rushing fearlessly into the fire where her husband's body burned. Nobody needed to push Mother. Nobody would dare in fact. She was burning more than a mattress. She was burning a part of her life. All the children had been conceived on that mattress. She had lain with my father for so many years on that mattress. Over the years she had filled and refilled the stuffing to keep it plumped up.

She watched it burning and it dawned on her that she had loved him. All those years she had loved him and not even known it. Even the unfamiliar twinges when he had first fallen she had ignored as foolishness. Perhaps she had known then but she had been too proud to tell him. She should have told him. Bitterly she wished that she had. It would have made him happy. Why, why, she berated herself, didn't she tell him? It might have even given him the will to live. She knew that it was his life-long ambition that she should come to love him. The last words that had escaped so painfully from his immobile mouth sang with bitter sweetness in her ears. 'I have been more fortunate than Thiruvallar.' She understood his message. In the string of stories that make the chain of Hindu legend, Thiruvallar was one of the greatest sages that ever lived. At his wife's deathbed he granted her a boon. 'Ask,' he said. 'Ask for anything your heart desires.' She could have asked for the most precious thing every Hindu aspires to – *moksha* – release from the necessity of further births, but instead she asked for the reason why he had requested, at the beginning of their marriage, a needle and a glass of water with every meal. As far as she could tell he had never used the objects.

'Ah, my dear wife, the needle was to pick up every grain of rice that might have accidentally fallen off the banana leaf, and the bowl of water was to dip them in and wash them before I ate them. Waste is a sin that denies entrance into heaven. But because you had never once allowed a single grain to fall by the wayside I never needed to use the needle or the bowl of water.' Because she had been such a good wife and so far beyond reproach, Thiruvallar granted her the boon of *moksha*. With his last breath Father wanted my mother to know that she was even more precious to him than Thiruvallar's perfect wife.

Tears ran down Mother's face. She knew she had made a mess of everything. She had inspired the children to despise him, taught them to ignore him, and ridiculed his gentle nature as dumb acceptance and even as sheer sluggishness. Then she systematically set about turning the gentle man into a foolish stranger. She had betrayed him. He who had loved her so dearly. She felt defeated by her own impatience, her own incredibly clever mind. Her head had ruined her heart.

Sevenese

Dreaming when Dawn's left hand was in the sky
I heard a voice within the tavern cry
'Awake, my little ones, and fill the cup
Before life's liquor in its cup be dry.'

All my life I was steadfast in my refusal to acknowledge the greater subtlety of Omar Khayyam. The real, mystical meaning to his verse is like a wine, so potent it becomes dangerous to the animal that consumes it. It seemed easier, the shallow Western interpretation. To have ever acknowledged that the 'voice within the tavern' was not the wheedling, mewling sound that slipped out of rouged lips in the early hours of the morning in some seedy hotel room in Thailand, could have solved the mystery of life. And I didn't want it solved. Solved, it slouched drab and boring in the distance.

Did Khayyam know about Apsaras, divine female nymphs that can be bought for a few American dollars a night? I will tell the great poet, should I come across him in the next world, that my life's liquor was a golden liquid too, but it came out of a Jim Bean bottle. And bloody good it was. Omar would understand. He was a man with a keen eye. He would guess that to deny myself the illusion of ignorance would have been to deny the

374

quality of the pot, even question the hand of the potter. The issue was a simple one. A vessel of a more ungainly make I was. Should I sneer at myself for leaning awry?

He who wrought me into shape also stamped me with the vine leaf of corruption. Dark green, it flowered early in life and grasped my very soul. What was to be done?

I am a compulsive cad. Strong liquor, rich food and the easy life move me in a way that is doubtless wrong. I look at my mother with horrified fascination. Material ambition is the compulsion that drives her. Is it possible, I think to myself, that she does not know how ugly a beast it is that she clasps so close to her breast?

Thwarted, it has slowly sucked the life out of her. So she wished it into us but the same seed of compulsion bears differently in different vessels. It looks different, smells different and demands a completely different menu. Mine smells like cheap perfume and dines on endless lengths of smooth flesh, but Lakshmnan's smells metallic, drives an impressively large Mercedes and lives in a grand house in the better part of town.

She was so strong, my mother, that she crushed all she came into contact with. Me, I rebelled. Took the long road home. The words were hardly out of her mouth and I had made the decision not only to enter the house of the snake-charmer but also to befriend his sons and learn their dark secrets and skills. Mother was right, of course, there was something very strange going on in that house. Even as a young boy I could sense that invisible aura, in places blacker than others, but mostly in the room with the black curtains where a large statue of Kali the Goddess of Death and Destruction stood.

Malevolently she stared at me and I stared back fearlessly. That was what my Maker did. His hand shook. He made me selfish, heartless and fearless in the face of the unknown. My point of no return is yet to be tested. 'Take me further,' I challenge recklessly.

Even now that my bones are aching and my muscles weary, it still urges inside me. It is damn near impossible to ask for just one beer or just one girl. I ask for four and line them up on the bar so that their stuck-on paper brands stare at me. Four girls lined up in a row and bent double is a mighty pretty sight too. Yes, I filled my cup until it overflowed and still I filled it some more.

I was waiting for my first prostitute. 'Wah, wah, wah,' played in my ear and the girls with the downcast eyes bored me. The sheer energy needed to take out a repressed Indian virgin with a fat mother attached to her knickers and the months and months of mild courtship with no guarantee of getting anywhere left me limp. I wanted less fuss, more variety. I hung about at the top of the school steps with my cool mates and we watched the girls coming up. Diligently asking them all if we could touch their mangoes. Invariably all the ugly, fat girls grew belligerent, cursing us soundly, while the pretty ones blushed or dropped their heads coyly. Once one of them fell in love with me, but of course I broke her heart. The thing I searched for didn't lie in the arms of a good woman. I wanted seasoned women who knew they ought to be paid.

All the way up to Thailand I went, on the Malayan Railway lines, for a short trip into the red-light district, and beautiful girls put their palms together and bowed deeply from the waist in the way of their kind. They removed their ornate headdresses and washed my feet in a basin of scented water while I closed my eyes and lay back with just one thought: *I am home.*

I know I am looking for something. Something I have not found. I traverse the streets of Chow Kit and watch the transvestites. Plastic women, they are called. They sashay boldly up and down the street; their flat chests thrust far out in front of them, their tight bottoms pushed far out behind them, pouting at passing men. Often they slide up to me in a vortex of self-denial – wigs, false eyelashes, stuffed bras, tight girdles, brightly painted fingernails and platefuls of vibrant make-up, their voices artificially high.

'How much?' I asked once just for sport, and instantly she snaked down beside me, and with a rich smile and a caressing hand ready to do my bidding.

'Depends what you want,' she bantered. I looked at her. The skin was soft but the eyes were wretched. An Adam's apple bobbed in her throat. It was impossible to sustain the mischief. I sighed regretfully.

She was instantly alert. 'But not much,' she assured me.

I know why she is far less than a prostitute – because she gives herself away as if she were a can of worms. Her sexuality can only be offered in the dark to strangers with deformed tastes.

'Maybe next time,' I told her.

'I show you strange things,' she insisted with a peculiar blankness in her face. I believed her. I believed that she could show me something strange and exciting but utterly abhorrent to her. The idea fascinated me. How misshapen is the vessel? Aah, if only she wasn't a man. But Sevenese, my lad, she *is* a man.

I shook my head and he stood up huffily, with exaggerated movements. Let it be known I had wasted his precious time. I watched him walk away and join another of his kind. Together they pointed and stared at me venomously. I know their tragedy. Their misfortune is not that they are not what they should be but that they are not what they want to be. Women.

Part Four

The First Taste of Forbidden Wine

Dimple

I have a memory of myself when I was very young sitting anxiously on a packed bag by the front door, my hair in pigtails, my feet encased in my best shoes and my heart counting the minutes like a very loud clock inside my chest. I was waiting to go to Grandma Lakshmi's home for the holidays but getting there was an obstacle course sometimes too difficult for a child to manage. The slightest infringement could lose me the privilege. Hardest of all, I had to pretend disdain at the prospect of the forthcoming holiday.

So it was only after Father came home and the two of us were sitting in the car on the way to the bus station that I could breathe a sigh of relief and know for certain that my trip was no longer subject to last-minute changes of plan.

At the door of the bus I kissed Papa goodbye and he waited at the platform to return my wave until the bus pulled out of sight. I closed my eyes and left all my troubles behind – my brother Nash's threats to tie me to a chair in the kitchen and burn all the hair on my head, and Mother's advancing, sneering face. Soon, very soon I would sleep so close to my darling Grandma that I would hear the asthma inside her chest. Like a tired engine. Worse every time I came back.

I sat very still during the journey, staring out of the window, not daring to nod off or leave the bus for refreshments at Bentong with everyone else. I was terrified of the bad men Mother had warned me of who spirited away little girls travelling alone. At Kuantan station Aunty Lalita would be waiting for me, a Big Sister cake in hand, and the wind from the jetty blowing her thin curls into her large, smiling face. I got down from the bus, put my hand in hers and together we walked, swinging our clasped hands, like best friends all the way back to Grandma's. In my mind's eye I can see the two of us walking through town, my luggage in her right hand and me barely able to contain my excitement. Kuantan hardly ever changed through the years. It was always dear and familiar. Like coming home.

As we turned the corner at Old Soong's house I would see Grandma, slightly hunched, standing by the door. Breaking free from Aunty Lalita's hold I would run towards the figure on the veranda. When finally I flew into her open arms and buried my face in her dear, familiar smell she always said the exactly same thing. '*Aiyoo*, how thin you have become!'

And always I think to myself: *If there be a paradise on earth . . .*

It is here. It is here. It is here.

How crystal clear is the memory of my early morning hours at Grandma's house before the sun crept up the horizon. I can see myself now waking up in the cool darkness, too excited about the awakening day. The light is still on in the living room and Uncle Sevenese is drunk. He had long claimed the night for his own and knighted himself 'a drunk Buddhist'. To be young and sit in the presence of effortless cynicism is to be utterly captivated. And my uncle was the master of cynics. 'How could one not revere a man who died because he was too courteous to refuse bad food?' he says of Buddha.

When he sees me peeping from the doorway he calls me into the living room.

'Come here,' he whispers, patting the seat beside him. I run to join him. He tousles my hair like he always does.

'What are you doing still up?' I ask.

'What time is it?' There, the slight slur again. I giggle inside my hands. I never saw the damage. I only saw a man of infinite sophistication celebrating a life of gorgeously outrageous ideas. The whisky bottle appeared incidental, if anything; its effects, amusing and friendly. When he was like this he discussed adult things with me that he and I both knew he really shouldn't. I poke my finger into his large tummy and my finger disappears into rolls of fat.

'Make your tummy shake,' I order and instantly his entire tummy vibrates. That brings forth peals of uncontrollable laughter.

'Sshh,' he warns, stuffing his bottle of Bells further down the cushions. 'You will wake the Rice Mother.'

'Who?' I demand.

'The Giver of Life, that's who. In Bali her spirit lives in effigies made out of sheaves of rice. From her wooden throne in the family granary she protects the crops she made bountiful in the paddy fields. So sacred is she that sinners are forbidden to enter her presence or consume a single grain from her figurine.'

Uncle Sevenese wags a finger at me. He is without doubt drunk. 'In this house, our Rice Mother is your grandmother. She is the keeper of dreams. Look carefully and you will see, she sits on her wooden throne holding all our hopes and dreams in her strong hands, big and small, yours and mine. The years will not diminish her.'

'Oh,' I exclaim, the idea growing large in my mind. I imagine Grandma, not frail and often sad, but as a Rice Mother, strong and splendid, grains of rice sticking to her body, and holding all my sleeping dreams in her substantial hands. Enchanted with the picture I lay my head on my uncle's pillow tummy.

'Dear, dear Dimple,' he sighs sadly. 'If only you will never grow up. If only I could protect you from your own future, from yourself. If only I could be like the Innu Shamans who can beat a drum from miles and miles away and make the deer dance while waiting for the hunters to arrive. While waiting for their own deaths.'

Poor Uncle Sevenese. I was too small to know that the demons and the ghosts were fast at his heels, their eyes huge and glowing like crocodiles' eyes in the dark. Chasing. Chasing. Chasing. I lay on his belly, innocent and wondering if a shaman very far away had already beaten his drum and the hunters were on their way. Was that why he was always out dancing the rumba, the merenge and the cha cha cha?

'Birth is only death postponed,' he tells me, the whisky warm on his breath. Then he takes the sleeper train to dangerous, secret parts of Thailand where it is possible to disappear without a trace. Where the girls have prized sets of impossibly clever muscles and extrude *kamasalila* (love fluids) as fragrant as fresh lychees.

Still craving for something he cannot name he leaves for Port au Prince in Haiti where he consorts with voo-doo doctors who have needle-thin fireworks sprinting out of their black auras. He watches seduced as they open the gates of the spirits and show him two beings called Zede and Adel. He sends a postcard of a large waterfall where 'everybody constantly spins into trances, shooting strange, unrecognisable words from their mouths and writhing uncontrollably on the rocks'.

Over the years I saved letters with pictures of him standing at the immense feet of the Egyptian pyramids. 'Finally figured out how ants feel when they stand at our doorstep,' he scrawls. He sleeps in the desert under an astonishing ceiling of millions of stars and walks through a sea of dead birds, their tiny eyes and beaks encrusted with the whirling sands, the ones that would never finish their migratory journey across the desert. He drinks strong camel's milk and notes how vociferously they complain when they are being loaded. They have feet as big and as soft as chapattis. He eats bread as hard as stone and watches amazed as tiny mice appear as if out of nowhere for the smallest crumb fallen on the sand. He informs me that the word for woman, *horman*, comes from the Arabic word, *haram* meaning forbidden, but the men there call the pretty girls 'bellaboooozzzz'.

He is offered pretty girls in shimmering veils and rich fabrics lying supine on luxurious cushions by the pool, protected by the stone latticework that allows them to watch life beyond the walls unseen. They gaze down into their swaying reflections on the water or into their antique Persian mirror rings. Their flashing eyes, surrounded by clusters of painted stars, look back, adolescent with a red dot in the inner corners. Their breasts spread with musk gleam and their belly buttons, inspired with precious jewels, sparkle in the setting sun as they playfully sprinkle rose water on each other. Uncaring and unaroused he wrote, 'Am I finally weary? What can be the matter?'

Cheerlessly he disappeared on safari for a month. 'The lack of company will do me good,' he said.

'He will lose his job,' Grandma lamented.

He returned restored somewhat, blackened to ebony by the ferocious sun and strangely unmoved by the impression he gained that it was only a matter of time before the African lion got tired of the Wheel of Life and went the same way as the Indian lion: an endangered species. I was terribly dismayed. I love lions. Their tawny eyes, their golden paws and that gorgeous roar of a full-grown male that sounds like it comes out of a cavernous hole in the earth. At dusk they look like they have been hewn out of the same rock they lie on.

He travelled down to Singapore, unenthusiastically inspecting the standards, and eventually took the over-night route north to the land of a thousand reclining Buddhas, saffron-clad monks beating giant gongs, and delicately carved spires glowing in the smoky, purple evening. There he closed his eyes and reached out to experience the familiar again, a yielding breast, a curving belly and a silken thigh.

At Grandma's the food was simple but healthy. She held my face by the kitchen window in the streaming sunlight and checked if my earlobes were healthy and transparent. Satisfied, she nodded and went back to chop-ping onions, quartering aubergines or tearing spinach leaves. She was curious about everything – Father, school, my health, my friends. She wanted to know everything and seemed especially proud of my good grades.

'Like your father,' she said. 'Before his bad luck pounced on him.'

We played many games of Chinese chequers, Grandma cheating a great deal. She hated losing. 'Bloody pool,' she shouted to distract me and quick as a flash she moved her pieces around.

Often Grandad and I sat quietly on the veranda watching the evening sun turn red in the sky to settle for the night. I read the *Upanishads* aloud for him. Once he fell asleep in his reclining chair. When I woke him up he looked startled for a moment, squinted in confusion and called me Mohini.

'No, it's me, Dimple, Grandad,' I said and he looked disappointed. I recall thinking that maybe he didn't love me after all. Maybe he only loved me because I looked a little like her.

The rest of the holiday always flew by, the sun setting faster and faster, bringing the holiday's end nearer and nearer. On the last night I always cried myself to sleep. The thought of going back to school, to Nash and Bella's jealousy and to Mother's fury, was almost too much to bear. She was always angriest when I returned from Grandma's.

While we were growing, Mother and Father were the most unpredictable element in our lives. They were like gunpowder and a match looking only for a flint or a rough surface so they could legitimately explode in a spectacular display of fireworks. In their time they found many flints and rough surfaces. Grandma said they were enemies from a past life tied together by their sins. Like two cannibals who feed on each other to live. They could have a conversation about the nuns in Andalusia, or how the breakfast eggs should be cooked, that could end with a black eye and a set of broken crockery.

'And what are you doing spying on us?' she would then scream hysterically at me.

'I've got a meeting in an hour – why don't I leave you

at Amu's house, hmmm?' Papa suggested, his handsome face sad.

Dear, darling Amu. I do love that woman. I can't remember a time when we didn't have Amu, when I haven't gone outside in the mornings and not seen her sitting on a low stool surrounded by plastic pails, scrubbing and scrunching our dirty clothes. Mother could never do housework because of her arthritis so she hired Amu to wash, mop and wipe. She was there every morning, squatting outside with her pails of dirty clothes when we awakened. When she looked up and saw me, her small, triangular face would light up.

'Mind the water,' she would say.

And I would carefully arrange my dress around my knees and sit on the kitchen steps watching her.

'Amu,' I would complain peevishly, 'I caught Nash trying to rip out the pages of the book Uncle Sevenese sent yesterday.'

'Oh dear, oh dear,' she would say, clicking her red tongue. And then instead of sympathising with me she would launch into a long convoluted tale about her brother's spiteful wife or she would produce a long-lost evil cousin out to swindle Amu's poor unsuspecting parents. Tales so full of intrigue and horrible people that I soon forgot my own petty troubles.

There were good times too. So exquisite you knew they could never last. Times when the entire family celebrated one of Papa's deals with a big Chinese meal in one of the better hotels, eating abalone and lobster. When Mother was in such a good mood that I would wake up in the night and hear her singing to Papa. In those intoxicated days it seemed she was consumed by her love for Papa, burning so brightly I was scared to touch her glowing face. Then it seems she was even jealous of the Malay dancers on TV that Papa glanced at. But the money was soon gone and Mother and Papa hastily returned to their ritual fighting once more as if I had dreamed the happy lapse.

Once Mother took Bella with her to beg a loan from an old friend. Bella said he pushed an envelope of money very slowly along the table with his middle finger, all the time staring at Mother intensely.

'Next time come without the child,' he called after their departing backs.

Our finances became so bad that Amu had to bring rice and curry from her house for us. I remember tears running down Mother's cheeks as she ate a piece of curried egg. She didn't save any for Papa. When he came home there was no food.

Three days later Mother went to see her friend again. She didn't take Bella with her. She came home with a brand-new pair of gold and brown shoes for herself, a large grocery bag full of food and a pair of strangely glittering eyes. When Papa returned they fought viciously and Mother shredded her new shoes in a fit, hurled herself on the bed and howled like a wolf. They did not speak again until the rainy weather arrived and Mother couldn't do anything but sit with her feet up. Her knees troubled her but her hands were so stiff and painful with arthritis she could hardly open a jam jar. Then I thought Papa must love her, for he cleaned her every time she went to the toilet.

One day I came home from school and Papa told me Grandad had fallen off his bicycle. By the time I was able to see him he was so thin his hands were like long pieces of bone covered with skin. He cried when he saw me that time. I knew then that he was dying. A shrivelled box full of history. Stories so precious I knew I must save them all on paper or perhaps on tape. I did not trust my memory. One day my daughter's daughter must know them. On my next trip back to Grandma's I found a boxed tape recorder waiting for me. 'Make your dream trail,' she said . . . and that is what I did.

After I had read the *Upanishads* to him I switched on my machine and let him talk. He spoke sadly but beautifully. Behind me, where his eyes focused, I turned around and saw his Nefertiti. More beautiful than anything I could have imagined.

Every day Grandma fed him a small, very special medicinal black chicken that she cooked in herbs for him. It was very expensive to buy but Grandma planned to give Grandad a chicken a day until he was better. She cooked a chicken a day for nearly a year. Grandad died on 11 November 1975, leaving in my care his voice. All the grandchildren stood around his shrunken body carrying lighted torches. Grandma did not cry. Mother came for the funeral too. She asked Papa whether there would be a reading of a will. I saw Papa slap her and walk out of the room. 'No, of course there won't be. The spider has it all, hasn't she?' she screamed after him.

When I was nineteen years old, a man dashed out of MINB bank's lift and told me the craziest thing ever. He joked that he had looked out of the eye of a telescope and fallen in love with me, but his eyes seemed as surprised as I was. I thought he was a madman in an expensive suit but I let him buy me an ice cream.

'Call me Luke,' he said, with a lopsided smile. He looked attractive then. Terribly sophisticated and out of my league. In the basement food court I listened to him as I ate my strawberry ice cream and wondered how to eat the banana in the bowl with him watching me so closely. In the end I didn't. It was too embarrassing. Leaving it was embarrassing too but not as embarrassing as eating it in front of his opaque eyes. They were strange eyes. That day they were filled with a wonderful light, and questions. Thousands of questions.

Where do you live? What do you do? How old are you? What's your name? Who are you?

'Dimple.' He tried it experimentally on his tongue and then he told me that the real beauty of a snake is not that its poison can kill a man in seconds but that, even armless and legless, it has buried terror of its species deep into mankind. So deep in our genes that we cannot get to it and are born to fear them. Instinctively.

For one second I was terrified. Instinctively.

Something inside me went cold. Like a dollop of strawberry ice cream. God whispered a warning but Luke smiled and he has such a beautiful smile it transforms his face. I forgot the warning. I forgot that his eyes when he spoke had been cold and opaque. Like a snake's.

'You, bright eyes, are keeping a table full of important people waiting,' he said with his charming smile.

I blinked. I thought men only said things like that to Bella's breasts. His ice cream melted in its glass bowl. Suddenly bold, I stared back. He wore no jewellery. His teeth were straight and his cheekbones sharp. There was hunger in his face. He looked at me with an extraordinary intensity. It held every line in his face together. Yes, I was definitely drawn. It is human nature to want the dark side of the moon. I knew that he was my destiny. He meant to have me. 'If you stay,' his eyes said, 'I will pour you into myself until you are no more.' And yet I did not run away. Perhaps for the same reason the sky-lark sings as it soars, dips and dives while it is pursued by the talons of a hungry merlin. Perhaps I have always wanted to be in somebody else's skin.

I agreed to phone him. I didn't think Papa would approve so I did not give him my number.

'Call me,' he ordered softly as he walked away and I saw the footprints he had left behind in the golden sands of my dreams and in my heart. I was so caught up with my own thoughts that I did not even see the blue car that followed me home until I turned around to close our gate.

Two days later I stood in the lobby of Kota Raya shopping centre and called his office. The card with his direct number on it had fallen into a drain while I was trying to pay for a glass of soya bean juice. It floated, white and pristine, in the murky green water for a moment before sailing away underneath the loose concrete drain coverings. A snooty receptionist asked me which company I was from.

'It's personal,' I said.

There was an audible pause. 'I'll put you through to his secretary,' she said, sounding so bored that it made me fidget uncertainly with the coins in my pocket. His secretary when she came on the line was equally cool. She made me regret calling. 'Yes, can I help?'

'May I speak to Luke, please?' I asked hesitantly.

She told me he was in a meeting and could not be disturbed, and so smoothly suggested I leave a message that I suspected she had done it millions of times before. Doubts that Luke would even remember me began to creep in. I imagined him a millionaire playboy. Hundreds of girls bugging him at the office. Maybe I had dreamed everything. I didn't even have his phone number.

'Er, actually he can't call me. Maybe I'll try later,' I babbled, embarrassed and with no intention of ever calling back. I felt young and stupid. Whatever must I have been thinking of?

'Wait a minute. What is your name?' the cool voice demanded.

'Dimple,' I whispered miserably.

'Oh,' the voice sounded undecided for a moment. 'Hold on, please. He is in a very important meeting but I'll check if he will take the call.' The line went quiet and I put another ten cents into the money slot, my poor stomach in knots. Just getting through to him had so unnerved me I was almost trembling.

'Hello,' Luke said abruptly.

'Hi,' I replied shyly.

He began to laugh. 'Why didn't you call me on my direct line?'

'Your business card fell into the drain,' I said, re-assured by the sound of his laughter. I knew then that it was going to be OK.

'Thank you for calling,' he said softly. 'Thank God I mentioned your name to Maria. Would you like to meet for dinner?'

'I can't really go out at night – you know, my mum, my dad . . .'

'Well, tea, lunch, brunch, breakfast, whatever?'

'Mmm . . . maybe I can do an early dinner on Friday but I can't stay out past nine o'clock.'

'Fine. What time do you want to be picked up?'

'Six o'clock outside Toni's hairdressers in Bangsar?'

'Done. See you at half six on Friday but will you call

again before that just to speak to me? This time use my direct line.'

'OK,' I agreed. He gave me his number and then he had to go back to his important meeting but by then I was happy again. He really did want to see me and I really did want to see him.

I got ready for my first date with Luke with a thumping heart.

'What shall I wear?' I had asked.

'Jeans,' he had said emphatically. 'I'm taking you to have the best satay you have ever tasted.'

'OK,' I agreed gladly. His voice on the phone did strange things to my heart. I felt helpless and gauche in his worldly presence. Jeans would even out the score a little, I hoped.

I didn't let him pick me up from home. He was not the right colour. Mother would have a fit to think I was going out with a man who was not Ceylonese. It was the main criterion. I wore a white shirt and jeans, caught my hair in a clip and wore too much make-up. Then I looked into the mirror, felt utterly disgusted, took all the make-up off and started again. A touch of mascara, dark-brown eyeliner on the top lid and pale pink on my lips. I slid the clip off my hair and shook it loose, still dissatisfied with my appearance and feeling fat in my blue jeans. He would look at me and wonder why he had ever thought I was attractive.

After much toing and froing I left the house wearing stretch black jeans, too much make-up and a clip in my hair. I was early. As I waited nervously a group of young boys stopped to chat and flirt. They were so persistent. I began to think the stretch jeans and the make-up were a bad idea. I turned away from them and began to surreptitiously dab away at the lipstick and the blusher. They milled about in a group behind me and tried to tease me into conversation. When I saw Luke's car, I practically ran into it. He looked at me carefully.

'You all right?' he asked eyeing the smudged lipstick.

I nodded quickly, feeling like a fool. His gaze moved to the youths who were already moving on good-naturedly. How to compete with such a car? I pulled the visor mirror down and I looked a mess. Self-consciously I repaired my face. It had all gone wrong. I felt almost tearful, thinking I had ruined everything.

At the traffic lights he took my chin in his firm hand and turned me to face him. 'You look gorgeous,' he said. I stared into those dark eyes. He was not a beautiful man but there was something compelling about him. In a room full of people he would shine like a light. It felt as if I had known him for a thousand years. As if we had spent a thousand lives together. We didn't speak any more. He didn't want to know about my family, my friends, my likes or my dislikes. All of it was unimportant. He put a tape into the cassette player. A woman sang a sad song in Japanese. I watched his hands. They had felt right on my chin. Strong and familiar.

In Kajang he parked near a shack crammed with people sitting around Formica-topped tables. A Malay man stood outside in front of a barbecue, fanning the fires that cooked two rows of satay sticks dripping fat. He smiled a huge toothy grin.

'Hello, boss,' he called out in a friendly manner.

'You're completely full. You're going to be richer than me soon,' Luke joked, looking into the wooden shack crowded with dining customers.

The man beamed with a mixture of pleasure and

modesty. 'Ahmad!' he shouted at a serving boy in Malay. 'Fetch the folding table from out back.'

The boy ran away nimbly and came out dragging an old table. Then he carted out two wooden stools. He had the same grin as his father. Soon we were sitting at the wobbly wooden table in the balmy evening air.

'You're Hindu so you probably don't eat beef, do you?' he hazarded.

I shook my head. 'No, but you go ahead,' I said.

'We will both have chicken.' He ordered forty chicken satay sticks.

Drinks, dips, sliced cucumber and onions as well as ground rice steamed in coconut-leaf packages arrived on the table.

'Your eyes are like a cat's,' he said suddenly.

'That's what my grandfather used to say. I take after my Aunt Mohini.'

'They really are the most beautiful pair of eyes,' he said in a softly assessing voice, the tone someone might use while deciding on the colour of their bathroom suite. The mullah in the golden minaret down the road began citing his evening prayers into the loudspeaker. I listened to the sound. There was something about the call that always filled a hole inside me. I could close my eyes and let the drawn-out sounds wash into my very soul.

The satay sticks arrived piled high on blue and red oval serving plates.

Luke dipped a stick into the rich peanut sauce. 'I want you to start thinking about getting married,' he said, biting into the yellow flesh.

When I arrived home Papa was watching TV in the living room. He looked up as I came in. 'What did you and the girls get up to?' he asked.

'Nothing much. Just hung around Pertama Complex.'

'Hmmm, good,' he commented, more involved in a quiz show than my answer.

Mother was in the kitchen. She was putting away some food.

'Are you back, then?' she asked.

'Yes,' I answered dutifully. Then I quickly crept upstairs and, picking up the extension in my parents' bedroom, I dialled Aunty Anna's number.

'Hello,' she said. Her voice on the other side was beautifully familiar in my rocking, slipping world.

'Oh Aunty Anna,' I declared almost tearfully. 'I think I am in trouble.'

'Come around, Dimple, and we'll talk about it,' she said in her dear, unflappable way.

Bella

When I was eight years old I opened Mother's old mirrored cupboard in the storeroom and found crushed among her discarded saris a rolled-up cloth picture. Unrolled it revealed a treasure beyond compare. Two splendid peacocks, their spread tails created with real peacock feathers and eyes fashioned from coloured glass, stood preening on a pink terrace ornately decorated with lotus-flower embroidery.

Against a black and stormy sky they shimmered deep blue and rich green.

I ran my wondering fingers over their cold glass eyes, along the fine blue stitches and shiny green beads that adorned their bodies. With a child's reverence for things of brilliant colour my clumsy hands tried to smooth out the gleaming eyespot on each ruffled feather. Some of the velvety fronds were broken and beyond repair but I still thought I had never seen anything so beautiful, until I remembered that I had seen the peacocks before. The picture, a wedding present, used to hang in a glass frame upon the wall until I was four or five years old when Mother smashed it during a ferocious quarrel and, with bleeding fingers and blazing hatred in her face, threatened Papa with a jagged piece of glass.

I sat on the stone floor of our slightly musty storeroom convinced I had found something very special, for the peacock is a holy, powerful creature. Even Buddha had passed one of his reincarnations as a peacock.

I laid my plans carefully.

One stormy afternoon while everyone was out and Papa slept in front of the television I carried the magnificent picture into my bedroom. I had decided to store my unhappy soul in the more resplendent peacock of the two in the picture and hide it under my mattress. Like any good Mongolian shaman I laid the soft cloth on my bed, carefully arranging and flattening each feather so they would not crush under the daily weight of my mattress and me. Rain blew sideways and beat steadily against the window. I ignored the sounds of the television from the living room and imagined myself in a shack with an orange fire in the middle of the room, the hypnotic sound of the rain exactly like a real Shaman's drum. I began to hum softly. Then I chanted secret, magic phrases now forgotten and in a rush blew my soul out of my body and into the waiting peacock. I cupped my hands over its face, its glass eyes cold and smooth under my hot palms until I was really sure that I had bottled my soul into the animal. Many minutes passed.

Slowly, finger by finger, I removed my hands. The beautiful eyes stared back. I exhaled carefully. It was done. It was really done. I had cast my soul into the bird.

Believing my soul thus entrusted, I was convinced, truly convinced that if the peacock was in any way harmed I too would fall dangerously ill or die. It was a serious business but I resolved not to retrieve my soul until the power of my chosen animal had turned me beautiful. Only when night came would I rest upon my soul. As long as Nash didn't find my peacock I was safe.

In my child's mind I was certain the transformation would not take too long. As in the best tales of the shamans I would only have to wait until the snow melted on the mountain. How long does snow take to melt? Surely not that long, but every day when I looked in the mirror I saw only a Japanese Oni puppet, fit for the task of frightening small children. Atop a face inflated with fat rested an untidy jumble of curls. Sadly I stared at eyes that were dull and ordinary when what I desperately longed for were eyes so enormous they whispered to my ears. There was simply no redeeming feature that I could see in my face.

'Make haste, thee,' my lonely heart begged the glossy peacock.

'Perhaps tomorrow the vermilion and the collyrium will arrive,' sighed the peacock wearily into my soulless body, its broken feathers swaying gently in the wind.

Is it not natural then that, for as long as I can remember, I resented my sister deeply, envying Dimple her shining, straight hair, her strangely light eyes, her slim figure, her effortless way with good grades, and that other family in Kuantan that only she seems to have inherited?

Oh, I know Mother said that Dimple was being banished to the 'great spider's web' for the holidays, but in our darkened bedroom I spied her secretly counting the days and struggling mightily to suppress her excitement at the onset of her holidays. I couldn't help the terrible envy that grew in my heart. At her command was so much devotion. I could imagine her walking with our aunt on their way to see the caged bear near the mechanic's shop. She is laughing and in her hand she carries the wild honey that our Grandma Lakshmi has thought to buy from the travelling aborigines and saved especially for that purpose – so Dimple may have the half-fearful joy of feeding a caged black bear with curving, grey claws.

She didn't see me creep up softly behind her when Grandma Lakshmi called her from Old Soong's phone. I listened closely to her nervously whispered conversation. 'No, Grandma, I'm fine. Everything is OK. Really it is. Please don't worry. I'll be there soon. I love you so much my heart aches.'

I tormented myself with images of Dimple sitting in the comfort of our grandma's lap, twirling a lock of her hair while the old lady fed her by the hand like a favourite child.

She didn't even notice my jealous eyes when the postman delivered packages wrapped in brown paper from our uncle Sevenese. No she was too busy turning the pages of *The Happy Prince*, *The Selected Poems of Omar Khayyam*, *The Secret Life of a Jasmine* or some other clever book that tells you how a female sea horse places her eggs into a pouch in the male. How he nourishes it with his own blood and finally suffers to give birth to the little baby sea horses. She was too busy giggling at outrageous excerpts from Vatsyayana's famous treatise or the romantic poems of Bhanudatta. I too wanted to be friends with Uncle Sevenese.

In my grey heart I coveted postcards sent to me from strange places in the world and sitting up late into the night listening to an uncle's wild stories of magic and supernatural beings. Is it so inconceivable that I too might want to listen to Daoist beliefs? Hear of an immortal flower growing on a submergible, mythical island where the trees are made of pearl and coral and the animals are glittering white? Or that I might want to know about Zhang Guolao, the great necromancer who folded up his white mule like a sheet of paper and kept it in a bag when he did not require it? Might not I, too, desire to be tickled so hard that Grandma Lakshmi has to come in and crossly tell Uncle Sevenese to stop tormenting the child? I wanted to fall asleep on his tummy and wake up to funny cartoons of me sleeping on a large belly with *zzzz* coming out of my mouth. Like her I would have saved and treasured the sketches for really they are exceptionally good.

I can't help remembering Grandad when he came to the Kuantan house to give Mother money. When we sat on the veranda and shared a banana. He was a mad fellow, giving me the fruit and eating the strands that he pulled away from the inside skin. He talked so little and looked so lost. Mother explained that he never spoke because he was afraid of Grandma Lakshmi. It entered my mind that she must be a horrid woman, our Grandma Lakshmi.

So through the years I consoled myself that these people who for some mysterious reason loved my sister and not my brother and me were exactly what Mother said they were. Poisonous and ugly. I let myself be persuaded that there was a valid reason for her fierce hatred. When Mother is in terrible pain, when her ankles are the size of footballs, she makes me sit at the edge of her bed and listen to her memories and the unthinkable injustices that have been heaped upon her. It makes my head spin.

Sometimes out of the blue her fingers will unclench and with surprising strength she plucks my chubby figure in her swollen hands and dashes me, my arms flailing, into her hard chest as if I am but a soft toy.

'Look at me!' she cries desperately. 'Look what that witch has done to me. It is because of her that I have become this cruel creature. I was a good person until she came into my life with her lies and promises.' She pulls my stunned face away from her hard breasts and stares into my shocked eyes. 'Is this a good life?' she asks malevolently. Then she throws her head in her hands and wails like a mourner at a Chinese funeral. I listen helplessly to the thin, long shrieks and I am relieved that I do not consort with people capable of such harm.

Then, I am certain that Mother is right. That wonderful Uncle Sevenese's skin conceals horrible rot. That he is no more than a vulgar cynic and Grandma Lakshmi an avaricious monster whose real jealousy towards Mother is rooted in incestuous tendencies towards our father. That Aunty Anna is to be avoided at all costs for she is a hypocrite of the worst order. Her soft shy smiles hide a deeply conniving mind. Often Nash is recruited to stand beside me by the bed and agree that the other two, Aunty Lalita and Uncle Jeyan, are two dim people best ignored. In fact they are detestable.

Still, when Dimple returns refreshed and glowing with a brand-new uniform for the new school year, a new box-style school bag, books and a fully equipped pencil case that dim Aunty Lalita has bought her, the feeling that Nash and I are excluded is like sandpaper on my skin.

And the exclusion is all-encompassing and stands guard day and night through thick and thin. Like the time Dimple had measles and Grandma Lakshmi phoned to ask Mother to tie together some branches of neem leaves and brush her skin with them. She said it would reduce the itchiness but Mother rudely replied that Grandma was talking nonsense. Frankly, she told Grandma Lakshmi, she did not believe in such old-fashioned rubbish and anyway where on earth was she supposed to get neem leaves from.

That was when neem leaves arrived in the post. They worked, too. Dimple brushed her body with the leaves and the itchiness went away. Then Nash and I had the measles but there were no neem leaves for us in the post. How small and petty our grandmother seemed to me then.

'Has she no feelings for us at all?' I asked Papa.

'Oh, Bella,' Papa replied, exasperated. 'There is a large neem tree growing in Mr Kandasamy's backyard two doors away.'

I agreed with Mother. That was not the point. Mother was so angry she almost didn't send Dimple to Grandma Lakshmi for the December holidays, the longest and best holiday period. It caused a terrible argument between Mother and Papa but I heard him come into our room and tell Dimple not to worry because she would be going to Grandma Lakshmi's house – as long as she did very well in her exams.

Yes, I resented that too. The soft spot Papa has for her. The more he tries to hide it, the more obvious it becomes. He treats her as if she is a princess made of spun sugar. So softly, so delicately so as not to break the little pink sugar hearts that decorate her white princess gown.

Then there was that Chinese boy who liked her when she was in Form Five. I never told anyone this but I liked him. I used to sit under the trees by the canteen and watch him staring at Dimple ignoring him. I heard that his father was very rich. He must have been, to have a chauffeur drop off that massive box of chocolates for her. Once I unscrewed a note he had written to her and read the untidy scrawl. How fast my longing heart beat in my jealous chest!

Then she began to record her dream trail. The piles of tapes in her box under the bed grew and grew, and one day I sat down and listened to them. Suddenly I saw myself as the frog that looks up into the cramped space under the coconut shell where it lives, unquestioning and satisfied that the world must be small and dark. I saw the richness of the lives of the people who loved her.

Finally I understood the sad reason our Grandpa didn't speak and I heard for myself the pain, the dashed hopes, the frustrations, the failures and the tragic losses that coloured our Grandma's fierce eyes. The floor-boards of the past that Mother had nailed down so viciously groaned and tore apart, leaving her lies bare. In the middle of a gigantic web I saw an enormous spider. It wore the face of Grandma Lakshmi but when I reached out and pulled away its mask, it was our own mother, her face full of cunning rage. It was all a damn plot to punish an old woman. A rich and precious association she has cost Nash and me, but for all her scheming, and all her machinations, I can extend my hand and touch her total, unrelieved unhappiness like a tangible thing. She is a connoisseur of excruciations, arranging her own insanity. Blackmailing the world with her suffering. Perhaps I have always mistaken my pity for love. Poor Mother.

Even as a child I had felt pity, watching her standing outside Robinson's craving the beautiful things displayed in their window. And even when times were a little better and I was standing quietly beside her as she bought, and bought, and bought things we did not need, I still felt pity for the clawing dissatisfaction inside her. She knows I know but she stares at me boldly, without the slightest shred of repentance for she is a shrewd one. She understands that I can never get rid of her. She is a karmic acquaintance. A venomous gift from fate. A mother.

I looked at my sister anew and she seemed far, far more than straight hair and the most gorgeous eyes I had ever seen. She had everything I wanted. I should have hated her but – you know what? – I loved her. I always have and always will. Another karmic acquaintance. Another gift from fate. A sister.

The truth is, I love her because she is genuinely enthralled by my unruly curls, ungloating about her exceptional grades, generous with her love; but also because I know what Papa doesn't, the real reason for all the times she broke her ribs. This I can never forget. The first time I saw Mother's back disappearing behind the green bathroom door downstairs, when Father wasn't home, she held in her hand the rubber hose Amu uses to fill her washing pails with water. First the lock rammed into place and then that fleshy thwack sound followed by a small, muffled cry and Mother's firm voice threatening, 'Don't you dare scream.'

I stood with my ear at the door. Fifteen times I heard the sound. Thwack, thwack . . . my sister hardly cried. When I heard Mother's footsteps turn towards the green door I ran to hide behind the stove in the kitchen. The bolt slid back and she came out of the room, her face serene, untroubled, unshakeable, the coiled tube held easily in her right hand. In the far corner of the bathroom floor my sister cowered in a small green blouse with red dots and no knickers. I knew then that Mother did not love her.

Poor pitiful creature. What was the good of straight hair, neem leaves in the post and an uncle who could tell the future if they couldn't protect you from Mother. If they could not even fetch a mother's love?

That night after she had cried herself into an exhausted sleep I stood over her evenly breathing form. I pushed her hair away from her swollen face and ran my fingers lightly over the frenzied welts on her suffering skin. So many hot waves for one small person to carry. And vowed then to love her deeply.

The years passed and the curls that had once so infuriated me are now a glorious thing of beauty. The forgotten old peacock under the bed has done his work. How the men run? See how they run. See how they run, Dimple. I look at myself in the mirror and there are cheekbones and eyes grown so large they whisper to my ears, 'Make haste. Time slips under the feet of beauty.'

The peacock will not have laboured in vain. Father says Dimple is spring and I am summer. I know what he means. My sister is the quiet beauty of an unopened rosebud still green at the tips and I am an exotic hothouse orchid, my fleshy petals open and voluptuous. A late-flowering summer flower with the colourful, elaborate beauty of a preening peacock. There is much to be admired: a waist like the tight mouth of an urn, breasts like fine jars and hips that sway like carried wine flasks. Mother eyes my vivid blue eye shadow, my immodestly jangling bracelets, my nails that refuse to blush a pale pink like my sister's and my white knee-length boots.

'The peacock adorns itself so heavily it attracts the attention of the tiger,' she warns, not knowing that the peacock is my animal. It was to him that I once entrusted my soul, but I sense her indifference, her ennui. I am the ignored inconsequential child. She doesn't resent me the way she does Dimple but she doesn't care. She has love only for Nash who in turn looks to her to serve him with bored, superior eyes.

'I will do what the peacock does,' I tell her brightly. 'When the first raindrop falls I will fly into the trees, for I know the prowling tiger uses the sound of the rain to creep up on unsuspecting prey.'

The men stare longingly. I flick my mane of curls to one side. They offer me their insipid hearts on a plate but I have no use for a weak man's heart. I want a man who will have a thousand secrets in his eyes and they will all open and shut like clams in the tide when he is talking to me.

And now it seems Dimple has such a man. A man that I would have wanted but I can see he has joined the army of people who adore my sister.

And now she has even more of what I want.

Dimple

'I've got a surprise for you,' Luke said, stopping his car outside the wrought-iron gates of a house called Lara. It was very large, brand new and set on hilly ground.

'Come,' he said, taking my arm. 'We will appreciate the grounds better if we walk up.' At the touch of a remote control the imposing gates swung open. I laughed. I had never seen the gates of a residential house operated in such a manner before. We walked along a driveway flanked on either side by conifer trees.

'Good. They finally did manage to get mature trees of the same size after all,' he commented to himself.

I looked at the perfectly trimmed trees and knew without a doubt that the house was his. I had known he was rich but . . . not this rich.

At the end of the curved driveway on a large piece of land dotted with big, shady trees, a house white and beautifully decorated with cornices and thick Roman pillars rose grandly from the ground. And at the entrance stood two huge stone lions. I let my fingers slide over their cool smoothness. Fearsome in expression, they were beautiful pieces of craftsmanship.

'They are beautiful.'

'Look there,' he said, pointing to a statue under the shade of an angsana tree.

I moved closer. It was a small statue of a little boy wearing a pleading expression on his blameless face and holding in his hands, like an offering, a man's sandalled foot ripped off at the ankle. I shuddered.

'Do you like it?' Luke asked very close to my ear.

'Not really. He's a bit gruesome, isn't he?' I said lightly.

'He's just a copy of a very famous statue. Come, I want you to see inside the house,' he said, turning away and taking me by the hand. He fished out a key and opened the door. I gasped. The lofty ceiling was painted with cherubs and robed figures from the time of the Renaissance. A curving staircase in the middle led to the first floor. Under our feet was an unbroken expanse of black marble and on the walls hung sumptuous paintings.

'Welcome to your new home, Dimple Lakshmnan,' he said, dropping the keys into my hand.

I swung around in shock. 'Mine?' I croaked. 'This house is mine?'

'Mmmm. It's even in your name.' He thrust some papers he'd picked up from a side table into my hand. I stood shocked. His voice faded into the background. I turned my head speechlessly and beheld, on the far wall, a very large painting of me. He had had me painted. Dazed, I walked towards it. There I was. Looking sad. My eyes. Somebody else had seen into my soul and captured some essence of me with a brush and some oil paint. When had it been painted? Who had painted me with that expression?

'Isn't it beautiful?' he asked from behind me.

'Yes,' I agreed faintly. *Was* sadness beautiful? I stared at myself, disturbed, excited and unable to look away.

'I like the eyes,' he said.

'Yes.'

'I like that pure, untouched expression.'

'Who painted it?'

'One of Belgium's best forgers. I sent a few photographs and, *voilà*.'

'Is this how I look?' I asked softly but he had already turned away and was pointing out another wonderful aspect of the house. I tore my eyes away from the girl who watched me with such unhappiness.

'Look, this is inspired by Nero's golden palace. Press this button and the mother-of-pearl squares in the ceiling slide back and look . . .'

I threw my head back and watched amazed as the mother-of-pearl decorations in various parts of the ceiling parted and out sprinkled drops of perfume. My favourite perfume. He must truly love me. I couldn't help beaming happily at him. Never in all my life had I seen so much opulence. Such an excessive display of wealth. His face animated, Luke took my hand and marched me through an elegant, well-designed kitchen. The evening sun slanted through and made squares of light on a chunky farmhouse table in the middle. He opened the back door to a large garden. A high, red-brick wall made it seem secluded, private. The way I had always imagined a walled garden would feel like.

'This way,' he said, carefully manoeuvring me down a small garden path.

'Oh, a pond!' I cried, enchanted. Inside, under green netting, large gold and red carp swam in tireless circles. He looked pleased with my joy.

A thought occurred to me. 'Who's your favourite painter?' I asked.

'Leonardo da Vinci,' he said without thought.

'Why?' I asked, surprised. I had not expected him to say that. Leonardo was restrained in his expressions of muted grief while the house and all its contents were gaudy. No, not gaudy. Perhaps a little ostentatious, a little too *nouveau riche*. Perhaps not even that, perhaps in my naïve mind I had hankered for a small white house and all that he threw at my feet seemed excessive.

'Look,' he said, dragging me along by the hand.

At the bottom of the garden stood a small wooden house. It was slightly raised off the ground, had large windows with wooden shutters and a small veranda with a rocking chair. He led me inside. My heart missed a beat. The whole house was only slightly bigger than my room at home but it was all white. There was a white desk with a white lamp on it and a white chair. On the other side of the room under a window was a pretty, white chaise. A white fan hung from the ceiling.

The white house of my dreams? I looked at him enquiringly.

'You told me about your white house just as the Taj Mahal over there was being completed,' he said, jerking his head in the direction of the house. 'So I built this summer house.'

Tears swam in my eyes. Yes, he definitely did love me. Only someone deeply in love would build a summer house in a country like Malaysia. Finally I had found someone who loved me. Loved me so much he had built me a summer house.

'The answer is yes,' I said, wiping away tears of joy. 'Yes, I will marry you.'

'Good,' he said with immense satisfaction.

We went to the Lake Gardens one day, strolling under

the large trees hand in hand, engrossed in each other like all the other lovers.

'You're the best thing that ever happened to me,' he declared under a huge tree. I looked into Luke's compelling face like a greedy child. Wanting more but not daring to ask. Sometimes I think he is too hard. All the edges of him are like badly cut sheets of tin. I feared I would cut myself even though he has never said no, never said a harsh word, has never been sarcastic or cynical. Yet there is something dark, unreachable and unexplainable about him. A place inside him that has 'No Trespassing' signs on it. I can see them clearly. They are on white boards with black writing in capitals and underlined in red. At the corner of the boards there are pictures of fierce-looking Alsatians that look quite ready to tear me to pieces.

He conjured a pendant out of his pocket.

'For you,' he said simply. It was a heart-shaped diamond as big as a five-cent piece. In the evening light it flashed in its dark-blue velvet box.

'I will lose it,' I wailed, thinking of the countless bracelets, anklets, chains and earrings Grandma had given me that I had already lost in my short lifetime.

'It is not irreplaceable,' he said, and that hard note crept into his voice like an old servant who no longer knocks before he enters his master's room. Then he looked into my suddenly apprehensive face and hastily bade the servant leave the room. With gentle hands he touched my hair. 'We will have the damn thing insured,' he consoled softly. He took me into his hard arms. 'Meet me for dinner?'

I shook my head silently. I didn't think Mother would buy two outings in a day. She already looked a little suspicious. I would have to hide the pendant very carefully. Sometimes I suspected that she went through my things. Bella said the same.

He bent his head and kissed me very gently on the lips. There was no passion in the kiss but his eyes screamed something that almost frightened me. The distance between the kiss he bestowed and the feeling in his eyes was the distance between Mother and Papa.

'Luke?' I whispered hesitantly.

His hand tightened on the small of my back and his head swooped down quite unexpectedly. Once I had been kissed in Form Six during orientation week but that was a form of humiliation. An unwelcome pair of lips and an insolent tongue wetly trying to force open my mouth to the delighted jeering of a gawking bunch of seniors. So I was totally unprepared for Luke's kiss. Suddenly I was in a dark vortex, spiralling upward from the bottom of my stomach. I forgot the long shadows made by the evening sunshine, the cooling breeze that blew from across the lake, the faint voices of children in the distance and the staring eyes of passers-by. The pendant dropped out of my hands. And still the kiss went on.

The blood pounded in my ears. My toes curled in my shoes. And still the kiss went on.

When finally he let me go I stared into his face in shock. The suddenness of his passion astounded me. It came out of nowhere and went nowhere. It was as though a different person lived inside Luke, a violently passionate person whom he normally kept in check with cold-blooded precision. For one second he had escaped and showed himself to me. My mouth felt swollen. He looked out to the lake. I closed my mouth and tried to compose myself. He turned back and smiled. The transformation back into cold-blooded precision was even more marked. Whatever battle he had fought with himself had been won. He bent down and picked up the fallen diamond.

'Yes, I definitely should insure this little bauble,' he commented lightly. 'Come, I will drive you back,' he said, taking my arm in a brotherly fashion. His hands were warm. I couldn't speak. I followed him, confused. How could he switch off just like that? I gave him a side-long glance but he stared straight ahead.

When I let myself in through the front door Mother was waiting. I could see immediately that she was furious about something. She was sitting ramrod straight in her chair, her hands clenched stiffly, but when she spoke she sounded so nice that I thought perhaps she was angry with Papa.

'Where have you been?' she asked me.

'To the park with Anita and Pushpa,' I said nervously. Mother in that mood frightened me. She was like a volcano getting ready to erupt and I was so close I could feel the blast of hot vapour and smell the acrid smoke.

'Don't lie to me!' she roared, suddenly springing up from her chair and advancing towards me in big, fast strides. For precious seconds I could only wonder what had happened to her arthritis. It seemed miraculously cured. She stood before me breathing hard. 'Where have you been?' she repeated. 'And don't even think of lying.'

I hesitated, frightened. It was a long time since I had seen her this angry. That time when she suspected Papa of flirting with the Malay girls next door while he was doing his press-ups in the backyard . . .

'Well, I have met a man—'

'Yes, I know. A bloody Chinese bastard. Everybody at

the park saw you kissing him like a whore in broad daylight.'

'It wasn't like that—'

'How dare you shame our family name like this. This is the last time you will see that yellow-skinned bastard. Which nice Ceylonese boy will have you if you carry on in this shameless way? Is this how you were brought up to behave?'

'I love him.' Until I said those words I hadn't been sure of it myself but now I knew it like I knew every month brought blood out of my body. I did love him. Ever since I had met him flowers grew in my heart.

She was so angry she wanted to hurt me badly. I saw it in her thin lips but in the end she settled for one blow to take the edge off her fury. She slapped me so hard I went flying. The strength in her hands never fails to astonish me. She glared at my sprawled body with disgust.

'You are only nineteen years old. Don't you dare cross me on this. I shall lock you in your room with no food for as long as you persist in this childish absurdity. What do you think that Chinaman wants with you, eh? Love? Ha! You are a very stupid and stubborn girl. Does he love you as well?'

I thought about it. It was true he had never said he loved me.

'Yes, I thought so too. So who is he then, this sly bastard?'

I said his name.

Mother took a step back in shock. 'Who?' she asked.

I repeated his name. She turned away from me quickly so her expression would be hidden. She walked over to the window and with her back to me said, 'Tell me every-thing and start from the beginning.'

So I told her everything. I began with the ice cream and ended with the diamond. She asked to see the stone. I took it out of my little beaded, tasselled purse and she held it up against the light and looked at it for a long time.

'Get up,' she ordered. 'Go and make some tea. I have terrible pains in my knees when the weather is like this.'

We drank tea together in the living room.

'The only way this man will have you is if he marries you. You will not meet him in the park or go out un-chaperoned with him again. I want you to bring him home for dinner and we will all sit like adults and decide the future together.'

That night Mother told Papa. He blanched and took a step backwards.

'Do you know who this man is?' he asked Mother incredulously. And then without waiting for an answer he shouted, 'He is one of the richest men in this country!'

'I know,' she said, hardly able to conceal the excite-ment in her voice. 'He has bought her a house,' she added, her eyes glittering.

'Are you both mad? He is a shark. He will use then discard our daughter when it pleases him.'

'Not if I have my way,' Mother said in a hard, cold voice.

'He is corrupt and dangerous. Don't let Dimple get involved. Besides, she must finish her education. There is no way she is not going to university. I won't allow it.'

'Your darling Dimple is already involved. She tells me she is in love with this corrupt and dangerous man. What can I do about that? It is not me that was seen by the whole of KL kissing him in the park,' Mother taunted.

'I will forbid her,' Papa said. 'She will marry that man over my dead body.'

'It's too late for all that now.'

'What do you mean?' There was confusion in Papa's voice.

'They have gone all the way,' Mother replied dryly.

'WHAT?'

'Yes, so now shall we talk about the future like adults?'

Papa sank into the sofa defeated. 'She will regret it,' he whispered, his big arms flaccid with defeat. Then the thought of a man despoiling his daughter made him drop his head into his hands. He whimpered very softly. 'These Japanese monsters. First they take my Mohini away and now my daughter as well.'

Mother sighed elaborately. 'You know, you don't have to behave as if our daughter is dead. She could have done a lot worse. Besides, he's only half Japanese.'

'No, you greedy woman, she could *not* have done worse. He will chew both of you alive and spit you out in the gutter, and I will have to sit here and watch it all happen.' There was so much anguish in Papa's voice that I wanted to run into the room and comfort him. Tell him that the deed hadn't been done. His daughter was still unspoiled. All that was needed was one sentence: 'Papa, we have not gone all the way.' It was not too late to tell him but then I would lose Luke. And more than anything else in the world I wanted Luke. Papa was wrong about him. In time he would see how wrong he was about Luke.

So Luke came to dinner.

He brought Mother a huge box of chocolates. Ribboned and imported. The sight of the thick creamy box and the velvet, hand-tied bow melted her grasping heart. She placed Luke at the opposite end of the table from Papa. Never had I seen her more animated, more sociable than she was that night. In fact, I wouldn't have thought she had it in her to sparkle in such a way. She played the hostess perfectly. There was not one thing wrong with the meal, the setting, the topics of conversation that she smilingly introduced, her understated but elegant dress and her complete mastery of the situation. Luke was charming and polite but I could tell he was unmoved by Mother. It made me secretly glad that he was beyond her machinations.

He watched the whole scene as if it was a play put on for his entertainment and Mother was the key actress. His bold eyes missed nothing.

Papa sat woodenly, saying nothing. Behind his glasses he looked impotent and miserable. I was just beginning to think that we were all too unsophisticated for the likes of Luke when he caught my eyes. 'Beautiful flowers,' he whispered.

I blushed, pleased that he had noticed my handiwork, but, catching Mother's sharp eyes, lowered my own demurely. I had a role to play. The shy bride.

'So, what are your intentions towards our daughter?' Mother asked after Bella brought in the dessert. Where had Mother learned to make lemon mousses like that? The room became motionless. Papa put down his spoon and leaned forward. Luke's hand stilled.

'All honourable and all in good time,' he responded.

Mother smiled. 'Of course, I never doubted your good intentions but it pays to question the motives of our daughter's suitors. After all, she is very young and *very* innocent.' I prayed Mother would stop there and she did.

Luke's eyes darkened. 'Just so. It was her innocence that first caught my attention,' he said, so softly that I had strain to catch the words. Then he complimented Mother on the lemon mousse. 'Absolutely delicious,' he said. Mother must give his cook the recipe.

Mother smiled smugly. After Luke left, Mother and Papa fought once more. Mother said that Papa had sat there like an idiot. 'An ironing board would have said more,' she jeered.

Papa accused her of licking Luke's boots. 'Be careful,' he said, 'Luke's boots are full of bits from other people's guts and intestines.'

Mother simply gave Papa a look of pure venom and opened her box of chocolates, her expression changing into one of greed, as if she had forgotten Papa and his pain. Incensed, he rushed towards her, his face a mask of anger, and knocked the box out of her hand. Startled chocolates jumped into the air. Bits of gold paper floated around Mother.

'You greedy whore. Can't you see what you are doing? You are selling your daughter for a box of chocolates,' he hissed.

Mother's shocked face began to twitch. Soon she was laughing heartily, her laugh mocking and superior. Papa punched the wall in pure frustration and strode out of the house with a bleeding fist and his wife's laughter ringing in his ears. Mother didn't even glance at the plaster crumbling in the indentation in the wall, seeming impervious to Papa's anger and his insults. She basked in the prospect of a rich son-in-law – in fact, one of the richest men in Malaysia. I helped her pick the chocolates off the ground. She dusted them off and ate them at her leisure, starting with strawberry crème first.

I took Luke to visit Grandma and they got on famously. I was relieved that she liked him. It was a nightmare with Papa. He refused to soften even slightly. When we were alone he would warn me sadly, saying, 'You will regret it, Dimple.' And nothing I said or did would make him change his mind. Grandma told me it would be better when the children started arriving. The patter of little feet would soon change his mind. Grandma played Chinese chequers with Luke. I could see that she was cheating because I know her game too well, but she did it so cleverly that I didn't think Luke noticed. She won almost every game they played. Luke was a good sport though. He enquired solicitously about her health, listened carefully to her troubles and agreed to make appointments with some top specialists in the city to try to relieve some of her ailments. I think he liked Grandma.

One Saturday Luke took Bella and me out shopping. Mother saw us off with shining eyes. Luke actually hates shopping so he gave us each five hundred ringgit and told us to meet him in an hour at the coffee shop downstairs. He touched my nose. 'Buy a dress,' he said with a wink and then he was gone, out of the complex and into the cool confines of his waiting car.

I bought a white dress. It was rather short but Bella said it looked cool. It had a little matching jacket that resembled something Chanel might have designed. In another shop I bought a pair of tan shoes. Bella went for a rather daring red dress with straps and another tube of bright red lipstick. We both decided to wear our purchases. I thought Bella looked simply stunning and wondered if Luke would think her prettier than me. She looked very sexy in her red dress and her masses of curls. Men stared at her.

She put her elbows on the table and her wonderful curls fell forward. That was the moment when Luke walked in. He looked her up and down and laughed. 'When you're all grown up you're going to eat men, aren't you?' he joked. Then he turned to me and said, 'You look dazzling. I love the dress. Purity suits you.' He said it so thoughtfully that I forgot about looking sexy from then on. Luke, I believe, doesn't like showy girls. He thinks I should wear white all the time.

'You look like a flower today,' he said after the waiter had taken the order, and Bella snorted in disgust and disappeared into the Ladies. He watched her go and I watched him watch her. He seemed mildly entertained by her. 'Is she always like that?' he asked.

'Always,' I said, wondering with pathetic insecurity if he found my sister attractive. Men were just so unpredictable and such a blank page to me. There was so much I didn't know about Luke.

An auspicious day was picked for my wedding. Mother wanted a big affair, Papa wanted no wedding at all and Luke seemed indifferent to the proceedings. He wanted me to wear a white sari but Mother nearly had a fit.

'What?' she screeched. 'My daughter to wear a widow's colours on her wedding day? The whole Ceylonese community in Malaysia will be able to laugh off all their problems at such a silly spectacle.'

So she set about ordering my sari from Benares where a small, brown boy would have sat weaving it in a tiny windowless room from five in the morning till midnight. He will have used a fine needle and rich gold thread to make the six yards of exquisite brocade that I will wear only once. Blood red with a matching blouse.

When it arrived wrapped in tissue paper Mother was especially pleased with the heavy material. Hers was a dark-blue, wonderfully grand brocade sari, and Bella, she decided, would look best in saffron. She had also ordered two sets of cream-coloured *dhotis* for Papa and Nash. There was fine decorative workmanship on the high Nehru collar and on the hems of the long flowing top and the trousers. Invitations embossed in gold handwriting were sent out and replies had begun to arrive. Hilton Hotel was the venue decided upon for the reception. A flawless Eurasian woman with a sharp suit and a crocodile-skin briefcase came to see Mother.

From the crocodile-skin briefcase came swatches of material, price lists, and colour-coded tags and a master floor-plan that included stage space. She had lists of appropriate wedding singers, brochures of wedding cakes, florists specialising in formal flower arrangements. Very subtly she vetoed Mother's colour scheme of pink.

'Peaches and pears with a touch of lime,' she said, with such a winning smile on her burgundy lips that Mother conceded to her better judgement.

Luke sent the jewellery I was to wear on the wedding day. Mother's eyes lit up when his driver arrived with satin-lined boxes filled with necklaces, chains, rings, earrings and matching bracelets. They were all studded with diamonds. I sighed. Somewhere I should have found the guts to tell Luke that I don't really like diamonds. Maybe one day I will tell him that I am particularly fond of emeralds and peridots.

Luke made the plans for our honeymoon. The destination was a secret.

The day before the wedding I couldn't do anything for

excitement. Every nook and corner of the house had been taken over with flower arrangements, banana leaves filled with rice, incense and silver pots of holy water, oil lamps and middle-aged women. Their chatter was incessant. In bright saris, impeccable buns set low on their necks and crowded with suggestions, ideas and ways to do things better, they were a force to be reckoned with. The kitchen, the living room, the bedrooms and I swear even the bathrooms were jammed with them. The fatter they were, the bossier they seemed to be. My sari hung in the wardrobe and my honeymoon suitcase was packed and ready to go. There were warm clothes, gloves, a beret, thick socks and sensible ankle-length boots. The rest Luke assured me could be purchased overseas.

I had also spent some money on a silk nightie. Deliciously cool and as light as wind it ran swiftly through my fingers. I blushed to think of Luke's reaction. It was pure white but really as far away from purity as was possible. I knew I had bought it because I wanted to see that stranger who lives inside Luke again. The one that I had glimpsed so briefly by the lake. He seemed an exciting fellow and made me feel dark things deep inside me. I confess I wanted him to press me against his hard body until I felt as if I were a part of him. Until I felt as if I had melted into his breastbone and entered his body. Once inside I would really know him. And then I would be able to prove Papa wrong once and for all. After all, I know Papa has been wrong about so many things in his life. All those deals, gone wrong because he misread his partners.

After all those days of hectic planning and waiting, my wedding flashed before my eyes like a movie on fast forward. I remember Mother looking resplendent and smiling proudly in her dark-blue brocade sari and all the colourfully dressed women whose sneers about Luke's race were thwarted by his enormous wealth. Their bubbling pot of malicious comments ruined by their own envy. Poor Papa stood in his marvellous cream *dhoti* and cried. Tears escaped from the corners of his eyes and ran down the sides of his face and the colourfully dressed women thought they were tears of happiness. Somewhere near a pillar at the back stood Aunty Anna. She wore a plain green sari with a thin gold border, red roses in her hair and a sad smile. I knew she was worried about me. Worried I would be chewed up by a monster called Luke. Then I remember the unending walk up to the raised platform where Luke was waiting for me, and finally looking into his dark steady eyes full of love and knowing without doubt that I had made the right decision.

'I love you,' he murmured in my ear. Ah, he loves me.

That moment I shall treasure for ever. Then I was forcing different pieces of food down my churning stomach and we were running to an open car door while being rained on by handfuls of coloured rice.

'Happy?' Luke asked. He wore an indulgent smile and made me feel like a child.

'Very,' I said.

London was beautiful but so cold. The trees were bare and the people, hunched into their thick dark coats, hurried along the streets. The English have long, pale faces and are quite unlike the tourists in Malaysia who are tanned and beautiful with golden streaks in their hair. At the bus stops they do not waste their time looking at each other in the inquisitive way of Malaysians. They immediately bury their noses into books that they carry on their persons everywhere they go. It is such a wonderful habit.

We stayed at Claridges. Oooooh luxury. Liveried staff with long noses. They had a ten-foot Christmas tree in the foyer with gold and silver bells and twinkling lights. I was very much afraid to venture into their high-ceilinged rooms without Luke. It was like walking into a page of a Henry James novel. So old-fashioned, so English and so grown up.

'Yes, madam, of course, madam,' they said in their lofty accents but I was certain they did not approve of me for they stared at me blankly with cold, light eyes from towering heights.

We went to a beautiful place called La Vie en Rose for dinner. Luke ordered champagne. I think I got quite merry in the process of breaking thousands of bubbles in my mouth but I found that I detest caviar. It must certainly be an acquired taste. Give me a plate of Penang noodles or laksa any time. The chocolate mousse dessert was heaven. I wondered, in a tipsy haze, why we didn't have such things in Malaysia. I was sure I could eat it all day.

After dessert Luke had cognac in a large balloon-shaped glass. He was very quiet during the meal. He smiled a great deal, sat back deep in his chair, ate very little and watched me so hard that I felt myself go quite wicked inside. I could never tell what he was thinking. Luke paid.

'Come,' he said, taking my arm so I didn't fall over, and hailed a taxi to the Embankment. Silently we walked along the black river, listening to the sound of it lapping against the stone bank. It was beautiful. A cold wind stung my cheeks and froze my feet but nothing could dim the beauty of the soft yellow lights reflected from the clusters of street lamps. Occasionally a boat chugged past. It grew so cold that Luke gathered me close to his body. I could smell and feel the warmth of it.

That night I loved him so much it hurt.

'Let's go back to the hotel,' I whispered. I couldn't wait any longer to lie beside him. To be his.

Inside the hotel room I felt shy once more. I thought for a moment about changing into that silk wisp that I had in my suitcase but the mere thought of it made my entire body flush. I decided that there was always tomorrow. On a glass table was a bottle of champagne in an ice bucket and a large bowl of bright red strawberries. I leaned against a pillar and watched Luke pick up the bottle. He raised an enquiring eyebrow.

I nodded. I had lost the merry feeling during our walk along the Embankment and could have done with that daring devil-may-care surge of courage that frothed out of that first bottle of champagne in the restaurant. There was a soft 'pop' and a friendly hiss and Luke held out a glass of bubbles in front of me.

I remember I accepted the glass laughing, giggling, happy. My eyes met his and the laughter died in my throat. The stranger was standing there looking at me out of Luke's face.

'To us,' the stranger said softly and then he was gone in a flash and Luke and I drank two glasses and fell on the bed in a tangle of arms, legs and faces. For one horrid moment I thought of Mother standing over the bed with her hands on her hips. She would certainly disapprove of such behaviour.

'Switch off the lights,' I said quickly.

The room, bathed in the Christmas lights from the

trees outside, spun when I closed my eyes. I remember lips, and eyes, and skin like raw silk and sometimes a voice thick with emotion called my name. There was a moment of pain followed by gentle hands and then rhythm. When it was over I closed my eyes and slept inside a pair of warm, strong arms. Outside, the cold English wind rustled in the trees but I was safe.

Sometime in the night I awakened, my mouth dry and my head throbbing. I stumbled out of bed and got myself a drink. Ooh my head. How it hurt! There was aspirin in the bathroom. I took two and in the mirror was Luke. He looked at me and I looked back boldly, unembarrassed by my nakedness.

'My Dimple,' he said, so possessively that I felt a quiver run down my back. Finally I belonged to him. We made love again. This time I remembered everything. Every kiss, every thrust, every sigh, every moan and that incredible moment when my body became liquid, when my closed eyelids turned red as if a million strawberries had been squashed so close together that they made a wall across my eyes.

Two weeks later we flew back, our bags full of Gucci belts, French perfume, Italian leather, beautifully packaged presents from England and a mountain of duty-free chocolates. I walked into the vast interior of my new home and felt rather intimidated. It didn't feel like mine. Too grand. Instead of a small white house I now had highly polished black marble floors, a richly painted ceiling and expensive furniture that I feared to ruin. Walking around the house the next morning I had the idea of asking Amu to move in with me. She could be my companion and we could do the housework together. So Amu came to live with us.

'This is not a house. It's a palace,' she gasped. She had never seen anything like it in all her life. Poor Amu had had a very poor life. I showed her the washing machine and she giggled like a little girl.

'This white box is going to wash the clothes?' she asked doubtfully.

'Yes,' I said. 'It can even dry them.'

She looked at the buttons and dials on it carefully before declaring it of no use to her. 'Just get me a tub and some pails and I'll show you how to wash clothes,' she said.

I showed her all the bedrooms and asked her to choose one but she only wanted the small room by the kitchen. She said that was the place where she would feel most comfortable. From her window she could see my summer house and she was pleased with that.

I sat on the bed and watched her as she built her prayer altar and lovingly filled it with old, framed photographs of Muruga, Ganesha and Lakshmi. She had found a new prophet, Sai Baba. Wearing an orange robe and a kind smile, he turns sand into sweets and brings his devotees back from the dead. Amu lit a small oil lamp in front of his picture. From a torn plastic bag she unpacked her five faded saris and some white sari blouses and put them into her cupboard.

Afterwards we had tea in the shade of the large mango tree. I sat there listening to her familiar voice recount stories about her spiteful second and third cousins and by and by I felt comforted once more. I was back where I belonged, beside the woman that I had loved for so many years like an aunt. No, like a mother.

One day Luke came home early from work and found Amu and me chatting amicably as we polished the curving banisters. He literally stopped dead in his tracks.

'What are you doing?' he asked very softly. There was a note of disbelief in his voice. Both Amu and I stopped working and stared at him. It was obvious straightaway that he was very angry but I couldn't understand why.

'We are polishing the banisters,' I explained, wondering if they needed special polish or something. God, how was I to know?

He walked up to me. He took my hands in his and looked at them. 'I don't want you to do the work that servants do,' he explained very softly.

I could feel Amu standing frozen by me. He ignored her completely. I felt embarrassed and hurt. Hurt for Amu and embarrassed that he had seen fit to chastise me in this way in front of her. My skin was growing hot under his cold stare. I nodded slowly and he turned away and walked into his office without another word. I was so shocked that I simply stared at the closed door until I felt Amu's thin rough palm on my hand.

'It is the way of men,' she said, looking deep into my miserable eyes. 'He is right. Look at the state of my hands. I can do the banisters myself. Why, I have done far more than this house in my lifetime. You go. Wash yourself and go to him.'

I went upstairs, washed my hands and in the mirror saw my surprised, confused face. Then I went downstairs and knocked on his study door.

He was sitting in his swivel chair. 'Come here,' he said.

I walked up to him and sat on his lap. He took my fingers and kissed them one by one. 'I know you want to help Amu but I don't want you to do the housework. It will spoil your pretty hands. If you want to help Amu, get another servant to come in three times a week to do the heavy jobs.'

I nodded. 'OK,' I said, eager for his anger to pass. Eager for that soft menace in his voice to go back where it came from. Eager that he should smile and ask, 'What's for dinner?' in his usual voice.

Sometimes Mother came to see me in my big house. Usually we sat for a while then I gave her money and she left, but one day she came troubled and frustrated. Nash was in yet another spot of bother. As we spoke I don't remember the reason but I must have displeased her for she raised her hand to hit me but the blow never came to pass because suddenly there was Luke with his hand in an iron grip around her wrist.

'She is my wife now. If you lay another hand on her you will never see her again or be a grandparent to any of her children,' he said in a pleasant voice.

I looked at him and saw the stranger. His eyes were cold and hard and in his cheek a small muscle jumped angrily. And I fell in love with the stranger all over again. No one but Grandma Lakshmi and sometimes Papa had ever stood up for me.

I felt like the god that lay peacefully asleep under the huge hood of a many-headed serpent. He was my scalloped canopy. My eyes moved to Mother. Her face was harsh with the thwarted rage of a bully. I could hear her thinking, '*She was my daughter first.*' She could have just given in gracefully, made it all right, but Mother is so proud that her mouth twisted into a sneer and when she turned and met the shining love in my face her scorn changed to disgust. She wrenched her hand out of Luke's grip, spat at my feet and stalked out.

Luke took a step towards me and held my trembling

body. I wanted afresh to enter him through his breast-bone, hear his thoughts, see what he saw and be part of him. I imagined him taking his arms away from around my body and seeing my limp body fall to the floor. Would he know that I was already inside him? A part of him. The words of a Sufi song that I had once laughed at as ridiculous and dramatic appeared in my head.

> *Can't you see my blood turning into henna?*
> *Just to decorate the soles of your feet?*

The mango tree in the garden blossomed. It was a magnificent sight. Amu built a hammock under it and napped there every afternoon. I watched her from my summer house and she looked enviably peaceful.

I went to see Uncle Sevenese at his bedsit. It was a terrible place; four flights up a dirty iron staircase, at the end of a smelly corridor black with dirt and behind a faded blue door. While I was climbing the stairs, careful not to touch the greasy banisters, I saw a woman step out of his blue door. She was attractive in a hard sort of way, with her hair in a smart bob. She wore white hot pants and white stiletto heels. Her heels were loud on the metal stairs.

Suddenly I didn't want to come face to face with her. I didn't know what I would see in her face. Quickly, I turned around and went back downstairs. I hid in an old-fashioned Chinese coffee shop where a tired fan whirled quite high on the ceiling and where old Chinesemen half sat and half squatted on three-legged wooden stools as they sipped their coffees and ate toasted white bread spread with kaya. I ordered a cup of coffee and felt in-explicably sad, remembering Uncle Sevenese telling me how he used to wait outside the baker's to steal little tubs of kaya. In those days it was not green but orangey-brown, and he used to open the tub, stick his tongue in it and lick every last drop of the sweet mixture of coconut milk cooked with egg yolks.

When I was younger he was my hero on a white elephant who could do no wrong but now he lived all alone in a tiny bedsit with hard-faced prostitutes in unsuitable shorts leaving his room at eleven in the morning.

When enough time had elapsed I tried the stairs again. He opened the door bleary-eyed and grunted when he saw me. He walked away leaving the door open. I let myself in.

'Good morning,' I said cheerfully, avoiding the sight of the unmade bed. He looked as if he was nursing a really bad hangover. I took the packets of cigarettes I had bought at the coffee shop downstairs out of the brown paper bag and put them on the table beside the bed. He plugged in a kettle.

'How's it going' he croaked, unshaven, his eyes smudged with ghastly dark rings.

'Not too bad,' I said.

'Great. How's your dad?'

'Oh he's fine. He's just got nothing more to say to me.'

He turned around from making his coffee. 'Do you want one?'

'No, I had one in the coffee shop,' I said automatically and then, remembering, blushed. My uncle watched me with a sly smile. He knew I had seen the prostitute. He was still a child who enjoyed shocking people. He lit a cigarette.

'And how's your husband?' There was a new note in his voice. I didn't like it.

'Fine,' I said brightly.

'You still haven't given me his birth date and time so I can work out his chart,' he accused, looking at the kettle through a haze of smoke.

'Yes, I keep forgetting,' I lied, knowing full well that I didn't want to give him the astrological details. I suppose I feared what he would find. 'I've brought you some cigarettes,' I said quickly to change the subject.

'Thank you.' He looked at me speculatively. 'Why don't you want me to do his charts?' he asked.

'It's not that I don't want you to do Luke's charts. It's just that . . .'

'I had a dream about you . . .'

'Oh, what about?'

'You were walking in a field and I realised that you had no shadow. And then I saw your shadow running away from you.'

'Ugh. Why do you have such dreams? They make my hair stand on end. What does this dream mean?' I asked, full of dread when I wished to be scornful of superstitious nonsense in my new happy life. In my large house with its crystal chandeliers, frolicking Renaissance figures and perfume compartments in the ceilings, Uncle Sevenese and his dreams had no place. I began to regret coming to see him. As soon as I saw that prostitute I should have simply left. Then I felt mean, entertaining such beastly thoughts. I looked around at the shabby room. I used to love him with all my heart.

'Why won't you let me help you?' I asked.

'Because you can only give me material things that I don't need and won't do my soul any good. Do you think I would be happier in a big house with a black marble floor?'

'So, what is this dream of yours supposed to mean?'

'I don't know. I never know until it's too late, but all my dreams are warnings of ill fortune.'

I sighed. 'I have to go but I'm leaving some money for you on the table, OK?'

'Thanks, but don't forget to bring the details of your beloved next time around.'

'All right,' I agreed wearily, my good mood entirely ruined.

What had happened to the times we spent talking for hours late into the night after everyone else had gone to sleep? There was nothing left to talk about. I knew it was me. I was frightened of letting him near enough to destroy the fragile wings of my happiness. I had never been so happy in all my life and I knew that he had the power to destroy it. In fact I was sure he could.

I knew things were too good to be true but the illusion of happiness had to be protected at all cost. I made a decision to stop seeing Uncle Sevenese for a while.

Three months later Luke was ecstatic when I told him I was pregnant. I wanted to call the baby Nisha if it was a girl. A long time ago Grandma Lakshmi had wanted that name for me and I wanted to please her by naming her granddaughter Nisha instead. Beautiful like the full moon. I hung pictures of Elizabeth Taylor all over our bedroom so that the first thing I laid my eyes on in the morning and the last thing I saw before I retired was beauty.

I began to feel sick all day. Grandma Lakshmi advised ginger juice. Luke brought me flowers wrapped in silver paper and ordered me to do no work at all.

It was while I was lying quietly in bed one night that Luke sat down beside me and started telling me about his past. He was orphaned when he was three years old. His mother, a young Chinese girl, was raped by Japanese soldiers and left for dead; she somehow survived and gave birth to him, but eventually died of malnutrition on the steps of a Catholic orphanage. The nuns opened the door one morning to a child crying by her cooling body. His poor little body was covered in sores and his belly distended with worms.

They named him after the nun who found him, Sister Steadman, and was brought him up as a Christian although he remained steadfastly Buddhist and strangely attached to all things Japanese. It was the strength of his will that kept him so. I cried when he told me how little Luke would wake up in the middle of the night and leave the softness of his bed to wedge his small body between the two bottom shelves of a cupboard. The nuns found him each morning for almost a year curled up between the familiarity of two hard surfaces. I thought of the child Luke with a distended belly and emaciated limbs and I wondered if his eyes had been opaque then.

The months passed very slowly. Every day my body changed. I lay on the cool floor of the living room and stared at the paintings on the ceiling. The truth was I wasn't sure I liked them all up there watching me. The artist had made all those people seem not just alive but present, as if they were a stern race that existed on another level inside the varnish on my ceiling. When I switched off all the lights and went upstairs, they came down and helped themselves to the food in the fridge. In fact, if I stared at them for too long I began to feel they changed their expressions. For the most part they seemed indifferent, but sometimes, just sometimes, it seemed as if they were quietly amused by our goings-on. The more

I looked at their foreign faces with their proud Roman noses, their vaguely smug expressions and their curved, spoilt mouths, the more sure I became that I wanted to take a brush and paint the whole damn thing white. But Luke likes them up there. He is proud of his ceiling. He says it is a work of art.

I suppose it is just that I was bored. I had nothing to do all day but wait for Luke to return. I missed the friends that I never saw any more. I had shopped enough to last a lifetime and I was, of course, not allowed to take walks in the evening on my own for fear of kidnap, rape and murder. Forbidden to soil my pretty hands with ordinary housework, or for that matter gardening, I was quite the useless wife. When would the baby arrive?

I went into Luke's study and he was standing facing the window with his back to me. Ramrod straight. Lost to me. Lost to everything but the swirling music around him, to a haunting lament of a jilted Japanese lover.

> *Mix me the poison*
> *For I wish to join the souls of the dead*
> *Unwanted as I am*
> *It is very pleasant the path to paradise*

It was the entreaty in the woman's voice mingled with the lilting flutes that carved him so still. Watching him standing there, I knew he was sad inside. Some deep part of him that I cannot touch. I felt it reach out like a thin wayward tentacle that refused his master's iron will. Gently, gently I had begun to understand Uncle Sevenese's desire for a cold lip, for I too had began to long for the coldly distant lips of my husband.

'Luke,' I called softly. And I saw the poor little boy with the distended belly rise off the floor, shake off the tattered clothes of his orphanage and step into the smart navy-blue bush jacket and trousers that Amu had ironed yesterday. And so attired Luke turned away from the window to face me.

'You're back,' he noted with a smile.

'Yes,' I said, walking into his outstretched arms. The baby lay between us. I loved him dearly.

'What did you buy?' he asked indulgently, stroking my belly gently. The room was cold but filled with sunset colours. Behind him the setting sun was deep red.

'A present,' I said, trying to look into his eyes. Into them, behind them.

He raised an eyebrow. His slanting eyes were curious. 'Well, where is it?'

I waddled outside and returned with a long, narrow box. He tore open the plain green wrapper, lifted the lid, looked inside and glanced up with a merry query.

'Now why would I want a walking stick?' he asked, lifting the cane out.

'A cane, a very long time ago, was an occasion to show one's rings off. This one is made of snakewood and the head of ivory,' I explained with mock reproach.

'Mmm, it's exquisite,' he said, examining the fine details on the small ivory terrier head. 'Where did you get it?' he asked, running his fingers over the wood so dark that it looked as if it had been soaking in snake blood for centuries.

'It's a secret,' I said, hoping to sound as mysterious as him.

He stood on his ice island and laughed. 'I shall treasure it for ever.'

And I loved him even as I felt the distance between us growing.

That night I dreamed that Mr Vellapan, our family doctor, came to visit. He sat outside in my summer house with me. It was hot and he had taken off his shoes.

'Is it very bad?' I asked.

'It's not good news, I'm afraid,' he said.

'How bad is it?'

He shook his head. 'You won't make it through the weekend,' he answered sadly.

'What?' said I. 'Won't I even have a chance to say goodbye to everyone?'

'No,' he said and I woke up. Luke was fast asleep. I snuggled close to his hard body and lay awake for a long time listening to his breathing. There was so much I still didn't know about him. He was not mine. What are you hiding from me, Luke?

I admit I stood outside the door for the express purpose of eavesdropping. It was the Whispering God that urged me on. Maybe I shouldn't have for I shall never be happy again. Happiness I know now to be the sole preserve of the ignorant, the simple, those who can't see or choose not to see that life, that all of life, is full of sorrows. Behind every kind word is a bad thought. On a bed upstairs love lies dying.

'What did you eat?' he asked into the phone and I knew instantly. *He has a lover.*

He has a lover.

The thought slammed into my brain so fast and with such impact that I actually reeled. Blood rushed into my head and the passage outside Luke's study span in dizzy, laughing circles. He had another. But it was only yesterday that he was in love with me. It is true, then, that love is heartless and has to fly from heart to heart.

Fool. Crazy, stupid fool. Did you think that *you* could hold him?

A man like him.

'OK, see you at nine then,' he said before I heard the click of a line disconnected. He had sounded neither tender nor voluptuous, as I knew he could be, but he was going to meet her the next day at nine. Nine. When he was supposed to be at a Directors' meeting.

I felt the baby kick. Hard.

My knees gave way and I collapsed to the ground. A small sound escaped my lips but he didn't hear. He was already on another phone call, his voice clipped and professional. 'Buy the idiot off,' he ordered coldly as I squatted, destroyed, outside his door. Then panic hit me. I had to get out of the passage. Outside his door I became cold with paranoia. I felt certain that he would open his door at any minute. I began to crawl away on my hands and knees.

The servants. They must never see me like this. He had a lover. My hands were trembling. I felt faint. I had been warned. A leopard never changes its spots. Who was she? What did she look like? How old? How long had this been going on? I crawled clumsily, my head reeling. I didn't want Amu to see me like that. I made it up the stairs, clinging desperately to the banister. I hated myself and hated the horrible thing inside me that made me so repulsive. So ugly. No wonder even my own mother hated me with such unexplained ferocity. Then a small thought arrived by late train. What if I had made a mistake? Hope poured through my veins like little bubbles that don't kill. They fizzed like Coca Cola in my blood. *What if I had made a mistake?* I sat on the bed heavily. The stitch in my belly was gone and my heartbeat slowed. I looked up and he was standing in the room.

I stared at him as if he were a ghost.

'Sweetheart, are you OK?' he asked, his voice concerned.

'Yes, I think so,' I said through numb lips. I looked into his blank eyes and he stared, alarmed by my stunned, bloodless face.

'You sure? You look a bit pale.'

I nodded and managed a smile.'

'Baby OK?'

I nodded again, stretching my lips further.

His anxiety eased, he smiled. 'I'll just dash into the shower before dinner.'

Tomorrow I would follow him. I must know who waited at nine o'clock.

I slept badly and awoke with the immediate knowledge of betrayal. There was no lapse between sleeping and waking. It was still dark outside and it would be some time before the sun appeared over the pine trees. The air was deliciously cool. I wondered what she had eaten yesterday. Cake, chicken rice, noodles, nasi lemak, satay, mee goreng, honeyed pork. The possibilities were endless, the variety of Malaysian food mind-boggling. She could be Chinese, Indian, Malay, Sikh, Eurasian or a mix of any of the above.

My head began to pound and ache. In the mirror my face was blotchy and swollen. I looked haggard. For some reason I couldn't comprehend, I didn't feel angry with him. I was furious with her. I went back to bed and lay in it until I heard the sounds of my house waking up. Music, toilets flushing, the use of pots and pans in the kitchen.

The expensive purr of Luke's Mercedes died away. There was a soft knock and Amu came in. She held a small tray in her bony hands.

'Go and brush your teeth,' she instructed bossily, laying the tray on the small table by the bed. The smell of my favourite breakfast, apam, wafted up. Two small white rice cakes, their middles glazed with sweetened coconut milk and the edges thin and perfectly crisp. I looked into their soft round faces as they eyed me, glistening coyly in their perfection, and I wanted to vomit.

'What's the matter?' Amu asked. Her lined face, sharp. Like needles her eyes probed mine.

Oh Amu, I wanted to say, he's having an affair. And those two apams are laughing at me.

'Nothing,' I said.

'Well, eat them while they are still nice and hot, then. I'm going to the market now so I'll see you later.' She watched me intently as I nodded and smiled. For a while it seemed as if she was about to say something else but she changed her mind, shook her head and left. I sat staring at the apams until I heard Kuna, our chauffeur, drive away with Amu in the back seat. Then I got out of bed. My feet carried me on the cold floor. Bright sunlight sat quietly in the silent house and waited to see what I would do. I opened his door and walked into his room. His room was like a freezer. I switched off the air-conditioner and the room became silent too.

It watched me with cold, disapproving eyes. I had become the intruder. I looked around that familiar room with a brand-new perception. Everything looked different. Shirts that I had bought laughed at my stupidity; handkerchiefs that I had lovingly ironed sniggered in corners. I opened a cupboard, a drawer and a small cabinet and always, continually, I touched things he had held, worn, slipped into, put on. I felt light-headed with the empty ache inside me. As if a large hand had reached in and scooped out everything inside me. I was hollow but for the baby. It hung in nothing. Like those wonderful Easter eggs they made in England with a plastic toy inside. The unmade bed was brazen with its rumpled sheets. All night it had lain with my husband. I climbed up onto the bed and stood right in the middle of it. The house listened and the four walls of his room watched as I began to scream. I screamed until I was hoarse.

Outside, the weather changed. Grim clouds gathered and the room darkened. Large drops of rain fell on the roof of the house. Exhausted, I fell into a graceless heap on the bed. I couldn't give him to her. He was too precious to give away to some street prostitute. I loved him too much to give him up. I straightened my ungainly body and lay flat on my back on his cool sheets. I would charm him back. There were certain men, bomohs, you could go to if you wanted to lure someone into your power. Yes, that was what I would do. I decided then that it was the only way that he would be mine for ever.

Suddenly Amu stood in the doorway. She looked flustered and horrified. Had she been calling? I had heard nothing. There was pity in her dark eyes. It was only when I looked into her compassionate face that my lips trembled, tears filmed my eyes and the burning pain in my heart screamed hysterically. I opened my mouth and howled. She climbed into bed and clasped my head against her flaccid breasts. She knew without being told that there was something wrong between the master and mistress. Against my forehead I could feel her breast-bone. She rocked me gently. Not a word passed her lips. Not a single story about a scheming aunt or an evil second cousin. She rocked me past the river of tears.

'The fish and the meat,' I reminded, in a choked voice.

In my mind I saw the plastic bags of market produce sitting on the kitchen table. I saw the glistening wings of the black flies that hovered so faithfully like veiled mourners at the scene of the dead. She nodded and left silently. I loved her more that moment than I had ever loved anyone in my entire life.

My limbs were still mine to command. I scrambled out of his bed and telephoned a car rental company. Would madam like to leave her credit card number or cash? Cash please. Two o'clock this afternoon. Fine.

At two the car arrived. I drove it to the end of the lane that met our driveway and parked it under a tree.

At six thirty Luke returned. He looked cheerful.

'Good day?' I asked.

'Very. What about you?'

'Brilliant. Baby's fine.'

He came to kiss me on my left temple, his favourite spot. The lips were cool and familiar. Judas. How easily he lied to me! I stared at him and to my horror tears welled into my eyes. Quickly they spilled onto my cheeks.

He looked startled. 'What? What's the matter?' he cried worriedly.

'Hormones,' I explained with a watery smile. No cause for concern.

'Really?' He seemed unsure.

'Yes, really. What time are you leaving for your meeting?'

'The meeting is at nine but I can cancel it if you're not feeling very well.'

I marvelled at him then. The absolute cool of the man. To stand there and show such sincere concern without the slightest trace of guilt.

'No, I'm perfectly fine. Maybe just tired. You go.' Did my voice sound as stilted as I felt? But he seemed satisfied. 'I shall rest for a while. If I say goodbye now . . .'

He understood immediately. He came forward and kissed me tenderly on my lips. 'Yes, rest a while.' There was a small, kindly smile playing on his lips.

I smiled back. You bastard. How can you be so unfeeling? I eased myself carefully out of the chair. I didn't want to seem clumsy. No doubt she was graceful and slim, but I had plans for her. Nothing but her head on a platter would do. I felt his eyes watch me as I toddled away. Upstairs I turned the key and sat on my bed to wait. When I heard him close the door of his bedroom noiselessly I let myself out of my room and slipped downstairs.

As I strolled down the driveway, my heart was thudding very loudly in my chest. What if he was standing at his window looking down at me? I would simply say I wanted a walk to clear my head. The sun had already set over the trees, the day russet and gold when I let myself out of the gate. His lighted window was empty. He was still in the shower. I walked down the lane that led to the main road. At the end of it was the dark-blue car I had rented. I got in, shivering. It was getting dark. I waited.

Soon his car drove past. For a precious second I was paralysed with fear. Then my hands and legs, like separate entities, took over. The key turned and the gears moved. The accelerator pressed down. It was easy to keep up with him. I followed him to where expensive shopping centres were climbing out of the ground like awakened giants. He stopped outside a Chinese medicine shop. On the first floor over the shop was a hairdressing saloon and on the top floor, a sign offered Golden Girls as escorts. Beside the Chinese medicine shop was a small narrow staircase protected by iron gates. As I watched it clanged open and released a young girl, incredibly beautiful, in a long black *cheongsam* embroidered with gold bamboo shoots. Flawless legs flashed through the high slits of her costume, and shoulder-length jet-black hair framed a smiling, oval face. The stunning girl waved at the man in the medicine shop who did not wave back. She glided down the few steps into the street and slithered into the passenger seat of Luke's car. He drove off without a backward glance.

I sat there gripping the steering wheel perhaps for an hour, or for ten minutes. Time ceased to matter. Cars passed. Other girls came out of the narrow staircase in an assortment of tight, revealing clothes and slid smoothly into large expensive cars and sometimes taxis, and I sat and stared. Until finally a hawker selling noodles passed by. He rang his bicycle bell very close to my window and woke me from my noiseless dream.

I started the car and drove home. Suddenly into my numb body came a small pain. It started in the left side of my stomach and spread like a drop of poisoned blue ink in a round pot of milk. Growing and growing. Soon I knew the whole pot would be infected, but finally I was turning into the lane of my house. How I had got there is a mystery of the power hidden in the subconscious. It had taken me back home.

I parked the car down the lane and began to walk. The

pain grew and grew. I clutched my stomach and sank to the ground helplessly. More than anything else he must not know that I had been out of the house – that I had seen. I began to crawl towards the house. In my delirious mind a slip of a girl in an adult costume slid into a glossy car. She was waving to me. The medicine man looked on expressionlessly. You could tell he didn't approve.

On my hands and knees I arrived at the front door. I rang the bell and curled into a ball of terrible pain. In my head the beautiful girl waved. In my stomach something was trying to tear through. The door opened. Amu fell on her knees. Her face was a blur but her thin hands rushed to cup my face. Then the stars descended and gave me blackness. Beautiful blackness.

I awoke in a moving vehicle but a passing goddess felt sorry for me and tossed me back into the beautiful black where the stars lived. I remember the hurrying wind at my feet and lights overhead. They were hurrying too. The sound of a trolley in my ears. Urgent sounds. And I remember hearing Luke's voice. The cool was gone from his voice. Serves him right, I thought, imprisoned in my black and red world. He sounded angry and demanding. He sounded far away and hazy.

The girl in the black and gold *cheongsam* waved to me. Her face was curved into a shining smile of youth and beauty. The man in the Chinese medicine shop sneered. He didn't like me either. The girl giggled and the man laughed. I was mistaken. He didn't disapprove of her, they were in it together. From far away I heard their laughter. Into the fading sound came another shot of pain. Pure white and then pure black. Blessed is the darkness . . .

I called her Nisha. I look at her with perfect wonder.

She shakes her tiny hands and legs and crows happily. How can anything so tiny and helpless be so powerful? She is the place I go to when the pain becomes too unbearable. At the glimmer of her smile the pain snakes away like a coward.

He still sleeps in the other room. I think I gave him a scare. His cold eyes are strange with concern. He looks me over carefully, protectively, but I am forever plagued by the waving girl. I sat in his study yesterday and looked through his drawers. Of course I found nothing. But today I went through the pockets of his car and found a picture. Yes, I found a picture of her. She stands in the middle of a hotel room. Her beauty is such that it spills out of the photograph and into my curious hands, making them shake. It is her eyes. There is something frighteningly timeless in them. It is like a lake at dusk. Unforgettable, mysterious and full of dreams.

Can a lake smile? Perhaps in the dark.

She frets inside a large T-shirt in a pool of sunlight. She is not a character but a vessel of irresistible temptation. What would she look like asleep on her stomach, her head fitted into the curve of his neck? Her hair is wet. She smiles without a care. There is something awfully innocent in her frozen smile. I recognise some deep need to be loved. She is in love with him. Her desire glows in her unmade face like morning dew on a blade of young grass.

I wish I could quote Terrence Diggory to her: 'Desire is defined as the pursuit of that which is already lost.' I wish I could tell her that what at first appears so clear fades like the past appears today, and so will today in the future ahead. She does not play fair, but I have the answer she doesn't.

'Who will replace me?'

Two years ago I was the vision with the dewy eyes in the picture but there are magical differences. It appears she smokes. Yes, I see the packet of Menthol cigarettes in the background. But when all is said and done such sophistication doesn't amount to much. Time is racing. Her dream will end. How will it not, ten years, five years, two years after. 'Who will replace you?'

In the background on the bedside table is the wallet I gave him two birthdays ago. A bunch of keys, of which one will open our front door, sits beside the wallet. Draped over a large armchair is a pair of jeans – hers, and his trousers. A towel lies carelessly on the seat of the armchair. It has been used. It is a communion of perfumes and shy thoughts. In view is just the edge of a large bed. The bedsheets are tangled. Ah . . . I have witnessed her love nest. I have seen the lacy black bra draped over his trousers. I will live in this portion of their hotel room for many years to come. I will know days, weeks, months, years when I will look out of the window and see motionless clouds in the distance and be back in their little love nest. It will always be there, day and night. Another woman's bra slung over my husband's trousers.

From the mosque down the road a mullah sings his praises to Allah into the loud speaker. His deep voice resonates and echoes into the dusk.

'Allah-o-Akbar, Allah-o-Akbar.'

I have always liked the sound of their prayer. As a child I used to listen to their call, so tangible that I could climb into it as if it were a magic building in the air. I could look out of its windows and walk up stairs made by those magical sounds until I reached the highest room where . . . No, those days are all gone. I slide the picture back into its leather pouch. I can hear Amu singing to Nisha. She is a good baby.

I went to see Uncle Sevenese. I asked him for the name of a good bomoh. A man who can cast a black spell for me. The picture shows me that she is dangerous. A woman in love will always want more. A prostitute wants only what is in a man's wallet. A woman in love wants to know the contents of a man's heart. If her picture is engraved on its walls.

Lakshmnan

There was a fine rain falling this morning.

Now it's in my head. Tap. Tap. Tap. Like a child's knuckle on a glass window. Ahhh, how tired I am. I will be fifty soon but I feel like a hundred. I have pains in my hand that travel up my shoulder, and when I lie sleepless in my bed, listening to my wife breathing beside me, my heart sometimes misses a couple of beats. It is tired too. It longs simply to stop.

I dream of her. She brings me baskets of flowers and fruit. She is glowing and only fourteen. How I envy her! 'Take me with you, Mohini,' I plead but she only places her cool hand over my lips and tells me to be patient. 'How many more years of guilt?' I ask, but she shakes her head and says she doesn't know.

'It was an accident,' everyone dismissed, safe in their cocoon of blameless sorrow. Not I. For it was I who caused the accident. It was my fault. I was the fool who slipped and fell into the crevice that should have kept her safe.

For each man kills the thing he loves. Yet each man does not die.

Yes, he does not die but how he lives. O God, how he lives.

Many years ago I read about a great Arab traveller, Ibn Battutta, who lived in the fourteenth century. He wrote that while the Sultan of Mul-Jawa was sitting in audience, he saw a man who held in one hand a knife resembling a book-binder's tool deliver a long speech in an unknown language. Then the man gripped his knife with both his hands and cut his own throat so viciously that his head fell to the ground. And the Sultan laughed, declaring, 'They are our slaves. They do this freely for the love of us.'

That is what I have done. I have slain myself for the love of my sister.

I thought I would never again speak of her and yet now, after all these years of silence, I feel as if I must. Nine months we spent lost somewhere deep inside my mother looking out of each other, sharing resources, space, liquid and laughter. Yes laughing. My sister made my heart laugh. She made the whole world bright and dazzling without saying a word. We never spoke. Why would anyone speak to their hand or their leg or their head? She was that much a part of me. When they took her away those Japanese bastards removed some necessary aspect of me. When I closed my eyes I used to see her face and the longing was unbearable. It made me want to scream and shout and destroy. I didn't scream. I didn't shout. I just destroyed.

At the beginning I simply lashed out and crushed the people closest to me, breathing fire and reducing everything in my path to ashes. I took an inhuman pleasure from causing strife, seeing the growing fear in my siblings' eyes, but that was hardly enough. Even twisting my heel on Mother's heart, engorged with love for me, was insufficient. I had to obliterate me. How could I be successful and rich and happy after I had killed my sister? Sometimes I sit and wonder which god smote me with that famous headache during my senior exams. Could it be Lord Lakshmnan himself at his first attempt to sabotage his own life? Could it be that the book-binder's knife had already done its gruesome work?

I know Dimple was surprised when I asked to be a part of her dream trail. After all, I had refused a thousand times in the past.

'Why now, Papa?' she asked, startled.

Now because the angry fires that burned inside me are dying away and the orange embers greying. Now because Nisha must hear my side because I too have a side, and now because it is time to admit and face the colossal mistakes.

Sometimes my rolling head looks up to my headless body in shock at the stupid, incredible things that my body has got up to. Yet I cannot stop. There was much to destroy but I mangled myself freely for the love of her.

The real damage was done in Singapore where I learned my vices well. A good family Mother knew offered me accommodation. They had a son, Ganesh, two years older than me, and a daughter Anna's age whom they called Aruna. She appeared to hate me from the first moment she laid eyes on me. She pulled bored faces and spewed sarcastic comments that were in a roundabout way surely directed at me. Her mother used to iron my shirts and once, in a great hurry, as she ran out of the door, she asked her daughter to iron the shirt for me. With disgust on her face Aruna picked up my shirt to iron it but I snatched it out of her hand.

'Don't bother,' I said rudely, turning away.

That night my door opened and in the half-light she walked in. She wore only a slip, the silky material clearly outlining her breasts. Startled, I stared at them. When she was close enough I reached out and touched them. They were large and soft in my hands. I had never known a woman's body before. She fell upon me ravenously. Countless times I loved her that night as she moaned and moved in my arms. Aruna never spoke. Before dawn she left, leaving behind the pungent smell of passion. I threw open the windows and smoked a cigarette. For a while there I had forgotten Mohini but the guilt returned.

The next morning at breakfast the girl was quiet. She did not meet my eyes. The sarcastic comments and odd faces were gone. That night she appeared again. We built a rhythm. By the time she left before daybreak she was familiar to my body. I opened the windows and let her aroma out.

We established a pattern. I looked at her in the eye less and less and I began to wait for her unclothed figure more and more. There were some nights she did not come. Those days I smoked until I fell asleep.

Then one day she whispered in the dark, 'I'm pregnant.'

How naïve I was then! That practical thought had honestly never occurred to my fevered brain and I recoiled in sudden horror.

She pulled me closer and clung desperately. 'Marry me,' she pleaded.

We did not make love that night. She left, sobbing. I sat stiffly on the bed. I did not even like her much less love her. I remembered her like a dream or a ghost one meets only at night. The memory is always vague and indistinct. What did I really remember? A velvet tongue on my back, soft lips on my closed eyes, the slip of her body against mine and the black vortex into which my guilt disappeared. And, of course, the smell of her – wet turmeric. I couldn't sleep so I dropped out of the window and went in search of an all-night food stall I often frequented in Jalan Serrangon. In the yellow light of his gas lamp Vellu's ebony face broke into a broad smile.

'Hello, teacher,' he called cheerfully.

I smiled listlessly and collapsed onto a wooden stool. Unasked he placed a steaming glass of tea in front of me. Then he went back to his job of cooling tea, pouring it high up from one enamel mug to another. For a while I watched the foamy liquid expertly stretched between two mugs take on the appearance of an ostrich plume then I turned my head and stared into the night. A stray cat came to mew by my feet and a mangy dog skulked and foraged among the rubbish dumped by the drains. All night long I sat watching the procession of people who took their tea from Vellu's stall.

At first the cinema-goers, loud and jolly, then students from the college nearby, young and carefree; after them the prostitutes and their punters, two policemen on the beat and then the incredibly beautiful transvestites. They glanced at me boldly. As the night moved deeper into itself the people became stranger and stranger until finally the dustmen arrived. I stood up and left.

In the morning at the breakfast table I told her father the good news. I had found lodgings with some friends of mine; their house was closer to the school where I taught. I did not look at her. I packed and left before night could fall and went to rent a cramped room with very little to commend it in Chinatown. I was washing my socks in the sink a week later when her brother came to see me.

'Aruna is dead,' he said.

She flashed upon my brain in the half-dark: half-clothed, her eyes slits of passion. 'What?' I said.

'Aruna is dead,' he repeated, his face dazed.

In my mind I saw her neck, stretched to the fullest when her head was thrown back as she arched atop me like a mighty Greek sculpture. She was the colour of earth itself.

'She committed suicide,' came his hoarse whisper, disbelieving. 'She simply carried on walking into the sea until she drowned.'

I saw her strong figure moving, moving away, but it was not painful. Tragedy. Clytemnestra is dead. She will never dance again in the half-light.

I went to her funeral. I met her father's shaken eyes squarely and her mother's uncomprehending sorrow with the kindness of a murdering impostor, but when I looked into her coffin I saw her again stretched on my bed, her thighs curving around my pillow, her dark, sad eyes watching me. To those eyes I couldn't lie. 'Sleep, Clytemnestra. Sleep. For I have remembered you better in the half-light,' I murmured to her tragic face. I sat frozen outside. My child was dead. And there was no one to cry for him. I returned to my little room and denied her a resting place in my mind. She became transparent. Goodbye, Clytemnestra. You know I have never loved you.

It was only by accident, through a friend of a friend, that I chanced upon my new lover. What goes around comes around, they say. And this time it was my turn to fall deep into the silken arms of a heartless lover. Mahjong. Her name works a miracle on me. She clicks to me. It is a secret language. An erotic command. You will never understand it because her red vinyl lips have not called to you. One click and I, my family, my grandiose plans, my waiting appointments, my half-finished meal, my sick wife, my barking dog, my troublesome neighbours all dissolve to nothing. I hold her cool tablets in my hand and I am king but, more, I forget my dead sister. I linger by her side till morning.

I'll tell you the real secret about us hopelessly compulsive gamblers. *We don't want to win.*

I know that as long as I am losing there is a reason to carry on. A big win would necessitate the intolerable: leaving the table when there is still money to be spoilt on my silken lover.

Yes, it's true I married Rani to clothe my lover. And I have remained faithful to my lover's possessive, unreasonable demands through the years even while my family have been poor and miserable. I have been a terrible father. A headless father.

I knew all the expensive things in Nash's room were stolen, just like I knew Rani poisoned Bella against my own family. Bitter though it is to swallow I even knew that the bitch used to beat poor Dimple black and blue, but in the end I always had to return to my mistress or the guilt was unbearable. She was my opium. She promised forgetfulness. Now death is nearing. Take courage. I do not fear. My father waits on the other side.

When we were first married, my unending grief for Mohini irritated my wife. 'For God's sake,' she exclaimed, 'there are families that are wiped out but for one during wars. I bet they didn't carry on in this ridiculous way. It's only one dead girl, Lakshmnan. Life goes on.' But as the years wore on she became angry and ever more jealous that my dead sister was more real to me than she was. 'How dare you insult me in this way?' she screamed. I have never told anyone but, you see, I have seen what the Japanese do to women they like. And the memory haunts me while I am sleeping.

It was while I was hunting in the forest with my aborigine friend Udong. Japanese soldiers in the forests are like Sumo wrestlers in a ballet. They stand out like sore thumbs. You can hear them crashing about from miles away. One Saturday we came upon them in a clearing. We crouched in the bushes behind the bastards and watched them with a Chinesewoman. Perhaps she was a Communist messenger braving the jungle for a cause. How they used her!

Oh God, I cannot describe what they did to her.

In the end she was no longer human. Covered in her own excrement and bleeding profusely, she was panting on the ground when one of them slashed her throat. Another cut off one of her breasts and stuffed it in her mouth as if she was eating it. This they found hilarious, laughing uproariously as they zipped up their gore-splattered trousers and moved off on their murderous way.

When their harsh, guttural voices had died away we came out of our hiding place and stood frozen and disbelieving over the woman, her naked legs askew, her face contorted with a bloody lump of meat sticking out of it. It was deadly quiet, as if the brutal jungle that daily fed upon itself had seen the appalling carnage and stood shocked. I still see her today. The silent hate in her face.

We left her there, as she was, a warning, a taunt to the Communists. Afraid of reprisals and unwilling to get involved in the war between the Japanese and the Communists, we took with us only the memory of her silent hate. In my nightmares I dream that we are not standing over a female Communist messenger's body but Mohini, her naked legs askew, a bloody lump in her mouth, and she is looking at me with silent hate.

I have done an unimaginable injustice to Dimple but perhaps she will forgive me, for my head has been rolling for a long time now. I watch her and I can see the unhappy shadows in her eyes. I have always known she would be unhappy by his side: I knew he would break her. For men like that, women are playthings and possessions. He should have married Bella. She is hardy. She knows what to do with such men.

I should demand to know the reason for the shadows in my daughter's eyes. I should confront him. It is my right, my duty as a father, but he is clever, my son-in-law. It is the yellow in his blood. Through the ages they have learned to bribe even their gods with sticky, sweet foods so why not a headless father-in-law? He has bribed me with this big house that I live in. He has sealed my lips with the sweet cement that built this house.

Aruna sits dreamy and ghostly at the foot of my bed in her slip, eyes empty but open and mouth closed. She watches me. No doubt it is all in my mind but I can't set aside the idea that she lives at the foot of my bed.

Part Five

The Heart of a Snake

Dimple

Uncle Sevenese yielded the address. At first he refused but my begging, bruised eyes hurt him. I went to see Ramesh, the snake-charmer's second son. He had learned his father's dangerous craft, meditated in cemeteries and was certified to chase away unwanted spirits and sell potent charms to people for a monetary reward. Daylight saw him in a hospital attendant's clothes, remarried with no children and attached to a rumour that his first wife had gone mad.

I drove out to Sepang. It was a very poor area. Small wooden houses lined the road. A group of youngsters stared at my BMW with a mixture of admiration and envy. Ramesh's house was easy to find. There was a large statue of Mariaman, the God of Beer and Cheroots, in the garden. A salt-dried, gaunt woman with very prominent shoulder blades came to the door when I called. She had the squashed face of a bat, only on a human being it didn't look so adorable. She was young, though. I could see my dress and person impressed her.

'Have you come looking for him?' she asked.

'Yes,' I replied.

She bade me enter. The house was wooden and small, the furniture shabby and sparse. A fan in the ceiling whirled, but other than that the place looked more deserted than inhabited. 'Please sit,' she invited, indicating one of the chairs near the door. 'I will go and get my husband.'

I smiled my thanks and she disappeared through a bead curtain. In minutes a man parted the beads and stood in the small room. He was dressed in a white T-shirt and khaki trousers. He made the room shrink into claustrophobic proportions, for he had the face of a hunting panther. Hungry, very black, and exuding a dangerously male smell. The whites of his eyes were so bright they were frightening. He smiled slightly and brought his palms to meet in the age-old Indian gesture of polite greeting.

'*Namasté*,' he said. Great culture flowed in his voice. It was all so unexpected I jumped up to return the greeting. He indicated I should sit. I sat and he prowled to the chair furthest away from me.

'What can I do for you?' he asked politely. He had not blinked. Disconcerted, I felt as if he could see through me. That he already knew what I was there for.

'I am actually the niece of Sevenese who you used to play with when you were younger,' I explained quickly. For a fraction of a second the lithe body stiffened and the eyes flicked as if he had received an unexpected blow. Then the moment was gone. I could have imagined it. Perhaps I had.

'Yes, I remember your uncle. He used to play with me – and my brother.'

No, I had not imagined it. I began to think that he bore a grudge towards my uncle. I should not have come. I should not have told him we were related.

But suddenly he grinned broadly. He had bad teeth. The flaw relaxed me.

'My husband has someone else. Can you help me get him back?' I blurted out.

He nodded. Once more he reminded me of that stalking panther.

'Come,' he said, springing up and leading the way through the bead curtain. Past the bead curtain it was windowless and shadowy. He turned to his right, pushed a green curtain and entered a small room choking with the smell of incense and camphor. A rambling altar grew upwards from the floor, holding a large statue of a god or a demi-god that I did not recognise. Small oil lamps burned in a circle around the statue. There were offerings of cooked chicken, fruit, a beer bottle and trays of flowers at his feet. The face of the god was hideous, with a huge purple tongue, bulging eyes that stared straight ahead, and a mouth stretched into a terrible roar of anger. Red paint dripped from the gaping hole. On the floor next to the altar was a curved knife and, beside it, a human skull. In the flickering light of the oil lamps both objects gleamed dangerously. I wondered if it was the same skull that Uncle Sevenese had told me belonged to Raja.

Ramesh beckoned me to sit on the floor and followed suit. Cross-legged he seemed far more comfortable than he had on the chair in the living room.

'She is fair, his lover, very fair,' he said. He lit another incense stick and stuck it into the soft flesh of a banana. 'Does he have two rather deep lines running vertically down his face from his nose to his mouth?'

'Yes,' I agreed eagerly, wanting to believe in his extraordinary power, wielded so casually without pomp or needless drama.

He poured milk into a bowl. 'Your husband is not what you think he is,' he pronounced, looking at me directly in the eyes. 'He has many secrets. He has the face of a man and the heart of a snake. Do not keep him. He has the power to destroy you.' .

'But I love him. It is her. He changed when she came into his life,' I pleaded desperately. 'He built me a summer house before she came. He sent me daffodils, knowing that I knew in the language of flowers they meant "for ever thine".'

He looked at me steadily. 'You are wrong about him but I will do as you ask.'

I felt a clutch of fear then. To disobey the panther seemed suddenly fatal. If he had persuaded me more . . . but his quick capitulation spoke of disenchantment. Disenchantment only came with superior knowledge.

'I will put his sickness in the milk and God will drink it.'

'Why do you say he has the heart of a snake?'

He smiled ever so slightly, sagely. 'Because I know snakes and he is after all one.'

I felt chilled to the bone with his answer. No, I would still keep Luke. He would be different when she was gone. Alexander the Great's mother slept entwined in snakes. No harm befell her. I would keep him yet.

'Make her go,' I whispered tremulously.

'Do you want to hurt her?' he asked softly.

'No,' I said immediately. 'No – just make her go away.' And then a thought came to me. If she went away, he would pine for her and that was not what I wanted. 'Wait!' I cried. The whites of his eyes floated before mine in the windowless room. 'Make him stop loving her. Make him afraid of her.'

He nodded. 'So be it. I'll need some ingredients from the provision shop,' he said, getting up. The panther was swift and graceful. He looked down at me. 'I shall be no more than twenty minutes. You can wait here or have a cup of tea with my wife in the kitchen.' As soon as the curtain closed over his dark figure the room took on a sinister appearance. Shadows in the corners came alive. The skull grinned knowingly. The oil lamps flickered and the shadows moved. I stood up and rushed through the curtain.

It was dark and cool in the corridor. I followed it and came into a bright kitchen. Everything was clean and tidy. The bat-faced woman turned from her task of scraping half a coconut to look at me.

'Your husband had to go and buy some provisions,' I explained hurriedly. 'He asked me to join you for a cup of tea.'

She stood wiping her hands down her sarong and smiled. Her gums and teeth were red from chewing betel nut. Her small bat face looked quite friendly when she smiled. I leaned against the door and watched her set about making the tea. She boiled water in a pan on a gas stove.

'My uncle used to play with your husband when he was a little boy,' I volunteered to start some sort of conversation going.

She whirled around from the task of spooning tea into a large enamel mug, her round eyes bristling with the first sign of animation and curiosity I had seen.

'Really? Where was this?' she asked.

'In Kuantan. They grew up together.'

She sat down suddenly. 'My husband grew up in Kuantan,' she repeated, as if I had said something unbelievable. All of a sudden tears welled up in her eyes and ran down her squashed face. I stared at her in surprise.

'Oh, I can't take it any more. I didn't even know that he grew up in Kuantan. He never tells me anything and I am always in fear of him. All I know about him is that his first wife killed herself. She drank weedkiller, burned her insides and lay in agony for five days. I don't understand what is happening to me either. I am so frightened and . . . and look at this,' she sobbed, running to a drawer and wrenching out a black handbag. She opened it, turned it upside down and shook it violently. All the coins, a few papers as well as her identity card and two square, blue packets dropped out. She picked up the packets and thrust them towards me. 'It's rat poison,' she informed me wildly. 'I carry it everywhere. One day I know I have to drink it. I just don't know when.'

I stared at her in shock. When she first opened the door to me she seemed a vanishing mouse, a world away from the raving lunatic confronting me. I licked my lips nervously. Her distress bothered me. Her husband bothered me too but I wanted Luke. I would have done anything to get him back. I could wait a little longer in the company of that strangely disturbed woman to get my husband back.

There was a sound at the front of the house and she quickly stuffed the blue packets, the coins and the papers back into her worn handbag. It was amazing how quickly she moved. She dried her eyes, poured boiling water onto the tea leaves and covered the mug with a lid in one fluid movement. Even before the sound of his footsteps arrived in the kitchen she had poured condensed milk and spooned sugar into two smaller mugs. Without another word she went back to scraping the coconut halves onto a large plastic platter.

When Ramesh appeared at the doorway, she threw him a hasty glance, furtive and full of fear before turning back to her task. I wondered what he had done to her to inspire such terror but I did not feel that he would harm me, and if he did I was fully prepared to suffer the consequences of my actions.

'Have your tea. I shall start my prayers alone. It is better that way.' He turned and left. The woman got up from the floor where she had been scraping the coconut, strained the tea into two mugs and offered me one without meeting my eyes.

'You can drink it in the living room if you like,' she offered politely. There was no longer any desperation in her voice. It was calm and neutral. The mouse-like bat creature was back.

I sat in the sparsely furnished living room and drank my tea. The hot liquid calmed me and soothed my ruffled nerves. Inside me was a fear of the black deed I was about to undertake. Soon Ramesh pushed aside the beads and stood before me, a red cloth package held in his hands. Hastily I put my mug of tea on the floor and took the lumpy package with the proper respect. With both hands.

'Keep the salt inside the cloth in a bottle and scatter it under your husband's bed daily until it is all gone. Whenever he goes out at night, take a small handful of salt, repeat the mantra I will teach you with as much force as you can muster and then in that same firm tone order him to come home.'

He took my hand. His was cold and dry. He turned it over and studied my palm for some minutes. Then he let my hand drop and taught me my mantra.

I paid him what seemed to me to be a pitiful sum. I wanted to pay him more but he refused. 'Look at this house,' he said. 'I do not need more.'

I took the salt and prepared to leave. As I was slipping into my shoes I looked up to say goodbye and found him staring at me with a peculiar intensity. His eyes were dark and unfathomable, his face closed and unreadable. He looked like a black marble statue.

'Be strong and be careful or he will win.'

I nodded and, clutching my red package, left as quickly as I could. The whole experience had unnerved me thoroughly. I could feel the blood rushing through my body in a great panic. I thought about calling Uncle Sevenese and telling him what had happened and then decided against it.

I stopped at a shop and bought a bunch of bananas. Then I threw the bananas by the roadside and put the red cloth and its contents into the brown paper bag. I didn't want Amu to see the red cloth. She would suspect its potential instantly. She knows all about the revenges that spurned lovers resort to. A big part of me felt ashamed. What would Papa say if he saw me sprinkling my magic under Luke's bed? What would Grandma say? It didn't bear thinking about.

I watched Luke prepare to go out. He put on his grey and white silk shirt. He looked perfectly charming. He smiled at me and kissed the top of my head tenderly. 'I won't be late,' he said.

I know you won't, you snake-hearted person, I thought to myself. I too had a secret now. It made me feel powerful in the face of his smooth deceit. He could look me in the eye and lie straight-faced. Well, so could I.

'Shall I wait up for you?' I asked with that special half

smile. He had not seen its face for a long time and seemed surprised.

'OK.' He nodded eagerly enough.

Maybe I had started to hate him then. I don't know. But there is old blood on the blade of my axe and the thought of life without him is still unbearable. I listened to the sound of his car engine dying away at the end of the driveway before I ran up the stairs enraged, scattered the salt under his bed and spat out the mantras coiled inside my mouth. I called him home.

In half an hour I did the same again. Angry tears ran down my face. I ordered him home.

Thirty minutes later I did it again. This time my voice had grown harsh and hateful. I ordered him home. 'Come home now,' I hissed venomously.

In less than twenty minutes he was back. I listened to the purring of his Mercedes with wonder. Ramesh truly knew his stuff. This was one battle I was going to win. I wanted to laugh. The key encountered the front door.

'Oh, you're home early,' I observed casually.

For a moment he stood frozen in the middle of the room as if confused. He looked at me strangely.

'What's the matter?' I asked. A small worry nagged in my head. I didn't desire him so lost. He was simply supposed to return home to his wife and love her like before. I stared at him and he stared back.

'I thought you might be ill,' he said, his voice odd. 'I thought something might be wrong at home. I felt anxious and restless. Is everything OK?'

'Yes,' I said feebly, standing up and walking over to hold him. It broke my heart to see him look so beaten. I didn't hate him after all. He was my life. 'Oh Luke, everything is fine. There is nothing wrong. Let's go to bed.'

'I thought I felt something crawl up my back inside my shirt,' he muttered to himself.

I led him up the stairs, limp and uncomprehending. In bed he didn't want to make love. He held me close as if he was a child that had been frightened by a nightmare. He frightened me. The power of the salt under the bed scared me. Over and over again I saw Luke's confused face say, 'I thought I felt something crawl up my back inside my shirt.' Luke without his glittering eyes was a frightened zombie. The responsibility of turning his brilliant brain into mush must not be mine. For hours that night I lay awake listening to the sound of his breathing. Once he shouted, breathing hard. I shook him awake and for some horrible moments he stared at me, hunted and without recognition.

'Everything is all right,' I comforted in the soft darkness, stroking his head until his breathing became deep and even once more and he fell asleep on my chest. Why does my silly heart desire the acid of his caress?

The next morning I swept away the salt. I gathered all the salt crystals together and flushed them down the toilet. Luke as he was the night before was too frightening a vista for me. The red cloth I put into the bin, and Ramesh's warning eyes into the furthest corner of my mind. Never again would I try anything like that. I would love Luke until I loved him no longer and then I would be free. That was the only option left for me.

To console myself I made a large flower arrangement. It drooped over a third of the dining table. Filled only with white rosebuds, yew and purple hyacinths it looked like a funeral arrangement, mourning for colour, but when he walked in, he said, 'Why, Dimple, that is beautiful! You really have a talent with flowers.' He did not realise that white rosebuds mean a heart ignorant of love, yew, sadness and purple hyacinths, my sorrow. Ah well, how to expect a lion such as him to know the emotions that gently reside in flowers? It must have been his secretary who found out the meaning of the daffodils he sent and the red tulips he brought to my doorstep after all. As I had suspected.

He was still seeing her. I felt it on my skin. Rubbing, rubbing like coarse material. She materialises in my dreams, waving at me from afar. Sometimes she laughs at me and shakes her head in disbelief. 'He is not your man,' she tells me. 'He is mine.' I wake up and stare at my husband, almost in fascination. He has no idea I know so he loves me gently like silk on my sore skin. He buys me flowers, velvet-textured and expensive. I look at him and smile, for he must never know that I know the face of his whore.

There is Nisha to consider now.

Amu really loves Nisha. In the afternoons they lie drowsy together inside the hammock. Sometimes I tiptoe outside to gaze at the two people that I love most in the world asleep under a tree. The sweat on their upper lips, the even breathing, and the minute veins that web their closed eyelids, like half-open windows, console me. It is funny the feelings that Amu arouses in me. When I see her in the temple in the company of other old people she looks frail and pitiful. Her life seems wasted, over, but when I see her with Nisha cradled in her arms I think her life rich and full.

Bella wanted to buy a house and I promised to supply the down payment. Surely Luke would not mind. Too bad if he does. For my birthday he bought me the largest diamond I had ever seen. I suppose he was doing very well with the economy on the up and up. It is freakish how completely blind he is to my pain and sorrow. Is it possible that someone could be so blind?

Mother came to see me, wanting money. Papa was not feeling very well and he had not been working. She needed twenty thousand ringgit. 'Of course, Mother.' Inside her mouth, her tongue is very pink and very sharp. It moves around her mouth like an energetic alien with a separate agenda of its own. I was quite fascinated by it. It reminded me of that time Uncle Sevenese got so drunk he likened Mother to the small-brained howler monkeys he saw in Africa. Black with a very pink tongue. 'If you saw their mating ritual, Dimple, you'd be shocked by how much they resemble your dear mother when she is talking.' Of course he was swaying drunk when he said that. But still.

A few days later Mother was back. This time Nash was in a spot of trouble with loan sharks. She needed five thousand. I gave her ten. I know Luke hates Mother and he does sometimes question big cash withdrawals but . . . Fuck him.

Two weeks passed and Mother found her way to my living room again. Nash was in serious trouble again. He had 'borrowed' forty thousand ringgit from the safe in his office on Friday night, hoping to double it at the Russian roulette tables in Genting Highlands at the weekend. Needless to say, he lost all of it. His employer lodged a police report and he was taken away. When Mother went to see him his bronze arms were covered with cigarette burns and his arrogant eyes cowed with wild fear.

'It is the policemen who did this,' he whispered desperately through a split lip. He clutched Mother's hand frantically and begged her to pay his employers off so they would drop the charges. Say no more, Mother dear. I went to the bank with her and withdrew the money in cash. I am developing a taste for giving Mother Luke's money. Papa phoned to say thank you but he sounded broken. I knew how he felt.

Let me tell you a story – a strange one but I assure you it is all true. You decide whether or not the heroine did the right thing for I, myself, fear she has made a grave mistake and there is no going back.

It happened not very long ago, at a party in a gorgeous house. Unsmiling, a splendid man watched our young heroine among the throng of guests, bejewelled, gilded and so very beautiful. Of course he couldn't hear what they were saying, the sleek waiter and she but he could see even the tiniest of nuances in their furiously young bodies. They were flirting with each other. He watched her eyes carefully. He could always tell all her thoughts from her eyes. They were upturned and moist with some strange emotion. Had he seen that look before? Mmmm, perhaps. He would look deeper into the shadows of his memory banks. The past seemed so far away now. Above all he desired objectivity.

There. There – a red fingernail tracing a crease in the waiter's shirt. In front of all these people! The shame. He thought about the delicacy of her neck. It fitted so prettily inside the circle of his entwined fingers. He knew because he had tried it for size. And it was perfect. His mind filled with a picture of the hussy, her legs, smooth and silky, wrapped around the waiter's naked torso. The liquid picture made him gasp for breath.

Suddenly he wanted to know what the reality looked like. Those small animal sounds she made in his bed, he wanted to watch from afar. Perhaps he was surprised by the perversion of his thoughts but he consoled himself that it was only an experiment. He might not like it, which of course would exonerate him of all perversion. He saw her offer the waiter a quick sidelong glance with her beautiful eyes and that half smile that looked more like a pout. That look he definitely recognised. It had once fired his blood and made the need to possess her sear his loins at night. He shifted uncomfortably in his trousers.

She tossed her long blue-black hair and swayed away. The waiter stared at her departing back.

The splendid man stood up and began to walk towards the waiter. She had chosen the cast, now he must hire them. Close enough, he clicked his fingers. It was rude but the waiter turned around, his expression polite and professional although his eyes were deeply offended. He was really quite good-looking in a dumb sort of way. The man smiled at the waiter and crooked a finger. He could see the resentment that stiffened the waiter's shoulders as he walked over. He had the walk of a pansy. The well-dressed man relaxed.

'Would you like to sleep with my wife?' he asked politely. There was a taunting smile in his cold eyes.

The waiter became rigid with shock. His eyes darted around the room quickly. It was beautiful, his act of dignified anger and disgust. 'I think you have mistaken me for someone else, sir. I have no idea who your wife might be. I am paid only to serve *drinks*.'

The bastard, there was pleasure in his voice.

'She is the one with the long black hair,' the man said, his face hard as he reached out and pulled a long strand of black hair from a button on the indignant waiter's white jacket.

The waiter visibly gulped. 'Listen, I don't want any trouble.'

'Hey, relax. I'm not looking for trouble either. I just want to watch.'

'What?' The young man's eyes widened with astonishment.

'I want to watch you with my wife.'

'You're mad,' the waiter stuttered, taking a step back. Obviously no one had suggested such a vile thing to him before.

'I will pay you five hundred ringgit if you can get my wife into one of the bedrooms in this big house and leave the connecting bathroom door open for me.'

'I will lose my job if I get caught.'

'Find another,' the unsmiling man suggested carelessly, letting his eyes wander around the room as if he was losing interest in the conversation. When his cold eyes returned to the object of his wife's attentions the waiter was waging a losing war with greed. Yes, greed. The cause of all man's downfall.

'How will you pay me?'

'Cash, now.'

'How does it work?' the waiter asked nervously.

In fact, the splendid man hadn't really thought about the mechanics of it all. Now he thought fast. The blue door down the corridor from the balcony had an en-suite bedroom that connected with the other guest bedroom. He started to walk away from the crowd of beautiful people towards the garden. The air outside was balmy. The waiter followed meekly.

'Take her to the bedroom with the blue door down the corridor upstairs and make sure you leave the connecting doors to the en-suite bathroom open and at least one light on,' he instructed in his hard precise voice as he reached into his wallet. Five hundred ringgit, still crisp from the bank and tightly wadded together, was counted and passed over to the waiter. For some reason it never crossed the man's mind that the waiter wouldn't succeed. It was true he had the face of a loser, but attached was an energetic body and flashing eyes. Exactly what she wanted tonight.

'What if she says no?' the waiter asked timidly.

'Then come into the bedroom next to the blue door and give me back my money.' The man looked at the nervous, ever so slightly aroused waiter coldly and smiled. It was a tense, terrible smile.

The waiter nodded quickly.

'By the way, she likes it rough,' the man tossed casually as he left to find his wife. She was coming out of the powder room downstairs.

'Darling,' he said, so close to her hair he could smell the clean scent of her shampoo. 'Something has come up. I have to leave but I'll send the driver back for you. Stay and enjoy yourself. I'll see you at home later.' He kissed her lightly on the cheek.

'Oh, what a shame,' she said very softly into his right ear.

'Good night, darling, and do try to *have some fun*.' He was suddenly eager to be away. Let the game begin. He closed the front door behind him and walked along the side of the house. A kind of cold despondency settled on his stiff shoulders. The initial excitement was fading. He stood behind some bushes by the bay windows and looked into the golden party inside. He saw her cascading length of hair. She was alone and staring out of the French window.

For a moment he stood transfixed by the sight and cursed the impulse that had possessed him to trap her, to watch her while she was unaware, to test her fidelity. Unexpectedly she looked small and lonely. Then the waiter was beside her. The man stood in the shadows and rooted for her.

'Refuse, refuse, refuse,' he whispered softly into a large, dark-green hedge. She stood staring out of the window, ignoring the creeping waiter. The man thought he would stop the experiment then. She was innocent. Then he saw her half turn and smile at the waiter. No, he must see this through. Expose her cheating heart.

The back door was open and he walked right through a busy kitchen. He was dressed appropriately and wore the right expression of arrogance so nobody stopped him. Quickly he slipped up the stairs before someone who knew him could waylay him. He passed the blue door and entered the next bedroom. The two rooms shared a bathroom. It was dark but cool in the room. The connecting door was open so he went through the bathroom and entered the arena where he would trap his beautiful wife. He switched on the bedside lamp and it threw a golden pool of light on the dark-green coverlet. Their hosts favoured a simple, uncluttered style. His mind imagined her gasping with revulsion, crying out, 'Stop! Get your filthy hands off me.'

If only she would pass his test. She had become so cold and withdrawn with the birth of the child. And with every year she froze a little more. Silently he left the room to wait next door. He sat on a large bed and smoked for about twenty minutes. Then he heard the connecting door to the other room open. Something thudded against his ribs. Someone was checking that his side of the bathroom was unlocked. In the dark he smiled cynically. The fish bites. He put out the cigarette and waited to see if she would use the bathroom first. Then he pushed open the door and stepped into the dark bathroom. The waiter had left the connecting door ajar. He could see directly into the pool of light.

'Do you—'

'Shhhh,' she said softly and began to kiss the waiter.

The man felt the blood begin to pound in his head. It was not pain that he felt but a strange excitement. It was such an indescribable rush that it startled him. He had stepped into the secret world of his wife and the waiter. The waiter took off her little beaded jacket, and her skin that he had admired for so long gleamed like polished ivory in the golden light. Her small breasts strained against the waiter's jacket. The waiter pushed her on the bed roughly. Good man. The waiter had taken his advice. *She likes it rough.* Until now the man had ignored the waiter, but now he could see a live thing writhing to get out of his trousers. This, this was the effect his wife had on men.

'Please don't be rough. Love me gently,' she whispered.

The man in the darkness was stunned. Love me gently? What did it all mean?

Then the nightmare began. He watched in pure shock as the woman who looked remarkably like his wife and the man whom he had paid clung to each other and moved so smoothly that their entangled limbs looked as if they belonged to a well-oiled machine. Out of her gorgeous mouth didn't come the curses, the harsh screams of passion and the grunting animal sounds that she made when she was with him, but quiet sighs and gasps so drawn out that deep pleasure was unmistakable. And eventually when she came, she came softly, elegantly. Her body stiffened and her head arched back, offering her slender white neck like a dying swan.

'Go now,' she instructed softly.

The waiter put his trousers back on and left immediately. As soon as he left she sat up and stretched, like a contented cat. From her handbag she extracted a cigarette. She lay back against the pillows inside the pool of golden light and smoked in silence, her face thoughtful. The watching man couldn't move. He stood transfixed. All these years she had fooled him. None of it was real. The animal cries, those hoarse cries, 'Harder, faster, deeper!' All of it was fake.

In the silence it came to him that for some time now she had been slowly moving money and property into her family. Money was being transferred to her uncouth, dishonest brother, many times to her avaricious mother and once even to her sister. She probably even had a secret account for herself. He stood trembling with fury. The bitch. The fucking bitch. She was planning to leave him.

He forgot that it was he who had engineered the encounter with the waiter and that it was supposed to be his new foray into depravity. So she didn't really enjoy watching her white skin redden with pain. She didn't like it rough. He had forgotten that he had hinted, gestured and tutored her slowly, subtly to pant and scream, 'Harder, faster, deeper!' He wanted to punish and at that moment he knew how to.

He would destroy her.

She was grinding out her cigarette. His legs unlocked and, moving through the connecting door, he closed it gently. Silently. Presently he heard the sound of the toilet flushing, paper rustling and a tap being turned on.

The door closed.

A thought flashed into his head. He wanted to see it all again. He wanted to be sure that he had seen it correctly. He wanted to see her white and gasping under the waiter. It was so unbelievable, her reaction, that it was like a dream. Surely it had not happened! Dear God, she was his wife of six years now. It seemed impossible that he had never seen this side of her. Yes, he wanted to do it all again. He must be sure that he had not imagined it.

That's what he told himself, but he knew the truth was that he just wanted to see her again with another. The really shocking truth was that he had enjoyed it. He had given his own blood and experienced an exquisite joy. He was not a learned man but even he recognised what had happened. Man has no real defence for the pain that he suffers. The only thing that comes remotely close to defence is to transform torture into pleasure. It was the basic dough that baked into a masochist. His eyes became flints in his face. It was her fault that he had gone down this thorny path. He was not even ready to accept the sadist in himself; the masochist could go take a flying fuck. He didn't want to continue down the terrible path. No way. No, he would not repeat the experiment; he would simply make her destitute, her and her entire family. He walked quickly across the room, closing the door behind him. He ran down the stairs and out of the front door.

You know, the hardest part had been sitting on the bed without my jewelled box jacket, calmly smoking a cigarette. Making sure my hands didn't shake, knowing that he was in the next room watching. And thinking, 'Oh God, please let him be so disgusted that he divorces me.'

I had seen him come back towards the house while I stared through the window but when the waiter slid up to me shaking with nerves, I knew. I didn't even need to see Luke slip up the stairs like a nasty shadow. I let the waiter into my body but everything else was the best performance of a lifetime. I always wanted to be an actress. Now I know I should have been one. I fooled him. I felt his eyes devour me, burn into me. I destroyed the purity that he so cherished. Sullied things sicken him. His best possession ruined right before his eyes. I wanted him to get rid of me.

After that I wanted to shower, to wash away the smell of the waiter. My hands were stained. My body was soiled. But I couldn't. His filth would always be my shame. I came down the stairs and the waiter was gone. After a while Luke sent the driver for me.

He was waiting for me in my room. A gasp of shock swam out from somewhere deep inside me to see him lounging on my bed like a dark fate awaiting me on my clean white sheets. I schooled the confusion inside me.

'Hello, darling. Was it a nice party?' he asked silkily. His voice was different. He was toying with me. A sort of new game.

'It was all right. I thought you might already be in bed,' I said weakly.

'I am in bed.'

I laughed nervously and walked to my dressing table. I knew I must not show my confusion. Act natural. I had taken my shoes off and my feet were soundless on the cold marble floor. I put my beaded purse on the dressing table and switched on a small light by the mirror. He stared at my brilliantly studded jacket. Remembering. I must have looked to him in the yellow light like a jewel box of secrets. His. His jewel box. I saw a change in him. He realised with a flash that he couldn't really let me go.

'Come here,' he said in a voice like a whiplash. It was the stranger inside him. Luke was gone. I shivered. But he had seen me with another! Why was he behaving like this? Where was the coldly angry stranger who should have turned me out mercilessly, clutching in my destitute hands my little Nisha? He clasped my trembling hand and brought it up to his lips. The stranger's shadowed eyes watched mine. Caught, I stared back helplessly. How could he have wanted to see me, the mother of his daughter, sordid and arching beneath another's body? To spy me thus, unobserved? His unblinking eyes said he must punish me as only he knew how to. And now he knew I didn't like it rough after all.

'Your hand smells different, dirty,' he whispered.

I snatched my hand away from his and began to walk away.

'Dance for me, my darling.'

'I'm a bit tired tonight. I think I'll just shower and go straight to bed,' I said. My voice sounded squeaky. I licked my dry lips and, panther quick, he had leaped off the bed, grabbed me by the arm and thrown me forcefully on the bed. I bounced slightly. For a few seconds I was too shocked to respond. I simply stared up at him with huge frightened eyes.

'Too tired to dance? How about something a little different then, my fussy pussy,' he purred nastily. From his hard lips I saw a creature, shadowy and terrible, plunge towards me. I recognised it. Pain. I felt the dark shape enter my body like a shiver. Inside me it will stay, devouring and malignant, and only when I am hollow and bitter with gall will it fly out of me and straight into the one dearest and closest to me. Nisha. Oh God, what have I done?

That night, there was pain like never before. When I opened my mouth to protest, to scream, he clamped his hand over it.

'Don't. You'll wake the child,' he advised coldly.

It is true that your mind can float out and hover over you when it can no longer endure what is happening to your body. It floats above, looking down quite dispassionately, and thinks of mundane things like a drop of sweat gathering on your abuser's forehead, or if the rubbish bins have been put out for the refuse collectors. When he was finished Luke left me with an expression of disgust on his face, the experience as distasteful to him as it had been to me. He knew that in his blood now ran a different fascination. Not to bed me but to watch me bedded by a paid stranger. To see me humiliated thus excited him. I had helped him discover an ugly perversion in himself. And now I was to pay for soiling myself, for soiling him.

During the months that followed, he tried everything to turn his attention away from this new perversity. But nothing worked. Even his lover with the carefree smile and all the techniques they must teach a golden girl could do nothing to abate the new passion. So he had me followed. Perhaps I had a lover. Perhaps he could recreate the party trick. Strange men with speculative smiles and slightly contemptuous eyes started approaching me at parties and in hotel lobbies. I did not turn around to see his greedy eyes; instead I smiled so coldly at them that they understood instantly that never, never, never would I willingly let them into me.

Then one night I came into my bedroom and saw all the paraphernalia of an opium smoker arranged neatly on the table. I let my hands slide over a fabulous antique ivory pipe carved with the most intricate elephants. I held up the cup and admired the oil lamp painted black and patterned with silver and copper flowers. It was my birthday. I was twenty-five years old and that was Luke's present to me. Nothing but the best for Dimple. He knew that I knew how those things work. Uncle Sevenese had long since disrobed the world of opium for me. I knew just how the skeletal old Chinesemen toasted opium on the lips of the oil lamp before shaking it and inhaling the fragrant fumes. I examined a small plastic bag of opium speculating where Luke might have got the aromatic brown stuff from. I understood the gift. He wanted me to destroy myself slowly. And why not? Didn't poppies symbolise release from all pain? Had not Emperor Shah Jehan mixed opium in his wine to enjoy its divine ecstasies? I walked away from my beautifully crafted birthday present. In the black sky outside the moon had waned into an upward-curving yellow smile.

Opium promised magnificent dreams. I thought of Nisha and the wind blew into the bamboo grove. It sighed and whispered. 'No, don't,' it said. 'Never,' I agreed but my hands were lighting the oil lamp and preparing a swab of raw opium over the glass funnel. Fragrant blue smoke rose from the pipe and flooded the room. Yes, yes I know. Thomas De Quincey has warned me too, but it was impossible not to succumb to beautiful dreams. Tell me how could I say no to music like perfume and living a hundred years in one night – even though I knew it would all end with the horror of thousands of years in a stone coffin, crawling through sewers and cancerous kisses from crocodiles. After all, what else was left but dreams?

Grandma's dead. I still couldn't really believe it.

Her small house was swarming with people. They sat, leaned against walls, talked in hushed voices and sang tuneless devotional songs in old, broken voices. I never knew that Grandma knew so many people. I suppose they must have been her temple cronies. Nobody was crying except Aunty Lalita. Even I didn't cry. All my tears were locked away somewhere where I couldn't find them. I knew I had made a terrible mess of my life and wished I was going with Grandma. It was only Nisha who held me back. I felt her holding on by her little fingernails. They were like small blades in my flesh, but every day the sky outside is a little greyer and the opium a little sweeter. No, I did not think of the blue smoke at the funeral. It would have been a terrible insult to succumb in that last time with Grandma. If she could have heard my thoughts, her spirit would mourn for my poor, wasted life.

Papa dashed about doing as much as he could to help, but when he met my eyes he came to sit beside me. He folded his long limbs under him.

'I was her favourite, you know,' he said looking out of the door at the place where the huge rambutan tree used to stand. Grandma's new neighbours had had it cut down when they saw the cracks in the cement drains around their homes, fearing that the roots of the tree were breaking through the foundations of their houses.

'Yes, she told me many times.'

'I wasn't a good son but I loved her. We suffered together during the Japanese time.'

I looked at him carefully. Poor Papa, how flawed his perception. Not only hadn't he been a good son; he had been a terrible son. He broke her heart and behaved exactly like the enemy the fortune-teller in the green tent had predicted he would become. Grandma had borne him like a rock in the face of the sea's angry waves. But it really was too late and there no longer any point in correcting him.

'We suffered together during the war,' he continued. 'I hid her jewels in the coconut tree. I was the only one brave enough to climb right to the top. Nobody else but I would do it for her. I was the man of the house. She turned to me for everything and I never let her down. I woke before everybody else to take the milk to the tea vendors. I tilled the land and took the ragi to the millers. I did it all for her. It was right that she loved me the best.'

He took off his glasses and wiped his eyes. Darling, tortured Papa. The carefully hand-picked selection of memories had undone him. He stood up suddenly and strode outside into the bright sunlight in the backyard. All of our lives twisted and ugly. When Papa smiled he had a dimple in his chin. I hadn't seen it for years. I saw Papa pass Nash without a word. My brother and father hold equal contempt for each other. Outside I could see Papa talking to Aunty Lalita. He wanted to wash the clothes that were soaking in a big red tub.

Aunty Lalita shook her head. 'No, no, I will do the washing later. I'm used to washing all the clothes now,' she protested.

'For one last time I want to wash what Mother wore,' Papa insisted, taking his shirt and his watch off. He put his watch on the old grinding stone where he and Mohini used to crush beans into paste many years ago. Then he began. I remembered what Aunty Lalita told me a long time ago about Papa washing clothes. He does not just beat the clothes on the smooth stone. He arches his entire body so the clothes are flying for a long time in the air and water droplets fly all around him, catching the sunlight and sparkling like precious diamonds. I could see Aunty Lalita standing by, watching him, and I knew she was thinking the same thing I was. My Papa is a Water God.

In the kitchen Aunty Anna was helping to prepare Grandma's body, laid out on her bench. That sturdy thing that had so enchanted her when she had arrived as an innocent in Malaya. Now it held her, dead. The bench will survive us all. I know for sure it will survive me. My time is short. It is true that I feel Nisha's fingernails in my flesh but her grip is not really that strong. My life is fading away. A cloth was held up to hide the naked corpse as Aunty Anna and three other women washed Grandma. I held little Nisha closer to me. She was quiet. I kissed the top of her head, and when she looked up at me with large questioning eyes, I smiled at her.

Mother slowly limped out of Grandma's bedroom where she had been lying down with terrible arthritic pains. Someone brought her a chair because her knees were too stiff to sit cross-legged on the floor like everyone else. I looked into her bitter eyes. She felt no sadness for Grandma. She had hated Grandma from the day she married Papa. Nevertheless she was there to pay her last respects and wait for the reading of the will.

I remember Grandma never wanted respect, had no time for it and scorned it when it was offered in lieu of real feeling. She gave deep love and unstinting loyalty and demanded the same in return.

'Love, Dimple, is not words but deep sacrifice,' she often told me. 'It is the willingness to give until you are crippled.'

Aunty Anna went into Grandma's bedroom and I followed her. She was sitting on the edge of Grandma's four-poster bed and when she saw me she smiled sadly and opened her right palm. It was full of hairpins, not the ordinary kind but the ones that Grandma wore. Kee Aa Pins. No one really wore those any more. They were like hair clips, but instead of staying close together, they were U shaped. Grandma used them to keep her bun in place.

'Years after I moved out of this house I would see a Kee Aa Pin and be immediately reminded of Mother,' Aunty Anna said. 'I shall always remember today, taking all these pins out of her hair for the last time. Her body is cold but her hair still feels exactly the same as all those years ago when Mohini and I took turns to comb her hair. Isn't it funny how these pins have suddenly made her death unbearable? Poor Mother. We were all such a monstrous disappointment to her.'

'Oh Aunty Anna. You were not a disappointment to her at all. She loved you, and of all her children at least you gave her the satisfaction of marrying well and made something of your life.'

'No, Dimple. None of us lived up to her expectations. Your mother calls her a spider without the slightest idea how accurate her description is. When Latin was spoken as a language the word spider meant "I stand above all". And she did. She towered above us all in talent, intelligence and sheer grandness. She could lend her hand to any skill, out-fox the most cunning of people, and yet we, her wonderful children, defeated her. Do you know what she told me at the hospital when we took her there this last time?'

I shook my head silently.

'She said, "I can smell Death in the air."'

'And blindly I said to her, "It's the antiseptic you smell."'

'No, Anna, you smell the antiseptic because it is not your time."'

I stared at Aunty Anna incredulously because that was exactly how I felt when I took Nisha to visit Grandma. I smelt Death in the air and saw him everywhere, but I held Nisha close to my body like a weapon and he backed down. I held the greedy ogre at bay with the little flower beside me. While I hold her close his perfume is not so alluring and his smile not so inviting. Aunty Anna began to cry softly and I hugged her. Her shoulders shook with sadness. Through the window I saw Nash smoking, his handsome face bored.

'Can I have one of the pins?' I asked.

She opened her palm and I took one. I am going to keep it. Aunty Anna is right – the pin will remind me most vividly of Grandma. I can see her now standing in front of the mirror in her white sari. There is still a lot of excess powder on her face and her mouth is full of pins as she does up her hair. One by one they go into her thick silver bun until it is secure on the back of her neck. Then she turns around to me and asks with a smile, 'Are you ready to go?' And one day I will say, 'Yes'.

After the funeral I went to see Uncle Sevenese. He looked terrible.

'When I was a boy I dreamed my mother's funeral. Everything was exactly the same. Only now I have names to put on the grown-up faces I didn't recognise before. I saw Lakshmnan and thought him a bitter stranger. The only person in my dream that looked vaguely like anyone I knew was you and I assumed you were Mohini all grown up. But when I saw you today with Nisha on your lap the dream broke.'

I gazed unhappily at him and he tossed an old copy of Sartre to me. 'Read it and stop simply *living the look*. You have the freedom of choice, you know. Don't stay with him if you don't want to.'

Once I would have taken the book. Read it eagerly. But now . . .

'All hope is gone – the Rice Mother is dead. There is no one left to protect my sleeping dreams, once lush with scented herbs, green moss, ripening fruit and glorious blooms, but now I can see the poor things, pale and without breath, buried at the bottom of a lost lake.'

Upon my words Uncle Sevenese turned speechless with horror and denied himself further knowledge. I could hardly tell him then how I need my blue smoke more and more and like it less and less.

Nisha told me there was a bird's nest in the mango tree. She said she could hear the chirping of baby chicks even from her bedroom window. She took me out to listen but for some reason their frantic calls made me anxious. 'Come on,' I said cheerfully, 'let's try the new coffee bar in town.' We sat at sienna tables, for the whole place was done up in the new terracotta palette. They had the strangest flower arrangement there using a new flower called the Kangaroo's Paw. I had never seen anything like it. It was beautiful and black. A black flower. How very strange – and yet how very beautiful, with little pad-like petals in the palest green. So unusual and so elegant. I went to the florist and ordered some.

They arrived on Thursday and looked beautiful in a clear glass vase on the coffee table. Nisha thought they looked like curled sleeping spiders on a stalk. What a child she is! But I will teach her to love them.

Luke won't touch her any more. Perhaps he is now afraid of what monsters lie sleeping inside him. What if he finds that he wants to lie with her? That is what he is afraid of – new perversions he will discover within himself. I feel sad for Nisha. She can't understand why her daddy pushes her away. I don't know what is to become of us. If only he would let us both go but I know that he never will. He will never let me go. He will use her to keep me here.

February 1983. Uncle Sevenese is dead. I was standing by his bedside at the hospital when he made the sign of writing, his eyes desperate. I rushed to put a pen and paper in his hands. Shakily he wrote, '*I see her. Flowers grow be*' and died. I can't stop thinking of that unfinished sentence. What had he seen that prompted him to request pen and paper? I felt numb all the way up the stairs to his room thinking about it. Troubled by the way I had lost him.

I see her. Flowers grow be—!

I put a greasy key into his door. That first whiff of his closed, stuffy room was so stale and horrible it made me want to retch. There was a small window in his kitchenette and I opened it as wide as the stuck mechanism would allow. The room was sordid. The cracks in the linoleum were caked in grease and black dirt, and there was a film of cigarette ash everywhere. This is the last time I will see this room, I thought in a surprisingly detached manner. Then I stood there and committed everything to memory.

In a strange way it was still fresh with his essence, as

if he had only gone downstairs for his morning coffee. His astrology books, his charts and diagrams lay scattered on the bed. He had been working on someone's chart when he was taken ill. I sat on the stained sheets; a picture of that prostitute in white lounging on the mattress smoking a menthol cigarette popped into my grieving head. She would never know he was gone. I opened the torn exercise book and looked at the notes he had been drawing up.

Keep away/short lifeline. Rahu/snake in marriage house/deadlock. Death, divorce, sadness, tragedy.

Pity the poor sod whose chart he had been working on. But when I lifted the notes, the charts and astrological details of my sister and me were underneath. I froze with disbelief. It was one of us. Bella or me.

In a drawer I found an envelope addressed to me. I did not open it but could feel that there was a cassette inside. He had taped me a message. A last story for my abandoned dream trail. I folded the brown envelope carefully and put it away in my handbag. It is still there. I cannot bear to listen to it yet. Perhaps one night just before the blue smoke, then it will not affect me so.

The funeral was brief. They had to carry out the body in a hurry even before the allocated time for the cremation. His badly damaged insides rotted so fast that the gases released bloated up his big body like a balloon. Even from where I sat I heard the hissing and spitting gases, as if his organs were conspiring to explode. They feared pieces of my uncle splattered all over the walls so they rushed him out. Soft-hearted Aunty Lalita reached down into the coffin and kissed him on the cheek even though the strong stench of decay that came from his body made me feel faint. It was not the smell of a corpse but the smell of rubbish. Even in death Uncle Sevenese refused to conform. Despite the two bottles of cologne, the reek of rotting rubbish and formaldehyde was so overpowering that a dignified funeral was not possible. The pungent fumes stung our eyes and two women even dashed into the kitchen to hide their distaste of the intolerable fumes. An old withered lady, too old to bother playing diplomatic games, covered her nose and mouth with the ends of her sari. I supposed Aunty Lalita would now hang up a garlanded, black and white, framed photograph of Uncle Sevenese to join Grandad, Grandma and Mohini. I felt cold. I felt cold all day. It was the blue smoke.

Aunty Lalita came to visit. She spent a lot of time with Nisha in the garden talking to her as if she too were only six years old. They watched the fish for hours then they studied the carefree dragonflies with the jade and turquoise patches enamelled on their long abdomens, hovering over the still water. She told Nisha what she told me when I was a child. That dragonflies are capable of stitching together the lips of wicked children in their sleep. Nisha's eyes became opalescent pools of wonder. 'Really,' my daughter breathed.

Watching them is like looking back in time. I used to sit in the shade with Aunty Lalita watching the dragonflies flitting back and forth at the back of Grandma's house. I used to turn my head and see Grandma sitting on the bench watching us through the window like I am now watching them.

Something is terribly wrong with Papa. He was rushed to the hospital with chest pains. They gave him some pills but he flung them into the air on the hospital steps. Poor Papa, I know his pain. He seeks the same oblivion I seek.

Nisha is having problems with a school bully called Angela Chan who leaves crescent-shaped fingernail marks on her arms. I will have to visit the girl's mother.

Have I told you about my horribly wonderful dreams? They must come from the blue smoke. There is a beautiful man in a thick glass case. His limbs are long and shapely and his curly hair gently sweeps against his strong shoulders. His face is shadowed yet I feel his beauty. I know when he gets out of the thick glass case he will be splendid beyond my expectations. His eyes are sad like mine are in the portrait downstairs, but I feel certain that he loves me. He has always loved me.

For many years now he has looked at me with deep longing, but now he is impatient to feel me, fill me, make me one with him. I don't know when exactly, but some time ago he began to cut through the glass. He is without weapons so he uses his fingernails. His fingers are bleeding and the glass is all red but he is tireless. His love is deep. Day and night he scratches. He will cut himself out one day, and I will be waiting. It will be a special moment when I kiss him. I like the way that mouth curves. I yearn for the day when I press my body to that lithe length and his mouth covers mine. When I give my life to Death. He is a beautiful man.

Part Six

The Rest is Lies
July, 2001

Luke

Brought to this uneasy landscape of sharply protruding bones and sunken flesh by a ravenous disease, I no longer dare shut my eyes. Day and night I watch the door feverishly. In this cold hospital room where butter-coloured tubes sprout sadly from my wasted arms and ride into blinking machines, I know Death will come to collect me. Soon. My breathing is hollow and loud in the silent room. Invisible hands have begun to pack me in a waxy, yellow material. Ready for my journey.

I turn my head to look at my daughter. She sits by my bedside on a black and chrome chair like a small mouse. But if she is a mouse it is surely my work. I have turned Dimple's beautiful child into a meek, inconsequential person. It is a cruel thing that I have done, but in my defence it was never my intention to hurt. Nor was it easy. It took many years and many lies to accomplish. She sits, innocent of my horrible deceit. If she knew she would hate me. She leans forward to clasp my stiff, clawed hand. The poor child's hand is freezing.

'Nisha,' my dry mouth murmurs. Faintly. The end is nigh.

Dutifully she moves closer. So close that she inhales the reek of decaying flesh. The rot within wags a long black finger; one day you too, it warns my drab mouse. I hear her gasp.

'I'm sorry,' I whisper, the words struggling out painfully. There is so little left of me.

'Why?' she cries, for she knows nothing of the past. An 'accident' and a convenient amnesia attack sixteen years ago is responsible. I'm afraid I rather took advantage of it and set about recreating her world for her. Feathered it with comforting lies. Decided she must never know the tragic truth. Never see the blood on my hand.

In her face I see Dimple's eyes but the girl lacks her mother's glamour. Oh, the regret, the regret. I have done them both wrong but I will right it today. I will give her the key. Let her meet my terrible secret, that hunched, deformed shape clinging relentlessly around my neck. Yes, the one I have so carefully sheltered and fed for sixteen years. The key that locked away my darling Dimple's dreams.

It must be said, I loved my poor wife badly.

There is a soft pain in my chest and the breath catches in my throat. Nisha looks at me with sudden fear. She runs out of the room, her heels loud on the polished floors, to look for a doctor, a nurse, an orderly, someone, anyone at all who can help . . .

Nisha

There was no peace in the open mouth and the staring eyes when I returned with a nurse. He died as he had lived. I gazed astonished, uncomprehending that the smouldering coals in the narrow slits of his face could so easily extinguish themselves into lifeless marbles, dense and black. Like the black marble floor that stretches endlessly in my nightmares. So highly polished that a child's face reflects back. A small face twisted with terror and shock. No doubt another fragment of an old memory, one missed by the memory-eating snake that has devoured my childhood. It winds and drips like mercury inside my dreams and whispers, 'Trust me. They are safest in the dark of my belly.'

I sank down slowly beside my still father and in a small mirror on the wall I stared at myself blankly. The blood of many races has infused my face with its mysterious eyes, high cheekbones and a small neat mouth that appears almost rueful to be sharing the same space as my exotic eyes. The mouth knew what the men didn't, that the provocation in the half-closed lids disguises an invitation to heartbreak. I have broken many hearts without meaning to. Without knowing.

In the lap of my brown dress my pampered hands mumbled that they had never done a day's work in twenty-four years. I looked at the key I had prised out of Daddy's tightly clenched fist. Could it be used to set free the memory pieces inside the greedy snake? Give them back their voices so they may explain silly little things like why a dripping tap should terrify me so. Or why the combination of red and black chokes me with inexplicable fear? I left my father's corpse without a backward glance.

Lena, my father's servant, let me into his house. Up the long, curving stairs I ran, bursting into the sparse coolness of his dull room. For a moment I froze in the sapphire shadows. I could smell Daddy. He had not been in that room for weeks and yet like a lost ghost his smell lingered helplessly on. I crossed the room, fitted the key into a door inside his dressing room and turned it.

The small, walk-in cupboard stored the thick, grey-white dust of many years. Its shelves were bare but for a startled rusty-brown baby spider and an old cardboard box that claimed in block green letters to have once housed twelve bottles of French Chardonnay.

'STORE THIS WAY UP' said the tired red arrow that had been pointing downwards for God knows how many years. Old duct tape gave way easily and a cloud of white dust like a pleasing mountain mist rose up.

All my life. All my life I had searched and not found. I opened the box.

A box full of cassettes. A box full of secrets.

On the inside cover of a yellowing collection of Omar Khayyam's poems small, childish handwriting proclaimed it the private property of Dimple Lakshmnan. Who the hell was Dimple Lakshmnan? Startled silverfish peered up from their dinner of black ink and old paper.

I rummaged through the cassettes. Each one had been carefully numbered and named – LAKSHMI, ANNA,

LALITA, SEVENESE, JEYAN, BELLA . . . I wondered who all these people were.

Downstairs, the phone rang. I heard Lena gasp loudly. Obviously the hospital.

'I'm sorry,' he had said so cryptically on the threshold of death.

'Don't be sorry, Daddy,' I murmured softly. 'There was never anything I yearned for more than an acquaintance with the secrets that lurked in your cold eyes.'

The Woman in Black

'I'm so sorry, Nisha,' a woman whispered very close to my ears, patting my hand sympathetically. I did not know her but she must have been a friend of Daddy's if she saw fit to attend his funeral. I watched her move away in a suitably funereal black and grey dress and felt quite numb.

I longed to leave. To return to my flat and liberate the voices trapped in the tapes. But dutiful daughters were expected to remain at least until the body had left the house. Daddy certainly knew a lot of people, for the whole house was crammed with flowers that didn't smell. There was even a massive arrangement from a prominent Indonesian Minister. How strange that he should send my father flowers. Daddy hadn't approved of him. Too obvious, he said. He preferred his corruption subtle.

I noticed that there was not a single Kangaroo's Paw in sight. It was strange the feeling of *déjà vu* that had flowed over me when I first laid eyes on it. I thought it strangely familiar and very beautiful. Thin and black with the slightest tinge of tender green as if unaware that it was its very blackness that excited the intense horticultural attention and wonder.

Like me. Unaware for too many years that my special attraction had lain in the unattainable curve of my cheek as I slept with my face turned away in the dark. Lying next to me, the men who came into my life became in-explicably and without exception obsessed with the mystery that lay so tantalisingly within reach and yet unconquered. They were gripped by the same fever, the need to possess me, to go where others had not gone . . . well at least at the beginning.

At the beginning they all came into my life rich with hope and glowing with expectation. To have actually ensnared the daughter of Luke Steadman! The possi-bilities seemed endless. The money, the power, the connections . . . but in the end they all left exasperated, frustrated by the knowledge that in the dark space between them and me was a terrifying gorge of unknown depth.

'Why,' shouted one of the more memorable ones in bitter amazement from the edge of the chasm, 'do I kiss you, suck you and fuck you, and you behave as if you've just licked a stamp?'

Of course an apology only made it worse. Perhaps an explanation . . .

'I can't help it if my eyes that have been claimed so many years ago by despair have the same expression when I am licking a stamp as when you are fucking me. You have mastered your technique,' I said. 'It is not you. It is I,' I soothed gently. Saved their pride. It is a precious thing pride, a man's pride.

'It is I,' I insisted mistily, my long, slightly Oriental eyes pleading for understanding. 'You see, I lost myself when I was seven years old. It was exactly like walking along on a zebra crossing and stepping off a white strip onto a perfectly innocent-looking black strip and suddenly tripping, falling. Disappearing into a limitless black hole with only the stars for company. And when

The Rice Mother

one day I climbed out of that hole I found myself on a white bed in a white room without my memories.'

At that point I had to stop for they looked at me as if I had concocted the whole zebra-crossing story to mollify them. So I never got to tell them about the stranger with the narrow eyes and the worried expression who I found staring down at me in that white room. I looked at him and he gazed back at me with a flicker of unease. I was afraid of him. He had distant, cold eyes.

He called me Nisha and claimed he was my father, though he didn't try to touch me or hug me. Perhaps that only happened in Hollywood movies, all that frantic kissing and hugging between fathers and daughters. Actually it has occurred to me that my father didn't even seem particularly happy that I had climbed out of the black hole with only the stars for company. I was left with the insolent impression that he was relieved I couldn't remember anything.

Sometimes I think I should have told the hopeful men that my father almost never touched me. In fact, no one was allowed to touch me. I grew up lonely in the company of servants. Perhaps then they would have understood about the unbridgeable chasm in the bed.

If I had not looked into the mirror that day on the white bed in the white room and seen looking back at me the same narrow eyes that he wore in his strained face, I would not have believed that I belonged to him. How could he have breathed life into me when his breath was so cold? His eyes so distant. Yet he told me he loved me and furnished my lonely life with the best of everything. For he was rich, very rich, and important. And powerful.

I stayed in the white room for a few more days and then he gently led me into a big car and drove me to a

506

very big house. Inside the house it was very cold. I shivered and he turned the air-conditioning down and showed me to a strange, pink room that I was certain I had never seen before.

'This is your room.' His black eyes stared closely at me.

I looked around the little girl's room where everything looked and smelt new. The clothes that hung in the wardrobe still had tags. In the bottom of the wardrobe expensive shoes with bright bows sparkled gaily without the dishonour of scuffmarks on their pristine heels.

'Do you remember anything?' he asked carefully. Not hopefully, but carefully. I shook my head. So vigorously that it hurt. There was still a red scar where I had hit my head when I had fallen through the hole in the zebra crossing.

'Don't I have a mother?' I asked timidly for I was afraid of the stranger.

'No,' he replied, sadly, I thought, but I could have been wrong. I was only a child then. I didn't know about daddies who pretend. He showed me a small picture. The lady in it had sorrowing eyes. Eyes that made me feel lonely. 'Mama died at childbirth,' he said. 'The poor soul haemorrhaged to death.'

So it was my fault that the sad woman in the picture had died. I wished then that I had my mother's eyes. But I had his. Cold and distant. I wanted to cry but not in front of the stranger. As soon he left I allowed myself to fall on the strange new bed. And cry.

I asked my father many times about those lost years but the more details he described, the more convinced I became that he was lying. There was a secret he was hiding from me. A secret so dreadful that he had invented a whole new past for me. Now I wanted those lost years back. Their absence has ruined my life. I knew the voices in the tapes were full of secrets. That is why my father hid them all those years ago.

I looked around at all the beautiful arrangements without any Kangaroo's Paws in them. Perhaps they are too expensive to waste on funeral wreaths. I suppose they are for the homes of the rich and famous. My father was a very rich man but he hated Kangaroo's Paws. Hated them with a passion. The way I hate the colours black and red together. For some reason the beautiful black petals made him sweat with nerves. It was interesting watching him pretend that the curly, spidery flowers didn't affect him. The first time I put some into a flower arrangement he stared at them as if I had curled an assortment of hissing snakes around each black stalk.

'Are you all right, Dad?'

'Yes, yes, of course. Just a bit tired today.' He had looked at me then. Carefully. As if it was I who hid something hideous. As if it was I who had bought a whole new wardrobe of clothes for him, painted his room a sweet, unrecognisable pink and told him a whole box of lies. I watched him with interest. I never knew him, my daddy. He never touched me. He never even came close enough for me to touch him. I didn't know his secrets. And he had many. Inside his cold, narrow eyes they burned like a funeral pyre.

'Did you remember something today?' he asked abruptly.

I stared at him with growing surprise. 'No. Why?'

'Nothing. I was just curious,' he lied with his politician's smile. Dishonest Daddy.

My eyes moved to a woman who had just walked in.

She wore her grief with tragic splendour, from head to toe in shades of black. Like a talented Japanese designer. She was startlingly beautiful. I had never seen her before. The woman's lips were too red. They made my fingers clench slightly.

Black and red. Black and red. How they coloured the nightmares that tormented me! The woman looked across Daddy's sitting room to where the coffin lay raised above the ground on a long, low table. Nestled in cool satin, yellow and still, he waited for us to feed him to the starving beast in the crematorium.

Suddenly the beautiful stranger broke into a run. Small, mincing, feminine steps. She threw herself dramatically on the still body and began to sob. I drew back slightly in surprise.

Another one of Daddy's little secrets come back for payment.

The sombre crowd were quick to realise her curiosity value. People covertly stared at me but I ignored them. For a moment the sight of the black figure sprawled over the thin yellow corpse made me entertain the intriguing idea of a large, black, female spider that curves over and devours her struggling lover. But whether it was only a wonderful performance was hardly the point. Even in death Luke Steadman was no struggling lover. My dear, dear father. True to the very end. Cold and certainly beyond silken webs.

The woman was not in his will.

His short will mentions nobody but me. His daughter. The one he gave the key to. The one he kept secrets from. As if the woman heard my unkind thoughts she looked up and met my eyes. There was something strangely abandoned in the scarlet of her lipstick. Poor creature. In my chest I felt my heart melt a little. I couldn't help it. I fancy I know what it means to be abandoned.

My poor mother's body expelled me into the world and then bled to death. So my father fed her bloodless body to the beast with the yellow saliva in the crematorium and I was left with Father. And he, he left me things – toys when I was younger and pieces of jewellery as I grew older – on a table outside my room just before he left for work. The stark truth was he left them outside my door so I could never give in to the spontaneous urge to run into his arms or kiss him as any daughter might. And to further negate the messy possibility of the dreaded hug when he came home, my devious father phoned beforehand to ask if I liked my new present.

He withdrew behind a wall of polite expressions, 'Please', 'May I' and 'Thank you'. Everyone believed in his wonderfully faultless act. Some even envied me the perfection of the tender love that they imagined existed between father and daughter. They held him up as an ideal. Only I stood behind the thick wall that he had built between us and screamed silently. Horrified by its terrible perfection and the truly astonishing amount of details that he had put into his distance. If only he would love me a little. But he never did. A baby monkey denied the warmth of its mother dies. Its sad heart simply stops the tedious business of beating. I suppose it is a good thing I am not a baby monkey.

I nodded and people moved like obedient dolls. I was the new master. Sole heir to a king's ransom. They pulled away the abandoned red mouth from the cologne-drenched body and guided her away, sobbing, to a corner. Gently, curiously.

Then they carried away his coffin on their shoulders.

No one wept except the beautiful woman in black with the blood-red lips. People began to drift away and I walked over to the sobbing woman. Up close she was not so young. Perhaps in her mid-thirties or even pouting at forty. Her eyes were startling, though. Huge and liquid. Like the glinting surface of a calm lake on a moonlit night. She, too, was full of secrets and some were surely mine.

I invited her into my father's study, away from the openly prying eyes. The woman followed silently. Had she been in the house before? In the study I turned around to face her.

'I'm Rosette and it's nice to finally meet you, Nisha,' she said quietly. Strangely, her voice matched her eyes. Cultivated to flow clear and liquid, like honey.

'Would you like a drink?' I asked automatically.

'Tia Maria on ice, please.' A smile bled onto the red lips. Too red.

I walked to the drinks cabinet. Well, well, it seemed my father did stock up on Tia Maria. I had a sudden picture of their bodies twisted and joined on the hospital bed. A sunken, yellow corpse of a man and this mysterious, beautiful creature. I shook my head to clear away the distasteful corruption of their unseemly coupling. What on earth was happening to me?

'Did you know my father well?'

I heard her take a deep breath.

'Fairly.' She was soft and feminine. And secretive. She was my father's woman.

'Have you known him long?' I persisted.

'Twenty-five years.' She said it lightly.

I spun around in shock. 'Did you know my mother?' The words ran out of my mouth before I could stop them.

Something rose out of the smooth moonlit lakes in her fair, carefully made-up face. It was alive and full of regret. The ugly lake creature looked at me sadly for a few seconds then slid back into the gleaming water. Her face became blank again.

'No,' she denied, shaking her head. The honey in her voice had thickened into dusky sediment. She had just lied. Loyalty to a man who was now dead – what was the use of that? There was still the rent to be paid and clothes in different shades of black to be purchased. I concentrated on the task of Tia Maria on ice. Just outside my skull, a clock ticked into the silence.

'My father didn't mention you in his will,' I said casually and heard the stillness that came to hug her. The clock ticked with determined precision. I let a few moments pass before I turned around, half-smiling, and presented her drink to her.

Still wearing the dead man's cologne, Rosette took the cold glass in her pale hands. Poor thing, it must be said she held it in her hand quite helplessly. The abandoned look returned. Oh dear, it was true the rent did need paying. As I watched, tears gathered in her lovely, sad eyes and slipped down her pale cheeks.

'The bastard,' she swore very, very softly before collapsing into a large, stuffed sofa behind her. She looked very small and very white against the dark green of Daddy's sofa. I liked her a little, then.

'I'm afraid I am the only person in his will. Not even the servants, some of whom have been here a lot longer than I can remember, merited a mention. I'm giving them something on his behalf.' I paused for a moment. 'The thing is, I didn't know my father very well and I didn't know my mother at all. If you can help to fill in some of the blanks I would be very pleased to help you with your finances.'

The lake creature undulated in the still dark lake. Perhaps with the realisation that it was looking at the shape of its new source of bread and butter from here on. Did I relish the power? She had certainly recognised and bowed low to it. Suddenly she laughed. A harsh bitter sound. It was the sound of a woman who has never been in control of her own destiny.

'Some things are better left in the dark. It is not kind the memory you seek. It has the power to destroy you. Why do you think he hid it from you? Are you really certain you want to know?'

'Yes,' I replied instantly, surprised by the clear conviction in my voice.

'Did he give you the key?'

I stared at her in amazement. She even knew about the key.

'Yes,' I said, stunned by how close this composed woman had been to my father. Truly I had never known my own father. The red lips smiled. I really couldn't stand that blood red. The colour was like a knife in my eye.

She drained her drink and stood before me. In her eyes was the knowledge that from here on was only old age and death, and the sad regrets of bad choices. Even I could have told her that my father was a bad choice.

'After you have listened to the tapes, come and see me.' She walked up to Daddy's desk and scribbled her address and telephone number on a memo pad. 'Goodbye, Nisha.' The door closed.

I picked up the notepad. She lived in Bangsar, not far away. Her writing was feminine and strangely inviting.

I wondered at her origins. She had the thin, very fair skin of a certain class of Arabic women. The type that have bodyguards waiting outside the changing rooms of Emporio Armani.

I tore the address off the pad and headed for home.

Inside my apartment it was stiflingly hot. The delicate, pink roses on the coffee table drooped. Pink petals lay where they had fallen. Time's up. Death waits everywhere.

Ignoring the muted rings of the telephone I turned on the air-conditioning and chilled, dry air poured silently into the room. Without changing out of my black mourning dress I switched on the tape recorder and closed my weary eyes. The voice of someone called Lakshmi filled the cooling room with shadows from an unknown past.

The next morning I jerked awake surrounded by cassettes and startled by the doorbell buzzing.

'Special Delivery letter,' a man's disembodied voice floated out of the intercom. I signed for the letter from Father's solicitors. They needed to see me immediately about a matter of the utmost importance. I called and made an appointment with the senior partner of De Cruz, Rajan & Rahim.

Mr De Cruz came forward and completely enveloped my hand in his large, leathery ones. In his veins ran the Portuguese blood that manifested itself as a high nose in his proud face and a condescending attitude towards the 'locals'. His hair sat stiffly like polished silver on his wary skull. From cavernous sockets his eyes shone with the merciless greed that had made his forefathers famous. There was something deeply unwholesome about him. Underneath his skin, I imagined, writhed a whole different creature.

I had met him once before at a dinner in the Stock Exchange. He had smiled with great charm but had not introduced the tall girl with the blank eyes who stood beside him. I found him, like all lawyers of my acquaintance, arrogant and too proud of his ability to have enslaved words to do exactly as he bid. He kept them inside his mouth and brought them out at the right time with the right inflection added. And look how rich it had made him.

'I'm so sorry about your father,' he commiserated in his deep baritone voice. I couldn't help but be impressed. It was surely a gift, this ability to sound so sincere at a moment's notice.

'Thank you. And thank you for the flowers too,' I said automatically.

He nodded sagely. The words waited inside his mouth for the right moment. He indicated that I should sit. The office was large and cool. There was a well-stocked bar in one corner. I had heard the rumour that he drank. Heavily. At the Selangor club.

He dropped into a large leather chair behind his table. For a moment he paused and studied me sitting in front of him. I imagined his thoughts: *Very pretty, if only she would make more of herself.* Then he let the words that had been waiting in his mouth jump out and scare the living daylights out of the poor thing who had not made more of herself. It was hardly his fault. It wasn't he who had made all those bad investments that had brought her father to bankruptcy as he died in hospital. It was the economy. The whole damn economy had fallen on its face after that fiasco with George Soros taking on the Malaysian ringgit and destroying the share prices like a fist on a house of cards.

Blankly I listened as Mr De Cruz used all the right words to tell me about the Stock Market crash, and the inevitable losses the high-risk investment portfolio favoured by Father had incurred. Basically, he said, there was nothing left to will over to me but enormous debts. In fact even my expensive apartment would have to go.

'Do you have any jewellery that you could sell?'

Horrified, I stared at him. 'But Father was a multi-millionaire! How is this possible?'

Mr De Cruz shrugged eloquently. 'The economy, as I said. Some unwise investments. A few sour deals . . .' All kinds of soothing words slipped out of his mobile mouth. 'Perhaps even fraud, shady characters . . .'

'So basically I am homeless.'

'Not quite.' Mr De Cruz flashed an uncomfortable, oddly guilty smile. I gazed at him expectantly. The smile broadened and the flash of guilt removed its unwelcome presence. No decent lawyer should suffer the likes of guilt too long on his person.

'Well, your mother left a house for you. You were meant to come into it when you were twenty-one but as you were comfortably ensconced in your apartment by then, your father decided not to concern you with the running of a decrepit old house. But as your circumstances have now changed, perhaps you should take a look at your inheritance.'

'My mother left me a house?' I repeated stupidly.

'Yes, a house in Ampang. Naturally the building itself is probably in a state of terrible disrepair but the land is another matter . . . Considering its location, it is quite a pile you are sitting on. The sale would solve all your problems, and of course this firm is perfectly qualified to dispose of it for you.' He set his lips in a businesslike manner and opened a file in front of him.

I should have been told about the house when I turned twenty-one but Mr Cruz had suppressed the information because my father had asked him to.

'Who has been paying the ground rent on the property?' I asked.

'There was an inheritance from your maternal great-grandmother that automatically paid the required amount, but that inheritance has been almost used up. There is also the matter of a sealed letter that your father left for you in the event of his death. Here are the keys and the address to your property.' He handed over a bunch of keys, the deed to the property and the mysteriously sealed letter.

I was speechless. My mother had left me a house and he had sat on such a vital piece of information for all these years. Words were still pouring out of the man when I stood up suddenly. He stopped speaking.

'Thank you,' I said politely and walked towards the glossy door.

Outside the building, the muggy afternoon heat hit me like a blow. Everything I had taken for granted died yesterday. The home that I had thought was mine was not and the mountain of money didn't exist. Yet nothing mattered but the keys in my hand and the house. I walked along the road until I spotted the Cherry Lounge bar. There was a light throbbing in my temples and the maddest desire to laugh in my mouth. I was poor. What a joke! A lifetime of wealth had left me helpless. A degree in social science that overqualified me for the job of secretary and left me underqualified for everything else. It was impossible to imagine my father's immense wealth reduced to a decrepit house in Ampang. I thought about the many politicians who came with arms outstretched and patted my father's back. 'Good, good. I know I can always count on Luke,' they said.

How was it possible? I became certain that while he lay in hospital my father was swindled and robbed blind. He was too shrewd, far too wily to have lost all the millions in real estate, shares and secret accounts. It could only be a scam, but the thought of unravelling his empire made me feel ill. The people who could make such colossal sums disappear sat in very high places and even my father had watched them very carefully from a safe distance.

I walked into the Cherry Lounge, bought a double brandy from a flatteringly curious bartender and found a dark corner to hide in. I leaned back into the seat. Was it possible for life to change in an afternoon? Of course. I lifted the heavy curtain at the window. It was raining outside. Obviously I couldn't go and see the house that afternoon and for reasons unknown the postponement was a relief. The house was more than just a house. I had felt its magic as soon as it fell out of De Cruz's mouth. I took off my shoes, curled my legs under me and tore open the letter. 'Let's see what new surprises you have for me now, Daddy dear.'

But the writing was not Daddy's. I uncurled my legs from under me and sat up straighter. It was in a feminine hand and addressed not to me, but to my father. I didn't want to read it there in that horrible and safe place but my seeking eyes moved to the top of the page.

Dear Luke,

My dying wish is that Nisha should have the tapes. They are simply memories of people whom I have loved all my life. They have no power to hurt you. The diaries I leave to you to do with as you please. You will heed this last request of mine if you have loved me at any time at all. I only want my daughter to know that she comes from a proud line of amazing people. None of them as weak as I have been. She must know she has nothing to be ashamed of.

Under her skin are fine ancestors. They are there in her hands, her face, and the shadows, happy and sad, that cross her face. When she opens the fridge on hot days and stands there cooling herself, let her know that they are the mist in her breath. They are her. I want her to know them as I have known them. Let her know that when they walked this earth they were wonderfully strong people who braved far more than me and survived.

I have been weak and pathetic because I forgot that love comes and goes like the dye that colours a garment. I mistook love for the garment. Family is the garment. Let her wear her family with pride.

Please, Luke. Give her the tapes.

The letter was signed Dimple. So my mother was Dimple Lakshmnan. She was not Selina Das as the birth certificate Daddy showed me claimed. And she didn't die giving birth to me. She knew me. *And I knew her.* Outside, big drops of rain hurled themselves at the smoked glass and slid down like fat, transparent worms in an awful hurry. 'What a liar you were, Daddy!'

Even from quite far away I knew it was the house. I stopped the car and climbed out. The name of the house, Lara, was almost obscured by the weeds that grew up the gates and over the red-brick wall that surrounded the house. Three young boys stopped their bicycles beside me.

'You're not going to go inside the house, are you?' one of them asked curiously.

'It's haunted, you know,' another added quickly.

'A woman died in there,' they all cried, their eyes formidable. 'It was horrible. There was blood every-where. Anybody who goes in there never returns,' they warned, completely caught up in the relentless need to shock the stranger out of her calm façade.

'This house belongs to me,' I said to them, looking through the iron gates at a winding driveway flanked by mature conifer trees.

The boys stared at me with open-mouthed surprise while I slotted my key into the gate. At the metallic sound of the key fitting into place they fled on their bicycles with hasty, backward glances.

The gates unlocked with a clang and a dark echo. *I have been here before.* As I drove up the winding road I was filled with a sense of loss. Loss of what? The conifers on either side of me were dark-green walls of silence. I parked the car by the house. Creepers covered most of the frontage and the red overlapping roof tiles. The wretched grounds, it seemed, had lost their battle with the waist-high wild grasses many, many years ago. Rambling rose bushes were abundant and savage with thorns. All in all it was a dismal, ghostly sight.

Yet it called to me, every dark window a pleading, beckoning eye. Under a tree, partially visible through the wild greenery, the statue of a small boy held something up in both his hands like an offering, but glossy weeds had thickly obscured his gift. I walked past two fierce lion statues that stood like silent guards at the entrance to a big mahogany door. In my hand it swung open smoothly. Inviting me in.

I stopped in the middle of the very large living room and smiled. The first real smile since my father died. The place was under a good inch of dust and cobwebs and quite ruined, but I was home. Without looking up I knew that the lofty ceilings were painted with gorgeously robed figures from the past. I looked up and sure enough even the thick froth of cobwebs could not disgrace the grand paintings. A small sparrow flew into the house through a broken window-pane, its flapping wings loud in the stillness. Landing on the banister it regarded me curiously. The banister that had once shone with polish. I knew that as clearly as I knew what colour the floor under my feet was. I swept my right shoe in a small arc on the floor, pushing aside layers of dried leaves, twigs, bird droppings and the accumulated dirt of many years and my own reflection looked back from a smooth, black surface. Ah, finally, the black marble floor of my nightmares.

Disturbed by the unaccustomed noise, lizards scuttled on the ceiling over the unflinching, plump hands of painted maidens and cherubs frolicking on clouds. My footsteps echoed eerily yet there was a feeling of welcome, as if the frozen people had been waiting for me.

As I looked around, it seemed to me as if the inhabitants of the house had left with the intention of returning soon. There was a chunky vase of dried twigs, a fruit bowl of dust-covered fruit seeds, and alcohol in the crystal decanters on top of a baby grand piano. I moved to the grimy pictures on the piano and blew at them. There I was with the beautiful woman from my dreams. The face that escaped the memory-eating snake's belly.

Who was she? Dimple Lakshmnan? If she was my dead mother, then the woman in the picture that Father showed me must be another lie.

On a rather fabulous, low, marble and stone coffee table was a stack of magazines. The top one was dated August 1984. The year, in fact the month I fell into that black hole. Well, well.

On the wall at the far end was an ornately framed picture covered in grey dust. Standing on a chair I cleaned the middle of the picture with my handkerchief. A woman's chest emerged. Slightly higher I found a face. A beautiful woman looked at me sadly and I knew for certain she was my mother, Dimple Lakshmnan. I cleaned the whole picture, climbed down and took a step back. Suddenly I felt as if I was not alone any more. As if all the dead people on my mother's side were huddled close to me. For the first time since I had climbed out of the black hole and known absolutely no one, I didn't feel alone.

Warm and strangely content, I walked away from the portrait and went up the marble stairs. I had a fleeting image of a small girl falling. I stopped, my hand rising automatically to my head. That small silvery scar. I had fallen down these stairs; I knew it without a doubt. I had tumbled down head first, screaming, 'Mummy, Mummy.' It was not as Daddy said. It didn't happen on a zebra crossing at all.

For some horrible reason my father had uprooted me from this house where I lived with my mother. He left behind absolutely everything that was familiar to me and transplanted me into totally new surroundings. And because he had taken nothing out of the house it looked as if someone had gone out for a pint of milk and never returned. I understood now why my father had taken nothing. He didn't want anything from my old life to trigger off my memories. He had always feared my memories.

Upstairs, I opened the first door on the left. Immediately I saw a vision of a small girl lying on the bed drawing. This had been my room, not the pink room my father had shown me to when I left the hospital. I recognised the blue curtains with the yellow sunflowers. The curtains were now grey with age but I saw them billowing in my mind. Blue with bright yellow sunflowers. Mother chose them.

I opened a cupboard curiously and drew back slightly with the unexpectedly strong waft of camphor. Inside was a wardrobe really too magnificent for a child of seven to have. What dresses! And in perfect condition too. My attention was drawn to a pair of red sandals with pretty pink bows on the top. I closed my eyes and tried to force the memories, but – nothing. 'Soon,' I promised myself. 'Soon I will remember everything.' I ran my fingers through the clothes, surprised at how well my old clothes had been preserved through time. From the back of the bed came scurrying noises. Rats. The wardrobe doors must be very secure.

All of a sudden I saw myself in the garden outside standing by a small pond filled with expensive gold and red carp. As suddenly as the picture had come it was gone. I hurried to the window. A dirty pond sat glumly in the middle of the overgrown backyard, very like the doubtful eye of the garden. I fancied it looked at me with some reproach as if it was my fault that its waters were green with neglect. Leaving my old room I walked along the curving gallery that overlooked the living room below. I opened another door and gasped.

The room had been decorated in the same manner as my father's bedroom in his house; everything identical. Curiouser and curiouser. Daddy had lived in this house with Mummy and me! Something had happened here that had made him take me and flee, leaving everything behind. Seeing the room made my flesh crawl. I crossed the spartan room and opened a connecting door.

The curtains in that room were drawn shut. It was pleasantly dim and the air so still I could hear myself breathe. Very gradually, almost imperceptibly, an impression swept over me that I was not alone. It was like falling asleep on a beach and being awakened by the soft warm lapping of waves against your feet. I felt safe and protected as if someone loved and very dear sat beside me. So strong was the feeling that I went around the huge bed and looked behind the curtains. Of course there was no one there. I pulled the curtains apart and evening sunshine filtered in curiously, turning the air into dust-filled magic spaces but banishing that strange presence from the room. I felt an unexplainable sense of loss. I walked past the large, four-poster bed, carefully made and hidden under the inevitable layer of thick dust, and opened the carved doors on a row of handsome, built-in cupboards.

Rack upon rack of exquisite clothes, beautifully preserved, met my eyes. The opulent 1970s in all their beaded, embroidered glory and rich colours hung before me. I thought I recognised a blue and green dress with an attached rhinestone choker. I thought I remembered myself saying, 'Mummy, that's pretty.' I closed my eyes and watched a slender figure twirl round and round so her pretty new dress cut on the bias could fly around her legs like a dazzling butterfly. It was her. Dimple Lakshmnan, my mother.

Carefully, I took the dress off the hanger and, standing in front of a mirror at the other end of the room, held it up against my body. My mother had been almost the same size as me. I took off my blouse and jeans and slipped the dress over my head. It smelt of mothballs and felt cool on my skin. I smoothed the satin carefully over my hips. The dress was beautiful.

As if in a daze I dusted off the padded cushion stool in front of the dressing table and sat on it. I cleaned the mirror with some tissue paper and examined the collection of make-up on the long dressing-table surface. I pulled off the top of a blue lipstick case. Frosty pink. It smelled strongly of old petroleum jelly but appeared remarkably dewy. Christian Dior and still raring to go. I twisted it up and applied it to my lips. Then I brushed on some shimmering kingfisher-blue eye shadow that was all the rage in the 1970s. I stood in front of the mirror and in the sunlight a ridiculous woman with bright blue eye shadow and painted lips looked at me. I felt sad. So unaccountably sad that I closed the curtains and sank uncaring on the dusty bed. It was then that I realised that with the curtains drawn the room had taken on an altogether different feel. I was again conscious of that feeling of companionship. And when I looked at myself in the mirror across the room I saw the woman in the painting downstairs. In the gloom I was beautiful, as beautiful as my mother had been. I didn't look like my father after all. I stared, enchanted by my own image, until I saw not my surprised reflection any more but a scene from the past.

Mother was downstairs wearing this very dress. She was going to a party. I saw the Romanesque living room clearly, with its impressively grand flower arrangements and big crystal bowls full of fruit, the floor, the crystal chandelier, the lamps, the banisters, the cream Victorian daybed, the mahogany dining table, the nest of large sofas – all polished and new, without the dust, the dirt or the animal droppings. And it was resplendent. While my mother waited for Daddy to return home from work she was arranging flowers on the dining table and crying silently.

Snip, snip, snip, she went with the scissors. She was making an arrangement for the dining table. Blood-red roses were teamed with Kangaroo's Paws.

'Why are you crying, Mummy?'

The memory faded and I was left staring at my subtly altered self in the mirror. I went downstairs in my mother's clothes. I not only looked different but felt different. The air was mild and peaceful and I felt at home, but soon it would be dark and there was neither electricity nor gas in the house. I spotted the pair of ebonised blackamoor statues standing on either side of the staircase, covered in dust and cobwebs, holding a candelabrum each, and began hunting around the kitchen for some candles.

The fridge had been cleaned out but the cupboards were full of old tinned food. Packets of instant noodles, tins of powdered milk, cans of sardines, empty boxes of cereal overturned by the rats, and jars and jars of home-made pickled mangoes. In another cupboard there was a bottle of wild honey that had separated into a solid dull-gold base and a thick dark-brown liquid. I found the candles. Then I noticed a bunch of keys. One of them fitted the back door. I gave the door a hard shove and it burst into the darkening evening. The sun had set behind the tall red-brick walls encircling the garden. In the half-dark of dusk I stepped out and walked along a short stone path almost completely overgrown on either side with wild plants. The garden was quiet. Wonderfully so. The sounds of the traffic seemed far away and the oncoming night was just beginning to dress the trees and grounds in subdued shades of purple. Because of the decay and the complete seclusion inside the high brick walls I experienced the delicious pleasure of having left the world behind, and discovered a fabulous secret.

What is paradise but a walled garden?

I passed a small vegetable plot long colonised by hardy grasses and large-leafed weeds. Like the skeletons of Red Indian wigwams, sticks weathered to the pale colour of birch bark had been stuck into the ground in a circle and tied together at the top. Once rambling vegetable plants had been trained on them. Now the top of each wigwam skeleton was studded with mauve and grey snails, curled up together in groups content to remain motionless high up over the riot of wild vegetation. Closer to the brick wall a mango tree's flowers had hardened into small green fruit. The hard knobs of pale green hung in low clusters. A tattered hammock hung from a mango tree. I had a memory of the hammock, brand-new and swinging slowly in the hazy shade of the tree. Somebody was in it. In the soft breeze I heard a small laughing voice cry, 'Race you.'

I turned around but there was no one. The stone path died suddenly and I found myself standing on springy moss. To the left there was a small brackish pond with a statue of a moss-laden Neptune rising out of it. By it a small shrub had flowered, and a lone pinkish-white flower, nearly as big as a small cabbage, hung heavy from a twig. I bent close to smell the flower and had a fleeting vision of bending over the pond and seeing another face in the clear waters. A smiling, dark, triangular face. The vision was gone as quickly as it had come. The pond was quite dead now. A brown, spotted toad stared suspiciously at me. I walked further down the garden.

At the end of it, almost completely hidden by creepers, was a small wooden shed. Orange roof tiles that had not fallen off lay hidden under large, glossy, heart-shaped ivy leaves. The leaves covered almost the entire doorway and threatened to bring down the whole roof with the sheer weight of their abundant growth. I pushed some foliage aside, squatted outside the door of the shed and peered within. In the darkening light I could make out a table and a chair and what looked like a small bed or a wooden bench. It looked far too dangerous to go in. Inside might lurk snakes. In the dark I thought I saw the glint of gold on a finger and fancied I saw, passing in the shadows, that same triangular face split into a big smile that I had seen earlier in the pond.

The face was old and the eyes were kind. There was something memorable about the face, a dark-green tattoo of small dots and diamond shapes that started on the forehead from the middle of each eyebrow and worked its way like a star constellation down the temples and onto the high cheekbones. A child giggled uncontrollably. The old lady with the tattoo was tickling her stomach. I strained to look further into the shadows but nothing else moved. The old lady with the gold ring and the giggling child must have been made out of tea biscuits for they vaporised into the darkness of the dusty shed like biscuit crumbs sinking into a mug of tea. The darkness was complete. I stood up and walked back slowly, retracing my steps past the pond. The tattoo. Who was she? All of a sudden I knew. Dear, darling Amu.

Back in the kitchen I locked the door and stood at the doorway until my eyes got used to the deeper darkness inside the house, and then I lit a candle and carrying it in one hand and the box of unlit candles in the other, I went back into the hall. One by one I stuck the candles into the candelabra. I dusted away the thick shroud of dust and cobwebs and lit all the candles.

The blackamoor boys looked grand lit up, their handsome ebony faces glowing like smooth black stones under a full moon. They put little dancing yellow lights on the walls and threw mysterious shadows in the corners. I did not remember their slightly surprised expressions but knew without a doubt that their names were Salib and Rehman. Once I had been no taller than them. The candlelight woke the ceiling. The plump nymphs, coy-faced women and perfectly proportioned, curly haired males were alive. The house and everything in it had been waiting for me. Perhaps the house *was* haunted but I felt quite unafraid and surely at home. I was home and far more comfortable in the crumbling, deserted house than in my cool, luxurious flat in Damansara, but as the corners of the room darkened into blackness I realised that though I didn't want to leave I must, for the delicate tapping of small claws on the marble floor grew nearer and bolder. I had no desire to make acquaintance with the rats that apparently lived in my house, so I put mother's dress away, blew out all the candles, and locking the door securely behind me, left with a heavy heart. As if I had left something important behind.

When I switched off the tape recorder it was two in the morning. Outside, a storm howled inconsolably. It rattled the balcony door like an angry spirit desperate to get in. I looked around at the luxurious things in my apartment and felt no regret. Their loss would not be felt. I had not put my heart into them. The most expensive fulfilled the highest expectation. Last week everything was different. In a week or so I would be like everybody else. I might have to go out and become a secretary somewhere. Buy my clothes from department stores, cook my own food, clean up after myself. I shrugged carelessly.

What mattered was uncovering the deep mystery surrounding my mother, solving the puzzle of the black marble floor that loomed, sinister, in my dreams, finding out why a dripping tap chilled me to the bone or why the combination of red and black was so gratingly offensive. Deep emotions were waking in me. I thought I remembered Great-Grandmother Lakshmi but it was hard to equate the vibrantly young Lakshmi in the tapes with the old grey woman I vaguely remember. Could she really be the same unhappy old woman in a rattan chair who always cheated at Chinese chequers?

I had been so involved in listening to the tape of Ayah's story that I missed dinner. In the kitchen my maid had left a selection of dishes in covered containers and I suddenly realised I was ravenous. I sat and ate furiously, out of character.

I stopped suddenly. Why was I behaving like that? Why the greed, the unseemly haste? I had a picture of a young boy vomiting into his own food. 'I can taste the food she's eating!' Laskhmnan cries wildly to the old lady with iron-grey hair and betrayed eyes. But no, then Lakshmi must have had wonderful thick, black hair and bold, angry eyes. I pushed my plate away.

Restlessly I walked into the living room and headed for the balcony. Instantly strong winds whipped my hair and pulled at my clothes. How I longed to be in Mother's house. Mine now. The wind blew rain into my face and I breathed its wild, wet smell. Thunder crashed very close by. The voices in my head clamoured for space, attention. Finally when I was very, very cold I went in.

I came out of the shower warm and exhausted and dried my hair in front of the mirror. It was already almost four o'clock in the morning. Tomorrow I would go back to Lara. I wanted to make arrangements to move in straightaway. I switched off the hair dryer and in the mirror my eyes surprised me. I stared at the green specks in my pupils. Nefertiti was dead but she had left her eyes behind, in me. I saw that aloof glaze in my eyes was gone and in its place glittered a feral excitement that made me look quite insane. I smiled at myself in the mirror and even my smile was different.

'Sleep now so you can leave first thing in the morning for your new home,' I told the glittering girl in the mirror. Then I lay down under the covers and listened to the frantic storm outside. I tossed and turned until finally I got out of bed, switched on the light and pushed the button on the tape recorder that read PLAY.

Ratha

I sent a very simply written letter to Nisha at her father's address explaining that I was a relative from her mother's side of the family. I noted that it had been impossible to be in touch with her before her father's passing because he had forbidden us all contact with him or his daughter. Since the appearance of his funeral notice in the newspaper I have wanted to meet her. If she was so inclined could she please telephone.

When she arrived my daughter showed her through to my favourite place in the house. My large kitchen. She was beautiful. She greeted me carefully, her eyes taking in my face, twisted on one side, and my scanty silver hair. I know I am a human gargoyle.

'Sit down, Nisha,' I invited, my smile crooked. 'Would you like some tea?' I offered.

'Thank you, yes,' the girl accepted. Her voice was elegant and cultured. If nothing else, Luke had given her poise. I decided I liked her.

I placed a small basket of eggs in front of her and said, 'Eat.'

For a moment she looked at me expressionlessly but I heard her thinking: Oh no, the old dear has more fat than protein in her brain.

My eyes full of mirth I took an egg, cracked it against the plate and broke it in my fingers. Runny white and yellow yolk did not flow out. The clever thing was made with cake, almonds and custard. The shell, coloured sugar.

She began to laugh too. Of course, Ratha, the mistress of sugar. Today she has done something simple. She has made some eggs.

'This is a gift,' she said picking up the cake in her hand. Small white teeth bit into the cake and her mouth declared it was gorgeous. 'A brilliant, marvellous gift,' Nisha said.

I seated myself opposite her. 'I am Ratha, your great-aunt and I want you to know that your mother, Dimple, changed my life. I am old now and soon I shall be no more but I should like you to know what she did for me so many years ago. She was the most caring, wonderful person I have ever met in my life. One afternoon, twenty-nine years ago, I was sitting alone icing a cake when I heard someone calling at the door. Outside stood your mother. She must have been – what? – fifteen years old then. Such a pretty little thing she was too.

' "I need to speak to you urgently," she said.

' "Come in," I invited, surprised. I should have slammed the door in her face because really I wanted nothing more to do with my ex-husband's family. Liars, cheats and thieves the lot of them. Each one a cruel hunter. But there was always something innocent, a little hurt, about that child. Her mother had always treated her very badly while I stayed with them. I wanted to help her but I didn't know she was there to help me.

'I offered her juice but she refused. "Why don't you love Grandma?" she asked, plunging straight in.

' "Well, it's a long story," I began, with no intention of telling such a slip of a girl anything, but suddenly I was pouring everything out. I started from the very beginning when her mother Rani had come to our home in Seremban full of smiles, looking for a bride. You see, Rani lied to us. She showed me a photograph of her husband Lakshmnan and told me my intended husband looked just the same.

' "They are brothers," the avaricious woman said, thinking of her commission. "So similar, people are always mistaking one for the other."

'I looked at the photograph and how I wanted him, your grandfather. Yes, that's right – the evil woman had guessed that her husband was the man of my dreams. She knew. She always knew. She knew which screws to turn.

' "Give me your dowry to help Lakshmnan," she said.

'How could I refuse? She knew. She always knew. But what she didn't count on was that one day her Lakshmnan might actually turn his head and look at me. She thought it amusing that a poor little rat living in her house harboured a secret passion for her husband. She thought she would torment me with her good fortune. She would rest her hand casually on his big strong chest and order him to bring her a pair of slippers from the bedroom because her arthritis didn't allow for movement. She thought she would tease me for fun. But she didn't count on a simple look that showed her just how tenuous her hold on him was.

'Anyway, I agreed to the marriage in principle and waited for the day of the first meeting. A week later I met my bridegroom in the flesh. Lakshmnan and my bridegroom-to-be were like day and night. I stared at that repulsive man in my aunt's living room with shock. I should have stopped the marriage arrangements right there and then but the people, the relatives, the flowers, the saris, the jewellery, the ceremonies – I got lost in them and my throat locked. I walked in a daze. I could not have your grandfather anyway so I lost myself in work. Every day from the moment I rose until the moment I lay down exhausted, I worked. I worked all day long so I didn't have to think about my terrible silence. The day of my marriage got closer and closer and I fell deeper and deeper into my pit of despair.

'Alone in bed I cried. The man I wanted would soon be my brother-in-law. No one could know my shameful secret. How could I tell anyone? Every night I took my poor love that dared not breathe during the day and stroked it to sleep in the dark. My silence grew and grew until it was too late to speak.

'It was the wedding day. And it was a disaster. There was nothing to do with my hands and so the tears flowed. A huge dam broke inside me and the tears refused to stop. Such a river that my nose ring slipped and fell. All those tears and nobody asked me what was wrong. Not one person opened their mouth to ask. "What's the matter, child?" If they had, I could have said it. I would have said it. Stopped the marriage. It was because I didn't have a mother. It was because no one cared about me. It is a question only a mother would ask.

'And then I went to live at your great-grandmother Lakshmi's house. She tried to be kind but I felt that she too had helped to deceive me. Together they had all plotted to marry me to her idiot son. I felt her contempt for him. It was never spoken aloud, in words, but in her voice, her look and her manner, and so subtly, that not even he noticed, but I saw it. I wouldn't let myself think of their terrible deception and so I cooked and cleaned all day long. I never stopped. It was a relief to clean under the cooker, between the rafters, and brush my skin until it was raw and red. The way I brushed the skin on my stomach where no one ever saw. Sometimes it even blistered and bled but there was a perverse pleasure to be gained by the pain I inflicted on myself. In the bathroom I examined the torn, angry skin with ugly satisfaction.

'Then came the dinner invitation from Rani. We went and during dinner she said, "Stay. Go on, stay." She insisted. "I could do with the company."

'I looked at my husband and he looked at me with doe eyes so I nodded shyly. It was the wrong decision to make but at that moment my foolish heart leaped and jumped at the thought that I would see Lakshmnan every day. "I only want to look at him," my errant heart whispered, to my shame. "Don't you see, that would be food enough," it pumped and sighed. It was my joy to cook and clean for him. When he sat at the table and smiled in admiration at my creations my heart blossomed. I waited quietly for each mealtime to see him turn more and more eagerly towards the dining table. Alas, he complimented me too often.

'I know she is your grandmother, but Rani has a fistful of dust for a heart. I saw it shrivel up and go hard with hate and venom. She watched me closely but I had nothing to be ashamed of or to hide. I was quiet, respectable and hard-working. Then one day, your grandfather brought home a piece of meat. He brought it into the kitchen and left it on the table wrapped in an old newspaper. It was as if he had given me a bouquet of scented flowers. I wanted to laugh out loud with happiness. He had never done anything like that before. I opened the package and it was the meat of a wild fruitbat.

'I began immediately. First I bathed the piece of meat in lemongrass juice then I beat it until it became a length of silk. Afterwards I wrapped it in a papaya leaf so it would become tender enough to melt on his tongue and the desire for more would haunt him after he had left my table. Hours I laboured, slicing, grinding, pounding, chopping and fanning the furnace lightly with a palm leaf so my pot would barely simmer on glowing coals. The secret was of course in the finely diced sour mango. Eventually my velvet-textured creation was ready.

'I set it on the table and called everyone to eat. When he put a violet piece of flesh into his mouth I saw him unconsciously inhale. Our eyes met and desire crept into his face. But even as he looked at me I saw the sudden realisation drop into his eyes that, just as the waves must leave the shore, his pursuit was of that which was already lost. No, it could never be. Confused, he dropped his gaze down to his food and, as if only then remembering your grandmother, abruptly looked up towards her. Rani was staring at him, her eyes dark slits in her throbbing face. Slowly, deliberately, she tasted the meat that had made her husband gasp with pleasure.

' "Too salty," she proclaimed tightly, pushing away the plate. She stood up suddenly. The chair fell back with a loud thud and she stalked off to her bedroom. In the dining room only Jeyan ate. The only sounds were his chewing. Blind to all the thick emotions pressing down on us he ate. It was truly the calm before the storm for suddenly she rushed back into the dining area, shrieking at the top of her voice. "I took you into my house and fed you and this is the gratitude I get. Get out of my house, whore! Is one brother not enough for you?" What could I say? It was true I wanted her husband but she had known that before she invited me to stay or took my money.

'She ranted and raved until Jeyan found us alternative accommodation, the little room over the Chinese dry-cleaning shop. It was nine o'clock at night when we climbed those creaking stairs lit only by a dim, naked light bulb hanging from the ceiling. I screamed when a rat as big as a cat ran in front of my foot. The room was tiny. It had one window and walls reduced to bare wood and planks. In some places tiny strips of unpeeled paint spoke of a room once light blue. In one corner was a wooden bed with a bare, stained mattress and in the other was a table with three stools. Dirt grew like light grey mould everywhere. My love affair was over. It disappeared behind a veil as if ashamed. And in that tiny dark room where we had to share a bathroom with the dirtiest people you could possibly imagine, I began to hate my husband. It crept on me so gradually that at first I didn't notice and then suddenly I hated him. I hated lying beside him listening to him breathing at night. I hated the children I would bear him. My hate was a solid thing inside my body. I felt it night and day. Sometimes I almost couldn't trust myself with a knife in my hand in his presence.

'And in this way I forgot about my untasted love for his brother. I told myself that there was no such thing as a field where flowers opened every day. I convinced myself that the world was ugly – a field of heartless human hearts pulsing greedily to live. The years passed and children fell out of my body. I looked at them and saw my husband in their eyes. And I despised that little bit of them too. That certain way they spoke or the way they ate. I tried to dig everything of him out of them and I punished them mercilessly. I made them ashamed of the bits in them that belonged to him. How cruel my frustration and hatred made me!

'Outside our cramped room on the telegraph wires and trees lived hundreds of crows. The children stood at the window and stared at the rows of bodies, black from beak to claw, and thousands of beady eyes stared back. Their organisation into so much unending black seemed ominous. Sometimes I had nightmares about them crashing through the dark window-panes, shards of glass flying everywhere and landing on the children. They would peck at the children's faces and gouge out bits of flesh from the screaming figures while my husband and I would sit and watch calmly. I was going mad in that room.

'Every night while my husband and children slept I heard Maya's voice murmur in my ear. Maya was the great-granddaughter of a chef during the golden age of the Mughal Empire and I had grown up in her lap. Every day of my childhood I had spent begging for and eating stories of the excesses indulged in the shady courtyards and the maze of private rooms where none but family, eunuchs and servants may enter. She whispered into my greedy ears unwritten stories handed down through the generations only by word of mouth. She knew about unpublished court intrigues, volatile passions, horrible jealousies, excesses beyond compare, tales of royal incest and instances of terrible, terrible cruelty on a scale never known before. "There are some things no one but the eunuchs and the servants see," the childless old woman once said to me. I never realised it but in her lap I had learned the art of exquisite cruelty. It lay inside me silently.

'It was my husband's birthday. I awoke early. The sky was golden and a mist still hung in the air. The children were asleep and my husband's hand was still on my stomach. A thought flashed into my head: *Are you awake now?* My poor heart. For years I had not thought about Lakshmnan; under my husband's heavy hand and the tangled bedsheets the thought instantly sickened me.

'Troubled, I got out of bed and leaving my tiny room, stepped neatly over the rats that were as big as cats and stood in the cool morning air. I remembered another age. Picking up Lakshmnan's shirts from the laundry basket and rubbing them against my cheek, the musk scent of him. I wanted to touch his face. Suddenly I missed him so much that tears burned in my eyes and a strange pain lodged itself in my heart. I decided to bake a cake. I went to the provision shop down the road and carelessly spent the money I was saving for a proper house for us on icing sugar, almonds, food colouring, eggs, chocolate butter and fine flour. At home I deposited everything on the table and got to work. It wasn't easy to get my cake into the shape I wanted, very much like a squarish egg. In my head I knew exactly what I was doing. It was early in the morning and the children were drawing quietly in one corner of the room.

'I hummed as I worked. The children stared at me in surprise. They hadn't heard me hum ever since they were born. When the cake was baked I trimmed off the excess bits and placed it on a clean plate. When my sugar paste was the exact dark brown I kneaded it until it was warm and soft. Carefully I rolled all the creases out of it and picking it up like a soft cloth I hung it over the squarish-egg shape I had baked. I cut circles the size of five-cent pieces out of onion petal and dyed them black. Onion flesh is best because it is curved and shines with the exact glimmer of a human eye. Then I moulded more coloured sugar paste onto the covered egg shape exactly the way the old lady had taught me until even I was surprised by the likeness I had attained. How very like him!

'I had learned my art well. I trickled food colouring into runny honey and I poured it around my shape. I slotted the dyed onion shapes into the blank circles in the oval of his eyes and I made his teeth out of the white sugar, glazing it carefully to get the glossy look of teeth. I drizzled fine strands of caramel to look like eyebrows then I cut the nostrils slightly wider and stood back to admire my handiwork. It had taken me five hours but the finished product was much more startling than I imagined.

'Pleased, I put it in the middle of the table and sat down to wait for my husband. He walked through the door and, just as I had anticipated, his unsuspecting eyes leaped to my masterpiece framed by the children and me sitting around it. Poor thing. The sight of his head resting comfortably in a sauce of blood on a large platter shocked him visibly. What a moment it was! Even the children recognised the head.

' "Papa," they cried in their babyish voices.

' "Yes, Papa," I agreed, exquisitely satisfied that they had recognised my work. Then I gave the knife to him. "Happy Birthday," I said and the children chorused it.

'For a time he was so startled he could only stare with

horror at the face on the platter. Its eyes wide and bulging. Its mouth open with terror. It was a Mughal revenge in the best tradition. It was the first time that poor Jeyan realised that I hated him. Until then I had kept it all inside, and the knowledge that he finally knew released me. The freedom was like the smell of fresh coffee in the morning. It woke me up. My brain yawned and stretched.

'Now I could hate openly. Because he refused to take the knife from my hand I stabbed the cake right through the nose. He didn't touch the cake but the children and I thoroughly enjoyed it, saving it for days. The children dipped their fingers into the gooey red blood under the head and licked it greedily. Their small fingers pushed into the soft lips and their small milk teeth eagerly nibbled the glazed sugar teeth. The pink tongue they pulled out and fought over. All this he watched with a hurt and unexpectedly stunned expression.

'And then one day I plucked up the courage to ask him to leave us.

'The day he left I spent on my hands and knees bleaching his smell out of my life. It was very hard at the beginning but we managed. Every year I worked harder and harder at my cake-making and decorating school. The children were growing up healthy and well but they were both terrified of me. We moved to a bigger house but I was so unhappy inside.

'My husband had become an old drunk.

'Sometimes I saw him with red-rimmed eyes where the poor labourers gathered to drink cheap liquor made from rice, coconut palm or even weeds. Once he stumbled past me on the street muttering to himself. He had not recognised me. I looked at the pathetic creature swaying back to his dirty little room and I felt not one bit of remorse. You see, I had become hard and cold. Nothing touched me. Not even my own unhappiness.

'Then one day your mother, Dimple, came to see me. She had taken a bus, got off at the wrong stop and walked all the way to my little terrace house in the burning afternoon sun. I looked at her, red-faced and clutching a plastic bag with her little tape recorder inside it. "Tell me your side of the story," she said.

'Nobody had ever asked for my side of the story. Nobody had ever asked me why I didn't love my saintly mother-in-law. So I told her. I said, I hated her grandmother because of all people she was the only person who really knew what it was like to be married to a man who disgusted you with his stupidity, his blindness, his ambling gait and his stubborn ignorance. She was the only one who should have understood, and yet she married me to him. It was because she didn't care about me at all. It was all a delicate, beautifully acted pretence. In the end she only loved her own flesh and blood.

'As soon as I poured all my smothered, cramped thoughts into Dimple's whirling machine they suddenly became unimportant. Layer upon layer of hate on what? "So what," my heart cried, as it soared free out of my body. What is this terrible hate that I have carried around with me for years? Who have I hurt with my hate but my poor blameless children and myself? I must have been mad to waste all those years carrying around such a pointless grudge. I let the hate slide away. The hate for my husband, his mother, Lakshmnan's wife and my dreadful cynical contempt for everybody.

'Suddenly I saw my untasted love again in your mother's little face. Lakshmnan became a person once

again. Time slipped back. The past called and I set back
the clock. I still loved him. I suppose I always will. Failed
desire is never the end of desire but the guaranteed
perpetuator of it. I sat down with her to have a cup of
tea and it was as if I was talking to Lakshmnan. It was
the strangest thing ever. After I said goodbye to her I
closed the door, leaned back against it and laughed until
I got a stitch in my stomach. Yes, I have to thank her. I
realised my children were a part of me. When they came
home that day I held their stiff, surprised bodies close to
my body and cried. Confused and frightened, they tried
to comfort me and I rediscovered them. That is what
your mother did for me. She helped me find my life again.
Allowed me to look again at the image of Lakshmnan. It
stopped raining in my world.

'That night I opened an old box deep inside the
cupboard of my soul and I took out the picture of that
colourful moment when he first put the violet piece of
meat into his mouth. That moment when he looked at
me to see if his look would be returned. That moment of
surprise and creeping desire. That moment when
sunshine flooded the room with silvery moonlight. Now
that picture lies like a treasure in my old heart and there
it will remain until the day I die. When I heard that he
had died the picture, far from fading, became brighter
still. Perhaps in another life we will meet again and be
the husband and wife that we were denied in this lifetime.

'Now, Nisha my dear, the reason I have told you all
this is because your mother wrote to me a few days later
to tell me that the tape she had used to record my story
had been chewed up by her tape recorder. She said she
would be coming back for the story again but she never

did. She never had much say in what she could and couldn't do in her life. Since I knew she was saving the stories for you I thought that this was something I could do for her. I could tell you myself what was in the ripped tape.'

Nisha

I stood in the middle of the hall and looked around me with a certain amount of satisfaction. The house was completely silent. Not even the old grandfather clock ticked or bonged. One day I would repair him but now I simply wanted to feel the house.

A team of robust women in blue had banished the thick cobwebs off the ceilings, polished the black marble floor to a high shine, put the gleam back in the curving banisters. The oil painting of Mother had returned from the restorers, a mysterious, wonderful thing of beauty. There was water in the taps and yellow light waiting in the light switches. Outside, the men had replaced the tattered hammock, dredged the pond and released flame-coloured fish into it. The weeds, painstakingly dug up, they burned at the bottom of the garden. The little summer house in the garden they strengthened and repainted in its original colour, pure white.

In the kitchen, most of the old-fashioned appliances were thrown out to make way for my own more modern items. A fridge that worked, a microwave and a perfectly good washing machine that did not meet Amu's approval. Oh, I forgot to say I found Amu. It wasn't easy but a blind man in a Ganesha temple led me to a priest in an ashram who in turn led me to an envious cousin who tried to throw me off the scent but I retraced my steps and finally I stood before her. She was begging in a night market, surviving on red ants she picked off dead lizards and the rotten food the market traders threw away. I saw her toothless, her twig hand outstretched, her feet thick with black dirt and stinking of rubbish, and knew instantly what it was to lie inside the loving circle of her brown limbs. 'Dimple,' she said in a moment of confusion.

'No, Nisha,' I said and she began to sob uncontrollably. So I brought her home.

I was officially broke but I didn't care. My needs were small. Nothing seemed more important than restoring the house to its former glory. Often I walked around in awe and disbelief, just touching things. Letting my fingers trail over smooth, shiny surfaces, still amazed that I had travelled countless times along the main road never suspecting that a left turn would lead to my own house. A remarkable house with the most wonderful treasures. I could hardly believe it was all mine. I turned yet again to look at Mother's portrait and to meet her sad smile.

I was determined to find my relatives. Meeting Ratha had given me a taste for it. I looked in the telephone book, there was only one Bella Lakshmnan in it. I dialled the number.

'Hello,' a strident voice answered.

'Hello. My name is Nisha Steadman,' I said. A moment of silence was followed by a loud wailing that went right through my skull. I held the phone away until another voice, abrupt and strong, said, 'Yes, can I help you?'

'Hello. My name is Nisha Steadman. I think you might be relatives of mine.'

'Nisha? Is that you?'

'Yes, and you are Bella with the beautiful curls, aren't you?' I asked half laughing.

'Oh God, I can't believe it. Why don't you come over? Come now.'

I followed her directions to Petaling Jaya. The traffic was bad and by the time I arrived it was almost dusk. I parked the car and saw a tall woman standing like a warrior at the door, peering into the darkening day. As I began to walk towards their gate she stepped out and started limping towards me, crying loudly. 'Nisha, Nisha, is it really you? After all these years . . . but I always knew you'd remember your old Grandma Rani. Look at you. You are the image of Dimple. She was such a good daughter to me. I loved her dearly.'

She enveloped me in a bear-hug and, grasping my right hand in both of hers, she rained dry, leathery kisses on my hand. 'Come in, come in,' she invited between sobs and kisses.

A lush woman with beautiful curls well past her waist stepped out of the house. She had the supple body of a dancer and she wore bells around her ankles. Her eyes in the dark were enormous and gleaming. Yes, this was the exotic flower of the family. As I walked closer I saw the fine lines around her eyes. She must be in her forties by now.

'Hello, Nisha. Gosh, you look so uncannily like Dimple.'

'You do the peacock credit,' I said.

'Ahhh, you've been listening to my tapes,' she laughed self-consciously, standing awkwardly to my left as my new-found grandmother monopolised the space around me and led me away into a sparsely decorated house. There was a knot of old, dark-blue sofas directly by the front door, and a few cheap paintings of Malaysian rural life on the walls. Against one wall a showcase filled with fussy little ornaments stood. Surprisingly, their dining table looked very expensive and sat completely out of place in their oddly decorated house.

Grandma Rani gathered together the two ends of her sari and mournfully wiped her dry eyes. 'I have prayed for this day for years,' she sighed. Then turning to her daughter said, 'Go and make some tea for the child and bring some of that imported cake.' Returning her attention to me she demanded, 'Where are you living now?'

'At Lara,' I said.

'Oh, do you live there all by yourself?'

'No, I live with Amu.'

'Is that old hag still not dead?'

'Mum, don't say such horrible things,' Bella admonished, shaking her head with disgust.

'So, how are you?' I asked my grandmother.

'Bad, bad, very bad.'

'Oh, so no change from before, then,' I wanted to say but I didn't. Instead I said, 'Oh, I'm so sorry to hear that.'

Bella left to make the tea and cut the imported cake. Grandmother Rani watched her daughter's retreating back with narrowed, suspicious eyes. When she was sure Bella was out of earshot she leaned forward and whispered fiercely, 'She is a prostitute, you know. None of our neighbours will even speak to me because of her. Why don't you take me to live with you at Lara? I can't live here any more. The whole world laughs at me.'

I looked at her shining, greedy eyes and felt sorry for Bella. I remembered what Bella had said in the tapes about her mother: *She is a karmic acquaintance. A venomous gift from fate. A mother.* I could well imagine how the vile woman in front of me must have bullied my poor mother. Dimple was too fragile a flower for such a python of a woman. Already the python was trying to squeeze me. Every time I exhaled she would squeeze tighter and tighter until she felt no more struggle, no more give within her strong set of muscles. Then her jaws would unlock to begin the task of swallowing me whole.

Aunty Bella leaned against the kitchen door. 'Kettle's boiling,' she informed us cheerfully.

'Listen, I remember us having ice cream in Damansara,' I said to her. 'You always had crushed nuts on yours.'

'Yes, that's right – I always have nuts on mine. Have you got all your memory back, then?'

'No, just bits and pieces, but I remember you. I remember the hair and the gorgeous, really daring clothes you wore. All the men used to stare at you.'

Grandma Rani snorted.

'You know what? Forget the tea. We'll have ice cream instead. Like old times,' I cried impulsively.

'Deal. Damansara, then,' she agreed, grinning.

'Damansara,' I said.

'Are you girls planning to leave me here all alone with my swollen feet and my crippled hands? What if I fall while you're out?' Grandma Rani cried peevishly.

'Please, Grandma Rani. I promise I won't keep Bella long. Just sit and wait for a little while, OK?'

Bella pushed back her heavy hair. She was still a very sexy woman. 'Let's go,' she said. In the car she said, 'I'm not a prostitute, you know.'

'I know that,' I said, putting the car into gear.

'It's just Mother. She's never been the same since she murdered my father with her tongue.'

*

The last tape was heard but the story remained unfinished. From inside a drawer I reached for Rosette's phone number.

'I have finished listening to the tapes,' I said into the receiver.

A rendezvous was agreed upon. I replaced the receiver and wandered up the curving stairs. Daddy's oh-so-mysterious mistress was apparently available for consultation at 6.00. Now what gifts would be acceptable for the meeting? I had promised the lady financial gain in return for information, but of course that was before I found out that I was virtually penniless. All was not lost though. In my bedroom I unlocked a safe in the wall and from inside the dark hole I extracted a small box encrusted with seashells. A seaside gift for a child.

I opened the box and inside was a tangled collection of jewellery – all the pieces that Daddy had left on the little table outside my room over the years. I tipped the precious contents on the bed. It seemed a rather careless thing to do with objects of such sparkling beauty. White stones flashed as they tumbled onto my bed. Diamonds were Daddy's favourite. He liked their undying brilliance best. Pearls were too understated and the other stones looked too much like coloured beads, but cold, hard diamonds held a special appeal for him. I untangled a small diamond choker set in white gold, the largest stone baguette cut. I remembered Daddy had insured it for twenty thousand ringgit. It dangled like a many-splendoured thing from my fingers. A change of address for the rope of stones looked imminent. I held it up so it swung at eye level.

'How would you like to go and live in Bangsar and

encircle the pretty neck of a whore?' I whispered softly.

I dropped the choker carelessly on the bed and stuffed all the other pieces back into their shell home. Downstairs I could hear Amu talking to herself as she kneaded dough for our simple dinner of chapattis and dahl.

Rosette's home was easy to find. It had the same sort of fir trees outside that surrounded Lara. Obviously my faithless father had a great liking for them. When I rang the bell, black electric gates opened soundlessly. I drove in and parked in the covered porch beside a rather aged Mercedes sports. A Chinese maid opened the door. My gaze wandered around the house, marvelling at my father's handiwork. The same marble floor, curved banisters and huge crystal chandeliers had been installed in the whore's home too. Father was certainly fond of the gilded palazzo look. Rosette smiled as she uncurled sinuously out of a large black leather settee. It looked new and modern. Certainly not to Daddy's taste. She came forward with her hand outstretched.

'How are you?' Her voice was friendly, her hand soft and dry.

'Fine.' This was the woman who had destroyed my mother. Look at her. How cool and poised she looked inviting into her lair the daughter of the very creature she had destroyed.

'Cognac, is it?' she asked already moving away.

'Thank you.'

'No ice, if I remember correctly.' She looked at me with a raised eyebrow. She no longer resembled my mother's distraught description of the waving young girl. Rosette had picked a whole suitcase full of sophistication along the way.

I nodded.

'So what would you like to know?'

'Everything. Start from the beginning,' I said and as I spoke I reached into a small velvet pouch and took out the flashing necklace. I laid it on a dark-green marble table. No setting could have given the choker more allure than the glossy darkness of the marble surface. Also, no doubt, Daddy's taste. I looked up and saw Rosette eyeing the gleaming stones, a look in her eyes that was difficult to decipher. Not greed exactly, not even happiness, perhaps a sort of dark longing. As if she was looking into her past at something very far away and no longer attainable. A glimpse into a life lost.

'As you probably know, my father was bankrupt when he died. There was nothing left but my jewellery and the house that my mother had left to me. I wondered if you would accept this little choker instead of the cheque I promised.'

Rosette came forward with the drinks in her hands. She wasn't drinking Tia Maria on ice after all. It looked like a glass of tea. She caught my eyes and laughed. 'When you are young, alcohol is allowed at all social occasions. At my age alcohol is allowed only on special occasions.'

'And my father's funeral was a special occasion?'

'Meeting you was.'

'What are you drinking, anyway?' I asked, thrown by the older woman's answer.

'A special Indonesian mixture of herbs and roots. It's horribly bitter but it has been known to keep its victims youthful.'

She was in her late forties and yet, relaxed in her own environment, she looked not a day older than thirty. Plastic surgery? But there wasn't that 'survived a wind tunnel' appearance. She watched me studying her and laughed. Fine lines appeared around her eyes and mouth. 'Youth makes a capricious friend. You can give him everything and he will still leave you. It is Age that is the real friend. He stays with you, giving more and more of himself until your dying day. Next year I will be fifty years old.

'All my secrets lie in a little village in Indonesia where a skull-faced old man with the most marvellous magic called *susuk* lives. He sharpens diamond-and-gold needles until they become the finest pins the eye could ever hope to see. Then he bottles the bloom of youth inside the fine diamond pins and inserts them under his customers' skin. Once under the skin they endow the wearer with an appearance of youth and indefinable beauty. A beauty that is not the sum total of all the features but in spite of it. The illusion I complete with these disgusting tonics.

'The problem with having these minute thread-like needles under your skin is that they have to be removed before you die or at least before you are buried, or your soul, earth-bound by *susuk*, will roam graveyards and roadsides for ever. Most of our top singers and actresses in Malaysia have it done as a matter of course. Look at their glow carefully and you will notice that behind it lies an ordinary face. Just before I die I will have all mine taken out and suddenly I will age before my very eyes. Macabre, isn't it?' she said, laughing at my surprised face. 'Anyway, you are not here to hear about the complications that my death will impose on my soul.' She swept her hands, white and beautifully manicured, out in front of her, indicating that I should sit.

I sat on a leather armchair. It was large and very

comfortable but I resisted the urge to curl up in it and relax. I wanted to watch the fascinating creature who cleverly and in turn managed to inspire pity and enchantment in me. I sat up straight in the chair. This was the woman who had held even in her young hands the power to lure away a man like Daddy and destroy Mother.

'Well, so where shall I begin?'

'Start from the beginning and end at the ending. Where did you meet my father? What do you know of my mother, and me for that matter?'

'I met your father while I was working at the Golden Girls Escort Agency. In fact, he was with your mother and she was introduced to me too but I don't think she remembered. I was sitting at a very large table with a lot of other beautiful women. I was dining with a friend of your father's that night but your father was immediately ensnared. His dark eyes devoured me. I saw him standing there and I felt his teethmarks in my heart. Your mother never realised; she never had a clue. She was young, innocent, without a vestige of corruption, and pregnant. When she looked into his face her eyes shone with happiness. She would never have believed the man who lived inside him. She was sweet and too pure for him to show her that ugly needful side that he hid from the rest of the world. In me he saw rice-white skin, but more than that he saw acceptance and recognition. I understood him. Ugly and deformed and yet wrenchingly appealing. There was no gentleness between us. We did unpleasant things together. Things that would have shocked your mother.

'I have never felt that I took anything away from Dimple. What I took she wouldn't have wanted anyway.

The desert wants the rain so it may be refreshed, sweetened and admired but the desert needs the sun to know it is a desert. Your mother was the rain in your father's life but I was the sun. She made him look beautiful and brought out the best in him, but he needed me. Anyway, he knew where to find me.

'He called for me the next day, and our mother hen, Madam Xu, arranged for us to have dinner at the Shangri-La. At that time it was the best hotel in the country. All night he watched me. He couldn't eat for the hunger inside him. I laughed and I teased the beast inside him until at last we went upstairs. Room 309 burns for ever in my memory. He opened the hotel room and I walked ahead of him, and when I turned around the man was gone and only the beast remained.

'He pulled out of his breast pocket a black silk handkerchief and unsmiling and unsurprised I pulled out a similar handkerchief from my handbag. Pain can be an exquisite thing but the man your mother married stood outside our hotel room. He remained faithful to your mother while the beast and I did our thing. Not a loving thing but something so vital that the mere thought of losing it was impossible to imagine. And it was a thing that burned bright for more than twenty-five years until he died. You and I could never have met while he was alive, although I have watched you grow. I sat in parks and watched you play from afar, for I belonged to a different life, parallel and never the twain shall meet.'

She stopped speaking and sipped at her horrible Indonesian concoction. I was spellbound. The things that poured out of this woman's mouth surely couldn't be true, but, her bitter sip done with, she opened her mouth and more words flowed out faster and faster. Like the river of water that rushes out of a crack in a dam, quickly rupturing and finally crumbling it altogether. Bigger and higher the waves became. Soon her words will engulf me, I thought wildly. Rosette looked directly at me. Her fine hair swung around her face and settled about her shoulders.

'Why do you look so surprised? Surely the tapes must have been the shocking aspect. This is merely the motivation that drove all the characters to do the things they did.'

I shook my head. 'When I listened to the tapes it was like reading a novel, a past that I couldn't relate to, but having you here in front of me makes it all suddenly so real – too real. You make my father a stranger. A monster.'

'No, he wasn't a monster. He loved your mother dearly and he loved you deeply.'

'Yes, so deeply that he couldn't even stand to touch me,' I cried bitterly.

'Poor Nisha. Don't you know your father would have filled his mouth with earth and lain down dead for you? Everything he did, he did with you in mind. I don't know much about your father's childhood but it wasn't the romantic picture he drew for your mother. Brutal, barbaric things happened to him that moulded his perversions, but he refused to acknowledge them until he met me. And then I became his deepest secret; after me he feared himself. Feared the poisonous night flowers that waited to bloom in his being.

'Luke told me that one night he was sitting downstairs having tea with your mother with the French windows open. A pleasantly cool breeze was blowing and the garden lamps were all on. The clock had just struck ten.

They had switched off all the lights in the house and lit just the candles in the ebony statues by the stairs. And he was feeling contented and peaceful in the mellow light. It was the way your mother made him feel. He looked up and you were coming down the stairs in a short white top that did not quite meet your white knickers, your long hair tousled and the back of your hand rubbing your sleepy right eye. In the light of the candles you were glowing. And his mouth dried. For one unguarded second he wanted you. And then he remembered himself and felt deep disgust. After that he hated himself and feared you. For that one unguarded second when that hideous night flower inside him, thick with horrible juices, had threatened to open. From then on he refused to touch your soft young skin. He wanted to be your father and not what the loathsome flower demanded. He wanted to be pure for you.'

I stared at Rosette with growing shock but she only looked back expressionlessly. I put down my untouched glass of cognac and stood up. I walked over to some windows nearby and stood looking out. 'Is there nothing good you can tell me about my father?' I heard myself asking.

'Your father loved you,' she said simply.

'Yes, he was a paedophile.'

'He could have been, if not for you. Be gentle with his memory. You are lucky. You have no dark compulsions that seethe inside, day and night whispering and urging you to things you are ashamed to admit to. Until your mother died, your father never knew that she had found out about me years before. She went about it the wrong way. If she had confronted him, things might have been different. The worst demon in the glare of light can look ridiculous, but in the shadows he grows in height and bulk to unbelievable proportions.

'After Dimple died your father listened to her tapes for the first time. As he listened, tears poured down his face. He realised then the reason for her growing coldness, her rejection of him. And when he heard about the waiter at the party he fell on the floor with remorse. You see, when your mother let that young waiter into her body she destroyed the good man she married. Standing watching her in bed with the waiter was the man that *I* held in my arms. The man your romantic mother had mistakenly, naïvely, thought she wanted to meet.

'He came to me that night angry and restless. He paced the floor like a caged tiger, looked at me with cold eyes. And when he took me in his arms he was deliberately cruel, denying us both any kind of pleasure. Afterwards he sat down to two large whiskys. He went home and began to hate her coldly. Began to devise ways to humiliate and debase her, destroy her.

'One night he came home and saw the result of his work. She was not dead yet. She looked at him like a dumb animal and he acknowledged that it was indeed his own handiwork. Long after her body was gone her suffering spirit remained. He couldn't bear to set eyes on anything she had worn, touched, or lain on. She was everywhere he looked. He saw her even in the eyes of his servants. Sleep was impossible. So he closed up the house as it was. He took nothing but the papers in his study that had no connection with her and her precious tapes.

'The tapes he locked away in a small cupboard in the dressing room of his new home and there they lay until you found them after his death. He didn't want you to remember her lying in her own blood, her mouth open and gaping like a stranded fish. And in her eyes the question, "Are you satisfied now?"

'Even years later a bottle of Chardonnay, a clever flower arrangement or a long black dress in a shop window would scream, "Are you satisfied now?" Those were the times he was happy that at least he had wiped the past clean for you. That while you lay in a hospital bed he had magically changed your entire world. Enrolled you into a new school, got rid of all the servants, brutally cut your relatives off – a job I might add that seemed to pleasure him. He hated your grandmother Rani.

'He bought a new home, gave you a new room and a whole new life. Is it so difficult to forgive that he didn't want you to remember Dimple like that? Is it so hard to believe that he loved you so deeply he didn't want you to suffer as he did? He always wanted to tell you about your inheritance and the past but the longer he left it the harder it became. He set himself target dates.

' "When she is eighteen," he said to me. Then eighteen came and went and he said, "Definitely when she is twenty-one." Twenty-one came and went and then you went overseas to study and he said, "When she comes back." Then of course he became ill and then he said, "When I die will be soon enough." '

'I wish I had known this sooner, when he was still alive. I always thought he didn't love me,' I said slowly.

'Nothing could be further from the truth,' Rosette said sadly.

I walked over to where the beautifully preserved woman sat. Her skin was astonishingly white. Looking up into my face, her eyes seemed very large and full of soft darkness. I wondered what my father had seen in them. What had he seen that had awakened the sleeping monster inside him? To think that this woman had felt teethmarks in her heart when she had first looked at Daddy. How utterly complicated and strange other people's lives are. How incomprehensible!

For several minutes Rosette and I simply looked at each other, each lost in our own private thoughts. Then I bent down and hugged her.

'Thank you for any comfort that you gave my father,' I said very softly.

Inside Rosette's eyes a sad, ghostly shadow passed. She lowered her eyes and bent her head. The beautiful, silky hair that I had admired earlier fell forward and hid her face. Somewhere inside me I felt the urge to stroke that silky, suffering head. I raised my hand and placed it along the side of her head. Her hair was indeed soft. Rosette rubbed her head gently against my hand like a blameless black and white cat would. I could never be her friend. Ever. Even then I had a vile picture of this woman entwined with my father.

'Thank you,' Rosette whispered. 'I may be a prostitute but I loved your father.'

'At least you have lived your life so you know what all your "what ifs" look like,' I told the bent head. Then I turned away and left. I knew I would never go back to that horribly gilded cage with its lonely black and white cat.

That night I woke up in the small hours for no reason at all. For a while I lay there confused and oddly restless. There had been no nightmare and I was not thirsty. And then I suddenly remembered another occasion when I had woken up for no good reason.

I saw myself pushing back my blankets, sliding off the bed and going to find Mummy. At times like these Mummy always knew what to do. We could snuggle up in her big bed and she could pull out from under her bed the adventures of Hanuman, the Monkey God.

As if in a movie I see myself walking to my mother's room. The whole house is quiet. I grip the cool banister and, looking down, see the living room full of shadows and dark corners. The hall downstairs is dark except for the soft glow from the night lamps. That means Daddy is still not home. My bare feet on the cold marble floor are silent. The door to Mummy's room is closed. Amu and the driver are fast asleep in their rooms downstairs. I see myself, small with shoulder-length hair, pause for a moment in front of Mummy's door before turning the knob. The door opens and quite suddenly I am wide awake. Somehow the room looks different. The bedside lamp is on. The room is quiet and still but for the sound of dripping. A soft, wet sound. Plop . . . plop . . .

Like a dripping tap.

Mummy has fallen asleep on the small table by the bed. She is slumped on the table, her face turned away from my view. She was so tired that she fell asleep on the table.

'Mummy!' I call softly.

The room is cold and silent and slightly smoky. There is a sweetish odour that I do not recognise. There is something weird going on that I cannot put my finger on but the hairs on my arms stand up and my mouth is dry. I turn away to leave. I will see Mummy in the morning. It is best. Things always look better in the morning light. And then I hear that thick dripping sound again. Plop. I turn around slowly and start walking towards Mummy's sleeping figure. She is wearing her pretty blue nightie. On the table where Mummy has fallen asleep are the strangest pipes and things that I have never seen before. I walk closer and closer.

'Oh, Mummy,' I say. The sound is like a lost whisper. I get closer and closer and then, instead of turning around to face her, I take two more steps past the deeply sleeping figure. If I go any further I will walk straight into Mummy's bed so I am forced to turn around. I turn around very slowly. For some secret reason that I myself do not understand I close my eyes. I take a deep breath and then slowly open my eyes.

I look directly into Mummy's eyes. They look at me and they look right through me. Her eyes are glazed and her mouth opens and closes like a fish. Deep in her stomach is that beautifully carved Japanese sword that used to hang in Daddy's study.

'*Hara kiri. Hara kiri. Hara kiri,*' Angela Chan, the bully in my classroom, sings in a taunting lilting voice.

My mind begins to whirl. 'Ring a ring a roses,' she sings, her voice nasty in my head. 'Stupid girl you shouldn't have told,' her mean voice hisses.

I shake my head and the voice disappears and once more I am looking into Mother's glazed blank eyes. Then my head is suddenly and confusingly full of nursery rhymes sung by taunting voices. They fill my head like a million buzzing bees so there is no room for my stunned brain to think.

Wee Willie Winkie runs through the town. Upstairs and downstairs in his nightgown. Rapping at the window, crying through the lock. Are the children all in bed for now it's eight o'clock. Poor Wee Willie Winkie with his bare feet.

The Dove says, Coo, coo, what shall I do?

Where are you going to up so high? To brush the cobwebs off the sky.

May I go with you? Aye, by and by.

Mary Mary Quite Contrary. And frightened Miss Muffet away. Cobbler, cobbler mend my shoe. Old King Cole was a merry old soul. And a merry old soul was he. I see the moon and the moon sees me. God bless the moon and God bless me.

Without warning the nursery rhymes stop. Silence.

Mummy has committed *hara kiri*. Will Daddy be proud? He always said that only the bravest samurais had the guts to commit *hara kiri* the proper way, finish the job themselves. I take two steps closer to Mummy. I reach out and touch her hair. Soft. Her mouth closes and opens. 'Mummy,' I whisper, 'you are bleeding to death because you didn't have the strength to finish the job properly.' The blood from her wound is flowing quickly down her open palm, down her middle finger and dripping into a red pool on the black floor.

Red on black. Red on black.

I stand frozen and watch a drop of blood poised on the end of her finger, then, as though in slow motion, it drops to the floor. I watch its graceful progress until it hits the spreading puddle of red and disappears into the thick liquid, and only then do I begin to scream.

I pull my hair out in fistfuls and, sobbing, run to the bedside telephone. There I find I cannot remember how to dial 999. My fingers get caught in the dial and the receiver springs out of my clammy hand. I run out of the room screaming.

'Mummy, Mummy, MUMMY!' I scream hysterically.

At the bottom of the stairs I see Daddy, his foot on the

first step. He has just come home. He is wearing his best Batik shirt, the one he only wears to dinner functions with dignitaries. The smile on his face freezes at the sight of me.

I lunge towards him. 'Help, Daddy, help!' I cry wildly.

At the top of the stairs stands a stern-faced Goose with a black neck. Hah, I recognise him. It's Goosey Goosey Gander wandering upstairs and downstairs in his lady's chamber. He must have mistaken me for the man who wouldn't say his prayers for he took me by my left leg and threw me down the stairs. I trip.

And I begin to fly down the stairs towards my stunned father. The marble steps confront me halfway down. There is no pain. I begin to roll. Images flash by. In the marble floor I see my terrified reflection. In the ceiling I see Mummy's glazed eyes accusing, her gorgeous laugh dead and trapped inside a bubble she is blowing, and at the bottom of the stairs Daddy's urgent, horrified face rushes towards me, his smile hurt and gone. Then just blackness. The black hole caught me. '*No more memories for you*,' it said in a soft soothing voice. It was a friend. It cared. It gave me a memory-eating snake for company.

Part Seven

Some I Loved

———

Nisha

I lay quietly in the darkness watching my memories one by one, like a stack of old movies found in a forgotten attic, until dawn broke outside my window. By five thirty in the morning I knew my father had loved me. I understood him a little now. The pain of vessels not quite perfect. Uncle Sevenese had taught my mother that. I buried my face in my pillow and cried silently for what might have been. 'I really did love you. I wish you had told me. I would have understood.'

I drove into Kuantan. Parking on the main road I walked into Great-Grandma Lakshmi's cul-de-sac. Memories flooded back. I knocked on the door and my Great-Aunt Lalita appeared. She held me in her feeble arms and she looked so old I didn't recognise her at all. Tears swam in her blurry eyes.

'Come in. Come in. You are exactly like your mother,' she half laughed, half sobbed. 'Do you remember me?'

'A little bit,' I answered. She was the last survivor. The rest were dead. They were a long row of black and white photographs wearing garlands of fake flowers.

'That's all right,' she said. 'You were only a child then. My mother always said, ' "One day, Lalita, that girl's going to be a writer." Are you a writer?'

'No.'

'Why not? It was your dream. You used to write beautifully, nice things about your terrible father. I suppose I shouldn't criticise the dead. Your mother was a beautiful girl. Did you know that your father fell in love with her the first time he saw her?'

I nodded.

'Would you like some coconut candy? It's the soft type. Very good for the toothless.'

'Yes, thank you,' I said smiling. She was lovely, exactly as Mother had described her. So innocent.

'Oh, wait a minute. Your great-grandmother left something for you.'

She disappeared behind a curtain and returned with a bracelet that she placed carefully in my outstretched palm. I looked at it. It had a place in my sketchily constructed past. I closed my eyes and fingering the cool stones of the bracelet called to the shadow of a clinging memory. By and by I heard my mother's voice say, 'And that was the day Grandma Lakshmi said to Grandad "Take Dimple with you. Sit there and make sure he doesn't exchange the stones for something less precious. These jewellers are all crooks."

'Bouncing on the middle bar of Grandad's bicycle, all the while cocooned by his long white sleeves on either side of me we rushed into the wind. The jeweller's room was dark. He worked by a small blue flame. Grandad handed over the jewels and we waited there with our arms crossed while the jeweller worked at his wooden table with sharp metal instruments setting Grandma's jewels. I remember wanting an ice cream but Grandad said we had to wait until the setting was complete.'

My mother's voice died away and I opened my eyes. 'Where did the stones come from?' I asked.

'The Sultan of Pahang and my brother Lakshmnan were sitting at the same gambling table once and the

Sultan lost. He gave the jewels in lieu of the money lost. One never argued with a Sultan and my brother accepted the jewellery hoping for a quick sale but my mother got hold of it first. She recognised their value instantly.'

'So these opals were actually won by my grandfather in a gambling game?' I asked, examining the pretty yellow lights in the green stones. Now I had something from my grandfather. I stood underneath his garlanded picture. I saw a handsome man, but in my mind his handsome head rolled on the ground. I turned away from the image. 'Thank you. Thank you so much for this. Can I see the Kuan Yin statue?' I asked.

'How do you know about her?'

'I listened to all my mother's tapes. It was you who spoke about the Kuan Yin, remember?'

From the dark depths of the showcase, behind the pipe-cleaner birds and the gorgeous white coral that Grandad had stolen from the sea, came the statue. She was smooth and beautiful. I ran an admiring finger down the jade noticing that it was not glossy dark green as it was described in the tapes but a very pale green.

'I thought it was supposed to be deep green?'

'Yes, it was gloriously deep green many years ago when first out of its box but every year since then it has faded a little.' My great-aunt's smile was dusty with age.

The jade was changing colour.

'You know . . . ?'

'Yes, I know. Return her.'

I took the statue to a Chinese temple in Kuantan town. As soon as I stepped into the darkened interior, a red inner door opened and a priestess in white walked out. She looked around expectantly and, spotting me, approached. Her eyes were fixed on the cloth package in my hand.

'You have brought her back. I dreamed last night that she was coming back to the temple.'

Astonished, I held the package out and the priestess unwrapped it reverently.

'Oh, look at the colour. She must have brought much ill fortune to the woman who kept her. Was it your mother?' she asked, looking up into my face.

'No, not my mother, my great-grandmother. And yes, the stone has brought terrible misfortune upon my family.'

'I am so sorry to hear that. Such statues have powerful energies in them. They need prayer and a clean mind or they will destroy the lives of the people who keep them. Now that she is where she belongs, she will regain her colour again.'

Evening was approaching. On the horizon the sun was a ball of liquid blood and for a while I tarried under the canopy of a large tree. Kuantan was small. I found places I recognised from the tapes and smiled to see them unchanged after all these years. I entered a newly built shopping complex. There was something I had to do. I walked aimlessly until I was outside a small boutique. My hesitation was almost imperceptible. Inside I browsed half-heartedly. What I really wanted was hanging on the mannequin in the window but I just needed a little courage. Courage to ask the bored sales girl to take it down so I could try it on. Eventually I stopped pretending to browse. It had to be done. It had to be said.

'Can you take down the dress that is in the window, please?'

The girl's face mirrored her thoughts: If I take the

damn thing down, you had better buy it. 'Which one?' she asked politely.

'The red and black one.'

'It's a very nice one, but it is two hundred ringgit, you know.'

I said nothing while the girl took down the dress. In the small cubicle the little dress looked rather short.

'Wah, so nice legs, ahhh,' the sales girl popped her head into the cubicle and commented in an exaggerated manner. 'Wah, very sexy lah,' she approved again. She made her reluctance to return the dress to the window display very obvious.

I was surprised to find my lifelong hatred of red and black muted into nothing more than slight disapproval at the shortness of the skirt.

'Sneakers no good, lah,' the girl commented, taking out a pair of black sandals that tied at the ankles. I put my jeans and T-shirt into a plastic bag held out by the girl, paid for the dress and the shoes and left the boutique. Walking past the shops I stared at my own reflection with surprise. I looked tall and elegant. In fact unrecognisable. Though I had hated red, red loved me. It brought out the best in my colouring and promised a long and happy acquaintance.

Red and black, I thought, was in fact a superb combination.

Watching Amu in the hammock one day I decided to try my hand at writing. Some days I wrote in my mother's white summer house and sometimes I wrote in her room, but always the fierce spirits that lived inside Mother's box came to me. Voices from the past descended like clouds of pink flamingos on the toxic lakes of East Africa. Each with a screeching voice of its own. Each demanding to add another pink silhouette on the land-scape of my story.

They whispered things into my ear and I wrote as fast as they spoke. Sometimes they sounded angry, some-times they were happy and sometimes they were full of regret. I listened to their sadness and I knew that my mother had collected their grief because she knew that some day her daughter would gain her freedom from them. Night seemed to fly in faster and faster. By the time I lifted my head it was dark outside. Amu was already lighting the prayer lamp downstairs and the faithful blackamoor boys were offering flickering flames of light.

'Come to eat,' Amu would call.

Then came the day I wrote the last page. I leaned back in the darkening room and something made me reach for the tape my mother had found in Great-Uncle Sevenese's room after his death. I put it into the machine and clicked PLAY.

> ' *"Then said another with a long drawn sigh,*
> *"My clay with long oblivion is gone dry;*
> *But fill me with the old familiar Juice,*
> *Methinks I might recover by and by!"*

'Rogue that I am, I whispered that into your ears and today you have brought me a magnum of Japanese Sake. I tease you about a secret lover and you blush a dull red. No, it is not a lover you have. It is a thorn in your breast. You will not tell me the nature of the thorn. Dear, dear Dimple, you are my favourite niece and always have been, but it hurts to love such a tragically sad and misguided creature. I have studied your charts and in your house of marriage sits the serpent Rahu. Have you not been warned about the man you married? I do not trust him. He wears his smile like his clothes, easily and carelessly. I have studied his charts too and I do not like what I see.

'He will be an adder at your breast.

'Did I ever tell you about the adder in Raja's chest? About three months after Mohini died, Raja died of a lethal snakebite. His own beautiful cobra bit him. I always remember him like a marvellous hero from an ancient world who thought to keep a huge, glistening cobra as a rat catcher. In the moonlight, his bronze body gleaming in the tall grass, all his secrets came alive. I can never forget that moment when he said, "Watch me," and approached that swaying black menace to stroke it as if it were but a plaything. Do you remember his answer to my question, "Is a snake-charmer ever bitten by his own snakes?"

' "Yes," he said. "When he wants to be bitten."

'I often think that inside me is a mirror image of me. A reckless, unwise fellow who does everything I am afraid to do. I have lived with him for many years and he tells me his ferocious older brother lives in your husband. I wonder if you have ever seen him lurking inside. Perhaps you haven't. They are cunning bastards. When I am shouting No, No, No, he is shouting On, On, On, with cruel glee in his eyes. When the cock crows outside and I turn away to go home he is the one who winks extravagantly down the sculptured cleavage of the woman at the bar and drawls, I think, very unwisely, "Would you allow those sweet domes to go to waste, unused?"

'I wake up in the bright light of the morning with only an indented pillow beside me, my toes sticky with marmalade, a jumbled, impossibly squalid memory and the grateful thought: *Thank God I left my wallet at Reception*. Once or twice when I push away my glass and resolve groggily, "Enough," he lights another cigarette, raises his hand and orders another whisky. "Straight," he tells the bartender. And then he leads me into the back alleyway where even the taxi drivers will not go. A young girl will pull herself away from the wall she has been leaning on and run her forefinger down my face. She knows me. She knows me from the last time.

'In Thailand you can buy anything. It is easy and I have bought a lot of things in my lifetime. As you are my niece and as I am not yet drunk it is neither proper nor necessary to speak of them all, but I must tell you that pure heroin is one of them. Why, I know not, but my experience seems to my befuddled brain somehow relevant to you. I sat on the bed in my hotel room and considered the syringe, the needle and the brown liquid inside. I examined myself minutely. Was it another experience I could add to my memorabilia of strangeness or a habit that will turn master? I have never said no to anything before, but heroin is the devil's machine. You walk into it and come out at the other end altered beyond recognition. Surely my compulsive personality would fling me without a second thought into the ravine of addiction. My God, I would come out of the machine gaunt, muddy-complexioned, vomit-splattered and wild-eyed. I have seen them by the railway stations; their eyes in their unwashed, shrunken faces blank of all but the unquenchable thirst for another score. Was that to be my fate?

'I hesitated but in the end I can be counted upon only to be weak. The prospect of stagnant waste was not equal to my compulsion for a new experience, for self-destruction. I tied the top of my upper arm with a belt and then I looked for and easily found a thick green vein in my arm. Health Inspectors know the best places to look for them. I let the needle slide into my skin and closed my eyes. The heat was instantaneous, followed immediately by a peaceful rush such as I have never known before. Life's troubles were indeed meaningless. I let myself fall into the abyss. Warm, dark, soft and indescribably fabulous. I fell and I fell and I would have fallen deeper but for the face that floated before me. Kutub Minar, my long dead cat, stared expressionlessly into my eyes. The only female I ever loved with all my heart. Perhaps, she is the only one I ever came across with a warm body and cold lips. Now . . . if I had found such a woman I would have abandoned myself to her the way an Alpha male baboon stretches out eagerly, patiently, on the ground, his limbs limp with remembered pleasure, and waits to be groomed by the dominant female.

'The cat mewed pitifully as if in pain. My limbs leaden with the drug slept on. Suddenly Mohini appeared. I stared, astonished. Since the day she died I had only heard her voice but never seen her. She stood in front of me as solid and as real as the bed I was lying on. Tears shimmered in her green eyes. Then the colours began. All around her, the most brilliant colours appeared, merged and disappeared. Shimmering colours that I had never seen, that I had imagined only dragonflies and goldfish did. I felt a strange pain, the pain of loss. I couldn't rid myself of their images. They fused and became one and made it impossible for me to push them away. I felt shame wash over me.

'When she reached out and put her hand on my head I felt the warmth of her skin. Was I dead? I thought I might be, so I tried to move my head slightly and her hovering hand slipped onto my face, her hand soft against my cheeks. Gorgeous colours moved and merged in the background. I heard the religious songs that old people sing at funerals. The voices didn't come from outside but inside my head. Those horrendous songs that I have always hated, songs that sound like a flock of sea-gulls wailing and crying as they pecked at the eyes of dead sailors. I felt a heavy weight on my chest. I looked into my dead sister's eyes. I had forgotten how green they were. Suddenly she smiled and I heard a tremendous rushing sound, as if I were standing too close to the edge of a railway track while an express train was passing through.

'The weight on my chest lifted. The colours were gone and she was gone too. Outside it was already dark. I heard the sounds of the food stalls in the street below coming alive. The scraping of plates and the rough, un-educated voices of the stallkeepers. The honest smell of cheap ingredients, garlic, onions and bits of meat sizzling in lard floated up through my open window. I felt hungry. The bloody syringe was still in my arm. I pulled it out and looked at the dark blood curiously. I would never repeat the experience. Mohini had made sure of that.

'Balzac said, "An uncle is a gay dog by nature." I am a clown dancing on the edge of an abyss and yet I tell you this now, though, like me, you will not listen: Don't walk into the machine, for you will come out at the other end altered beyond help.

'Don't do it, Dimple.

'I walk into the doctor's surgery and he says, "What? Are you still alive?" He cannot believe that such an abused body survives. But you won't survive the machine. Leave him. Leave the adder in his jungle. Leave the child in the jungle, for surely the adder will not hurt its own child. Nisha has good charts. She will do fine things with her life. Save your fragile self now, darling Dimple. I see bad things in your charts and at night the demons send me dreams finely drizzled with blood. I am once more seven years old and hiding behind the bushes watching Ah Kow's mother slaughtering a pig. The panic, the screams of terror, the spurting fountain of blood and that unforgettable reek. In my dreams you are walking in a rain of blood. I shout and you turn and smile fearlessly, your teeth red with blood. I fear for your future. It is drawn in blood. Leave, Dimple.

'Leave. Please leave.'

Sevenese's voice ended and only the sound of the tape whirling remained.

Downstairs I heard Amu finishing her night prayers, ringing her little bell. I closed my eyes. In the red shadows of my eyelids I see Great-Uncle Sevenese sitting in the middle of a desert, bare-chested and wearing a white *veshti*. The desert night has painted him gleaming blue. The sand shimmers but here and there lie dead birds, their tiny, open beaks and throats holding miniature sand storms. He turns to me and smiles. His smile is familiar. 'Look,' he says, sweeping his arms out to the sky. 'It is the desert night's one conceit, the zillions of stars that decorate her raven hair. Isn't it the most splendid thing you ever saw?'

I opened my eyes to a room full of dusk, and suddenly knew. I knew what Great-Uncle Sevenese had desperately tried to write for my tormented mother on his deathbed. As if he had whispered it into my ear I knew what the unfinished message was. Stretched on a hospital bed, horribly bloated and voiceless in his dying world, he wanted to say, '*I see her. Flowers grow beneath her feet, but she is not dead at all. The years have not diminished the Rice Mother. She is fierce and magical. Stop despairing and call to her, and you will see, she will come bearing a rainbow of dreams.*'

Outside the wind rustled the indigo leaves and at the bottom of the garden, the old bamboo grove burst into song.